C000263149

PRODIGIES

Also by Francis King

ᢍ

FRANCIS KING

PRODIGIES

A ARCADIA BOOKS
LONDON

Arcadia Books Ltd
15–16 Nassau Street
London W1W 7AB

www.arcadiabooks.co.uk

First published in the United Kingdom 2001

Copyright © Francis King 2001

Francis King has asserted his moral right to be identified as the author of this work in accordance with the Copyright, Designs and Patents Act, 1988.

All rights reserved. No part of this publication may be reproduced in any form or by any means without the written permission of the publishers.

A catalogue record for this book is available from the British Library.

ISBN 1–900850–44–3

Designed and typeset in Monotype Ehrhardt by Discript, London WC2N 4BN
Printed in the United Kingdom by The Cromwell Press, Trowbridge, Wiltshire

Arcadia Books distributors are as follows:

in the UK and elsewhere in Europe:
Turnaround Publishers Services
Unit 3, Olympia Trading Estate
Coburg Road
London N22 6TZ

in the USA and Canada:
Consortium Book Sales and Distribution, Inc.
1045 Westgate Drive
St Paul, MN 55114–1065

in Australia:
Tower Books
PO Box 213
Brookvale, NSW 2100

in New Zealand:
Addenda
Box 78224
Grey Lynn
Auckland

in South Africa:
Peter Hyde Associates (Pty) Ltd
PO Box 2856
Cape Town 8000

For

Abdel-Karim Deham

fellow explorer

We carry within us the wonders we seek without us: there is all Africa and her prodigies in us.

Sir Thomas Browne: *Religio Medici*

Book 1

1 AS A CHILD she would often think about her father's distant plantations. Halting in the corridor to the nursery, overlarge head tilted upwards on its long, thin neck, she would peer up at the coloured engraving, foxed with damp and fretted at the edges by the jaws of white ants, with its wide, chlorotic expanse of sugar-cane and, dotted here and there about it, half-naked, black figures – savages, Nanny Rose had told her. The women stood erect under bundles that looked like towering head-dresses, the men were armed with machetes. From those spears of vegetation a viscous liquid was extracted; and eventually that liquid was transformed into gold.

'What's that place?'

'Demerara,' Nanny Rose said.

'Is that where Daddy is now?'

'No. Was. He's not there now.'

'Where is he?'

'In Liverpool. I think. Yes, that's what your mother said. With your brothers. Half-brothers,' she corrected herself. She herself came from a village in the Wirral. It was the wife of one of the two half-brothers, a haughty, long-faced woman with a nervous habit of constantly licking her lips, who had recruited her, after the death from diphtheria of the child – such an adorable boy and so unlike this sharp, capricious, disobedient, spoiled little madam – who had been her previous charge.

'Where is Demarara?'

'Oh, a long, long way away. In the West Indies.' Nanny Rose put up a hand and fidgeted with the widow's lace-fringed cap surmounting a plain, square face scarred from small-pox. She often fidgeted with the cap, as though uneasy with the premature widowhood it represented.

'Too far for us to go there?'

'Oh, yes, dear, far too far. What an idea! In any case, it wouldn't be the right sort of place for a little girl like you.'

'Why wouldn't it?'

'Well, you can pick up all sorts of diseases. And it's very hot. And you wouldn't be able to lead the sort of life you lead here.'

'When is Daddy coming back?'

'Well, we don't know, do we? We never know. He has so much to occupy him. I heard your mother say he might have to go to Jamaica. There's been some sort of problem there.'

'What problem?'

'Oh, I don't know. I really don't.' But she knew perfectly well. She had overheard a conversation between madam and madam's sister, the one who was lady-in-waiting to the Queen, when they had spoken of some sort of rebellion of the coffee-plantation workers, so recently awarded the gift of their freedom but not in the least grateful for it.

'There are always problems for Daddy.'

'Well, every important man has problems. Problems are an important man's meat and drink.'

It was after that conversation that Alexine began her habit of stationing herself in front of the engraving and, on tiptoe, staring up at it. She would try to imagine that she was one of those women with the towering headdresses that were in fact their burdens. The air would be hot and damp, wrapping itself around their half-naked bodies, like the towels that were wrapped around her to make her sweat out a fever at that time when, on holiday in Naples, she had fallen so suddenly ill; and everywhere there would be a scent of caramel, like that scent of burned sugar that arose when her mother, helped by Liliane, made toffee on the wide verandah overlooking the garden at the back of the house. *Demerara.* She repeated the word to herself. *Demerara.* It sounded strange, frightening, seductive, a magic password.

Her father also owned coffee plantations, rubber plantations, ships and factories; but when she thought of his money, it was always as sugar, piled high, mountain after mountain of immaculate snow, in warehouses in The Hague, in Paris, in Liverpool, in Milan, in all of those mysterious, far-distant places to which he was constantly travelling. Why could she and her mother never travel with him? 'Oh, I'll be far too busy to have any time to spare for you,' he would reply when, as so often and so pressingly, she put that question to him. Only six though she was, she could already bend her mother, Aunt Addy and Nanny Rose to her will, but never him.

'Why are those people black?' she asked Aunt Addy, pointing at the engraving.

'Why are you white?' Aunt Addy countered. Then she said: 'They – or their parents or their grandparents or their great-grandparents – were brought from Africa.' She almost added 'As slaves', but instead said 'To work.'

Pale and extremely thin, the rusty shadows under her eyes suggesting either extreme fatigue or ill-health, she smoothed down the grey taffeta over her thighs with long, narrow hands as she said: 'Without all those black people we shouldn't be living in this beautiful house – or making journeys – or having Nanny Rose and Mademoiselle and Daan and Liliane and all the others to look after us.'

∽

At six, Alexine was already fluent in three languages: her native Dutch,

English, and French. She had inherited that gift from her father, everyone was always saying. How many languages did he speak? Sometimes he said six, sometimes seven, sometimes even eight, when people asked him. Alexine used to wonder: How could he be so vague? Didn't he remember?

When he returned to The Hague, after many weeks of absence, from his estates in Sumatra, Alexine urged him: 'Papa, say something to me in the language that they speak out there.'

He stroked his forked beard with that mischievously enigmatic smile of his, tilted his head to one side, tongue between teeth, in deliberation, and then brought out something that sounded so odd – did those people really speak like that or was he making it up? – that Alexine burst into delighted laughter. 'What does that mean?' she asked.

'It means "I love you".'

'Am I the first person you've ever said that to? I mean – in that language of theirs?'

Again he gave that mischievously enigmatic smile, head tilted to one side. 'What do you think?' Thirty-three years older than her mother, his second wife, he was a powerfully built man with wide shoulders, an outjutting paunch and a head that, like a battering ram, he held thrust forward as though to demolish any barrier that might obstruct him from achieving his visionary ambitions. The veins stuck out like grey-blue caterpillars on the backs of his huge hands and at his temples. Early every morning, when he was at home, a perky young barber would arrive, worn leather bag in hand, in order to shave him and to clip and comb his grey forked beard. Sometimes, if she pleaded for long enough, Alexine would be allowed to watch this event. As a beard clipping slithered down and off the sheet wrapped around him to the floor, she would often stoop to retrieve it. It felt dry and sharp in her palm, like a pine-needle.

'Now, pussycat, you must let me get on with my work.' He sighed, pushed at the armrests, decorated with an elaborate scrollwork of flowers and foliage, of the chair that he had brought back from one of his English visits – 'school of Grinling Gibbons' he would tell people invited to admire it, adding, in case they were ignorant of it, that Gibbons had been born in Rotterdam – and then rose to his feet.

'Oh, do let's talk a little longer!'

'Sorry, pussycat. But work is work – and must be done, if Mama expects to go to Paris next month to buy even more of those expensive dresses.'

'Why can't I just sit in your study while you're working? I won't make any noise.'

'Because other people come and go. And because, if you – or anyone

5

else – is watching me, then I can't concentrate. I've told you that. Many times.'

She had learned the futility of arguing with him, just as, in the years ahead, people would learn the futility of arguing with her.

With his slight limp, the result of being thrown from a horse startled by the sudden emergence of some black, overawed children out of a thicket in Demerara many years before, he hurried off through a succession of doors, opening and then decisively shutting them behind him, towards the study. Its entrance flanked by Corinthian columns wrapped in palm fronds, this room was the termination of a tunnel-like, vaulted corridor.

Sometimes, after he had disappeared into the study, Alexine would follow, careful to make no sound. She would reach up for the first of a succession of door-handles and then, with an effort, turn it. She would slip through and gently, oh so gently, close that door behind her. Then no less silently she would move on to the next. From time to time she would glance up at a portrait. Few of them were of his family, most of them were of Mama's and Aunt Addy's. When she had once asked Mademoiselle why this should be, she had replied in an indignant, even angry tone of voice, '*Historiquement la famille de votre mère est beaucoup plus importante.*' It had always been clear to Alexine that Mademoiselle did not like Papa, and she had often wondered why this should be.

Stationing herself on the thick Aubusson carpet with its pattern of birds of paradise perched on the grey-green branches of olive trees, Alexine would peer through the keyhole into the study. But it was only rarely, as he stooped forward to take something out of a drawer of his large *bureau à cylindre*, did she glimpse Papa's face. For the most part she would see only an expanse of his waistcoat, the watch-chain glittering across it, the taut protuberance of his belly, or one of his large, amazingly white hands, far whiter even than Aunt Addy's, which contrasted so oddly with the hectic flush of his cheekbones and forehead. She found an excitement in observing and not being observed. That excitement was to remain with her for the whole of her life.

Sometimes, Papa would not be alone. Mysteriously, most of his visitors did not come up the imposing main staircase with its Venetian windows and Ionic pilasters, but up a small, corkscrew one, with direct access to the study, which had been added only a few years earlier to the house. No member of the family other than Papa ever used that small staircase. When, exploring the house, Alexine had attempted to do so, she had found the entrance to it barred by a locked iron grill.

It was as rare for her to be able to catch a glimpse of the visitors' faces as it was for her to be able to catch a glimpse of Papa's. But, if they spoke in one of the three languages known to her, she could sometimes make out, here and there, something of what they were saying. But since most of their talk was about business and money, it was so tedious to her that she never strained to listen. The other voices were often raised in excitement, disagreement, pleasure or dismay; but Papa's always maintained the same even, strong tenor. That tenor never left any doubt of his superiority to all those who called to see him.

Once, suddenly jumping up from his chair, striding to the door and flinging it open, as he went to protest about a bell too long left unanswered, he caught her scuttling away down the passage, like some small animal surprised when foraging for food.

'Hey! What have you been up to? What? Hey!'

She halted, turned. She put a hand up to a cheek as though anticipating a slap. The slap came, to the other cheek. 'I don't like eavesdroppers,' he said. 'Go back to the nursery! Go! Go!' He marvelled that, when he slapped her, she never cried. His boys, now grown up and far away in England, would at that same age begin to blub even before palm met cheek with stinging force.

Later, after they had eaten their midday dinner together – now that his English first wife was dead, he refused to follow the English custom of banishing children to the nursery for meals – he called her over to him. Defiant but pale, she scrambled out of her chair, crossed the floor between them and stood before him. She thought that he was about to punish her again. But he extended his arms and then, placing his hands on either side of her narrow waist, jerked her up on to his knee. 'You are my Benjamin,' he said. 'Except that Benjamin was a boy and you're a little girl.' He kissed the top of her head and then the side of her neck. She did not know what he meant by 'Benjamin', and she did not like the touch of his full, damp lips on her flesh. But Harriet, her beloved Mama, looked across at them through her lorgnette and smiled indulgently, and Daan, the gnarled, wheezing manservant, stationed behind Mama's chair, also smiled.

It was this Benjamin who was to inherit most of Papa's money.

Papa had once said that the proof of whether you were truly rich or not was whether you could make a reality of every one of your dreams. She was to be rich in that way.

2 PAPA HAD BEEN AWAY for such a long time that sometimes, lying in bed, she would have to make an effort to recollect what he looked like and what his voice sounded like. She could visualize the grey forked beard, the whimsical, mocking, sometimes even cruel smile on the moist, full lips, the aggressively out-thrust head and the small, brown mole on one side of his nose; but somehow, as though she were attempting an insoluble jigsaw puzzle, she could rarely fit all these features satisfactorily together. With her amazingly retentive memory for a foreign language, she could even remember that way in which the Sumatrans said 'I love you' – unless, of course, he had invented those weird sounds. But, that apart, it was hard to hear in recollection that firm, low, vibrant voice of his.

She would repeatedly, with a growing impatience, ask Mama, Aunt Addy, Mademoiselle and Nanny Rose when Papa would return. But none of them could say with certainty – answering 'Soon, dear, very soon,' or 'You know what it's like when your father goes away on business' or 'He said he'd be back at the end of the month at the latest.' Strangely, whereas she felt his absence like a constant, dull ache, often distracting her from paying attention to Mademoiselle's explanation of the French subjunctive, from eating up the food placed by Daan or Beatrice before her, and even from playing with her lead soldiers, her mother, aunt, Nanny Rose and Mademoiselle, like the servants, seemed far more carefree, even far more happy for it.

When he did return, it was wholly unexpectedly – so that Harriet chided him, in incredulous anger, 'But why on earth didn't you tell us that you were on the way?', only to receive the off-hand, smiling answer: 'Oh, I wanted to surprise you. Surprises are good for the health.' 'Not for mine,' Harriet retorted. But he was right. Her life, she secretly acknowledged, was so dull because nothing surprising ever happened in it. A surprise of any kind stirred her sluggish blood with the sharpness of its challenge.

It was already growing dark on that autumn evening when the barouche first clattered over the cobbles and then, having squeaked through the high, narrow gates, each bearing the crest of this newly rich and newly famous family, crunched up the semi-circle of the drive. Alexine was playing cards with Mama and Aunt Addy on the glazed front veranda that extended along the rusticated ground floor of the house, under an upper floor of seven broad bays. Nanny Rose had twice come to fetch her charge for bed and on each occasion Alexine had protested 'No, no!

We must finish the game.' Nanny Rose knew that Madam and Miss Addy would give in to the child, as they always did. On each occasion she marched off, brows drawn together and chapped lips moving soundlessly as she repeated to herself; 'Spoiled. Utterly spoiled.' They were words that she was often silently to utter in the years ahead.

It was Alexine, with her extraordinarily acute hearing, who first heard the carriage. She threw down her cards on the table, with such force that some slithered to the floor, and then ran to peer out through the rain-spattered glass. The carriage drew up under the porte cochère, the horse tossing its head. Then the coachman descended and hurried over to open the door. Before she could see who was in the coach, Alexine shrieked, 'It's Papa! Papa! I know it's Papa!'

Mama and Aunt Addy leapt up, their cards still in their hands, and hurried over to join her. All of them peered out. Papa, his hat pulled down low over his forehead and a voluminous grey cloak swirling about him, jumped out, refusing the outstretched hand of the coachman. Despite his age, he hated to be physically dependent on anyone.

'Yes, it's him! It is! It is!'

Aunt Addy had already gone over to the bell-pull to summon Daan and the footman.

It was then that Harriet put to herself the question that she was so often to put, in one form or another, to her husband and to others in the days ahead: Why on earth hadn't he warned them?

Suddenly and simultaneously, she, Addy and Alexine realized that there was someone else in the coach. Papa had turned to peer into its interior. They could see him beckoning, head lowered, to whomever it was who still lurked inside. What he was saying, though they could not hear from behind the glass, was: 'Come! Come! Come on! Don't be frightened!' Again he beckoned, this time in command, not invitation.

Eventually, a figure not so much stepped as stumbled out of the barouche. He was wearing a brown, billycock hat and a military-style brown overcoat with elaborate frogging. Daan had now arrived, and in the light of the flambeau that he was holding aloft, the teeth of this sturdy but diminutive figure – at first, because of the adult style of his dress, all three women had, in their amazement, assumed him to be a dwarf – gleamed as though phosphorescent. His face was black.

Now all of them rushed out to greet Philip. Alexine was the first: 'Papa! Papa!' She threw herself into his arms, feeling the dampness and roughness of the cloak against her cheek, before he whirled her up and away in his arms. He began to kiss her wildly, making her first giggle and then scream in joy as he pressed his lips to her cheek, her forehead, the side of her neck. His companion stood silent and impassive beside him, while all this was going on. He seemed unaware that the two

9

women, in their fashionable Paris frocks, and the two menservants were staring at him, each wondering: 'Who is this? Who is this?'

It was only after he had set Alexine down and had embraced Harriet and Addy that Philip said: 'Now let me introduce to you all...' He put a hand on the shoulder of the figure that everyone had by now realized was a boy of twelve or thirteen at the most. 'This is Samuel. Sammy. He comes from Jamaica. From Kingstown. His family saved my life, and in return I promised to bring him to Europe with me. He has been looking after me all through my travels since I left Jamaica, and I want him to go on looking after me.'

Was he to be a servant or a member of the family? All of them, even the two servants, wished to put the question. None of them dared to do so.

Harriet extended both hands to the boy. 'Welcome to our home.' His already muscular body held stiffly erect, the boy made no response. He did not even smile or nod.

Addy was staring at him, in frowning bewilderment.

Impulsively Alexine stepped forward. 'Do you speak Dutch or English, Sammy?' she asked in English. Then, when he impassively failed to make any response, she repeated the question in Dutch.

'It's no use speaking to him. He doesn't speak English or Dutch. Or any other language. He's deaf and dumb.' Philip tapped the boy on the shoulder with commanding forefinger and middle finger and then indicated to him that he should enter the house. The boy hesitated for a moment, glancing around him. Then, with a little shrug, he did as he was bid, preceding the two women, the girl and his master.

In the hall, decorated by ten large paintings by a painstakingly mediocre mid-century artist, representing the history of the sugar trade from its earliest years to the present, Philip slowly and silently took off his cape and hat and handed them to Daan. He had all the appearance of someone not returning to his home but arriving for the first time at a house which he has rented. He looked about him. The two women and the child watched him anxiously, as though afraid of what he might do next.

Sammy crossed the hall to a round-backed fauteuil and, having stared at it for a while, then placed himself on its edge, legs wide apart and large hands dangling between them. Addy gave him a look of distaste, then turned her head away. How dared he sit down when the rest of them were standing? In her mind, it was already decided: he was a servant and should be treated and behave as one. The boy, a dreamy expression on his face, appeared to be totally at his ease, even though a house built on such a scale and crammed with objects of such value was something that he could never even have imagined, much less entered.

Suddenly, Philip was smiling around at them all. 'Well, how have you all been? The last letter to reach me was Harriet's at St Thomas. Oh, I'm tired, tired. But it's wonderful to see you.'

'You probably want something to eat.'

'No, no, nothing. I ate something at Josquin's before coming on.' The restaurant, popular with the richer sort of traveller, was by the harbour. Harriet was taken aback that he should have stopped off to eat there, instead of returning home immediately. 'But I should like a drink.' He turned to Daan and ordered some cognac. Then he put one arm around Alexine's shoulders and another around his wife's and began to propel them forward into the drawing-room.

Addy, bringing up the rear, called out: 'Philip – what about the – the boy?'

He turned, striking his forehead with the palm of his right hand. 'Yes, the boy, the boy...' It was as though, on an impulse, he had bought some piece of furniture in the course of his foreign travels and now, having had it shipped home with him, did not know where to put it. He again turned to Daan. The boy was to be taken up to a seldom used guest-room above the study. He was to be given whatever he needed. That trunk – Philip pointed at a brand-new valise – was his. Daan could help him to unpack it.

Help him to unpack it? So perhaps, the two women thought with alarm, he had indeed arrived so surprisingly at the house not as a servant but as a guest.

As Daan picked up the valise, his fury barely concealed – couldn't the nigger rascal carry it for himself? – Philip turned to the boy and with a few, decisive gestures indicated that he should go along with the servant. Reluctantly the boy slowly got to his feet. Perhaps, Harriet thought, his dreamlike manner was the result of exhaustion.

Suddenly Alexine was pulling at her father's sleeve. 'Oh, Papa, Papa! Can't he come with us?'

'No.' The monosyllable fell like a sword-blade. 'He must go to his room. Tomorrow Daan will show him the house. And then – somehow – he must learn his duties.'

Duties? What duties? The women could only surmise what they would be.

Alexine watched the boy as, at last removing the brown billycock hat, he followed Daan out of the hall and up the staircase. Harriet wanted to protest that surely the boy could relieve the old servant of the valise, but she had by now learned when it was propitious to say such a thing to her husband and when it was not. It was not propitious now.

As he sipped at his cognac, one fork of his beard glistening from some drops that had spilled from it as he had first tipped up the glass,

Philip answered, with increasing weariness, all their questions about his travels. Yes, he had visited his sons in Liverpool, they had turned out well, he was pleased with them, business was thriving. Irene, the daughter-in-law who had recruited Nanny Rose, had been delivered of twins, identical boys. The other daughter-in-law was suffering from anaemia, but the consumption of raw liver every day had made a marked improvement. Alexine pulled a face at the mention of the raw liver. She hated liver even when it was cooked.

No, he went on, the hard part of his journey had been in Jamaica. There was a new governor, a popinjay, his only interests being the collection of rare plants and butterflies. Can you imagine? The young fool was far happier with a butterfly net or a trowel than with a gun. No wonder there was so much unrest.

It was then that Alexine asked: 'Papa – tell us, tell us! How did Sammy's family save you?'

He sighed. 'Oh, it's too long a story to tell you when it's long past your bedtime.'

'No, please, Papa! Please!' The mystery of Papa's deliverance was part of the greater mystery that the boy, with his black face, his brilliantly white teeth and his inability to communicate in any way, already represented for her.

Philip told the story hurriedly, almost negligently, as though he had told it many times before and was no longer interested in it. He had been out riding, alone, because his companion's horse had gone lame, and then, all at once, this gang, this gang of lawless ruffians, men whom he had sacked from the plantation because of their utter uselessness, had surrounded him. Like a fool, he had gone out unarmed, he did not even have a riding-crop with him. Well, he thought that was the end. But then miraculously, out of nowhere it seemed, these three men appeared. They were workers, not on his estate but on a neighbouring one, and they were carrying machetes. At first he had thought that they were allies of the others but in fact they had proved to be his rescuers. There had been an altercation, no, not a physical fight, and then, mercifully, the gang vanished as swiftly and silently as they had first appeared. The leader of the three rescuers was Sammy's father. He was a carpenter, so skilful that he had even been able to copy for his English employer some Windsor chairs brought out from England. When Philip had tried to reward this man with some money, he had instead proposed that Sammy should accompany him back to The Hague. 'He wants me to make a gentleman of him. Or, at least, a gentleman's gentleman.'

As a guest or as a servant, the women again wanted to ask; and again neither of them did so.

There was a silence. Then Philip said: 'Apart from his – his disability, his cruel disability, Sammy is an extraordinarily intelligent little fellow. Like you' – he turned to Alexine – 'he forgets nothing once he's learned it. But' – his eyes softened and saddened – 'when he can't hear, there's a limit to what he can learn.'

'Are they all like that?' Alexine asked.

'Are all who like that?'

'These black people. In Jamaica.'

He laughed, and the two women joined in. 'Of course not! You talk of them as though they were animals. The problem with a lot of them is not that they can't talk but that they won't stop talking.'

'Perhaps he and I can find some way of talking to each other.'

'I doubt it.'

Again the two women and the so much older man laughed, while Alexine looked at them in hurt, reproachful bewilderment.

3 WAS HE A SERVANT OR A GUEST? Still, no one could be sure. He seemed to have no specific duties. At times, all by himself, he would be wandering the house and garden, throwing sticks by the canal and even into the canal for the golden retriever brought back by Philip, like so much of the furniture, from his visits to England, or turning over the pages of some picture book discovered in the library. At other times he would be laying out Philip's clothes and even helping him to dress for dinner, accompanying him as gun-bearer when, on some clammy winter afternoon, he practised shooting at the gulls on the flat, dun polder that stretched behind the house, or tidying, with slow, finicky care, the papers on Philip's desk or his bedside table. Harriet and Addy had expressed to each other the fear that, savage that he was, unused to washbasins, let alone baths, he would be dirty; but in fact he was scrupulously clean, washing his clothes for himself and then manoeuvring the iron, pink tip of brown forefinger having first gingerly touched its base to make sure that it was hot, back and forth with an artistry far superior to the laundry maid's.

For many days, Alexine merely watched him – lingering on the threshold of the library or the laundry-room, peering down into the garden from an upstairs bedroom, looking across at him as, in a far corner of the room, he turned the crisply rustling pages of a newspaper as though he could read them. He would avoid meeting her gaze; but, as soon as she looked away, she would become aware, with a tingling, embarrassed pleasure, of his scrutiny.

There was a cat in the household, a huge tabby stray, adopted by Nanny Rose after it had slunk into the kitchen and miaowed imperiously for food. Its tail had been broken and it had lost one eye. These disabilities had only endeared it the more to her. Because Addy had a terror of cats it was barred from any of the rooms frequented by her and spent most of its time either in the kitchen regions, up in the attics, where the servants slept, or on Nanny Rose's bed. To the jealous fury of Nanny Rose, this cat, which she had called Ginger, a name inappropriate for a creature so lethargic, fell passionately in love with Sammy, following him about the house and continually jumping into his lap whenever he was seated. Mademoiselle, wrinkling her nose, said that the improbable attachment must have something to do with the smell of 'those people'. More than once, in search of him, Nanny Rose had eventually stormed into Sammy's attic bedroom to scoop the cat off his narrow truckle bed. 'Naughty boy!' she would scold Sammy as much as the cat.

One day, looking out through the glass of the veranda, Alexine saw that Sammy was seated out on one of the elaborate wrought-iron benches flanking the rose-garden, Ginger on his lap. He was staring out ahead of him, lips slightly parted to reveal those extraordinarily white teeth of his, with that dreamy expression, or lack of expression, that, during many days of observation, she had come to know so well. With one hand he was rhythmically stroking the cat, from time to time pausing in the movement to tug at a burr of fur. Each time that he tugged, the cat raised its head and emitted a squawk, whether of pleasure or protest it was impossible to say. For a long time, observing but unobserved, Alexine watched the brown hand, the cat and that wholly uncommunicative face. She might have been watching not one animal but two, the second so rare that she was terrified that with any movement she might frighten it away forever. Then, on an impulse, she went to the door from veranda into garden, pulled it open and slowly and, as she hoped, silently descended the steps.

At the sound of her feet on gravel freshly raked by one of the two gardeners that morning, Sammy looked up. But it was the cat, leaping off his lap and scuttling off into the privet hedge behind the bench, that was alarmed, not he. Sammy did not turn his head; after the brief glance he went back to staring out at the roses. The only movement that he made was to place the hand that had been stroking the cat on the back of the bench. It rested there, oddly inert.

Alexine seated herself on the bench beside him, turned her head and smiled. It was the first time that she had ever smiled at him, indeed shown him any acknowledgement of his presence. But the smile was unreturned. His head averted, he might even not have noticed it. The cat now crept out from the bushes and, with its single, rheumy eye, gazed up unwinking at her. There was something eerie about the animal's total stillness, as there was about the boy's. She had never tried to make friends with the cat, because she had sensed that, possessively, Nanny Rose would not have wished her to do so. Again she turned her head towards Sammy and again she smiled. Then, since there was still no response whatever – his face, glistening in the spring sunlight, never changed from its somnolent expression or lack of expression – she nudged him.

At that, he turned and abruptly jerked up from the seat, as though to run off. She put out an imperious hand and grabbed at a sleeve. 'It's all right. Don't worry. Sit.' She then realized the futility of saying these things to someone who not merely could not speak Dutch but who was incapable of hearing her. She tugged at the sleeve, once again smiling. With the hand not tugging, she patted the seat beside her.

Reluctantly he sat. She noticed that the hands that, leaning forward, he had rested on his knees, were trembling and that his wide nostrils were quivering. She put out her left hand and tremulously, as though she were making the first contact with a wild animal, placed it over his right. She patted, patted again. With joy she sensed, through the hand, that his whole body was beginning to relax.

She raised the hand and pointed at the cat. Then she faced him. She mouthed, exaggerating the two consonants, 'Cat, cat, cat!' She pointed once more. Again she pointed, again she mouthed the word. He was staring at her in panicky bewilderment. She pointed at his chest, then at his mouth. '*Cat!*'

After many attempts, she suddenly saw, with delight, that his lips were moving as hers had been moving. But, instead of the expected word, what emerged was merely an incoherent grunt, followed by an effortful groan.

She persevered for a long time, until Mademoiselle called to her from the upstairs window of the schoolroom, to ask what she was doing, she was late, hurry, hurry! Through all Alexine's efforts with Sammy, the only response had been a series of other incoherent noises, while the dark, mysteriously handsome face had increasingly glistened with sweat and that once somnolent expression had become an anguished one.

'I must go now. *She* wants me.' Again Alexine had forgotten that he could not hear, much less understand, anything that she said to him. She patted his hand in reassurance and, bursting with an unreasoning joy, scampered back into the house.

'What were you doing with that boy?' Mademoiselle demanded. She already had her suspicions about that little savage's presence in the house. Later, she would pass those suspicions on to Nanny Rose, the two women would discuss them, as they discussed everything concerning their employers, and eventually, overheard, the suspicions would come to circulate among the servants, and through them to other people's servants, the tradespeople and the whole outside world. 'I'm sure you're not supposed to be with him.'

'Why not?'

Mademoiselle shrugged, drawing the Latin primer towards her. 'He is hardly *bien assorti*.' She had arrived knowing no Latin, and now constantly had to keep a lesson or two ahead of her pupil, who, at nine, was displaying an aptitude far superior to her own.

∽

Alexine constantly sought Sammy out, when he was not performing one of his vaguely prescribed duties for her father. That he so often himself seemed to be avoiding her was no deterrence to her. She remembered how, when Ginger had first arrived in the household, he had, as a result of years of mistreatment, been totally unapproachable. But

Nanny Rose had eventually succeeded in her wooing of him, so that, instead of arching his back and hissing when she put out a hand, he now came to it, prancing up, head tilted sideways, eager for her to scratch him under the chin or stroke his long, lean back. That was how, with infinite patience, Alexine now herself wooed Sammy.

Seated beside him, she would point to objects around them – a table, a chair, a picture, a vase. Then, with a piece of chalk (Aunt Addy would put her hands to her ears, gritting her teeth and rocking from side to side each time that she heard its squeak) Alexine would carefully inscribe on the schoolroom blackboard the letters representing it. She would hand the chalk to him. He would copy what she had written. Then, with a duster, she would hurriedly wipe out both sets of words. She would point to the same object again, then hand the chalk back to him. Sometimes his transcription was totally wrong; but, increasingly, it was, with a few errors, more often right.

None of the women around her approved of what she was doing, but none of them actually forbade it. Had they been sure that Sammy was in the house as the master's servant, they would certainly have done so. But they were not sure and therefore uneasy. From time to time Harriet or Addy would, in conversation with Philip, make devious attempts to define the intruder's status. But he seemed to take pleasure in its ambiguity and would not let himself be drawn.

Once, as Harriet and Philip were going through her housekeeping accounts together, she looked up abruptly, as though intuiting that something was amiss, to peer out of the window of his study. She frowned. 'Those two are at it again!'

'What two?'

She fingered the large, taut chignon at the nape of her neck. She was a plain woman, whose best feature had always been her luxuriant, shiny auburn hair. She therefore took great care of it, having Liliane wash it daily with a shampoo of glycerine and lemon juice and then massage macassar oil into it. 'Alexine and the boy.'

He said nothing, merely smiling, as with one hand he stroked his beard.

'Do you think it a good idea?'

'A good idea? What do you mean, my dear?'

'That they should be friends.'

'Why not?'

'Well, they're so different. And their future lives will be so different.'

'Does that matter? They're happy together. So . . .' He shrugged.

At the time, Harriet was exasperated and bewildered by his indifference. Surely he could see that a friendship between his daughter and that little savage was highly unsuitable – and might even have its dangers in the future? But then, as Sammy slowly began to learn to write isolated words – 'Come', 'Dinner', 'Carriage,' 'Master', 'Horse' – on the slate that he now always carried, along with a piece of chalk, in a bag worn over a shoulder, she too began to share her daughter's excitement. 'It's a miracle, darling,' she more than once told Alexine. Even those once incoherent sounds, the groans, yelps and rat-tat-tat stutterings, now seemed to be gradually coalescing. Any day now, she was sure, something intelligible would emerge.

Alexine had many friends who, not unnaturally, were curious about the mysterious black boy who had taken up residence at the house. But just as Nanny Rose was possessive of Ginger, not in the least liking it if he showed friendliness to anyone but her, so Alexine was possessive of Sammy. 'Couldn't he join us in our game?' one of these friends, invited over for Alexine's tenth birthday, suggested, and the others agreed 'Yes, yes, yes! Go and fetch him!' But Alexine shook her head. 'Papa and Mama don't allow me to play with him,' she lied. 'He's really a kind of servant. He helps Papa. That's why he's here. To help him.' 'Oh, please! Come on!' But Alexine was adamant.

∞

One evening Addy returned from her duties at the palace, to hurry upstairs to her sister's bedroom. Philip and Harriet had ceased to sleep in the same room or even to have sexual relations soon after Alexine's birth.

'Oh! I didn't realize you were having a fitting.' Addy was so eager to say what she had to say that she felt an upsurge of unreasonable anger when she opened the door and saw the young Hungarian dressmaker, Madame Molnar, with pins in her mouth, and Harriet standing, with uncharacteristic docility, head bowed and arms hanging limp, in the half-sewn evening gown before the cheval glass. Madame Molnar was a lithe, ample-breasted, beautiful young woman, with high cheekbones and long, glistening eyelashes.

'It'll soon be over. What do you think about these sleeves? Aren't they too long.'

'No, no, madame. They are perfect,' Madame Molnar said, even though the question had been put to Addy and not to her.

'Yes, they're perfect,' Addy concurred. Madame Molnar had the reputation of always being as right about the cut and fit of a dress as Philip about business.

Addy seated herself in a chair by the chimney-piece, torso stiffly erect, chin tucked in and foot rhythmically tapping against the fender. Only the day before Harriet had noticed that the brass of this fender was smeared and dull, and one of the two housemaids, having been scolded, had energetically polished it, so that it now shone in the late sunlight slanting through the window.

'Was she in a better mood today?' Harriet asked. 'She' was how they usually referred to Queen Sophia, so that others would not know about whom they were talking and so carry gossip to the outside world.

Addy shook her head. 'It's her time of life, I suppose.'

'Oh, surely she's long past that!' Harriet laughed.

Addy shrugged. 'She was making a fuss over not being able to find one of those wretched water-colours of hers. Of Windsor Castle. She even accused me of having thrown it away. If I'd produced such a daub, I'd have certainly done so. Out of shame.' She gave her brittle, dry laugh.

'You have a lot to put up with.' Harriet had been alarmed by that reference to Windsor Castle. Might it not enable Madame Molnar to infer the subject of their talk? Addy was always so indiscreet, and Madame Molnar was notorious for taking advantage of her clients' indiscretions.

After Madame Molnar had carefully folded and packed up the dress, she asked: 'For the French Embassy Ball next Friday?' She was aware of even far smaller events than this in the social calendar of The Hague.

'Please. Do you think that you can have it ready by then?'

'Of course, madame. Even if my girls have to stay up all night.'

Madame Molnar gone, Addy jumped to her feet. 'I heard something rather disturbing today. It was from Juliana. You know what a poison-ous little gossip she is.' Juliana, the daughter of a Dutch nobleman and his Bavarian wife, a cousin of King Ludwig, had recently joined Addy as one of the Queen's ladies-in-waiting.

Harriet, unlike Addy, had no interest in gossip, so that it was with some weariness that she went over to her dressing-table, picked up a comb and began to draw it slowly through her fringe, looking at the same time at her reflection in the glass. 'So what titbit did dear Juliana produce for you today?'

'There's apparently been a lot of talk about the boy.'

'The boy? What boy?' But Harriet knew perfectly well.

'Sammy.'

'Yes?' Harriet prompted, since her sister, now fearful of upsetting her, was hesitant about whether to go on or not.

'It's all too absurd but apparently people are saying that he's – he's Philip's son.'

Addy was amazed by the calmness of her sister's reaction. 'I've often wondered that myself.'

'You have!'

'Well, it's all been so odd. Bringing him here like that. Treating him now as one of the family and now as a servant.' She put down the comb, peered into the mirror to examine her large, pale face, and then sighed, dissatisfied, as so often, with the image before her. It was because of that dissatisfaction that, like her equally plain mother before her, she spent so much money on clothes. If only she had been born with the looks of Addy and the rest of her siblings, who all took after their handsome father, instead of their mother!

'Well, to tell you the truth, I've also often wondered. One senses something between them. *Une tendresse.*'

Harriet moved away from the mirror and walked briskly to where the dress that she had been wearing before Madame Molnar's arrival lay over a chair. She reached for it. 'Well, there's nothing I can do about it.' She spoke in a matter-of-fact voice. 'Philip will always lead his own life. That's how he is.'

4 THE TWO SISTERS – Harriet born only a year after Addy, so that they were often assumed to be non-identical twins – had always been far closer to each other than to any of their seven siblings. People, even when the sisters had grown up, would often refer to Harriet as 'the plain one' or 'the brainy one'. What they did not realize was that she was also the tough one and the adventurous one. Always she had felt that there were things within her – a capacity for the sort of work that no woman was allowed to perform, an emotional response that no man had ever demanded of her, an ability to surmount obstacles that had never been placed in her privileged path – that had lain idle and that, she had by now decided with melancholy fatalism, would always remain so.

Her father, Jonkheer Van Capellen, an Admiral in the Dutch Navy, had been taken ill with dysentery on board his ship when on duty in the Caribbean. All his life, despite the courage that he had displayed in the Battle of Algiers and the subsequent decisiveness with which he had taken the lead in the restoration of the House of Orange after the fall of Napoleon, he had been a man prone to panicky attacks of hypochondria. Some minor ailment – a prolonged attack of influenza, an unusually sharp bout of indigestion, a headache that persisted despite repeated doses of laudanum – would at once convince him that he was dying. It was said derisively of him that he spent far more money on his doctors than his wife did on her dressmakers. But the attack of dysentery was genuine enough. It made this once-commanding man shrivel away to a mere seven stone; indeed it seemed to everyone, even to the uppity, over-confident young English doctor called in to attend him, to be a death sentence,

Philip, then on the threshold of middle age but already growing rich, heard of the Admiral's presence on the island, and at once called at the house of the Governor, where the Admiral had been carried on a stretcher, to offer his help. Had the Admiral not come from a family so distinguished, he would probably not have done so. All through his life he was to show remarkable shrewdness not merely in predicting all the vagaries of the market but in befriending people who, in the future, would be of use to him. Daily he would arrive on horseback. With solicitous insistence he would then reassure the Admiral that, no, he wasn't dying, of course he wasn't dying, he was putting on weight, his colour was so much better, his hand-clasp was so much stronger. The Admiral was short-sighted, and night after night Philip would read to him into the early hours. Since the Admiral was also religious, what Philip was obliged to read were theological commentaries, collections of sermons and even the Bible. He hated the task but performed it with an appearance of enjoyment. Why, he used to wonder, should a man on such good terms with his Maker, be in such terror of His final judgement?

When not reading, Philip would play chess with the Admiral – who, though crass at the game, showed peevishness if, as was usually the case, he failed to win. In the early stages of the illness Philip would also perform tasks even less agreeable, removing the Admiral's soiled nightshirt and washing his soiled body, after he had repeatedly complained, in his high, rasping voice, of the roughness or incompetence of the two black male servants appointed to his care.

Of that period of illness, slow recovery and then prolonged convalescence, the Admiral would often say: 'He was like a son to me,' even though the difference in age between the two men was merely sixteen years. He would also often say: 'But for him I should now be in my grave.'

When Philip returned to The Hague, it was not surprising that he at once got in touch with the Admiral, as the old man had repeatedly urged him to do. But it was to find Van Capellen once again distraught – not, on this occasion, because he feared, as so often, that he was dying, but because some unwise investments in the East Indies had brought him near to bankruptcy. He needed money quickly, and Philip, after a series of brilliant financial coups, was in a unique position to advance it.

Cautiously, over a period of months, interrupted by a visit that Philip could not avoid paying to Constantinople, the men, as in one of those interminable games of chess that they had played in Demarara, edged their way, each in turn offering a piece, to a check-mate. As almost invariably in those games of chess, Philip was eventually the victor. For a sum small in his eyes, though not in the Admiral's, he saved the old man and his ancient family from ruin; and in return he married one of the old man's daughters, Harriet, and achieved the entrée to the Court that he had always thought to be unattainable by someone of his birth.

It was not Harriet, the plain one, whom he had first wanted to marry but Addy, and he had been bewildered by the Admiral's embarrassed rejection of this proposal. They had been sitting together, wholly relaxed in each other's company, once again circling and then edging towards a conclusion to their prolonged and wholly amicable negotiations.

'Addy! Oh, no, my dear fellow. She wouldn't be suitable for you. Not at all. But my Harriet! She has a wonderful nature and she's so talented – she paints, she plays the piano, she sings, she has virtually run the household since her mother's death.'

For a while Philip persisted. He had a passion for what was beautiful – whether the mansion that he was soon to buy for his renewal of residence in the Netherlands, furniture being sold by impoverished aristocrats in barns of houses in England, or Addy, so tall, so grave, so often silent, with her huge, dark eyes and her magnificent embonpoint and profile. 'She is one of the most – perhaps the most – beautiful woman I've ever seen.'

The Admiral gave an embarrassed laugh. 'Many men have thought that. But believe me – it's because of my affection for you and for no other reason that I think that Harriet is the one. I promise you! She'll make you a wonderful wife.'

Later Harriet would say that hers had been an odd betrothal: it was the man who brought the dowry to the marriage, not the woman.

By then, she had begun to think that she would end her life as a spinster. Men never seemed to notice her as they noticed her sisters, and particularly Addy. She was plain, yes, she had overheard that said of her and she knew it. Her eyes were too small, her brow too low, and her ankles were thick. When she smiled she revealed an eyetooth broken in childhood. Philip's proposal therefore came as a wonderful surprise to her. 'Oh, but Harriet, he's *old*!' Addy protested. 'You can't, you can't!' But Harriet could. She was intoxicated by the sense of power that exuded like a rare musk from him. That power seemed to be symbolized by the broad, muscular shoulders, the thick neck and, above all, the huge, white hands, with their perfectly manicured nails. The brutality of his love-making in the first months of their marriage only made him even more irresistible to her.

As a young girl she had been invited to a party at the Palace at which Clara Schumann had played. When, after that thrilling performance, Harriet had been introduced to the great pianist, noticing how after the effort of playing the monumental Liszt *Transcendental Studies,* a number of tiny beads of sweat still nestled in the wrinkles around her down-turned mouth and on her sallow neck, her father had said: 'My little girl also plays the piano. But as an amateur, a total amateur of course.'

The hump-backed woman, dressed entirely in black, stared at Harriet with dull, hooded eyes. Then she smiled, nodded. 'Why don't you play something for me?' She added, with a fleeting smile: 'But nothing too long.'

Harriet looked at her father. She felt no fear, only a steely resolution. She would play, she would play well.

'Do you really wish – ?'

'Yes. Yes, certainly. Play!'

The Johnkheer, having spoken to the Queen and received her permission, led Harriet over to the Pleyel grand. Totally without any nerves — she might, she thought later, wondering at her own behaviour, have been practising in the drawing-room of her own home, her mind half on other things – she waited, head bowed, for the chattering to die down around her. Then, taking a deep breath as though before a plunge into an icy sea, she began to play the Schumann *Humoresque*. By a fortunate coincidence, she had only recently learned it, so that she still retained every note of it in her memory.

Clara Schumann appeared hardly to listen. There was an abstracted expression on her face, she never looked at Harriet, and from time to time, since the room was hot and she had not yet recovered from her previous exertions, she agitated before her face a huge, black, lace-fringed fan, with spokes of mother-of-pearl that from time to time caught the reflection of the giant chandelier above her. But, as soon as Harriet, head once again bowed and hands now resting on knees, had finished, the great pianist jumped to her feet. '*Brava!*' She raised the by now closed fan in her right hand and brought it down, with vehemence, on the palm of her left. The applause from everyone else, even those who had no knowledge or love of music, then swelled to a crescendo.

Clara Schumann crossed over to Harriet, who at once jumped to her feet. She tapped the girl on her shoulder with the fan, in accolade. 'You made one or two mistakes – you know that, of course. Twice that B natural instead of B flat – and those final arpeggios – well, that doesn't matter. You can play, yes, you can play! You played that with all the necessary caprice – imagination – allure. Now you must study, study every day. Who is your teacher?'

Harriet told her. He was a once-famous Dutch pianist, who had succumbed to a creeping paralysis as the result (so the rumour went) of syphilis contracted in the brothels of Paris in his boisterously dissolute youth.

'Excellent. You couldn't find a better teacher – not here, at any rate.' She gazed at Harriet, at once questioning and imperious. Then she said: 'Do you promise me to work, work, work?'

Harriet nodded. All the nervousness that she had failed to feel when playing, she felt now.

'Yes?'

Harriet swallowed visibly. 'Yes.'

The older woman appraised her. Then she said: 'That's a beautiful dress.'

Harriet was humiliatingly aware that people constantly remarked on the beauty of her dresses, never on her own beauty. She began to blush.

The Queen, gigantic in mauve, rustled over. 'Thank you, my dear. Perhaps one day – one day – you will be our Madame Schumann.'

'There can be no second Madame Schumann,' the Admiral, who had been standing behind Harriet, said with the decisiveness with which he would once give an order on the bridge.

∽

Harriet worked at her music, for four, five, or even six hours each day. When the rest of the family complained of the incessant noise – to them, even Addy, it was always noise, never music – she eventually arranged with a neighbouring family to use the piano, far inferior to the one to which she was habituated, in an empty dower-house of theirs next to their mansion. Often, as she played, she would suddenly become aware that a child of this family, a sickly-looking boy with large, famished eyes, would be standing in the doorway listening to her for many minutes on end. But if she broke off to speak to him, he would barely answer and then vanish. Later, he was himself to become a pianist of note, before his premature death in the first railway accident to occur in the country.

Harriet's teacher soon became ill, with recurrent losses of vision and memory and a growing inability to enunciate the criticisms and suggestions that he struggled, in a manner agonizing to her and no doubt to him, to express. With the desolation of a bereavement or a broken love-affair, she then realized that she would soon have to find a successor. Already she had decided that she wished for a professional career.

On an impulse she wrote a letter to Clara Schumann. Would she be willing to accept her as a pupil? Harriet had not yet spoken to the Admiral about her ambition, having decided that she would defer that fight until she had received the great pianist's reply. Weeks passed and then finally a letter arrived, from Rome. It was so formal that Harriet inevitably wondered if an amanuensis might not have written it. Madame Schumann presented her compliments to Mademoiselle Harriet Van Capellen and her family and thanked her for her letter, too long left unanswered, owing to her travels on a concert tour just completed. Unfortunately, she was now too busy to accept any pupils. She wished Mademoiselle Van Capellen good fortune in finding a teacher worthy of her gifts.

Harriet brooded, in disappointment, on the letter for a long period. Then, on another impulse, she again wrote to Clara Schumann. Could she perhaps recommend a suitable teacher, since sadly she herself was unable to accept that task? That letter was never answered. Harriet would sometimes decide that, following Clara Schumann around on her ceaseless journeying, it had got lost; but more often she would accept, with a fatalistic melancholy, that such a great executant must be far too busy to concern herself with one of no doubt innumerable young aspirants who badgered her.

Nonetheless, Harriet did not yet give up on her ambition. In neighbouring Amsterdam she found an elderly woman teacher, in no way famous, married, with a brood of children and grandchildren to provide incessant distractions and noise. But the two women got on so well that Harriet would often sleep in the little canal-side house for two or three days on end, not in the least caring that there was no room for her to bring her own maid, that the attic assigned to her was tiny and damp, and that all through the night noise reverberated upwards from the cobbled towpath just below the window.

Eventually, the time came when, at Addy's urgings, Harriet at last steeled herself to speak of her dream to the Admiral. The result was disastrous. What was so bruising for her was not merely his absolute refusal to allow her to proceed with her plan, but his failure even to take it seriously.

'Oh, no, my dear!' He laughed. 'No, no! That's not the life for my Harriet, not at all. Look at the sort of life that Madame Schumann lives. Wretched! No wonder her husband went mad. And what happens to those children of hers when she's traipsing around the world? No, my dear, you don't want that sort of life – and I certainly don't want it for you. I want you to find a good husband, well-connected, rich. I want him to be able to look after you as your Mama and I look after you now. I want you to have lots of children, as we have – yes, even ten like us! That's what I want for you. You don't need to make money, not at all. Of course, you can go on playing,' he went on. 'Why not? At parties, for us, for your husband, your children. You have a talent, of course you have a talent. Madame Schumann said that. I remember well. But, – he gave a benevolent smile – 'my little girl doesn't want to have all the trouble and anxiety of making that talent public. For what? For what?'

Harriet did not immediately give up her dream in despair. From time to time she thought of running away from home, to Paris or Vienna or Rome or Munich. But how would she pay for a teacher, since certainly her father would not do so? And how would she live? If she did run away, despite those objections, a scandal would also engulf her family, so that it might well be that her father's post of Grand-Marshall would be compromised, as might the marriages of those her siblings who were still single. Oh, if only she had been born a man! If only!

෴

When Harriet's mother, long ailing with pulmonary tuberculosis, was advised to spend the next winter in Majorca with a younger, unmarried, much put-upon sister of hers, it was Harriet who, in effect, took charge of the household. She was so brilliant an organizer that the Admiral often remarked that she would have made a superb Chief of Staff. She was also, unlike her querulous, parsimonious mother, extremely popular with the numerous servants and the tradespeople. When, after a brief return to The Hague, the Admiral's wife died, and Harriet once again took charge of the household, there was a general feeling of relief among both staff and family, though of course the latter would never have admitted it. 'How are we all going to manage without you?' the Admiral repeatedly asked when her engagement was announced, since he knew that Addy would be neither so dedicated nor so efficient and that the only other unmarried sister was far too young to shoulder the responsibility of a household so large.

In the weeks immediately after her wedding, it was enough for Harriet to be thrilled vicariously by what she saw and heard or overheard of Philip's resourceful and decisive administration of a commercial empire that had already extended from the West to the East Indies and was now about to encroach on the North coast of Africa. Then she began to be consumed by the desire to cease to be merely a wondering observer of his manifold activities and to become his partner in them or, at least, his lieutenant.

Instead of merely inferring what was going on, as in the past, she now began to question him; and instead of waiting patiently for his repeatedly delayed return from some foreign city in which he was conducting his business, she now began to propose that she should accompany him. To her questions, his answers were always evasive and vague – oh, it was too complicated to explain to her, it was really all so boring, why on earth did she want to trouble her pretty head about things, when she had to make plans for that New Year's Eve ball and she must practise the piano part to those Schubert *lieder* for her performance with the youngest of the princesses at the Palace? To the suggestion that she should accompany him, he only once acceded, taking her to Paris with her maid, and then in effect leaving her wholly to herself, after he had pressed her to buy anything that she wanted anywhere and to have the bills sent to his Paris office. Subsequently, he would always say: 'You know what it was like in Paris. We hardly saw each other. Let's wait to go abroad together until I have a holiday. Or take Addy on a holiday with you. Why not? That would be far more entertaining for you.'

Eventually, after Alexine's birth, Harriet resignedly gave up, contenting herself with running her husband's household even more efficiently than she had run her father's, with playing the piano merely for her own pleasure, and with indefatigable work for a host of charities.

She was constantly occupied.

She was constantly bored.

5 ALEXINE HAD COME TO THINK OF SAMMY as her brother.

She had a way of moving soundlessly about the house, even into areas forbidden to her, and her ears were sharp. From fragments of the servants' conversation, she began firstly to suspect that there was some secret link between her father and the newcomer, and then to decide that, yes, that must be it, the boy was his son by some woman met on his ceaseless travels. She had always wanted a brother of an age closer to her own, and here in the house, in addition to those two half-brothers, both now married and fathers, in distant Liverpool, a city that she had never visited, one had suddenly and mysteriously appeared.

But she was ambivalent in her feelings, alternating between a joyful acceptance and an anxious resentment. Among Philip's children, she had grown used to being always the first in his affection. Although his two sons ran the English side of his business and although, as old age began to whittle away his once unbounded energy, he was now increasingly deputing to them other duties as well, he had over the years felt more and more distant from them as he had seen them less and less. The letters between father and sons had long since become oddly formal, even stilted, not all that different from those that passed between Philip and managers and agents in no way related to him. But his letters to Alexine were full of puns, nicknames, childish jokes and professions of love.

Now Alexine began increasingly to suffer twinges of jealousy, like the sudden spasms that herald a fever, whenever this beloved if often absent Papa of hers showed to the boy even a small part of the love that previously had been hers alone. One late autumn evening, in the course of her restless wanderings, she was looking down from the schoolroom window, the lamp unlit since lessons for the day were over, a hand to the curtain. She was waiting, though she did not acknowledge this to herself, for the return both of her father, who had been shooting on the polder, and for Sammy, whom he had insisted should go with him. Not only Philip carried a gun but also Sammy, who had been presented with one only a few days before. Why had she not also been given one? When she had demanded that of her father, he had laughed. 'Girls don't shoot. I gave you that new easel and box of paints only last Tuesday. What are you complaining about?'

Out of the misty dusk, two blurred figures at last appeared. They were extraordinarily close, one of the man's arms around the already muscular shoulders of the boy, while the other held his gun. The boy's gun was slung around him. As they passed under the window, the boy, body erect and chin raised, was laughing. He often laughed like that, seemingly at nothing, from no more than an excess of high spirits or pleasure in life. That closeness of the two bodies represented for Alexine an emotional closeness, from which she felt herself to be cruelly excluded.

Now they had entered the house and a moment later she heard her father calling to her: 'Alexine! Alexine! Where are you? Come and watch Sammy and me play billiards.' He had never allowed her to play billiards; that was not a game for a girl, he had repeatedly told her. She had no wish to sit and watch them at an occupation as stupid as hitting balls around a table. 'I'm busy!' she called back. After that, she remained for a long time at the schoolroom window, looking out, with a restless melancholy, at the dusk thickening over the dreary landscape.

Two day later, however, her mood had changed. By then Papa had left for Brussels and, in his absence and in the absence of Harriet and Aunt Addy at a luncheon party, she led Sammy into the billiard room and indicated to him, now scribbling on his slate with the piece of chalk that kept screeching like a living thing under the insistent pressure of her hand, and now making imperious gestures, that he should show her how to play. It took a long time but eventually she decided that she had mastered what was required. She had always been able to learn new skills with amazing quickness, just as in later years she was always able, like her father, to learn new languages. In the subsequent game she had no difficult in defeating the boy, who was laughably maladroit.

Having returned from Brussels – once more, days later than he had announced at his departure, because things, as he explained, had been so much more complicated and delicate than he had expected – Philip brought Alexine a magnificent French example of a *poupée modèle*, a cut-out figure with a number of gowns, with enormous sleeves, tight cuffs and elaborate hair-styles, all in the height of fashion, and a number of head-dresses. But for Sammy he brought a box of Andreas Hilpert tin soldiers in garish Prussian uniforms and shakos that towered above them far out of proportion to the size of their bodies. Had he forgotten that she had no interest in dolls, so that Nanny Rose had long since packed away a huge, neglected collection of them and placed them in an attic ('For your own little girls,' she had said) and that, instead, she was now building up a collection of soldiers herself? Sulkily she pushed the doll back into its box and, mouth pinched and eyes blinking back tears which she was determined not to shed, tugged at the tissue paper, until it wholly covered the gift again.

'Don't you like it?' her father asked.

She shrugged, putting the box containing the doll down on to the table and then giving it a push.

'It cost a lot of money.'

Again she shrugged, in assumed indifference.

'The trouble with you is that you're spoiled. Thoroughly spoiled.' It was what Nanny Rose constantly grumbled.

The next day, Alexine came on Sammy squatting on the floor of the glazed veranda, the soldiers spread around him. Totally still, he was not playing with them, merely staring at them. She knelt down beside him. Suddenly she felt an extraordinary, thrilling kinship with him, her brother and, yes, her friend. She had never felt that kinship with the two tall men, typical Englishmen of the upper middle-class in voice, dress and manner, her half-brothers, when they paid their visits, never together and rarely with their wives, to consult with their father about something to do with the business. She put out a hand and took up one of the soldiers. She placed it before Sammy. Then she picked up another and placed it beside the first one. 'Wait!' She gestured imperiously and he nodded, seeming to understand. She left the veranda and raced up the stairs to the schoolroom, where, from a high shelf – she had to stand on a chair to reach it – she took down one of a number of boxes, piled one on top of the other. It contained a set of English soldiers, from the Crimean War. She returned, set out these soldiers for herself, and then the rest of the Prussian soldiers for him.

∽

The next day, Philip, who for once had nothing more important to occupy him, took the two children out to shop with him. In the shop where he bought cigars and snuff, Alexine and Sammy watched while he raised a cigar to his nose, twirled it and sniffed, then another, and yet another, until at last he decided, yes, he wanted a hundred of those. A new mix of snuff had just arrived from London and that too he tried, putting some of it in the hollow on the back of his left hand between thumb and forefinger and then sniffing first through one nostril and then the other. He nodded at the owner of the shop, a Silesian Jew, who always puzzled Alexine because he wore a strange, circular little hat on the back of his head, even though she had always been told that, whereas ladies wore hats in indoors, gentlemen never did so. On a whim, Philip held out his hand, on which some of the powder still remained, and indicated to Sammy that he too should take a sniff of it. Reluctantly the boy did so and was at once convulsed with not one but three sneezes in succession. Alexine was herself convulsed, but in her case with derisive laughter. Philip and the tailor also laughed. Then Alexine said, 'Me, me, Papa! Let me try!'

'Oh, no, no! Girls don't take snuff. They don't smoke, they don't take snuff. What an idea!'

'Please! *Please!*'

On another whim, he yielded, amused and even charmed, as so often, by her importunity. He would often say that she had twice the spirit of her half-brothers. He put another pinch of snuff on the back of his hand and extended it. She bent over and sniffed, sniffed again, until nothing of it was left. She made a superhuman effort not to sneeze and, despite the insane tickling at the back of her nose and then in her throat, she managed not to do so.

Philip patted her on the shoulder in approbation. 'You took that like a man! Bravo!'

They next visited Philip's tailor. In his youth, in the West Indies, he had been careless of appearance, often wearing a soiled shirt, a frayed jacket or ill-fitting trousers. But wealth and his English first wife had changed all that. He was now regarded as a dandy, bringing back an embroidered waistcoat from Budapest, a perfectly cut suit from London, a shimmering silk cravat from Lyons, or a pair of beautifully flexible calf-skin boots from Florence.

Seated on two spindly chairs, japanned in black, the children watched in silence as the diminutive tailor, swiftly removing pins from the lapel of his jacket, went about his business. Alexine had often watched her mother having fittings, but this was the first time that she witnessed her father having one. From time to time he would turn to examine himself in one of the three panels of the mirror. He raised an arm, he shrugged a shoulder, he adjusted a sleeve, while anxiously the tailor waited. 'H'm, h'm. Not bad. But there's a small crease here. Just here. Don't you see it? *Here!*' Unlike Harriet, he easily became impatient with the people whom he employed to do things for him. 'Surely you can see it, man?' 'Oh, yes, sir, yes, I think – yes, I see what you mean.' Alexine hated the man's obsequiousness. She was sure that, however poor she was and however much she depended on other people's patronage, she would never debase herself like that.

Eventually, the fitting over, Philip was about to put on his hat, held out to him by the tailor, when suddenly, on one of the whims that became more and more frequent as he grew richer and richer, he said: 'I've an idea. How about making a suit for this boy over here? He's growing out of that one, and in any case it never amounted to much. Made in Jamaica and made – you'll never believe this – by a black woman, I swear to God by a black woman, not by a man.'

'Certainly, sir. Certainly. What sort of cloth did you have in mind? I've just received a new consignment of worsted from Bradford.'

The discussion took a long time, as Philip fingered now one bale of cloth and now another. The measuring took almost as long, with Philip admonishing Sammy 'Stand up straight, straight!' as though the boy could not merely hear him but also understand him. When Sammy's body still remained slouched – it was as though he were limply submitting himself to something painful or degrading – Alexine jumped up and taking hold of his shoulders eventually jerked him into the posture required. The two men laughed.

As they left the shop, Alexine felt mortification surge up in her, like an acrid bile. Her father had never ordered any clothes for her, but here he was ordering a suit for the boy from a tailor known to be the most expensive and exclusive in the country. It was useless for her to tell herself that her father was hardly the person to choose the cloth and cut of a dress for a girl and that that was a task for her mother and Aunt Addy. Jealousy continued to simmer within her, until Philip took the two of them into a Swiss teashop recently opened and ordered for each a cake, piled high with whipped cream and surmounted by the last wild strawberries of the year, and a glass of lemonade.

∽

On the night before Philip's departure on another of his journeys, this time to Spain, Portugal and Italy, Alexine, in the room next to his, could not sleep. Downstairs a farewell dinner party, for members of Harriet's family and the closest of the family's friends, was in progress. At one point, unable to hear what the distant voices were saying to each other, she crept out of bed and went to the top of the stairs. But strain though she might, she could make out only a little here and there. Philip's voice, though by no means the loudest, dominated the others with its deep vibrancy. The Admiral's eldest daughter's laugh soared out, an eldritch shriek, whenever her brother-in-law said something that amused her in that whimsical, slightly mocking manner of his.

When her legs and arms became chilly, Alexine returned once more to her bedroom, only to be awakened by the sound of her mother playing the piano. Alexine had already displayed a talent for a variety of things – languages, history, painting, calligraphy – but music was not one of them. Eventually she slept.

What roused her was the sound of footsteps outside her door, hurried but firm, which she could only suppose must be her father's. Then whoever it was – yes, it must be Papa – was mounting the narrow staircase that led up to the attics. She listened with beating heart, sensing something strange and even perhaps sinister, but not able to guess what it was. Then there were the sounds of footsteps descending, one set clearly once more her father's and the other faint and draggingly irregular. Who was this second person, descending with Papa?

She lay back again on her pillow and stared up at the ceiling, luminous in the moonlight that came through a window spider-webbed with a premature frost. Then she heard a sound, unmistakable and, in that context, late at night, when everyone had long since gone to bed, unnerving, even terrifying. It was Sammy, it could not be anyone else. It was the strange guttural, yelping sound that he made when he wished to refuse something or protest about something. Startled, she raised herself on her elbow, straining to hear more. After several seconds, the sound was repeated.

She got out of bed and stood in the middle of the icy room, wondering what was happening and what she should do. Then she edged to the door and finally opened it. Gathering courage she crept down the corridor. Outside her father's bedroom she halted, hands pressed to mouth. Then she said: 'Father! *Father!*' She repeated it more loudly. She put out a hand, hesitated, rapped, once, twice.

She heard him cross the room swiftly, and then the door had been pulled open and they were facing each other. 'What are you doing?' he demanded, with a mixture of astonishment and anger.

'I heard – noises. I was frightened.' She looked past him and saw Sammy, barefoot and in his nightshirt, seated rigidly on an edge of her father's four-poster bed. One hand was gripping one of the inlaid satinwood posts. His lips were drawn back oddly, to expose his teeth in what looked like the snarl of a cornered animal.

Philip, his nightshirt revealing a gold cross on a chain, nestling in the grey hair of his chest – Alexine had never seen that cross before – came closer to her. He took her by the arm, tightened his grip on it, turned her round and began to lead her back along the corridor to her room. 'There was nothing of which to be frightened. I heard a noise from Sammy's room. He'd had a nightmare – at least I supposed that he'd had had a nightmare, since he was making such a noise. So I went upstairs and brought him down to sleep with me.'

She herself had heard nothing from Sammy's attic, which was directly above her own room. If he had been making a noise and her father had heard him, then she would have heard him too. But she did not dare to say that, so clearly was Papa angry with her.

'Now go to sleep! Go on!'

He all but pushed her back into her room. Then he closed the door and she could hear him marching back to his own room and Sammy.

6 PHILIP WAS GREY-FACED and almost silent at breakfast on the morning of his departure. Out of habit, he helped himself lavishly to the elaborate meal set out, as always, hot dishes above spirit stoves, on the heavily carved oak sideboard. But he ate with an effort, bleak eyes staring out of the window at the frost-whitened lawn that sloped up to a row of bare trees, and said hardly a word.

'Are you feeling all right?' Harriet asked him at one moment, when her attempt to make conversation had received little more than inert monosyllables – 'Yes', 'No', 'Perhaps', 'Really?' – in answer.

'Of course I'm all right.' He struggled to swallow some cheese. 'What should be wrong with me? I'm thinking.' He added: 'I have a lot to think about.' Feeling nauseated by all that he had forced himself to swallow, he was aware that not merely Harriet and Addy but also the two children were now looking at him – the women with darting glances from under lowered lids, Harriet and Sammy with their hurt, bewildered eyes directed fully at him.

Suddenly he pushed his chair away from the table, the food less than half consumed, and jumped to his feet. 'There are things I still have to see to.' He hurried out of the room.

'Is he all right?' Addy asked.

Harriet shrugged. 'I hope so. He's getting too old for all this travelling. He should retire – I keep telling him that.'

'What would happen to the business?'

'Well, the boys could see to it perfectly well.' Harriet and Philip always referred to his two sons as 'the boys' even though they were both now middle-aged.

'Could they? They haven't got his gift.'

'I sometimes think that his gift is really a curse,' Harriet said quietly, pouring out some more coffee for herself.

They were talking, as so often, as though Daan, standing beside the sideboard, the white napkin that was his badge of office over one arm, were merely an automaton.

'Oh, look, mama! Papa is walking in the garden.' Alexine pointed out of the window.

Without either hat or coat, head bowed, Philip was slowly walking, large, white, ungloved hands clasped behind his back, up the lawn towards the stunted trees. All of them watched him. When he reached the trees, he put his hand to the bole of one, an elder, and then, as though exhausted, rested his body against it. He raised his head, he looked back at the house that for more than a decade had been the hub of his empire.

'What *is* he doing? He'll catch his death,' Addy said.

Again Harriet shrugged. Her impulse was to run out through the french windows and up the lawn to urge him to come in out of the icy cold. But she knew that, if she did that, she would only anger him, as she always did if she attempted to deflect him from a chosen course. She was peripheral to his life, she had realized for a long time, and she had come to accept that without either recrimination or pain, merely with an intermittent sorrow.

ॐ

Philip embraced the two children with a suffocating intensity of emotion, taking them in his arms and pressing them close against his chest, with such force that Sammy, hardly able to breathe, eventually squirmed to free himself. Alexine, in contrast, was as inert as one of her many rejected dolls. Within her there were feelings both of terror and of loss, such as she had never before experienced when her father had left on one of his journeys.

Philip, though she did not suspect it, was consumed with the same emotions as herself. He knew, he could not have said why, that he would never return. Yes, this farewell, the icy wind buffeting them even under the *porte-cochère*, while one of the horses, a handsome bay mare presented to him by an English client, repeatedly shook her head violently from side to side and neighed as though in distress, was to be the last.

'Be a good girl,' he said and then gave a long sigh, as he set Alexine down.

She tried to make a joke of a situation that she felt to be eerily beyond all of them. 'Oh, no, Papa. I want to be a bad girl. That's much more interesting.'

Now he embraced Addy, with the formality that had always existed between them, and then, finally, Harriet, kissing her first lightly on the forehead and then on each cheek. 'Don't worry, my dear. I'll soon be back.'

'I really don't know why you have to go on all these journeys.' She spoke with uncharacteristic fretfulness. He stared at her, frowning. He was so used to her being always cheerful, calm and resourceful, whatever the occasion.

'You know why I have to go,' he said. His voice was hollow and listless. He blinked his eyes and then removed his pince-nez – he had only recently taking to wearing them – folded them and put them in the breast pocket of his jacket. Without them, the eyes looked small and myopic.

With a sharp pang of sorrow, Harriet thought: 'He's an old man!'

Her lessons over, Alexine sat on at the schoolroom table, trying to concentrate on her Latin primer but unable to do so. As so often in the past days, she was thinking of her father. Where was he? What was he doing? Above all, why had he acted so strangely on that evening before his departure and at the departure itself? She wished, oh, how she wished that she could ask Sammy why she had found him seated like that, body rigid and lips drawn back from his teeth, late at night on an edge of the four-poster bed, the cone-shaped canopy above him looking as though it might at any moment crash down to snuff out his life.

Of one thing she was sure. Her father was in danger. But what danger could possibly threaten him? He had been on so many of these journeys; his young male secretary, Hans, a shadowy, handsome, taciturn figure with a faint stammer, little more than a momentary hesitation, was, as so often, accompanying him; he travelled in the utmost luxury, always putting up in suites in the best hotel on offer; and, as he himself would often boast, he had never had a day's illness in his life. But, for all that, she felt a constantly fluctuating anxiety.

She jumped up from the schoolroom table, almost knocking over her chair, and hurried out. 'Sammy! Sammy!' Then, as so often, she realized the futility of calling him. A maid, upstairs at work, leaned over the banisters to shout over them: 'I think he's in his room, miss. I heard him going up there.'

Sammy lay out on his bed. He had not taken off even his shoes or the jacket of the suit that, at such expense, Philip had had tailored for him. His face was twisted sideways on the pillow, the eyes expressionless. He did not turn his head when Alexine walked in, since he did not hear her. Then she moved into the periphery of his vision and he started up. He stared at her for a moment in alarm, then the large mouth opened in a smile. He slung his legs off the bed, preparatory to getting off it. The room was full of that musky odour of his. It always excited her, so that, in the years ahead, whenever she smelled a similar odour, she would always think, with a sorrowful longing, of him.

She beckoned, then mouthed: 'Come, come, come!'

Miraculously, he repeated what he could just recognize as 'Come!', the sound emerging from far back in his throat, almost like a cough. He knew, she was sure, that she was summoning him to the schoolroom.

Some days before Alexine had asked Mademoiselle if Sammy might attend her lessons. But Mademoiselle had given a derisive laugh: '*Chérie*, what would be the point? He would take in nothing. And he would be a distraction for you. No, no, that's not a good idea.' When Alexine had appealed to Harriet, she too had at once dismissed the notion out of hand. 'No, I'm sorry. The idea's ridiculous. I know that, with your father away, the boy has little to occupy him. But he would be bored to tears, sitting there and hearing – and understanding – nothing. Mademoiselle is right.'

'Please, Mama!'

'No. I've said no.'

'*Please!*'

'No! No, no, no!'

On this occasion, Alexine began by setting Sunny a simple sum. As, frowning, biting on the end of his pencil, he worked at it, she stared fixedly at him. With an intense exertion of her already formidable will, she was once more struggling, as she had repeatedly struggled in the past, to enter into a being so alien from her own. No use! She gave up, baffled and exasperated by her inability to communicate at anything deeper than a totally superficial level. Unlike any other member of the household, whether above or below stairs, she had developed an extraordinary instinct for what those inchoate noises that he effortfully jerked up from his diaphragm, were indicating. But, fatally, they indicated merely objects and actions, never thoughts or emotions. The desire to know what it was like to be someone other than herself, always an obsession with her from her earliest years, now became, in his case, an unappeasable longing.

Eventually, he pushed the piece of paper towards her and watched her as she put a tick against one sum and then another. 'Good,' she mouthed at him, and his face then broke into a smile. 'All correct.'

For a while she set him some further tasks, this time of subtraction, at which he was less adept. Then she reached for the slate beside her and, taking up a piece of chalk, wrote on it in capital letters 'RIDE?' At once, relieved, he jumped to his feet. Riding was the one occupation at which he surpassed her. Back in Jamaica he must have had practice in it, she had decided, to show such mastery of even the edgiest of mounts. Philip would often say of him in mingled admiration and amazement, 'He's a natural, an absolute natural.'

The groom or the under-groom usually accompanied them on their rides. But that afternoon the former was ill and the latter had taken the bay mare to the blacksmith to be shod. They themselves therefore saddled the horses, before setting off, she ahead of him, across the polder in the greying autumn light. The air was damp, the sky low, but Alexine was filled with a mounting exhilaration, such as she often now felt when he and she went out riding together.

At one point they saw two other riders in the misty distance, a girl who had been one of Alexine's closest friends since childhood, and her mother, who had been one of Harriet's. The two figures at once reined in their horses, then a moment later veered off in a different direction.

Alexine realized that the mother must have decided that she and her daughter should avoid the nigger ragamuffin – as the girl, taking her cue from her mother, had, to Alexine's indignation, more than once referred to Sammy.

In a bid to escape from this uncomfortable realization, Alexine brought down her riding crop, urging her horse into a gallop. Her hair, long, lustrous and thick – she had inherited that hair from her mother – streamed behind her in the wind. Sammy galloped behind her.

From a low, bedraggled clump of bushes, a skeletally thin dog emerged. On a number of occasions it had been caught foraging for food in the dustbins of the house; it was also suspected of having from time to time killed a chicken or a duck. Philip had said that he was going to shoot it, but Alexine, always tender-hearted to animals, had begged him not to do so. The dog now stood its ground, front legs wide apart and ears cocked, as the horses hurtled towards it. Then it began to bark on a single, high-pitched note. Alexine's horse reared up and swerved away. Insecure from riding side-saddle, as her mother always insisted, Alexine knew herself to be falling, attempted to right her balance, and then crashed to the frozen earth. She felt a sulphurous taste at the contact, and simultaneously a fiery pain shooting up her left forearm.

Sammy dismounted and ran towards her, while the two horses waited in total insouciance. The dog had slunk away, back into the bushes from which it had emerged. Sammy knelt down beside her, making incoherent noises. She endeavoured to smile. Had she broken her arm? She moved it. She decided that she had not done so, even though that brief, cautious movement had sent that fiery pain once again shooting up her forearm. She struggled to get to her feet, all at once aware that, since in her fall she had shattered the ice glazing a deep puddle, her skirt was spattered with mud.

His face was extremely close to hers. Then his arm was around her. She leaned against it, and once more struggled, now with his assistance, to get to her feet. She had never before touched him, not once. She could feel the muscular hardness of his body so close to hers, and could smell, with a hallucinatory intensity, that musky odour of his. Suddenly, astoundingly, he was gripping her to him, both arms around her shoulders, his cheek against hers. She could feel all the violence of his desperation. Overcome with a momentary terror, she pushed him away from her and, a moment later, wished that she had not done so. Frowning, lips pursed, she rubbed at her arm, rubbed at it repeatedly, while he stared down at it. Then going to her horse, she made a number of efforts to remount. She was only able to do so when, putting his hands to her waist, he assisted her by half-lifting her up.

They rode home slowly, side by side. The dog had reappeared and now, at a distance, it followed them, head lowered, picking its way carefully over the icy terrain. As they approached the house, the animal mysteriously disappeared. She was never to see it again. In the days ahead, she would often think of it, with its dull coat, sticking up in tufts, and its long, greying muzzle, and wonder whether perhaps someone had shot it, as her father had threatened to do.

The arm was badly bruised but not broken, the doctor, hastily summoned by Harriet, assured them. He rubbed some embrocation, smelling of turpentine, into it and then bandaged it up. It ached all that night, so that Alexine could not sleep, despite a dose of laudanum prescribed by the doctor and administered by Nanny Rose. But for once her chronic insomnia did not worry her, so that, instead of tossing fretfully, as she usually did, she lay absolutely still. All the time she thought of that frenzied embrace. It was as though by holding her so suffocatingly close, he had wanted to become one with her and so to wrest from her the knowledge of her inmost being, just as she had continually wanted to wrest that same knowledge from him. But the effort had been futile, and the belief that it could be anything else was only an illusion. She now no more knew what it was like to be him; and he, she was sure, now knew no more what it was like to be her. Physically, they had been closer than ever before; but they were no closer to each other in any other way.

7 EVEN THE MOST ARDUOUS TRAVEL, across the winter wastes of Russia or, on one occasion, by ship through often raging seas to Shanghai, had never before tired Philip or daunted him. But now he felt an ineluctable weariness. This was not a weariness of the bones or even of the flesh, such as he had often experienced in the past after some prolonged physical exertion – a day of riding over rough terrain, an ascent of a mountain, more than an hour of swimming in a rough, icy sea – but of the spirit.

Even people who had seen him only a few months before were shocked by the change in his appearance – the eyes dull, the cheeks fallen in, the skin a leaden grey – when they first set eyes on him. 'Are you all right?' they would ask him, suspecting some mortal illness in a man of his age. But then, in the course of doing business with him, having found that his mind was as alert and decisive as ever, that he could still drive the sharpest of bargains and that he could at once see through any attempt to deceive him, they would decide that they must have been mistaken.

In Geneva, between a morning appointment that had ended sooner than he had expected and a late afternoon one, he had set off alone for a walk around the lake. But after a few minutes he had thought, as he had repeatedly been thinking, 'What is the point?', and had sunk on to a bench. Moodily he had stared out over the placid water, while two children, now screaming at each other and now laughing hilariously, repeatedly threw a stick for a chocolate-coloured labrador to retrieve. The noise jarred on his nerves – oh, why couldn't they go and play somewhere else? Eventually they did so. But almost immediately an overdressed woman, with heavily rouged cheeks and yellow, high-buttoned boots, parasol in hand, walked towards him, with seductively swaying hips, peered at him, an elderly and obviously rich man in a homburg hat and a long black coat with a sable collar, and then seated herself on the other end of the bench. She kept stealing glances at him, clearly waiting for him to address her. Eventually she asked him for the time. Without answering, he rose with a sigh and began to trail slowly, leaning on his cane, back to the hotel.

In Rome, he ordered dinner to be brought to his room. The waiter wheeled in the trolley, each of its dishes lurking under a silver cover, but the mere smell of the food nauseated him so that he continued to sprawl out on his bed, fully clothed, his gaze fixed on one of the covers, unnaturally dazzling under the light of the elaborate gasolier reflected in it. He thought: *One hears of being love-sick. I am life-sick.* It was not only the prospect of all that elaborate food, prepared in one of the finest kitchens in the country, that turned his stomach and made him want to retch. He had also lost all appetite for the intrigues, the jugglings, the confrontations and the collaborations that had once made these business tours far more thrilling than any love-affair. Now, like some great executant who has lost all interest in performing but who continues to do so with no loss of technical mastery, he could still outwit or outcharm all those with whom his business lay. But the work and the results of the work were dust and ashes. What was the matter with him? He repeatedly asked himself the question and could find no reply.

In Bologna, shaving himself on a whim – his beard was always carefully demarcated to an area below his lips – instead of calling in the hotel barber to do so, he stared at his grey, doleful reflection in the bathroom mirror and then lifted the razor and laid its blade across his throat, just above the prominent adam's apple. Gently he drew it across the sagging flesh, feeling nothing. Beads of blood appeared, like a dotted line incised in red ink across a sheet of parchment. He reached for the towel and held it to his throat. Later that morning, a chamber-maid would retrieve the towel from the floor, see the blood on it, and call to another of the chamber-maids to show it to her. But they repeatedly found even odder things in the rooms that they cleaned, and soon the maid had thrown the towel into a huge wicker basket with all the other soiled towels. For the next few days Philip wore an unusually high collar and cravat.

At last, after a visit to Milan, all his lucrative business had been transacted, and he thought that, if he were now to die, his wealth would be even more impressive than ever. It was then that he added a codicil to his will, leaving a major part of his fortune to Alexine and nothing whatever to the boy whom all those who knew him in the Netherlands and many who knew him in other countries, assumed to be his son. He summoned the manager and one of the assistant managers of the hotel to his room and had them witness the document, which he then sealed in an envelope and handed to his secretary, Hans, telling him: 'Keep this – in case anything should happen to me.'

Later, as he said goodbye to Hans, one of whose aunts lived in Florence and whom he was about to visit, he handed him a wad of banknotes, amazing him with a generosity remarkable even for him, and said tersely: 'Enjoy yourself.' In two weeks, he said, he would be back at the hotel, where he would spend a night before the two of them returned to the Netherlands together. 'Are you sure you don't wish me to accompany you, sir?' Hans asked, since he had so often done so on previous occasions when Philip had taken a brief holiday. 'I'd be happy to cancel my visit to my aunt.' 'No.' There was no explanation. On his departure, Philip left most of his luggage behind at the hotel.

He had decided to journey south, first by the newly built railway and then on by ship to Sicily, to visit his friend the German Baron. He had visited him twice in the past, and on each occasion, free of all the stress of doing business now in one city and now in another in a variety of languages and with a variety of characters, he had at last been able to relax and to enjoy himself in a manner that was rarely possible anywhere else. As he now sat in the railway carriage reserved by Hans for his sole use, he was conscious that an essential part of his being had fallen away, as the flywheel might detach itself from the machinery of a watch, and he thought, though with growing pessimism, that perhaps in the tranquillity of the little seaside village he might now find it again.

Physically the long journey was nothing to him. But still that aching weariness of the spirit persisted. On the ship there were three Italian men known to him, through the business, for many years. They too were going to Sicily, to Palermo, where they planned to build an hotel. The men tried to get him to drink and play cards with them, but he made the excuse that he preferred to remain up on deck to watch the changing coastline. In fact, the coastline, with huge, ungainly black birds – what were they? he vaguely wondered – wheeling above it, interested him not at all.

The Baron's small thatched house, in a cranny by the sea between two abrupt cliffs, was deserted – as the coachman who took him there had already warned him. Philip tried the doors but all of them were locked. In the distance a dog, alerted by the sound of the carriage wheels jolting over shale, barked with a maniacal persistence. Finally, Guido, the male of the elderly couple who looked after the Baron in their lazy, laughing fashion, limped down the hillside path that led from their ochre-coloured villino high up above the main house, to say that two days before the Baron had had to leave for Frankfurt. The wife whom he so rarely saw was dangerously ill, perhaps dying, perhaps already dead. Since the old man knew Philip, who had always tipped him and his wife lavishly, he offered to fetch the key, along with his wife to prepare a meal and a bed in the guest-room.

At once, as soon as he had set foot in the untidy, dusty, sprawling house, that broken fly-wheel trembled, jerked forward, jerked forward again, and then began to move with all the strong, pulsing regularity of the past. As he smelled the sauce cooking for the pasta and simultaneously gazed out through a window encrusted with dead flies at a long, empty stretch of sand, with a horizon streaked with orange and yellow behind it, he felt that what he had lost, seemingly forever, he had miraculously regained. He went into the kitchen, where the woman stood at the stove and the man was, with extreme deliberation, placing dishes and cutlery on a tray. He began to talk with them in an Italian far superior to the Baron's – even though the Baron had been living in the house for at least a decade. Soon all three of them were laughing. As their joking continued, Philip even caught the inflections of the Sicilian dialect and was able to reproduce them.

That night, a lamp beside him, he took down at random from their shelves one work of pornography after another from the collection built up by the Baron over a lifetime. Many of these books were centuries old, some extremely valuable. They were arranged without any system and many of them had suffered from damp and the depredations of insects. Philip turned the pages, reading a sentence or a paragraph here and there, and pausing to smile over a woodcut or etching. Eventually he opened a desk drawer and found in it some of the sepia photographs, each subject carefully posed on a rock, at the prow of a boat, on the long, narrow, crumbling veranda, or on the shore with the wide sea and the even wider sky as a background, that the Baron, a pioneer photographer after he had abandoned his sketch-book for the newly invented camera, himself had taken. The Baron would not object to this opening of the drawer or the viewing of its contents. The two men had often passed the photographs back and forth between them in the past. Looking at the photographs, Philip felt a joy well up in him from a source that, in the past days, he had thought to have dried up forever. For the first time since he had started on his travels, he slept deeply, hand under cheek, with no troubling dreams.

He was up early the next morning. After the chill of the Netherlands and even northern Italy, it seemed unseasonably warm. In only his nightshirt and a wrap found in the Baron's wardrobe, he sat out on the veranda and watched the sun rise, spokes of orange light radiating out with increasing intensity from around a huge, pink bank of cloud, as he awaited the arrival of Guido's wife, Maria, to prepare his breakfast for him. For the first time for several days, he had an appetite. The appetite was not merely for food, but also for life. As she made the coffee and sliced the rough peasant bread, Maria sang to herself in a throaty voice that might almost have been a man's. The song, *La Piccola Colomba,* was a sad one, about a small girl's pet rock-pigeon that one day flies up into a clear blue sky and is lost forever, but the sound of it, coming through the window now open behind him, only increased his feeling of joy.

Having eaten his simple breakfast, so different from those brought to him in the luxury hotels in which he had recently stayed, he sat on out there on the veranda, doing nothing and happy to be doing nothing after so much frenetic activity. He stared out to sea, at one moment wishing that he had the energy to go back into the house and fetch the Baron's telescope, in order better to see a steamship that, trailing a

43

ribbon of greyish-blue smoke behind it, was crawling past, an iron insect, far out to sea.

When he did return to his bedroom, he saw that Guido, trained in the task by his employer, had laid out his clothes – the suit, the shirt, the cravat, the clean underwear – for the day ahead. The soiled underwear and shirt of his long journey south had vanished, presumably to be washed and ironed by Guido's wife. He put on the clean underwear and reached out for the shirt. Then he dropped it to the floor. He was used to servants constantly picking things up for him, and so thought nothing of leaving it there. He went into the Baron's room, next door to his, and opened the vast Biedermeyer wardrobe. The wood of it was warped and he had to tug at the door. He inspected the clothes hanging inside it and then opted for an open-necked peasant shirt of a rough, yellowing cotton, and a pair of worn trousers, one leg of which was frayed at the end. Then his eye caught the wide-brimmed straw hat on the shelf above the clothes, and he reached up for that.

Out in the overgrown garden, its grass a yellowish brown and its flowers almost all shrivelled, he heard Guido chopping wood. Soon, when this strangely unseasonable warmth – *una estate di San Martino*, Guido's wife had called it, shaking her head and saying that such a second summer always meant a subsequent winter of illness – had ended, fires would be needed. Philip walked out into the garden, the sun warm on his face and his neck bare, so that a number of dot-like, dark brown scabs showed where the razor had cut it. He wanted a boat, he said. Was he going to fish? the old man asked. No, no, he didn't think so. He might swim. The old man was astonished. The season for swimming was long since over, he protested, it was out of the question, even the two English *padrone* who lived on the other side of the headland and who swam long after everyone else had ceased to do so, had given up. Philip laughed. 'Well, we'll see,' he said. Then he added boastfully: 'I've swum in Norwegian fjords in October.' But that meant nothing to the Italian. Guido put down his axe on the chopping block and hurried off up the hill. Eventually a boat appeared. A thirtyish man, unknown to Philip, was pulling at the oars with brown, muscular arms, Guido was seated in the prow, and a boy, of about the same age and build as Sammy, was seated at the tiller.

Guido and the man, but not the boy, got out of the boat and the man then tethered it to the rotting jetty with large, ungainly but surprisingly deft hands. Guido and the man were both disappointed when Philip made no protest at the high price first quoted by the man in what he had imagined would be a long period of bargaining. 'Fine. Good. Let's go.'

'Do you want to take some water with you, *signore*?' Guido asked.

'Some wine would be better.'

Guido walked back to the house, eventually to return with a *fiaschetta* of the raw, almost black wine of the district, and a tumbler. In his absence, Philip talked to the boatman, marvelling that, in this warmth, he should be wearing a knitted woollen vest. Eventually the man seated himself on the beach and began to pick with the nail of a forefinger at a callus on the sole of his bare foot. From time to time Philip surreptitiously glanced over to the boy. But the boy, now perched on the farther gunwale of the boat, was looking out to sea, totally uninterested in the conversation between Philip and the man who was presumably his father.

With long, steady strokes the man rowed the boat out over the placid sea. Then he stopped, his forehead glistening with sweat, and called out to the boy to take over. Philip was amazed that, when the boy rowed, the boat moved far faster than when his father did. Philip pointed to three high rocks, which he remembered from previous visits, when he and the Baron had taken it in turns to row and the Baron had kept catching crabs and had eventually given up, 'absolutely worn out' as he put it in the English that they usually spoke to each other, and let Philip once more take over. 'Let's go over there,' he said. 'There!' The boatman said that those rocks were known as *Le Tre Madre* – no, he did not know why, he added when Philip asked the reason. The highest of these rocks arched over to make a tunnel, wide enough for a boat to enter.

Philip said that he thought that he would swim in the tunnel. The water was so beautiful, a limpid blue, and he could see small fish flickering about just below its surface. But he did not give that as his reason for wishing to swim there, since he thought that the boatman would think that fanciful of him. The boatman protested – No, no, it was far too cold, if he was determined to swim than it was far better to do so closer in to shore. But Philip, already stripping off, only laughed. The boatman was stupefied that a man so much older than himself should be prepared to undertake something so unpleasant. Not since he was a young boy had the boatman ever entered the waters to swim.

In only his drawers, Philip poised himself on one side of the boat. He looked across at the boy, but once again, staring back through the tunnel of rock, he refused, with what struck Philip as a deliberate obstinacy and even unfriendliness, to return the look. Then he dived.

After a long summer of intense heat, the water was still amazingly warm. He first swam out through the tunnel to the other side and then, glimpsing the ruin of a church high up on a hillside, made for its direction, almost as though, despite its distance, he was proposing to visit it. At last tiring, he turned over and floated on his back. He shut his eyes, he almost slept.

To his amazement, he was aroused by the sound of splashing,

approaching nearer and nearer. It was the boy, who was clearly a swimmer quite as strong as he was. Now, for the first time, the boy looked straight at him. He grinned. Then he executed an elaborate series of dives, twisting and turning, head over heels, heels over head, his head or his whole body disappearing and re-emerging sometimes within a second or two and sometimes after so long an interval that Philip feared that something had happened to him. They faced each other. Philip laughed and the boy laughed. Since the boy was now near enough, Philip put out a hand and rested it on his shoulder. The boy did not dart away, as Philip had half expected.

'I'd like to take a photograph of you,' Philip said in Italian, with the Sicilian accent that, with his faultless ear, he had so easily acquired.

'Of me?' Treading water, the boy pointed to his still entirely hairless chest. 'A photograph? I've have never had a photograph of myself.'

'Well, you will now.'

'The Baron takes many photographs.'

'Yes. I'll use his camera. He gave me some lessons. But whether I'll be any good at it ... You'll have to sit very still. As you were sitting in the boat,' he added.

Side by side, they began the long swim back. When they had traversed half the distance, Philip paused for a rest and the boy, though he did not need one, paused too. Once again they faced each other, treading water. The boy put up a hand and pushed the seaweed-like hair up off his sunburned forehead. 'When?' he asked.

'When?'

'When does the *signore* wish me to come for the photograph?'

'This afternoon? About four? We need light, sun, a lot of sun.' He gazed up at the cloudless sky. He pointed. 'A lot of light, a lot of sun.' A thought came to him: 'But perhaps in the afternoon you have a siesta.'

'It doesn't matter. I'll come. About four.'

'About four.'

As the boy's father propelled the clumsy boat back to the shore, and the boy, his head averted, once again gazed out to sea in a detachment totally at odds with the intimacy of their encounter in the water, Philip looked up again into the cloudless sky and ran a hand over his shoulder, feeling its smoothness and warmth. He thought: This is happiness. Yesterday I was life-sick. Now, by some miracle, I have been cured.

∽

After a lunch of pasta and grilled red mullet, the Italian couple disappeared, to Philip's relief. He stood at a window and watched them trudge up the hill. She was carrying a basket, presumably with his soiled clothes in it. She, but not he, was going to return in the evening to get him his meal.

Eventually the boy arrived, heralded by his whistling of the same song, *La Piccola Colomba*, that Maria had been singing in the kitchen. Philip had never heard it before. He assumed that it must now be popular in Sicily. It could not be a folk-song, it was too sophisticated for that. Away from his father, the boy was wholly relaxed. He strutted about the room, examining the various objects in it. When he picked up a silver cigarette box, Philip thought that perhaps he was going surreptitiously to pocket it. But he merely raised the lid, removed one of the Baron's black Egyptian cigarettes and, having looked enquiringly over to Philip – 'May I take it?' the look said – put it in his mouth when Philip smiled and nodded. Philip rummaged in a trouser pocket and produced a small enamelled box, bought on a visit to Constantinople, in which he always carried his vestas. The boy, standing close, head tilted upwards, let him light his cigarette for him. He drew deeply, drew again, and then began to cough, his eyes filling with tears. Philip laughed and, after a moment of looking annoyed, the boy joined in the laughter. Then he threw himself down on to the rickety *chaise-longue* and leaned back, his cap, which he was still wearing, tilting down low over his forehead. He grinned and drew again on the cigarette. He held it out before him and stared down at it through narrowed eyes. There was something over-familiar, even impertinent about all his behaviour. But so far from upsetting Philip, that merely excited him.

Eventually, after they had talked for a while – Philip had offered the boy some of the wine left over from the previous evening, and had then poured out tumblers for each of them – Philip got up and lugged out of a closet the cumbersome plate camera and then searched for the black hood, which he eventually found on the floor of the closet, behind a cabin trunk. The boy made no attempt to help him as he carried the camera and the plates for it out on to the veranda. There was a well of sunshine there, in one corner, and the three rocks could be seen far beyond it, with the sea, now a wholly unreal cerulean in the afternoon light, stretching out between. If only it were possible to photograph in colour! He wanted to catch that grey-green of the rocks and that extraordinary blue of the sea; but most of all he wanted to catch the flesh-tints – the honey-colour of the shoulders, the ivory of the torso, the brown of the arms – of the body that had been revealed to him in the water.

Having set up the camera to his satisfaction, Philip went back into the house and climbed up to the attic where he knew, from his previous visit, that the Baron kept his props: a goatskin; Pan pipes; a wreath of laurel; a pair of sandals, painted gold with thongs of red leather; a toga. He thrilled, even as he descended the stairs, at the thought of dressing the boy in them.

'What's this? I'm not going to put those on. Not on your life! No, no!'

He might have been asking the boy to dress up as a girl.

'Please! For the photograph. I want you to look like a young Greek god, oh, hundreds and hundreds years ago.'

The boy burst into derisive laughter. 'A Greek god!' He pulled a face. 'Are you crazy? I heard that some odd things went on with the Baron in this villa but I never thought...'

Philip went back into the house and returned with a handful of bank-notes. He held them out. 'Yes? Well?'

The boy stared at them in stupefaction. Then he put out a hand, the nails bitten to the quick, and snatched at them with a joyful laugh. 'Now you're talking!'

Philip exposed plate after plate. Having first been uncooperative, the boy was now altogether too co-operative, adopting ludicrous attitudes and pulling extravagant faces. At one point the laurel wreath tipped over and all but covered his face, at another he somehow managed to snap the Pan pipes in two.

Eventually, his excitement constantly mounting, Philip indicated that he wanted to photograph the boy in the nude. 'No, no! Certainly not! No!' The boy was vehement, shaking his head, his cheek flushed with both wine and his outrage. Again Philip went back into the house, again he returned with a fistful of banknotes.

'Oh, all right then. All right!'

The sun was beginning to sink when the photography session ended. Between them, they carried all the equipment – the ponderous camera, the two heavy boxes of fragile plates, the black cloth, the ludicrous costumes and props – back into the house. The boy took hold of Philip's hand, not as an act of intimacy but to examine the rings on it. He pointed at one ring, a Roman intaglio of a bull in an elaborate early nineteenth-century setting. 'For me?'

'No, not that one. That was given to me by my wife. On our marriage. But you can have this one.' He held out his hand and pointed to his signet ring. It was incised with the crest of the Admiral's family, since his own family had none.

'Really? Truly?' The boy was overjoyed.

'But first you must do something for me. Something small but important to me.'

The boy nodded, dubiously. He understood, of course he understood. The Baron had often said that all these Sicilian ragamuffins understood.

'Yes?'

The boy nodded.

∽

Philip once again slept deeply. But this time the sleep was not dreamless,

48

as on the night before. He dreamed of the polder, stretching on and on behind the house, far vaster than in reality. In the distance he could see Alexine and Sammy trudging hand in hand across it, with that emaciated dog, that dog that he had wanted to shoot, trailing, shaggy head lowered, behind them. He set off determined to catch them up. But though he constantly quickened his pace, eventually breaking into a sprint, he could not do so. The distance between him and them inexorably lengthened.

All at once he heard a flapping, as of clothes put out to dry in a high wind, all around him and above him. He looked up. The sky was darkening with a vast flock of those huge, ungainly, black birds that he had seen from the ship. What were they? What did they want?

It was then that he awoke. A door had slammed – or was it a window? He must have left one or other open. He sat up in bed and almost at once, hearing footsteps, jumped out of it, knocking over the table beside it as he did so, so that a half-drunk glass of the raw, black wine overturned and crashed to the floor, shattering to fragments and splashing its contents up on to the ragged silk that covered a settee. 'Who's that?' For a moment he thought that it must be the boy. Then he could see the intruder in the moonlight. His face, expressionless, implacable, like that of some piece of statuary, was not the boy's but his father's.

'What do you want?'

But Philip already knew, as the man, arm outstretched, rushed at him.

8 THE HEAD OF THE OLD MAN, Frederick van der Warsenberg, who had succeeded the Admiral, now dead, as Grand-Marshall, appeared around the carriage door like that of a beetle. He clutched the extended arm of the coachman and stepped unsteadily down from the carriage. He had been obliged to do many unpleasant things in the course of a long and adventurous life, but this, he thought, was one of the most unpleasant. As he tottered forward on his stick, Hans leapt out of the carriage behind him. His narrow handsome face was extraordinarily pale and it was disfigured by a stye angrily erupting along the left eye-lid. Both men were dressed entirely in black, their shoes and top-hats gleaming.

As soon as she saw them, Harriet knew, as though she herself had been pierced by the knife that had abruptly ended Philip's life, that something terrible had happened. But she smiled and held out her hands to the old man in greeting, as she said, with an assumed easiness: 'General – how good to see you! When I got the message ... What brings you here?'

In a voice husky both with the winter bronchitis from which he was suffering and from emotion and stress, he said: 'Madame – please sit down. Please.' He pointed to the sofa.

But Harriet had now turned to Hans. 'Hans! I'd no idea that you were back. But what's become of my husband? Didn't you return together?'

'Please sit. Please,' the General repeated on a note of desperation. He clutched his top hat before him with hands swollen with arthritis and blue with cold from the long carriage ride.

Harriet crossed slowly to an upright chair, not to the sofa at which the General had pointed, and seated herself. Her manner was outwardly calm, despite the turbulence within her. She had been brought up in the belief that any public show of emotion was unladylike.

'I have some terrible news. You must be brave. I know you will.'

She stared across at him, plump chin uptilted and lips compressed. She waited. Then, as he floundered, emitting a rasping cough, hand raised to mouth, she prompted: 'Yes, General? What is it?'

'Your husband ...' Again the hand went up to his mouth and again the cough shook him before exploding upwards. Stricken, he looked over to the young secretary, as though expecting him to rescue him. But Hans's head was bowed. His grief for his master, whom he had also come to regard as a friend, was intense.

'I'm afraid . . . He died. In Italy . . .' The General broke off.

Harriet stared not at him but straight ahead of her. As soon as she had received the message that the General wished to see her that morning, she had known in her inmost being that Philip was either dying or dead. But now that the death had been put into words it seemed even more dreadful. 'How? How did it happen?' She turned to Hans. 'Hans – tell me.'

The young man moved towards her. He realized, despite her outward composure, the extent of her shock, and he wanted to comfort her. But the social gulf between them precluded any physical contact – the taking of a hand, an arm around a shoulder, even an embrace – of the kind that he could have shown to any one of his friends or relatives in a similar situation. 'He was k-killed, madame. M-murdered.'

'*Killed!*' She was astounded. Until then her scenario for his death had been totally different. He had looked so pallid and worn at his departure, he was still working so remorselessly. A man of his age who lived such a life of ceaseless action could all too easily succumb to an apoplexy or a heart-attack. 'Where? How?'

Hans glanced over to the General. He was hesitant to usurp the other man's function as the bearer of the news. To do so might seem presumptuous of him.

'The details are not yet fully known,' the General muttered, looking down at his highly polished boots. 'He left for a holiday in a village in Sicily,' he continued in a louder voice. 'He had a friend there, a German Baron. His – his name now escapes me. The Baron was not in his villa, he was away in Frankfurt – or was it Düsseldorf? No matter. No doubt you know him – or know of him.'

'I've never heard of any German Baron friend of my husband's. Why should he have chosen Sicily for a holiday with this – this German Baron?' The corollary to that question was: Why didn't he come back home as soon as his business was finished? She looked first at the General and then, when he remained silent, at Hans.

Hans sighed. 'He s-seemed to be exhausted. He needed a rest. There had been a lot of difficult n-negotiations, first with the Bank of Geneva, then in Rome with . . .' He broke off. Why trouble her with all the details?

'Why were you not with him?' Her tone carried a hint of accusation.

'I have an aunt in Florence. A w-widow. The master said that I could go and visit her. I offered to accompany him s-south but . . .' He shrugged and rubbed with a forefinger at the stye. He swallowed. 'He said that that wasn't n-necessary.'

'But why was he murdered? Why?' She jumped to her feet as she put the question and crossed over to the window giving on to the garden. Her back was to them.

'The police are not sure,' the General answered, repeating what Hans had told him. 'So far we have only the preliminary report from the consul in Palermo.' Again the old man was racked by the barking cough. His wife had scolded him that it was madness to go out in such a cold, but he had an unyielding sense of duty. Philip had been a close friend, even if he had often made cruel fun of General's pomposity and fussiness; the General and the Admiral had fought in the same campaigns. 'He was alone in the villa. The two servants live somewhere else. It was during the night. It is all – nothing is clear at present. The police at first thought that the motive was theft but it seems that nothing was taken. He had a lot of money with him, the villa was full of valuable objects. Nothing touched.'

The General fell silent. Hans looked at him, waiting for him to go on, and then, when the silence prolonged itself, he volunteered: 'Perhaps there was a dreadful m-mistake. The Baron had lived there for many years, he may have made an enemy – or many enemies ... In Sicily – you know how it is. Assassinations are c-common. It might have been a hired assassin who entered the house.'

'At all events the police are still investigating,' the General took up.

'I see.' Harriet turned to face them, still outwardly calm, and then went back to the sofa and sat down on it. She mused for a while. Then she said: 'How am I to tell Alexine?'

The General, though not in the least wanting the task, volunteered: 'Would you prefer that I ... ?'

'Oh, no. No! That's something I must do.'

Hans again rubbed at his inflamed eyelid. He could feel it throbbing, as he could feel his heart throbbing. Ever since he had heard the news, he had been wondering what would become of him now. No doubt he would find other work, perhaps even one of the two sons would take him on. But, he was convinced, he would never find an employer as brilliant, as resourceful or as kind as the man now dead. 'I took the liberty, as I passed through Paris, of t-telegraphing your sons – step-sons,' he amended. The telegraph between Paris and London had only recently been inaugurated. There was still none between any city of Italy and London. 'I imagine that one – or both – will arrive here soon.'

Harriet nodded, hardly taking this in. She was thinking of Alexine.

'I also have a c-codicil that he added to his will. He gave it to me in Rome when we said goodbye. Of course I have not broken the seal.'

'Our lawyer can deal with that,' she said abruptly. She was not in the least interested. When she had married Philip, the Admiral had secured a generous settlement. She had always assumed that the bulk of his fortune would go to the sons. That was only natural.

∽

'Well, thank God that's over,' the General said, as he settled himself in the coach. 'I'd rather lead a cavalry charge than go through that again.' Since the survival of a dreaded ordeal always brings an exhilaration with it, all at once, previously so wan, the General perked up. He no longer coughed. Tapping his knee with his palm, he began to hum a Strauss waltz, as he looked out of the carriage window to survey the passing scene. His choice of that waltz was not fortuitous, though he did not realize that. On the last occasion when, at a Palace ball, he and Harriet had danced together, it had been to its cheeky, sexy lilt. He was one of the few men who thought her, even in middle age, to be attractive.

'She t-took it well.'

'Yes. Of course. As one would expect from someone of that family.'

'Perhaps I should have stayed. Or at least have offered to stay.'

'Oh, no, no, dear boy. Much better in such circumstances to leave people to their grief. Grief is a private thing,' he added sententiously. 'Unlike happiness, it is not something to be shared.'

But Hans continued, throughout the rest of the silent journey back into the city, to brood. Perhaps the master would have wanted him to stay. Perhaps he had failed in a last duty to him.

∽

'I'll tell her before she goes to bed.'

Addy frowned. Her eyes were still red from tears, even though she and Philip had never been close and she had never greatly liked him, thinking that he neglected her sister and took her too much for granted. Harriet, on the other hand, had not once cried over the death, and was never to do so, not even in the privacy of her bedroom. 'Why not tell her now? As soon as she comes down from the schoolroom.'

Harriet shook her head. 'No. If I tell her when she's already in bed, then she can have a good cry and sleep on it. Better that way. Don't you remember that that was how Mama told us of Grandmother's death?'

'But she'll guess, of course she'll guess. Nanny Rose or Mademoiselle – or even one of the servants – will let something slip.'

Without an answer, Harriet got up and began to mount the stairs to Philip's study, a room which she had rarely entered in the past. As she opened the door, she half expected to see him seated at his desk. He would look up, startled; he would frown briefly at the interruption; then he would say, 'Yes, dear?' in that voice of controlled impatience which made it clear that she should not be there.

She pulled out a drawer of the desk and looked down at the papers that Hans had set neatly in order before his departure abroad with Philip. The letters were all to do with the business, in which she had never been allowed to play any part. The boys would now take over and she still would not be allowed to play any part. Nor would Alexine. But she was convinced that she – and Alexine in due course – would be quite as capable of taking over from the dead man as those two tall, pale, prim sons of his.

She sank into Philip's leather-covered armchair and inhaled the lingering smell of the countless expensive Cuban cigars that he had smoked while sitting there. In that far distant past when they had made love, she had hated most of all that smell of cigar-smoke that wafted from the mouth seemingly set on devouring her each time that it fastened on hers. But now, suddenly bereft of him, she found solace in it.

She got up, went to the humidor and took up a cigar in trembling fingers. With its band still on – Philip would have exclaimed in horror as much at that social solecism as at the sight of a woman putting a cigar to her lips – she lit it and then took one cautious puff after another.

Suddenly she began to feel dizzy and sick. She crushed out the cigar in an ashtray. What would the housemaids think when they next came to do out the room? No doubt they would decide, giggling among themselves, that old Daan had lit the cigar while his master was absent abroad and had then thought better of smoking it.

∽

'Is she in bed?'

Nanny Rose nodded. 'Yes. The poor dear.' Alexine had always struck her as too bossy and bumptious to be deserving of the wholehearted love that she had lavished on that dear little lad who had died so young of diphtheria; but now, as she herself had put it to Mademoiselle, her heart ached for the poor little dear.

Harriet entered the room. She had dreaded this moment.

'Darling.'

The lamp still lit on the table at her bedside, Alexine went on reading.

'Darling!' Harriet repeated, more loudly.

Now Alexine raised her head. The braids of thick hair, falling on either side of her pale, expressionless face, gleamed in the lamplight.

'I have something to tell you. Something – something very sad.'

'Is it to do with Papa?' The voice was alarmingly matter-of-fact.

So the child had guessed! 'Yes. Yes, I'm afraid it is. I'm afraid that – that he won't be coming back.' All through the day Harriet had been rehearsing what she should say; but what now emerged at once struck her shamingly inept.

Alexine gazed fixedly into her mother's eyes, with what at the time Harriet thought to be contempt. Later, alone in her bedroom, seated in her nightdress before her dressing-table mirror, she tried to persuade herself that no, of course not, of course it wasn't that, why on earth should the child be contemptuous of her? But then, as on many occasions of later brooding, she was unable to do so.

'Do you mean – he's dead?'

After a long day during which everyone had been retreating into euphemisms – 'Now that he's gone', 'Now that he's no longer with us', 'Now that we shall never see him again', 'Now that he's passed over' (from Nanny Rose) – Harriet recoiled at the brutality of Alexine's monosyllable. 'Yes, darling. I'm afraid so. What can I say?' She sank on to the bed and bent forward to put her arms around her daughter. But Alexine rolled away to the far end of the bed. Having crossed her arms over the bolster, she rested her face on them.

Yearningly, Harriet again reached out and, having now placed her hands on Alexine's shoulders, attempted to ease her round. 'Darling. Look at me. Listen to me.'

Muffled by the pillow she heard: 'Go away. Leave me.'

'But darling...'

'Please. Please! Go away!'

Harriet got up off the bed with a sigh and went and sat on the armchair that faced it. She stared at Alexine's prostrate body, willing her to turn, to speak to her, at least to make some acknowledgement of her presence. Then, after several minutes, she again sighed, got up, walked over to the bedside table to extinguish the lamp, and left the room.

Downstairs, Addy was waiting for her. 'Well? How did she take it?' Harriet told her. 'She's such a strange child,' she concluded.

'We all have to cope with grief in our own way. Even children.'

'Then I'd better leave her to cope with it,' Harriet said with uncharacteristic bitterness.

'Precisely.'

∽

The next day Alexine continued to show no emotion.

'It's the shock of it all,' Addy said. 'She hasn't fully taken it in. That's the way with children.'

'I'm not sure that I've fully taken it in myself.' Harriet pulled a face as she inadvertently pricked her finger with the needle with which she was doing her *petit point*, and then raised the finger to her lips to suck it. 'When I told her that there would be no lessons today, she merely asked me if Mademoiselle was ill. And now she's gone out riding.'

'Riding! On day like this! With that boy?'

Harriet nodded.

'What's going to become of him?'

Harriet shrugged.

But she had already decided.

∽

No one, other than Alexine, had wondered how to convey to Sammy that Philip was dead, much less had attempted to do so. Throughout their ride together, during which they rarely broke into even a trot, Alexine brooded on the problem. Somehow she would have to tell him. But how? It was useless to write PAPA DEAD on a scrap of paper, as she would write ALEXINE LESSON or COME TEA.

From time to time, as the two horses paced slowly along beside each other through the flat, dreary landscape, she glanced over to him, in the riding-breeches and the highly polished boots bought for him by Philip only a few days before his departure. She felt increasingly oppressed by the feelings of pity and exasperation that his isolation in the prison of his deafness always brought out in her.

When, the ride over, they had once more entered the house, she put out a hand and firmly gripped his arm. He looked at her in bewildered questioning and she smiled and nodded her head. She mouthed 'Come' and, as always now, he understood that. She released his arm and, taking his hand instead, she began to lead him up the stairs. Eventually, she was walking briskly down the corridor to her father's study and, trailing fingers along the panelling, he was following after her. She hoped that the door had not been locked.

They went in and she shut the door behind them. It was difficult to see anything because the curtains had been drawn, and so she crossed over and, reaching up, jerked one of them back. The weak winter sunshine briefly touched one side of her face and her outstretched arm, but without any warmth.

On the wall above the chimney-piece there was a crude but still recognizable portrait of Philip in his youth, painted, during a period when Liverpool was his home, by a mediocre itinerant artist. Addy had once made fun of this portrait in Alexine's hearing – remarking that the left hand looked more like a dog's paw, and that any art-student of average talent could have improved on the perspective of the house behind the seated figure. Alexine pointed up at the picture and mouthed 'Papa'. She repeated the procedure. Sammy nodded. Then he produced his version of the word, as he had done more than once in the past: 'Baba'. Alexine nodded, So far so good. What had to follow would be far more difficult, perhaps impossible.

Again she pointed at the portrait, then she waved a finger back and forth. No use. She waved it again, shutting her eyes. He stared at her in perplexity. Could it be that, having inferred that she was forbidding him something, he was trying to work out what it might be? She lay down on the floor, crossed her arms over her chest, and again closed her eyes. She opened them and looked up at him. His perplexity had intensified. He began to look panicky. Suddenly she thought of the dumb charades that she and her friends would often play at parties. On those occasions, when an attempt to communicate ended in either total failure or some bizarre misapprehension, there would always be shrieks of laughter. But now she felt no impulse to laugh, only a frustrated vexation.

An idea came to her. It was ludicrous but it might just be effective. She jumped up off the floor and once more went over to the chimney-piece. Resting on it, at its centre, was a bird of paradise, its plumage still a brilliantly unfaded kaleidoscope of colours, which Philip had shot somewhere in the East Indies and had then had stuffed. He had brought the bird back to Europe as a present for Harriet, but when he had given it to her, in its glass case, she had pulled a face and shuddered, exclaiming, 'Oh, the poor thing! I'm sorry. No, I just can't bear to look at it. How could you have brought yourself to shoot something so beautiful and harmless?' Philip had been annoyed both by her squeamishness and by the criticism. In a cold voice, he had pointed out that she thought nothing of wearing the feathers of dead birds on her hats. He had then said that, if she really did not want it, he would keep the bird in his study. He had not really wished to have it there, but had hoped that that would shame her.

Having carefully removed the glass dome of the case in which the bird perched on a branch as dead as itself, Alexine no less carefully placed it on the desk. Then, extricating it from the branch, to which its legs were fastened by wire now grown rusty, she took down the bird. She showed it to Sammy, like a conjurer about to perform a trick. She stooped and laid it, legs in air, on the carpet. She looked at him in enquiry, head on one side.

He stared at the bird, then at her, then once more at the bird. He was frowning. She pointed at the bird, again at the portrait. Once more she mouthed 'Papa', and followed that with 'Dead', though there was no chance that he would understand the word.

At last, with a rising sense of triumph, she could see that comprehension was about to dawn. His brows went up, stretching the skin on either side of his eyes, his mouth began to open, he tilted is head backwards. Finally, he nodded eagerly. There was always this feeling of triumph, even more for him than for her, when one of them at last succeeded in communicating something difficult to the other.

She picked up the bird and, carefully twisting the rusty wire – one strand snapped off in her fingers – eventually managed to restore it to its perch. Then she picked up the glass dome. But as she raised it, it somehow slipped through her fingers and crashed down into the grate. In horror, she let out a brief cry, raising her hands to her cheeks. Looking across to him, she saw the change in his expression. A moment ago he had been smiling in triumph. Now his face was rigid with what could only be terror. What had terrified him? Was it the smashing of the dome? Or was it the news of the death? Once again she cursed the impossibility of their ever having anything more than a vague, fleeting communication with each other about their inmost feelings.

Suddenly overwhelmed both by the sadness of his situation and by her desire to console him in it, she rushed over to him, put her hands on his shoulders, leaned forward, and gently laid her right cheek against his. It rested there for several seconds, until she hurriedly jerked it away as she heard the sound of feet hurrying down the corridor. That heavy tread could only announce either Nanny Rose or one of the male servants.

'What are you both doing in here? I heard a crash from the linen room.'

Alexine did not answer, looking not at Nanny Rose but at Sammy.

'Alexine, answer me!' Only then did Nancy Rose notice the broken dome. She stared down in horror. 'How did that happen? What were you doing with it? Alexine!'

Still Alexine remained silent. Going down on her hands and knees, she began to pick up the jagged fragments of glass, cupping them in the palm of one hand as the other retrieved them.

'Leave that alone! You'll only cut yourself. It needs a dustpan and brush. Liliane can see to it tomorrow morning. Did your mother give you permission to come in here? I'm sure she didn't. Come on! Out, out! I really don't understand you. At a time like this! What's the matter with you?'

Alexine jumped to her feet and hurried out of the room. After a moment, during which he seemed to be at a loss what to do, Sammy followed her.

Nanny Rose's voice pursued Alexine: 'What would your poor father think if he were still alive? You know he never liked anyone to go into his study. He'd be horrified. I'll have to report this to your poor mother. As though she didn't have enough to upset her at the moment . . .'

Although Alexine was now almost nine, Nanny Rose still treated her like a small child. In the years ahead she was to continue to do so.

9 TWO DAYS LATER, John Tinne and his wife Irene arrived. The younger brother, William, invalided out of the Navy because of epilepsy, was too ill after a cluster of attacks to have come along too.

Harriet and Addy would often privately mock at the clothes, extravagant but dowdy, that Irene's Liverpool dressmaker produced for her. Once they had even urged her to accompany them on a trip to buy clothes in Paris, but Irene had replied that there was little point in making the journey when at home there was Madame Loussière, herself French, the best dressmaker in the whole of England. On this occasion, Madame Loussière's mourning dress was made of a jet silk so shiny that it looked as if Irene's painfully thin body had been sealed in lacquer. Irene's face was still yellow from sea-sickness – 'We were being thrown about, here, there, everywhere. I'm such a terrible sailor. You'd never believe that I'm descended from Drake.' Because her maiden name was the same as the seafarer's, she was in the habit of claiming, with no other justification, her descent from him.

Both she and John were eager to know the contents of the will, but only she showed that eagerness. 'Have you any idea what his last' – she sought for a genteel word – 'dispositions were?' she ventured, as Nanny Rose handed her a cup of camomile tisane. As soon as she had come down from her room after a preliminary reconnoitre, she had requested the tisane 'to settle my stomach'. She ran her tongue over her lips and then raising her veil and hitching it back over her hat with the hand not holding the cup, lowered her head on its long neck, and took one sip and then another.

'Not now,' John told her in a low voice. 'Let's consider that later.' He was an essentially decent man, with none of his father's appetite for money and power. If he had been so successful in managing the English side of the business, that was solely because of his unspectacular but formidable intelligence and his sense of duty.

'The lawyer is coming the day after tomorrow,' Harriet said. In its lead coffin, Philip's body was awaiting burial on the following day. 'That's the usual way of doing things, isn't it?' she added with a sharp edge to her voice. She and John had always got on, but she had, from their first meeting, decided, as she put it at the time to Addy, that Irene was 'coarse-grained'.

Later Irene announced, 'I think I'll go up to my room for a rest – I couldn't sleep a wink on that packet', and then, with many pauses for breath, mounted the stairs and vanished. Harriet and John, left alone together, talked of the circumstances of Philip's death. 'I can't help thinking that Hans must be right,' Harriet said. 'He could only have been killed by mistake for the Baron – that friend of his. Why else should anyone have killed him? Apart from his business connections, he knew hardly anyone in Italy. And nothing, nothing whatever was stolen.'

John leaned forward in his chair, bony hands, disfigured by chilblains, clasped between his knees. 'I wonder,' he said. 'I wonder. All through the crossing – I left Irene down in the cabin and spent most of the time on deck – I was wondering. There was always something mysterious about Papa.'

'*Mysterious?*' Her tone expressed surprise. But she too had felt that mystery. Often, even after years of marriage, she would remark to Addy, always her confidante: 'I don't feel I really know him.' There was some small part of him that persisted in remaining inviolable and unapproachable, like a locked attic in a mansion otherwise always wide open to inspection.

'You know how he started life?'

'Vaguely. The family was poor, he struggled in inferior jobs – just as Hans is struggling now. He went abroad. He started to make money. When the English took over Demerara, he became Secretary to the Governor. That's about all I know. He never wanted to talk about the past, even about your mother. He was someone who was impatient even of the present. What interested him was the future.'

'Did you know that his first job was in the Foreign Service?'

Harriet was astonished. 'No. He never told me that. How did he manage to get such a post? I mean, with those beginnings.'

'He was helped by an influential cousin of his grandfather. Or his grandmother. I don't remember. And of course he had that remarkable gift for languages. He served for a while in London and after that he came back here. He never spoke to me about what his tasks then were, but he once told my mother – oh, in the vaguest way – that he had been somehow involved in intelligence. Opening letters, examining documents. Assessing what was in them. That sort of thing. When Napoleon invaded, he at once fled the country – unlike most of his colleagues in the Foreign Service. It was then that he started his career in the Caribbean.'

Harriet struggled to take all this in. 'You mean that, as a young man, he was a *spy?*'

'Perhaps not only as a young man. It was odd that, as soon as he arrived in Demerara, he was at once taken under the wing of the English Governor. And, as you know, soon after that he was granted British citizenship. That was something rarely granted to a Dutchman at that time.'

'So he might have been working for the British?'

John shrugged. 'Who knows? For the British, the Dutch, the Prussians? For all of them or two of them at the same time? He was an extraordinary man. With him – anything is possible.' John knew that he was not an extraordinary man himself, in fact a totally ordinary one, apart from his knack for making money. Again he leaned forward in his chair, bony, chilblained hands clasped. Like his father, perhaps in unconscious emulation of him, he too had a forked beard. But his was sparse and straggly, as though, even in that respect, he lacked his father's luxuriant energy. He unclasped his hands, raised one and stroked the beard repeatedly. 'All those journeys of his,' he said, ruminating as much to himself as to her. It was only as he was clutching the rail of the bucking and heaving boat, the upthrown spume salt on his lips and sometimes almost blinding him, that a possibility had come to him. 'Were they all really necessary? Not for the business, I'm sure. Perhaps, as a side-line, he was still doing that same sort of work.'

'But he didn't need the money!'

'No. Of course not. But people who do that kind of work rarely do it for money. It becomes a habit. And he loved power. You know that, of course you know that. And to deceive people is to have a kind of power over them. And he loved secrets. That was why he never told anyone – even you or my mother or William or me – anything that he didn't feel that we *had* to know.'

A plump hand to her forehead, Harriet was thinking. She nodded. 'He had an odd way of just – just disappearing for two or three days at a time. He would give me no explanation – except to say that he had to be somewhere on business. And if I tried to make him be more precise, he'd say something like, "Oh, I shall be travelling about France", or "I have to be in Amsterdam and Antwerp and one or two other places". Often he didn't take either Hans or his valet with him.'

'Well, there you are!'

But where was she? She did not know.

∽

Dressing for dinner, after the lawyers had departed, Irene suddenly twisted away from the maid who was doing up some buttons and told her: 'All right! That's enough. I can manage on my own.'

'Are you sure, ma'am?' The girl too had been violently seasick on the packet and even now, five days later, had still not fully recovered. When she walked, the floor seemed to tilt from side to side and then to rear up before her. She was not in the least sorry to be told that she could go.

'Of course I'm sure!' Then, relenting, Irene asked: 'Are they looking after you all right?'

'Oh, yes, ma'am. Thank you.'

Irene nodded. The question had not really been necessary. For all her faults, Harriet certainly knew how to run a household.

Her dress still half unbuttoned, Irene picked up a hairbrush and, without using it, went to the door separating the bedroom from the dressing-room. John, already dressed but not wishing to disturb her, was once more looking through the copy of the will and its codicil left with him by the lawyer.

'What are you doing? Reading those things isn't going to change them.'

Patiently he said: 'Of course not. But such a will is a long and complex document. Inevitably. I want to be sure of everything.'

'There's one thing you can be sure of already. That little minx is going to get most of the estate.'

'A large part of it. But we're not going to be left exactly penniless.'

'What made him add that codicil – so late in the day, just before he was murdered?' Her tongue moving restlessly over her lips, she crossed to the chair facing his and sank down on to it. She pressed a hand to a bosom pushed upwards and out by the constriction of her stays. 'My heart is horribly unsteady. Racing one moment, then feeling as though it were about to stop.'

'You had that ghastly journey.'

'And now this shock. What made him do it? What came into his head?'

'Perhaps he loved Alexine more than William and me. Why not? Anyway, it's useless to speculate. William and I have the business – and a handsome legacy each. I'm not complaining.'

'It's only because you're so weak that you're not. You ought to complain.'

'Who to? What would be the point?' He drew his gold repeater watch – a twenty-first birthday present from his father – out of his waistcoat pocket and glanced at it. 'You'd better finish getting dressed. We'll be late for dinner.'

'I haven't any appetite. I couldn't eat a thing.'

'Well, you'd better come down anyway.'

'Oh, all right! Anything to oblige! But I hate the idea of sitting there while those two women gloat over us.'

'Harriet isn't the sort of person to gloat. Addy might,' he added with a small smile. He had always secretly envied and even admired Addy's candour and her willingness to show herself in an unfavourable light if an occasion demanded.

'You'll have to help with this dress.'

'Isn't Barbara helping you?'

Laying claim to a kindness that she had not in fact shown, Irene said: 'The poor little thing looked so peaky that I told her I could manage without her.'

'You're always so good to them all. I hope they appreciate it.'

Was he being sarcastic? As so often, she could not be sure.

∽

Nanny Rose was seated before the smoking fire in night-dress and slippers, in the long, low-ceilinged room, next to the now empty nursery, which served as both her bedroom and sitting-room. Harriet had offered her the nursery when Alexine had moved out of it into the room, next to her father's, that she still occupied, but Nanny Rose had replied in that grumpy, ungracious manner of hers, even though she was secretly touched: 'Oh, no, that's not necessary. Not at all. What I should like is a really comfortable chair.' It was in this really comfortable chair that she was now slumped, her darning held up close to eyes that were becoming increasingly myopic.

The knock startled her. Once again Alexine had been allowed to stay up far too late, because she had pleaded to be allowed to finish a drawing of Sammy. It could only be she. But, in fact, to her surprise, it turned out to be Irene. Nanny Rose staggered to her feet, the half-darned black woollen stocking trailing from a hand.

'Oh, Nanny, forgive me for disturbing you like this. But I wanted a little chat before we leave tomorrow. It's an early start, you know.'

'Yes, madam.' Nanny Rose made no effort to conceal her displeasure at being disturbed at an hour so late for her, if not for the rest of the household. She pointed to the chair that she had just vacated. 'Would you care to sit down, madam?'

Irene sat. 'This is a very comfortable chair,' she said in surprise. 'And a pretty one. Very pretty.' It was the sort of chair that she would not in least object to having in her own drawing-room.

'Yes, madam kindly let me have it. It used to be in the breakfast room. No one ever used it.'

'What I really wanted to know – are you still happy here?'

'Happy, madam?' She repeated the word as though it were a foreign one, stressing it unnaturally.

'I mean – now that Alexine is – what? – almost nine, there can't be all that much for you to do for her.' Nanny Rose did not answer. Now seated on another, upright chair, she had resumed her darning. 'Is there?'

'Oh, I hope I still make myself useful to madam. And to Miss Addy and Miss Alexine too, of course.'

'She's a funny girl,' Irene said. 'But everyone seems to think her someone quite out of the ordinary. Well, I suppose she's talented – with her drawing and her gift for languages and so on.' Her tongue moved over her lower lip as she fingered the cameo, of John's dead mother, at the low vee of her dress. 'What I really wanted to ask you is – have you ever thought about a move back to England?'

Nanny Rose considered, head on one side. Then she raised her darning and snapped the black woollen thread with her teeth. 'I can't really say I have. No, that hasn't really entered my head.'

'I ask for a reason. It struck me that you might be homesick for the Wirral. I mean, you can't have many friends here, it must be rather lonely for you. And then there are your children – two, is it?'

'Three.'

'Yes, three. Of course, of course. And the grandchildren. Don't you miss them?'

Head again tilted to one side, Nanny Rose once more considered. Then she replied: 'Sometimes. But I'm sure they manage very well without me.' It was only rarely – although she would never have confessed that to anyone – that they wrote to her. On her last birthday, only the youngest of her children had remembered to send her greetings – and those were perfunctory.

'If you *did* want to return, then I have an idea. My daughter – the older daughter, I think you met her that time you came for your' – she almost said 'interview' – 'came for our little chat.'

'Yes, I remember her,' Nanny Rose said laconically, thinking, 'That one really gave herself airs.'

'Well, she needs a nanny now. The one she had was not really – not really all that satisfactory. She had a – a *problem*.' Nanny Rose could decipher the code: the nanny, like many of her kind, drank. 'So I thought – she and I thought – that perhaps...'

Nanny Rose said nothing, as she picked up another stocking to darn.

'What would you think about returning to England with us – now – yes, now – why not now? – in order to work for her? Yes? She'd be a generous employer. And that house of theirs – it has *the* most beautiful nursery, overlooking the garden.'

Nanny Rose lowered the stocking to her knee. 'Thank you, madam. It's very kind of you to think of me. But...' She shrugged. 'I'm too old a dog to change my ways. I've been here a long time and ... and ...' She could not bring herself to say, 'I'm happy here', although that was the truth. To say that she was happy was something that she had been unable to do even on her wedding day. 'I think I'll stay,' she concluded. 'As long as I'm wanted. Yes, that's what I plan to do.'

'Well, there it is! No harm in trying. If you should change your mind...' Irene fumbled in her bag and brought out a card. 'I gave you my card, I think, all that long time ago. I don't imagine you still have it...'

She held out the card and reluctantly Nanny Rose took it and, without glancing at it, placed it on the table beside her.

With a rustle of black bombazine, Irene got to her feet. 'I'm sorry to have disturbed you,' she said. Before, her tone had been wooingly sweet; now it was vinegary. 'It was just an idea.'

'I'm sure I'm very grateful, madam.'

'Well, goodnight, Nanny. I don't know whether I'll see you so early tomorrow morning or not. In case I don't see you, I'll say goodbye now.'

'Goodbye, madam.'

When the door had closed, Nanny Rose pulled a face and reached out for the heavily embossed card. She looked down at it, frowning. Then with a 'Tsk', she began to tear it into fragments.

*

After they had waved goodbye to Irene and John and had then watched the carriage wheel out through the high wrought-iron gates, Harriet and Addy re-entered the house.

Harriet sighed and slipped an arm through Addy's.

'He's a decent sort,' she said.

Addy laughed. 'And she's a horror.'

'You must have made that clear to her.'

'Did I? I thought I was being extremely polite.'

'*Too* polite.'

Again both of them laughed.

'I feel I can trust him,' Harriet said. 'I'm glad that Philip made him one of the three trustees.' The other trustees were William and Philip's lawyer.

'Galling for him.'

'No, I don't think so. Galling only for her. Yes, I trust him. He'll do his best by my little girl.'

In this confidence Harriet was not mistaken. John handled Alexine's money so well that before her majority she had become the richest woman in the Netherlands. Harriet often used to wonder whether, if she had been in charge of it, she would have done as well.

10 AS SOON AS THE GUESTS HAD GONE, Harriet at once set about burning, unread, the personal letters that, always kept apart from Philip's business ones, lay compressed together in a number of cardboard and wooden boxes up in the loft above the stables. Hans and Philip's valet, Jean, carried the boxes out to a far corner of the garden, and she then joined them out there, in a black pelisse trimmed with sable, which she had gone out with Addy to buy expressly for her mourning. Despite the protests of the two men, she stooped and took up damp armfuls of the letters, many of them tied into bundles with a dark-blue tape, and then hurled them down into the devouring flames. From time to time she would make out a phrase or even a sentence. One bundle, curling up at the edges, contained, she suddenly realized, letters that she herself had written in her small, neat, schoolgirlish hand. Another, added to the flames by Jean, contained letters from her father. She made no attempt to rescue either.

Later, she would say to Addy, 'I felt as if I were burning the past'.

'That must have been horrible for you.'

Harriet shook her head. 'No, not at all. I felt as if I were opening a window that I'd always thought to be locked.'

Alexine, followed by Sammy, wandered out, alerted both by the blue smoke wavering up in the still winter air, and a persistent, acrid smell of burning. 'Do you want us to help?'

'No. No, thank you. I have Jean and Hans, as you see.'

Alexine and Sammy remained standing just beyond the fire. Neither was wearing a coat, but neither, in that icy air, felt cold, since the glare of the fire gave them an illusion of the warmth that they could not feel in reality at that distance from it.

'Go back into the house, *chérie*! We don't want you to catch another cold. Go! Go!'

'Oh, please, Mama, please!'

'No! Go! Now, now!'

Pulling a face, Alexine turned and began to trail back to the house. Sammy, dragging his feet over the frost-hard ground, followed after her.

There was a white heart to the fire and, when the last bundle of letters had been emptied on to it, Harriet stared into that heart. She felt the tears pricking at her eyes, and her throat began to ache with them. But no tears fell.

∽

Later, she, Hans and Jean went up to Philip's bedroom and began to turn out his drawers and cupboards. Harriet marvelled at the size and variety of her husband's wardrobe. She knew that, like herself, he was extravagant about clothes. But such an accumulation of shirts, suits, cravats, overcoats, gloves ...

She crossed over to Hans, as he spread another armful of clothes over the armful already lying on the bed. 'Have what you want. Anything.'

He was taken aback. 'But, madam, don't you want to keep ...?' He shook his head in disbelief.

'What would be the point? He's not going to come back. And these things will never be of any use to me or my daughter. Or to my sister.'

'You could sell them, madam. I know of someone ...' The someone of whom he knew was an aunt, who carried on a sporadic, rarely profitable trade in used clothes, when not occupied with looking after an invalid husband and a large and demanding brood of children.

'*Sell* them?' At once, as she said the two words, he realized the enormity of what he had suggested to a woman of her wealth and class. 'Oh, I shouldn't dream of doing that. Go on, take what you want.' She turned to the valet. 'And you too, Jean. The rest we can give away.'

Hesitantly, first Hans and then Jean began to pick out things – a shirt, some breeches, some stockings, a stock, a riding-crop. Then, emboldened, no longer aware that, with the trace of a melancholy smile, Harriet was watching them from a chair in a far corner of the room, they became more and more acquisitive.

'Do you want that?' Hans asked.

'Well, only if you don't.'

'It would go so well with the shirt.'

'All right. Go ahead. In that case perhaps I can have this suit. It's just my style. I can't do with anything too bright.'

Jean gathered up the suit, bending stiffly because he favoured tight-waisted trousers, and then, having deposited it on the ottoman covered with the clothes that were now to be his, gave a lady-like, self-congratulatory sniff, knuckle of delicate forefinger raised to a nostril.

'I like this.' Hans held a cravat up to his neck. 'What d'you think?'

'Suits you. Yes. I'd go for that.'

At first embarrassed and therefore keeping their voices almost to a whisper, they were now talking as though Harriet were no longer with them.

'I don't think much of those boots. Most of his boots are real quality stuff. Made in England. But this pair ... I'd guess they were made here. Anyway, I'll take them.' Hans was taking them not for himself to wear but for his aunt to sell.

67

'They'll be too big for you. You'll see. The master had big feet. Look at these socks. Look at their size.'

When the plunder had been divided up between the two men and their discards put on one side, eventually to be distributed among the numerous charities supported over the years by the family, Harriet told Hans that he could borrow as many of Philip's valises that he needed to pack up his share. Jean helped him in this task, fastidiously folding each garment before Hans placed it in one of the three valises. The valet, with his vast quiff of upbrushed red hair above a pale, narrow face, took pleasure in the task, familiar to him from the years of repeatedly packing for Philip, and was skilful and amazingly quick at it.

Harriet continued to watch them intently. At first, as she had handled the dead man's clothes, she had been overcome by sadness. It was like entering a once familiar and much loved house, to find it suddenly emptied of its furniture, inhospitable, cold. But now, as the room was gradually stripped of everything that might remind her of him, she felt, to her surprise and shame, a tide of exhilaration slowly sweep into her, as into some secret, narrow creek. She was alone now, and she had never been alone before in her life. But she was also something else that she had never been before. She was free.

'You can't carry all those valises,' she told Hans, when at long last he and John had finished the packing. 'You'd better get Harry to take you in one of the carriages.'

'Oh, no, madam. I wouldn't dream of that.'

'I insist, I insist!'

'Well, in that case . . .'

'Since the master's death, Harry's had an easy time of it. He won't mind.'

Hans, who was used to the Englishman's truculence, was not sure of that. But he did not care. If the mistress said that he was to be driven home in the carriage, then he would be driven home.

∽

The house and the near-slum in which Hans lived with his widowed mother, in a three-roomed attic apartment under the eaves of gaunt, grey tenement, were at opposite ends of the city. On the long drive home, he therefore had ample time to busy himself with plans for the future. Philip had left him a legacy far bigger than he had ever expected; and the two brothers had, in effect, promoted him in the business, making him their agent in The Hague. Now, like Harriet so shortly before him, he realized that, as a result of the wholly unforeseen death – Philip, so vigorous and decisive even in his seventies, had always struck him as immortal – he had suddenly achieved the one thing that he always thought to be beyond his grasp: his freedom.

For years Hans had shared the small apartment with his mother, because neither of them could afford a separation. She had once been a dressmaker, of a far humbler sort than Madame Molnar, but failing eyesight had eventually obliged her to give that up. Former clients were generous to her, and her husband, a bank clerk, had left her enough money to buy a small annuity. She spent most of her time seated in the tiny little parlour, under the open dormer window in the summer, hunched close to the stove in the winter, knitting on large wooden needles, since it was only with them that she could see what she was doing, and carrying on endless conversations with a tiny, mongrel bitch, herself as frail as her mistress, which Hans (how much he regretted it now!) had found straying in the street and, on an impulse, had brought home with him. She would, he had decided, be the companion to his mother that he himself, constantly going abroad with Philip, could so seldom be. The bitch had long since become incontinent, filling the house with an ammoniac stench. When he could not walk her himself, Hans had to pay the young son of a neighbour to do so.

Yes, he mused, looking out of the carriage window but seeing nothing, he would rent a large, sunny apartment on a ground floor of a house in a decent quarter for his mother; and he would persuade his spinster sister, now discontentedly working as a lady's maid in Delft, to return to The Hague and look after her in it. He himself would rent another apartment, not as large, not as expensive, near them but not too near. At last he would get away from his mother's constantly prying, censorious presence, and that voice that pursued him to his own room with incessant questions and demands, when she herself was not lumbering up out of her chair to do so. At last, like his former master, he could lead the sort of life that he had always wanted to lead. Only money could give one that sort of freedom.

Yes, he would be happy, at last he would be happy.

11 AT BREAKFAST less than two weeks after Philip's death, Harriet announced to Alexine that on the following Monday Aunt Addy would be taking her to Paris. Aunt Addy had a number of things to do there, Harriet said, and it would be nice both for her to have Alexine's company and for Alexine to see a city so much larger and more beautiful than The Hague. Harriet did not specify the nature of the things that Addy had to do. Prey, like her father, to bouts of hypochondria, she had in fact decided to consult a Russian physician, a disciple of Mesmer, widely reported as being extraordinarily successful in his treatment of nervous disorders, particularly in women.

'Why can't you come?' Alexine at once demanded.

'Because I have so much to see to here.'

'Can't you see to it later?'

'No. You know how I hate putting things off. Papa's death left me with a lot of things to do, and I want to get them done as quickly as possible. So that I can then got on with my own life,' she added.

'If you came with us now, I could help you when we got back.'

Harriet laughed. 'That's sweet of you, *chérie*. But I think that you're still too young to do that.'

'If you can't come, can Sammy come?'

Harriet and Addy looked at each other. Addy raised her eyebrows, Harriet shrugged her plump, rounded shoulders.

'I don't think that's a good idea,' Harriet said. 'A journey like that would only be wasted on him. He'll be far happier here, in a familiar environment, among people he knows.'

Addy nodded. 'Yes, he would feel totally lost in Paris. You must try to understand what it must be like for him, wholly cut off from the world around him.'

It was, in fact, something that Alexine had often tried to understand.

'I'd always be with him. I'm sure he'd like to come. Oh, please, mama!'

Harriet shook her head. Addy used often to say to Alexine, 'You are the girl who always gets what she wants' – sometimes in admiration and awe and sometimes, since she herself had rarely got what she wanted, in envy. But on this occasion it was clear to Alexine that she was not going to get what she wanted. Her mother, so often criticized for giving in to her, was not going to do so now.

Nonetheless, though knowing the fruitlessness of continuing the argument, she persisted. 'But why can't he come with me? Why? Why? It's so unfair. I want him to come.'

'Well, I'm afraid you can't always have what you want.' Since her father's death, Alexine had sensed, with puzzled apprehension, a new toughness in her mother. In the past, it was he who had denied her things and her mother who had then pleaded for her to have them.

'It's only for a week,' Aunt Addy said. 'What are you making such a fuss about? Don't you like my company?'

Alexine did not answer.

Later that same day, Harriet announced that, since Aunt Addy would so often be occupied in Paris, Mademoiselle would also be going, to look after her pupil.

Alexine, who did not like Mademoiselle and who knew that Mademoiselle knew that, was aghast. 'Oh, no. *No!*'

'You can't be left on your own in an hotel,' Harriet told her severely. 'You're far too young for that. Mademoiselle can take you to the museums and churches and parks.'

'Why does she have to come? Why can't Nanny Rose come?'

Harriet and Addy laughed. 'Nanny doesn't speak a word of French. And she's never been to France. Don't be silly! You'd both of you get lost as soon as you set foot outside the hotel.'

∽

In fact, Alexine all too often found herself alone in the suite that she and Addy shared, with Mademoiselle occupying a smaller room next to it.

'I just have to slip out for an hour or so,' Mademoiselle announced to Alexine, who was alone in the suite, on the second day after their arrival. She was resplendently dressed, in a frock passed on to her by Harriet and then altered by one of Madame Molnar's drudges to fit her much slimmer figure. Her dark eyes under finely arched eyebrows were lambent with expectancy. 'Now don't leave this room, remember? Just ring for the maid if you want something. Do not leave this room! And don't' – suddenly she looked furtive and embarrassed – 'don't say anything to your aunt about my leaving you like this. Promise? You know how she fusses.'

Alexine, busy with drawing at a table under the window, nodded.

'Now you promise me to do what I've told you?'

Again, without looking up, Alexine nodded.

Sometimes Alexine would disobey such instructions and slip out of the room, to trail along the labyrinthine corridors or up and down the two vast staircases. It was absurd, she thought, that a girl of nine should be kept a prisoner like that. Once or twice, she became so bored and exasperated that she even wandered out into the street. But the crowds streaming up and down the rue de Rivoli, the deafening clatter of horses and carriages, and the fine snow drifting from the leaden sky, soon drove her back.

On one occasion, Mademoiselle returned to the hotel before Alexine did. Hearing the girl enter the suite, she at once jumped up and rushed out of her own room to scold her. Her eyes were even brighter than when she had gone out, her cheeks were unusually flushed. When she approached, Alexine could catch the same smell that she used to catch when her father returned from a dinner-party or from playing cards with his cronies.

'Where have you been? I told you, told you, not to leave this room!'

Alexine lied. 'The bell wasn't working. I rang and rang. I was hungry. So I went out to see if I could find a maid.'

'And . . . ?' Mademoiselle did not believe her.

'I got lost.'

'Lost?' At that, Mademoiselle gave up. She did not really care. She was far too much taken up with her own thrilling, totally unexpected love-affair with a young man who had walk-on parts at the Comédie Française to bother about her charge.

One day, Addy announced to Alexine that a French friend of hers, a Monsieur Thierry, had invited them both to lunch at Le Grand Véfour. He was about to go to The Hague as Head of Chancery at the French Embassy. Would Mademoiselle also be coming? Alexine asked. Addy gave a derisive laugh. No, of course not. Would this Frenchman be bringing his wife? 'No, I don't think so. I think he said she was on a visit out of Paris.'

Monsieur Thierry was plump and pale, with soft hands, sparse, unnaturally dark hair parted in the middle, and a crooked smile under a small, heavily waxed moustache, the ends of which stuck out like wires. He was deferential, in a stiffly formal way, to Addy – like a courtier to a queen, Alexine thought. But with Alexine he was totally relaxed, pulling faces, performing simple tricks of sleight of hand with coins on the starched white damask table-cloth, and making silly jokes – many of them puns which, being in French, she could not always follow. At first Addy laughed far more than was usual with her, throwing back her head, while a blush flooded up her throat. But then she began to look wary and even, by the end of the meal, vaguely displeased.

'He's a silly ass,' Addy told Alexine, when they had got into their carriage to return to the hotel. He had offered to see them back there, but Addy had told him that that wasn't necessary. 'He has a little girl of about your age,' she added. 'She'll make a nice friend for you.'

'I have too many friends already,' Alexine said peevishly.

'Yes, you have too much of everything,' Addy said sourly. 'You're lucky in that.' Then, repenting, she put a hand on Alexine's knee. 'It's lovely being with you like this. I'm so glad that Mama agreed to my bringing you with me.'

Addy was now taking drops prescribed by the Russian doctor. 'They make me feel so much better,' she said. 'I'm a changed woman.' She certainly seemed to smile and even laugh far more than in the past, and she was uncharacteristically restless in her desire constantly to be doing something. 'Remind me to take my drops,' she would tell Alexine. 'Dr Pavloski says that I must be sure to take them every four hours.' She would even wake up in the middle of the night in order to take them, the sudden flare of the gas all too often arousing Alexine in the bedroom that they shared.

The three of them had a reserved carriage for the journey home. They had just settled themselves into it when, suddenly, there at the window beside Alexine, was Monsieur Thierry, a porter hefting two valises behind him. He had a carnation in his button-hole. A gold-capped tooth, unnoticed by Alexine at their previous meeting, gleamed as he smiled. 'May I join your party?' he asked.

'Of course, of course,' Addy said. 'But what a surprise! I'd no idea that you'd be travelling on the same train.'

Was it really a surprise for her? No. Alexine knew that Addy was lying – something she rarely did, and then so clumsily that the lie, as on this occasion, was instantly apparent.

Monsieur Thierry began to explain. He had decided to arrive at the Embassy ahead of his wife and family. That way, he could, as he put it, 'acclimatize' himself without distractions. It was, in any case, more convenient and – he laughed – cheaper if he were to put up alone in a hotel while looking for a suitable house to rent. The lease on the house rented by his predecessor had unfortunately expired and the owner did not wish to renew it.

Mademoiselle had begun to turn over the pages of a woman's magazine as soon as Addy had made the introductions between her and Monsieur Thierry. For her, he was too old to be of interest, let alone attractive.

It was a slow journey. At first Monsieur Thierry chattered away, constantly turning to Alexine, as though she, rather than Addy, was the most important person in the carriage. Mademoiselle pursed her lips, sighed from time and time, and went on with her reading. Addy laughed, but the laugh was increasingly artificial. Eventually she rested her head back on the cushioned seat, pulled her cashmere rug higher up over her knees, and shut her eyes. Soon she was snoring discreetly. When Alexine glanced over to Mademoiselle, she saw that she too was asleep. A moment later the magazine slithered across her knees and dropped to the floor. Quietly, Monsieur Thierry reached for it, picked it up and placed it on the seat beside her.

After a few minutes, during which he kept peering at Alexine, as at a picture in an art gallery, Monsieur Thierry produced from a pocket a metal puzzle, of a number of rings that had to be disentangled from each other. 'See how you get on with that,' he said in a whisper, so as not the disturb the two sleeping women.

Reluctantly Alexine took the puzzle from him.

She manipulated the rings for a time and then, with characteristic impatience, began to tug at them, her fingertips growing white with the pressure. Monsieur Thierry chuckled, leaned forward and put one of his soft, cold hands over hers. He eased her fingers away from the rings and then began deftly to manoeuvre them. Suddenly they were separate. Then, no less suddenly, having been manipulated by him for a few seconds, they were joined again. He handed the rings back to her. 'Try again,' he said. At that he jumped up from his seat opposite to her and sat down beside her. She could feel his body close to hers, pressing her up against the side of the carriage. Once again she tried to separate the rings. But she was even more maladroit than before. He was still pressing up close against her. Then she could feel his hand on her knee, resting there, like some inanimate object. He leaned his head towards her, and all at once she felt his waxed moustache pricking her cheek.

Terrified, she jumped up, crossed the carriage and stood by the farther window. Hands gripping its ledge to steady herself, she looked out at the flat, monochrome winter landscape slowly unrolling under her gaze. She saw a canal, with a horse-drawn barge stationary at a lock; a carriage lurching over the hump-backed bridge that spanned it; a small detachment of soldiers marching, in ragged order, down a narrow dirt road. She could see that the soldiers were singing but she could not hear them. Then he was standing beside her. Again he was extremely close. She could smell his cologne, at once bitter and sweet.

'Look, look!' she cried out. It was really a summons for help.

Aunt Addy jerked up. Her eyes opened. Mademoiselle stirred, her eyes also opened. She yawned and then, this time putting the back of a hand to her mouth, yawned again.

'What is it?' Aunt Addy asked.

'Some ducks on the canal,' Alexine said, since that was the next thing that she saw at that moment.

'Well, you don't have to wake me up for that. You've seen ducks often enough before.'

∽

The train arrived more than an hour late; and they were made even later because Addy offered Monsieur Thierry a lift to his hotel before they travelled on to the house.

'When my little girl arrives, you must come and play with her,' Monsieur Thierry told Alexine.

Alexine said nothing.

'That'll be nice, won't it?' Addy prompted.

Again Alexine said nothing.

'She's tired,' Addy said.

'Yes, the poor child is tired,' Monsieur Thierry agreed.

Once more in the carriage, Alexine said: 'I don't like that man.'

'What do you mean? There's nothing wrong with him.'

Mademoiselle was humming to herself a little tune that she had heard in a café to which the actor had taken her. The sound was getting on Addy's nerves.

'He touched me.'

'Well, what's wrong with that? He has a little girl of his own. You know that.'

'I don't like being touched. Not by a man. Not like that.'

Mademoiselle gave a little laugh. Then she went on humming, more loudly.

'You *are* an odd girl,' Addy said.

Harriet was overjoyed to see them. It had been a long week, and the house had, despite the presence of Nanny Rose and all the servants, seemed empty and cold.

'Did you have a lovely time?' she asked Alexine, as they all, with the exception of Mademoiselle, went into the drawing-room and Addy began to take off first her hat and then the dark blue redingote that she had bought on the Paris visit. Its cutaway front, hardly suitable for a long journey in an unheated train, revealed the extremely narrow waist of which she had always been proud.

Alexine shrugged. 'I prefer being home.'

'Well, that's nice. And I prefer having you home.' Harriet drew Alexine to her and once again hugged her. 'You're all I've got.'

'Oh, you have a lot of other things too,' Addy said with a laugh tinged with bitterness.

'Where's Sammy?' Alexine asked, having hardly responded to her mother's embrace.

All through the ride from the station, Alexine had been thinking of him. She had brought him a box of sweets, a bow and arrow, a real one, not another toy one like the one that she herself possessed, and some French lead soldiers, from Napoleon's Grande Armée.

Harriet and Addy looked at each other, and at once Alexine knew,

knew with absolute certainty, as she so often knew things still unspoken by her mother, that something was wrong.

'He's gone, darling,' Harriet said.

'Gone!'

'Yes. He's gone back to his home. That seemed the best thing for him.'

'To Jamaica?' Alexine was incredulous. How could such a thing have happened?

'Yes, darling. One of your Uncle John's people was about to sail there, and so we decided that the best thing would be for him to take Sammy with him.'

'The best thing! For whom is it best? For him?'

'Yes, darling. I've explained. I don't think he was ever really happy here. He'll be far happier among his own people.'

'How do you know whether he was happy or not?' Alexine was now white with fury; her heavy jaw was set. 'You've never known anything about him. I'm the one who's always known about him. He was my friend. He wanted to be with me. He did, he did!'

'Now, come on, *chérie*. That's enough of all that. You're tired after your long journey. You ought to get up to bed.'

Her fury boiling over, Alexine suddenly rushed at her mother and began to pummel her with her fists. Harriet grabbed her arms, at the same time as Addy put hands to her shoulders from behind her. Alexine began to scream.

Nanny Rose, who had been drowsing by the fire in her room, heard the scream and realized that the Paris party had returned. What was going on? She lumbered to her bare feet and then pushed them into slippers, at the same time readjusting her shawl.

As she shuffled crablike down the stairs, hand to bannister, she heard Harriet's voice: 'Now that's enough of that. Quite enough. Just pull yourself together. Get up! And stop that din!' Alexine was lying on the floor, sobbing and kicking her feet in a violent tattoo. Nanny Rose had never before heard the mistress talk to Alexine in that commanding, implacable voice.

'Oh, Nanny, do see what you can do with her. She's worked herself into this state simply because that wretched boy has gone.'

Creakily Nanny Rose knelt down and put a hand on Alexine's shoulder. 'Now come along, darling. Come upstairs with me. It's time for bed. Bed.' Her voice was coaxing, gentle, maternal. That was how she used to talk to Alexine when she was still a small child.

Alexine raised herself, turned to her, put out her arms. Nanny Rose enfolded her. 'There, there!' she muttered. 'Come on, sweet. I'm going to make you some hot chocolate. That's what you'd like, isn't it?'

As Nanny Rose and Alexine mounted the stairs, Addy turned to Harriet. 'What a fuss about nothing!'

But suddenly Harriet was overcome with guilt. She bit her lower lip. She was unnaturally flushed and her hands were trembling.

'You couldn't have kept him here. How could you? John agreed about that, we all agreed. His family will be happy to see him. And they'll be even happier to have all that money. It may not seem much to us but to them it will be a fortune.'

'I hope I've done the right thing,' Harriet said.

'Of course you have.'

Upstairs, Nanny Rose did not think so. As she brushed Alexine's hair with long, rhythmical strokes, the cup of half-drunk chocolate on the dressing table beside them, she was saying: 'I don't understand it. Why did they have to send that poor creature back? What sort of life will he have out there? And he was such a nice friend for you.'

'One day I'll find him again. I'll go out there and find him. You'll see. I'll find him.'

Book 2

1 BOTH AGED SEVENTEEN, Alexine and Monsieur Thierry's tiny, pretty, frivolous daughter, Sophie, had become the closest of friends. A day rarely passed when one of them did not visit the other. Impartially, they would talk to each other now in Dutch, which Sophie spoke with so many grammatical mistakes and with such an appalling accent that Alexine was always laughing at her, now in French, and now in English. Together they would feed and exercise the unruly pack of dogs, some pedigree but most mongrel strays, that Alexine had collected over the years. Visitors would put their hands to their ears in horror at the constant barking and yapping. For her favourite among these dogs, a mongrel called Flopsy, Alexine had even had a visiting card printed, which she would deposit along with hers when paying an obligatory call – as though to say 'I'd have so much have liked to see you, but Flopsy was in such a hurry to get on with his walk.'

Sophie had a sweet, small, pure soprano voice, free of all vibrato. Alexine would listen entranced as, accompanied by Harriet, she would sing some drawing-room ballad at a party. Before meeting Sophie, Alexine had, like her father, been indifferent to music. Now she would creep into the room whenever she heard her mother playing, as Harriet so often did when she had nothing else to occupy her, and struggle to come to terms with an art for which she lacked any natural affinity.

Monsieur Thierry did not care for the closeness of the relationship. He now only half remembered how the precocious girl, with the touchingly fragile arms and neck and the luxuriant, shiny hair, had enthralled him so many years before in Paris. Recently he had succumbed to a secret, never to be fulfilled yearning for another young girl who, when not occupied on some task to do with her father's confectionery shop, would perch, chin propped on palm, on the railings outside it. As he entered or left the shop, making seldom necessary purchases, he would address her as '*chouchoute*' and she would then giggle behind a raised hand, since the word sounded so bizarre to her.

What Monsieur Thierry had against Alexine was not that, so many years before, she had decisively rebuffed him in the railway carriage, but that her unconventionality of behaviour was so often a subject of gossip. That she was vastly rich sometimes mitigated this gossip, but more often, because of envy in that close-knit society of people often living far beyond their means, exacerbated it. 'If only she were more ladylike!' or 'If only she were more womanlike!' was the usual tenor of the criticisms. She was, people complained, so independent and emphatic in her views, brusquely contradicting her elders. There was something at once too vigorous and too awkward about all her movements, as she strode down a street, arms swinging, or decisively mounted a stile, unaided. Her voice had such a vibrant, impatient tone to it.

Such criticism also took in Harriet. Coming from such an old and distinguished family, people would say to each other, she knew perfectly well how a young, unmarried woman should conduct herself. But, instead of attempting to restrain her daughter's behaviour, she indulged and even encouraged her in it. When other girls of her age would have their chaperons, Alexine would appear on her own; on more than one occasion, she had been glimpsed riding astride instead of side-saddle; and, though as extravagant as her mother in her patronage not merely of Madame Molnar but also of a host of other dressmakers, she all too often did not care, even on formal occasions, how she looked.

More than once Monsieur Thierry asked his aristocratic, blue-stocking wife, seven years older than himself, whether she did not think that there might not be something 'unhealthy' in the relationship between their only child and the heiress in the large house visible, in its extensive grounds, from the upstairs windows of their far smaller one. Often from those windows they would see Alexine, surrounded by her dogs, toiling in the garden, along with one or both of the gardeners, as if she were a gardener herself. Madame Thierry would laugh and shake her head, dismissing her husband's suspicions. Young girls of that age would often form these intense friendships, she said. She herself had had such a friend, a Russian girl, long since dead, who had been a pupil in the same convent. Madame Thierry was a sensible woman; and in any case an innate laziness made her retreat from any possibility of friction or fuss.

Monsieur Thierry's worry was that, if the close friendship of his daughter with Alexine were to cause any scandal, he might never achieve the ambassadorship that, despite his wife's powerful connections, was already overdue. Madame Thierry did not care about the ambassadorship, which might prove an inconvenience if it took them too far away from Paris for her to pay her frequent visits to her friends and family there.

Harriet's parties were always lavish; but they, too, were often the focus of criticism. Inevitably among the guests would be members of the aristocracy and of the *corps diplomatique*. But so too would be writers, composers, artists, and people who, often far less successfully than Philip, were dependent on commerce for their livelihood. Harriet's sole criterion for issuing an invitation was whether a prospective guest was amusing, interesting, talented or attractive.

It was at a Palace Ball that Alexine first set eyes on Count Adolf Franz Joseph von Königsmark, though she had already heard of him, newly arrived as Prussian military attaché, from friends. He was so handsome, these friends had enthused, he had such beautiful manners, he was so full of fun.

Alexine had, with her usual unpunctuality, arrived late, with a flustered Harriet and a fuming Addy, at the ball. One of her dogs, an English mastiff bitch, was pupping and instead of leaving it to Harry to cope with the situation, she had insisted on being present to ensure that all went well. Repeatedly her mother had sent servants out to the stables to tell her to hurry, she must get dressed, they could not possibly arrive late for a palace ball. Eventually, in her finery, her small feet in their delicate shoes picking their way over mud and straw, Harriet herself had gone out. 'Please, darling! *Please!*' The lateness of their arrival did not go unremarked. Even the Queen noticed it and commented on it to the lady-in-waiting, Addy's friend Juliana, who was already beginning to supplant Addy in the royal favour.

Arm in arm, Alexine and Sophie swayed down the ballroom, looking to right and left. Then Sophie gripped Alexine's arm and, on tiptoe, put her lips to Alexine's ear. 'Over there! Look! That must be him!'

'Who?'

'The German count. You know. They were talking about him yesterday.' She giggled. 'He's beautiful, really beautiful. So broad and tall!'

Alexine looked over in the direction that Sophie was now indicating with an inclination of her head. The young man was standing with the Prussian consul, who was his uncle, the consul's wife and Madame Thierry.

'Maman's talking to him. Let's go over.'

'No.' Alexine felt an immediate attraction, but she was determined to resist it. 'No!' She pulled at Sophie's arm. 'Oh, come on!'

But Sophie would not come on. Eventually, reluctantly acquiescent, Alexine allowed herself to be led across the floor.

Königsmark was surprisingly shy. At first, after the introductions had been made, he kept turning his head aside, to gaze out over to the dancers, as though wary of even looking at the two young girls, much less talking to them. But Sophie was bold. Repeatedly she questioned him – when had he arrived from Prussia? was he happy in his post? where was he living? – until, at long last, he was prepared to focus all his attention on them. But Alexine, with an appearance of detachment, even disdain, kept aloof from the ensuing conversation.

To her amazement, it was she, not Sophie, whom he first asked for a dance. Capriciously, she refused him – 'I'm so sorry. My card's full already' – and then at once regretted it. He turned to Sophie: 'And you, mademoiselle? Is your card also full?' Sophie said that there was still one dance unclaimed. 'Then you will allow me to have it?' Sophie nodded.

She was overjoyed, as was her mother. Everyone in Dutch society had already agreed, less than a week after his arrival in the city, that the Count, with his striking looks and his aristocratic forebears, was highly eligible.

Later, as she herself danced with a lumpish, spotted young man, with a faint body odour, a nephew of the King, Alexine repeatedly glanced over to Sophie and Königsmark. How happy they seemed, constantly smiling at each other as they met, joined, separated, took each other's hands! What an idiot she had been!

'Did you enjoy yourself?' Harriet asked Alexine in the carriage going home.

'Oh, it was so tedious! All these balls are so tedious! The same people, the same food, the same music. Nothing ever changes.'

But something had changed.

∽

Alexine was surprised that at their next meeting, on the following afternoon, Sophie had lost all her enthusiasm for the Prussian. He was too tall, she complained, she had got a crick in her neck from being obliged constantly to look up at him; he was so solemn, talking endlessly about politics; he had such a deep, slow, guttural voice and, though his French was correct enough, he had a weird way of accentuating it. She began to give an uncannily accurate imitation.

'But his eyes!' Alexine protested. 'Those extraordinary blue, blue eyes! And his hair! That blond, blond hair!'

'The blond beast,' Sophie said, with a laugh. That evening, she had also danced with a Prince Caradja, a small, swarthy, prematurely balding man, a First Secretary at the Turkish Embassy, with whom her father played chess, and she had suddenly decided, on no more than a whim so it seemed to Alexine, that he was the one whom she wanted to marry.

'Oh, but everyone says that Caradja has no money at all!' Alexine protested. 'You'll end up having to wash his one shirt for him, while he lies in bed smoking those horrible cigarettes of his.'

Sophie gave a joyful laugh. 'I shouldn't mind doing that at all. After I'd finished washing the shirt, I'd jump into his bed and smoke a cigarette with him.'

'Oh, Sophie, how can you?'

Secretly, Alexine was relieved that there would be no competition between them.

∽

That year archery had become the craze among the members – men, women, children – of society at The Hague. All through a summer that was a sequence of one hot, cloudless day after another, people held their archery parties out on their lawns or, if those were not extensive enough, on some nearby stretch of open ground. Lavish refreshments were laid out on trestle tables, servants were loaned from one household to another. When Harriet gave such a party, the dogs wandered among the contestants, causing a lot of secret annoyance. One, a Pekinese, was, to Alexine's horror, all but transfixed by a wayward arrow.

Two days after the Palace ball, Alexine arrived with Harriet at one such party – Addy, with her dislike of any strenuous physical activity had declined to come – to see that the Count was already performing at the butts. Leaving her mother with their hostess, after a few perfunctory words of greeting, she strode over, closed parasol extended like a stick to hasten her passage through the crowds, and took up her position just behind him. Through his white silk shirt, she could see the powerful muscles of his shoulders. He was sweating in the heat, and between the shoulders the shirt was sticking to his vertebrae. Sweat had also dampened his thick, unusually long, wavy hair, and glistened on a cheekbone, each time that, preparatory to shooting, he half-turned his head, without seeing her behind him.

'Bravo!' an elderly man standing next to Alexine called out. At once there was some clapping from a small group of women also watching. With a decisive smack, the arrow had hit the bull's eye. Another followed it to the same place, to even more applause. Then, as though he had become suddenly bored, Königsmark's aim became increasingly erratic, until, obviously annoyed with himself, he gave up.

As he was about to lower the bow, Alexine stepped forward and put out a hand: 'Let me try!'

He stared at her in amazement. There were separate butts for the women, who shot over a shorter distance and used smaller bows. Then he laughed, half embarrassed and half pleased. 'I'd be happy to do anything for mademoiselle. But this bow isn't for a lady.'

Alexine laughed. 'Oh, come on!' Again she held out her hand. 'Let me try. I'm not a lady,' she added. 'Everyone says how unladylike I am.'

'Very well, mademoiselle. Try. But it'll be far too heavy for you. I warn you.'

Alexine took the bow, and Königsmark handed her an arrow. Amazed by the sight, more and more people gathered round them. To everyone's surprise, the first arrow not merely reached as far as the target but struck the inner ring. The next arrow overshot it. The third grazed the outer edge. The remaining three arrows all fell just short. But everyone agreed that, for a woman, Alexine had done amazingly well. Whether they approved of her doing amazingly well was another matter. 'Typical!' 'That girl's just doesn't know how to behave.' 'She might be a boy.' 'Why doesn't her mother have more control over her?' As the crowd slowly dispersed, the familiar criticisms were repeated.

'You're a marvel,' Königsmark told her. 'Now, after that exertion, let me get you some iced tea.'

How could Sophie have taken exception to that slow, deep, guttural, heavily accented way of speaking French? Alexine thrilled to it.

She put an arm through his. 'Thank you. Yes, I'd like that.'

'I hadn't realized that you were such an Amazon.'

'Don't Amazons have only one breast? As you can see, I have two.'

It was a bold thing to say to a man whom she hardly knew, and he was startled by its boldness. He turned his head and stared at her with those amazingly clear, pale blue eyes of his under eyebrows glistening golden, like his forearms, in the sunshine. She thought, with a brief pressure of her fingers on his arm: A golden man.

He laughed. 'You're all that everyone here says that you are.' Then he added: 'And I like that. Yes, I like that.'

∽

In the days and then weeks ahead, the gossip intensified. There were reports of the couple walking arm in arm, heads bowed, deep in conversation, along the canal, and even of their kissing, unmindful of whether anyone could see them or not; of their constantly riding together, early in the morning, soon after dawn, before Königsmark went to work at the Prussian embassy; even of their having been seen in a disreputable café, in a slum area of the city, known to be largely frequented by prostitutes and their clients.

Inevitably, the gossip reached Harriet, when her friends, sometimes genuinely concerned but more often affecting to be so, passed it on to her. Shouldn't she have a word with Alexine? Of course there was no substance in what was being said, they quickly assured her, but the dear girl ought to be more careful. People could be so malicious, they could do her real harm.

Harriet was dismissive. 'Oh, I trust her,' she would say. Or, 'I'm afraid I can't be bothered with all that kind of malicious talk. Life's too short for it.' So far from arousing her disapproval, Alexine's reckless behaviour secretly excited her. The girl was behaving as she herself had always wanted to behave. It was only now, with extreme slowness, that she was herself gathering the courage to follow her example.

It was Addy, goaded by sly remarks made directly to her or in her hearing at the Palace, who eventually tackled Alexine. After a long and exhausting day, during which she had accompanied the increasingly tetchy Queen on an interminable visit first to an orphanage and then to a home for the blind, she was standing at her bedroom window in a loose peignoir, a hairbrush in her hand, gazing out with a vague dissatisfaction into the garden, where the shapes of the distant trees were beginning to blur in the gathering summer dusk. All at once she saw them. Flopsy, the mongrel favourite, scampered out of some bushes and then, from the rough path snaking through them, Alexine and Königsmark eventually emerged. The path had been so narrow that she had had to walk ahead of him. But now, out on the lawn, she waited for him and then took his arm. She said something, her overlarge head uptilted on the long neck, and both of them laughed. She put her mouth up to his in what, to Addy, was blatant invitation. He responded with ardour.

Addy watched them with reawakened anguish for her own recklessness in the past and with anger at her niece's now. If that girl was not careful, she was going to wreck her life, as she herself had done. Königsmark might well marry her, but it was by no means certain. His parents, many of the family estates heavily mortgaged, had higher ambitions for him, according to gossip at the Court. There was even talk of a royal match, some said with a daughter of Queen Victoria and others with one of the Wittelsbach princesses. There was also said to be another heiress, daughter of an Austrian entrepreneur almost as wealthy as Philip had been, with whom Königsmark was said to have been infatuated while *en poste* in Vienna before his arrival at The Hague.

༄

Harriet was playing the piano in the next room, and Alexine, kneeling on the rug before the unlit fire, was teasing at the matted hair of an English sheep-dog with a silver-mounted comb. Addy decided that now was the time to speak out.

'May I say something to you, *chérie?*'

Alexine looked up. From far back in her early childhood that was always how her aunt prefaced some complaint or reproof. 'Of course. What is it?'

'I hope you won't take it amiss. But I feel I must say it. For your own good.'

'Yes, of course.' Alexine continued to tug the comb through the matted hair. Though entirely motionless on the rug, the dog would from time to time emit a little, high-pitched whimper, whether of pleasure or pain it was impossible to say.

'Why are you using that comb? Isn't it one of the ones you use yourself? It's hardly suitable for a dog.'

'It has wide teeth,' Alexine said. 'Is that what you wanted to talk to me about?'

'No, of course not.' The notes of the piano from the other room became more and more clamorous. The old fortepiano had been so much less disturbing. Why did Harriet have to go and replace it with an instrument better suited to a concert-hall than to a drawing-room? 'No.' She made an effort to shut out the din. 'You know how malicious people can be. Particularly when they're envious.'

'Envious?'

'Remember that you're the girl who always gets what she wants. That's how they think of you. Whereas so many of them want so much and get so little. So, with their tittle-tattle, they set out to harm you. Us,' she added. 'Us too.'

'I'm really not interested in tittle-tattle,' Alexine said, as her mother had had said before her.

'It's all very well to say that you're not interested in tittle-tattle. But I know – I know from my own experience – how destructive it can be. Do be careful, my dear. Try – try to be more *discreet*.'

Her task finished, Alexine jumped up, comb in hand, from the rug. She began to remove strands of hair from the comb and dropped them, without a thought, to the floor. Tomorrow one of the servants would sweep up the hairs – with difficulty because they would become enmeshed in the thick pile of the rug – just as they constantly picked up the clothes that she discarded on the floor. 'I don't care about being the things that people want me to be. What's the point of being rich if one cannot be oneself?'

'Oh, very well. If that's how you feel about it.' Addy, who had merely a small annuity, thought that to talk like that of being rich was crude and insensitive. But of course Alexine was right. It was only the rich who were able to be wholly themselves. Bitterly, she had learned that through her service at the Court, constantly adapting herself to the capricious demands of the Queen, never arguing, never expressing or even hinting at an unconventional opinion, always saying and doing precisely what was expected of her.

2 HANS, TRUDGING DOWN THE COBBLED STREET to the cottage that he had rented for his mother and sister, after a tiring and tiresome day of dealing with John's unnecessary instructions as to how he should conduct the negotiations to buy a firm on the verge of bankruptcy, was deep in thought. The legacy and the job had gained him some freedom, but not as much as he had expected. Although absent in Liverpool, John was a far more exacting master than Philip had ever been, since he was both unsure of his abilities, when he contrasted himself with his forceful, brilliant, reckless father, and suspicious that they might also be inferior to Hans's. The girl whom Hans had so often put off marrying because he must stay with his mother and in any case could not afford to have two women dependent on him, had, when he had at long last proposed to her, announced that she was sorry but her affections were, as she stiltedly put it, elsewhere engaged. To add to his despondency, he was extremely hot in his tightly buttoned blue serge suit, and his new elastic-sided boots, fashionably narrow and extremely expensive, were pinching him.

Suddenly he raised his head from his examination of the cobbles and there, in front of him, the two of them were! Alexine, taller than any of her women friends, was unmistakable even when seen from the back and from so far away. Her arm was intertwined with that of the man with her, her head bending forward as they swayed along together. Who was he? The man, who had the build of an athlete and a strutting, slightly bow-legged walk, had removed his hat, so that the tardily setting sun, which was causing Hans to screw up his eyes and from time to time even to raise a palm to shield them from its glare, glinted on his thick golden hair, creating an evanescent halo. Then Hans realized: this must be that Königsmark about whose relationship with Alexine he had heard some gossip only the previous day in the office.

The couple slowed their pace. Then the man put a hand in a pocket and drew out two keys. He inserted one key in the front door of the mean little house beside which they had eventually halted and stood aside, to allow Alexine to enter first. Then, with a laugh at something that, now out of sight, she must have said, he entered.

All at once Hans's mood of weary depression lifted. He had knowledge of something of which, in all probability, no one else had knowledge. Merely to possess it gave him a sensation of power and therefore of happiness.

As he walked on, he began to whistle to himself.

Having washed herself in the chipped enamel bidet in the alcove concealed by a tattered curtain from the rest of the room, Alexine emerged naked. She stared down at Adolph, lying out, also naked, on the bed, and then, with a sigh, crossed over to the mansard window. She looked out over the roofs, glinting in the late afternoon sunshine from the rain that had recently fallen in an abrupt, powerful downpour.

'Oh, this place is so squalid!'

He smiled. 'It's not that bad. It's good of Franz to let us have it.'

'It would be even better of him if just occasionally he had it cleaned.'

'You know he hasn't got a job. And his father gives him only a tiny allowance. Even smaller than mine.'

'That bidet was filthier than ever. I had to scrub it out before using it.'

'Oh, please!' He pulled a face and patted the bed beside him. 'Come on! Come!'

Reluctantly she strolled over to the bed and clambered on to it. He put an arm around her and tried to draw her to him, but she resisted him.

'Oh, not again!'

'What's the matter with you? What's put you in this mood?'

'This has gone on too long. I hate these furtive meetings. In this awful, awful place.'

'Where else can we go? It's better than nothing – or doing it out in the open, against a tree, as we did that last time.' He laughed and again tried to pull her towards him. 'You wouldn't like to go back to that, would you?'

'Why can't we get married?'

'I've told you why. We've only known each other for – what? – seven weeks. And I've been only a short time longer at the legation. Let's wait until, well, the New Year. That'll be the time for a decision.'

'What do you mean – a decision? Aren't we both decided?'

'I said – everything in good time.' He was now faintly exasperated, but his tone remained patient and reasonable. 'I must establish myself in my job. I must get a better one. My pay is very small.'

'You know that I have money. Lots and lots of it. Far more than I know what to do with.'

'I don't want to be a man who lives on the wealth of his wife – like that awful Monsieur Thierry.' Although Alexine had never spoken to anyone about that scene in the railway carriage, it was as though Adolph, by some miracle of extrasensory perception, knew of it, so extreme was his hatred of the Frenchman. 'As a younger son – one of so many – I have little from my family now, and I can expect even less in the future. Over the years we've become poorer and poorer. And it's going to go on like that, unless my brothers and I can make some change. And that's unlikely. No Königsmark has ever been any good at making money – only at spending it.'

'It's so silly to be proud about these things. I have enough money for at least a dozen husbands.'

'I don't think I'd like to be part of a harem. I want you to myself.'

Once again he put a hand up to her shoulder, in an attempt to pull her towards him. Once again she resisted him, this time actually thrusting him away from her.

'And this wedding – your sister's wedding.' The following week he was going home to his family. 'I really can't see why I can't go with you.'

'Because they haven't met you yet. Only my sister knows of your existence.'

'Well, tell them about me! Let me meet them!'

∽

Back at home, Alexine brooded moodily. He was as affectionate as ever to her in public and as passionate as ever to her in private, but she was enraged by his refusal in any way to commit himself. All her behaviour was based on the assumption that eventually, more likely sooner than later, they would get engaged and then married. Harriet, Addy and everyone close to her shared that assumption. But whenever the subject of their marriage had arisen, he would either make no positive response, as just now in that filthy garconnière, or else he would veer away from it with some irrelevance or a joke.

∽

Harriet stared down at the jostling capital letters, some tilting this way and some that, in which the anonymous note was written. Daan had just brought it to her. Out in the hall, she could hear Adolph saying his last goodbyes to Alexine before his departure. They sounded not sad but boisterous, as repeatedly their laughter rang out. Having said her own goodbyes, she had decided to leave them alone for theirs.

It was disgusting. And cowardly. If people wanted to write such things, then they should have the courage to reveal their identities. Who could be the perpetrator? At a first reading, the clumsiness of the handwriting and the crudeness of the language had made her decide that it must be some former servant, sacked for dishonesty or inefficiency, or some disgruntled tradesman. But now she had her doubts. People equating money with happiness might well envy Alexine for a happiness that they imagined to be far greater than their own, and so attempt to destroy it.

When Harriet heard the front door open and then a minute or two later close, she got to her feet. She hated the task ahead of her but it was imperative to perform it.

She opened the door. '*Chérie!*'

'Yes!'

'Could you come for a moment?'

'Is it important? I'm late for Sophie.'

'Well, yes, I'd like a word now.'

Alexine entered the room. 'I ought to feel sad, but somehow I don't. I really do think that when he gets back, he'll at last decide that the time has come. But it's such a long wait. He says that it won't be more than two weeks at the outside but...' She broke off, at last noticing the look of strain on her mother's face. 'What's the matter? What is it?'

Harriet held out the flimsy sheet of paper. She did not know it, but it was on such sheets that the clerks in what had once been Philip's office and was now Hans's, jotted down notes or made rough calculations.

Alexine frowned down at the paper. Then she looked up. 'Who wrote this?' she demanded angrily.

'I've no idea. The question is – is it true?'

Alexine hesitated, once again frowning down at the clumsy letters sprawling across the page. Then she raised her head. She held it high. 'Yes.'

'Oh, *chérie!* How could you, how *could* you?'

'I love him.'

'Yes, yes! But think of the possible scandal – the possible danger. If you'd told me – if you'd really wanted ... I'd have hated it but we could have found some pretext for his coming to stay here ... That area is notorious, you must know that. And to be seen going into a house there with him...'

'Well, that's how it was. I'm sorry. But' – she shrugged and then stooped and placed the letter on Harriet's desk – 'there was nothing else for it.'

'I don't want you to ruin your life! I – I don't want you to be another Addy.'

'Aunt Addy? What has she got to do with it?'

Alexine had always sensed some mystery in her aunt's past. It was odd that a woman so much more beautiful than her sister had never married, and that, for as long as Alexine could remember, had never once had a relationship or even a close friendship with any man.

'Oh, sit down!' Harriet said, in a weary, cross voice. 'She was an idiot. But she had more excuse than you have. And ever since she's been paying for her idiocy.'

. . . It was when she was only seventeen that the Admiral procured for Addy the post of lady-in-Waiting to Queen Sophia. But soon after her arrival at the Court, she caught the attention of the sombre, dumpy Queen Mother, Anna Paulovna, sister of the previous Tsar, Alexander I. After months of inexorably declining health Anna Paulovna had decided that, as she put, she was nearing the end of the road and, for the last time, wished to revisit her native Russia. Fascinated by the young girl's beauty and vivacity, she asked her daughter-in-law if she might 'borrow' her for the trip. Queen Sophia was unaccommodating, as always with Anna Paulovna, whom she suspected of making trouble between herself and her estranged husband and secretly disliked. 'But I'm just breaking her in,' she said, as though Addy were a recently acquired filly. But Anna Paulovna persisted, until 'Oh, very well!' the Queen impatiently gave in. 'But I must warn you that she's terribly unpunctual and can come out with the most tactless things.'

Anna Paulovna laughed. 'Well, then she resembles me!'

When the party from The Hague reached the Imperial summer palace, the German-born Tsarina and the seven children were in residence but not the Tsar. Anna Paulovna, whose condition at once deteriorated on her arrival, was increasingly obliged to take to her bed. Because the old woman's eyesight was also failing, Addy would then be summoned to sit for hours on end reading to her. Addy did not in the least mind a task that her fellow lady-in-waiting, a spinster in her forties, hated. Fortunately for the spinster and no less fortunately for Addy, Anna Paulovna soon decided that Addy read so much better than her colleague that this duty should, for the future, be performed by her alone. The two women, one so near the close of her life and the other so near the beginning of hers, soon established a powerful and surprising intimacy. When Anna Paulovna had one of the fainting attacks, it was Addy who held the smelling-salts, always kept in readiness, to the old woman's nose. When she took a rare bath, it was Addy, with two maids in attendance, who supervised the lengthy operation. When her feet ached intolerably, it was Addy, kneeling before her, who would massage them between her strong, capable hands.

Eventually, tired and irritable from dealing for days on end with affairs of state, the Tsar arrived from St Petersburg. He was perfunctory with his wife and aunt, reserving any show of pleasure for the younger of his children. He seemed hardly to notice Addy, nodding to her in greeting if they passed each other and then moving on, rarely addressing her on those occasions when she joined the family for a meal, a stroll in the garden or music after dinner, and even from time to time absent-mindedly calling her by the name of the other, older lady-in-waiting. Anna Paulovna confided in Addy that it was clear that he was bored with his wife, whose only interest was in her children and the embroidery that she carried everywhere with her, even on their excursions to the seaside, and that she surmised that this had aggravated his natural moodiness.

When not busy with her duty of reading to the Queen, Addy passed the time reading by herself. She would go out into the extensive park and seat herself on a bench, with a copy of a novel by Balzac, Stendhal or Dickens. Fluent in both English and French, she had no need of translations. One afternoon, when she was absorbed in a French translation of Turgenev's *A Sportsman's Notebook*, she looked up to see, in the far distance, the Tsar striding out – he always seemed to be in a hurry, even when arriving for a meal – with his two Borzoi dogs now scampering ahead and now lagging behind him. She watched him, wondering where he was going. Then he swung round, as though some thought of things to be urgently done had suddenly come to him, and was striding towards her. As he drew nearer, she saw the familiar look of petulance on his grey, heavily lined face. That face would have been handsome if, below the high forehead and dominant nose, the chin did not slip away so disastrously, as though a rock-face had, near its base, suddenly suffered a landslide.

'What are you doing here?' It was almost as though he were accusing her of doing something that she ought not to be doing.

She rose to her feet and held up the book. 'Reading, sire.'

'Sit, sit!' He motioned to the bench. 'There's no need for formality. Not here.'

She sat and he sat down beside her.

'So you're reading, are you? You always seem to be reading. I've so little time for it.' He reached out, took the book from her and examined it, first the title page and then the spine. He stared at her. 'How can you read such dangerous nonsense?'

Boldly she replied: 'Excuse me, sire, it's not nonsense. And it's beautifully written.'

'I favour reform – reasonable reform. But this fool's ideas could precipitate a revolution.'

'If there isn't enough reform, then that is far more likely to precipitate a revolution.'

'Are you arguing with me?' He burst into laughter. It was the first time that she had heard him laugh in all the days of the visit. 'Well, I like your spirit.'

For a while they went on talking. He drew out a cigarette, placed it in a long gold holder, and drew deeply on it. The cigarette finished, he jerked it out of the holder, flung it away, and jumped to his feet.

'Why have we never had a conversation before?'

'Because you've never started one with me.'

Again he laughed. Then, without any farewell, he strode off, the dogs in attendance.

From then on, he repeatedly placed himself beside her. 'So what revolutionary nonsense are you reading today?' he would ask her. Twice he invited her to join him and two of the children in a game of croquet. Once he invited her to go for a walk with him and the dogs. If the Tsarina was present when he showed some such attention, she would move with a strange jerkiness or sit with a strange tenseness, her clear blue eyes fearful and wary.

One evening, having asked her to dance, he held her unusually close, his cheek almost touching hers. Surely someone, perhaps even the Tsarina, would notice? Addy tried to distance herself, but each time his hand round her waist tightened and he drew her closer again. Eventually she terminated the embarrassment by saying: 'It's too hot, sire. I feel giddy. May we sit down?'

The next evening, the Tsar's private secretary, a dark, daunting young man, already going bald, knocked on her bedroom door at the moment when, having seen to Anna Paulovna's exigent needs, she was on the point of undressing for bed. His Imperial Highness wished for a word with her.

'With me?'

He nodded. He almost smirked. Then he held the door open for her to pass out into the corridor.

'Why should he want to see me at this hour?'

The secretary shrugged and pulled a little face.

It was the first time that any man had made love to her. So far from being repelled by all the indications – the small paunch, the varicose veins, the wheezing – that the Tsar was long past his youth, she merely felt an additional excitement because of them. On three more consecutive nights she received the same summons.

On the morning after the last of these summons, she came down to breakfast to find that the Tsar was not at his usual place at the head of the table. When she sat down, she was aware that the Tsarina was eying her, with a faintly sardonic expression, over her raised coffee cup. Addy tried to meet her gaze fearlessly. 'His Imperial Highness had to leave early this morning for St Petersburg.' The Tsarina appeared to be announcing the news to the whole company; but Addy felt, chilled and desolated, that the announcement was really for herself.

The stay protracted itself because the doctor said that Anna Paulovna was too ill to make the arduous journey back to the Netherlands. 'You don't want to leave me, dear, do you?' Anna Paulovna asked, her once formidable character now pitiful in its dependence.

Addy replied that, no, of course she didn't. Day after day she sat in the stuffy bedroom, reading if the old woman was awake or merely staring into space and thinking of her lover if the old woman was sleeping.

At first Addy refused to believe that she could possibly be pregnant. She had suffered from dysmenorrhoea ever since the menarche, and her periods were all too often late. But eventually, obliged to rush out of Anna Paulovna's bedroom, where the two of them were eating breakfast alone together, in order to vomit, she realized, with horror, that there was no doubt whatever.

Two days later, in the midst of her reading from *Notre Dame de Paris*, Anna Paulovna raised a hand and rapped out in interruption: 'What's the matter? Tell me, tell me.'

'The matter? Have I done something wrong?

'Now, come on, tell me tell me!'

'There's nothing, madame. Nothing at all. I don't understand.'

'There's something on your mind. I know you so well now. Don't try to pretend to me.'

In her guilt, Addy thought this to be an accusation. She bowed her head. 'I – I can't speak about it.'

'Of course you can! Don't be foolish. We have to think what to do next.'

∽

Anna Paulovna had inherited a hunting lodge in Finland from an aunt. She decided that Addy must go there to have the child, in order to avoid any scandal whether in the Netherlands or in Russia. Harriet must accompany her. Back at The Hague, the old woman told the Admiral all this. He was horrified by the news but also, though he would never have admitted it, secretly proud that Addy should have had such an exalted liaison. Before her departure, he was constantly demanding of her: 'What's the matter with you? What made you do such a thing?' and telling her that she was sick, evil, depraved, mad.

In Finland the winter had already started. The hunting lodge was situated, far from any town or even village, by an already frozen lake, with silver birches all around it. Later in retrospect it seemed to the two sisters that in the long winter months that followed Addy did nothing but read and Harriet did nothing but practise on the piano. But, when the weak sunlight glinted on the snow, they would trudge arm in arm round the lake. Because of the barrier of language, they could barely communicate with the three servants who looked after them. From time to time, however, they would go into the kitchen and, seated on straight-backed, unpainted wooden chairs, silently watch the preparation of a meal. Eventually they would themselves join in the cooking.

Late one morning, as they sipped coffee beside the smoking fire, they suddenly heard a dripping sound, as of a tap not properly turned off. Together they listened, heads on one side, frowning in bewilderment at each other. Then Harriet jumped up and ran to the window.

'The thaw! The thaw!'

The water from the thawing ice was dripping from the steep eaves.

Five days later, the baby was born. The midwife did what she had been instructed to do. Having washed and dried the wrinkled, scarlet boy, she swept him up and hurried out of the room with him cradled in her arms. Addy never saw him again. When she asked what had become of him, she was told that he had been adopted by a farmer and his wife. Were they local people? No one, not even Anna Paulovna, who died a few weeks later, would tell her.

∽

'. . . So somewhere in Finland a Romanov must be working as a wood-cutter or a cowman or a poultry-man,' Harriet concluded.

'But later – why did Aunt Addy never marry?'

'Oh, the poor dear's foolishness continued. She seemed to be incapable of learning any sense.'

Less than a year later, Addy had fallen in love with a country boy, two years younger than herself, gawky, reckless and ardent, who was employed in the stables. Inevitably, the other servants had begun to gossip first among themselves and then to the servants of neighbours and friends of the family. A servant of a neighbour or friend must have said something to his or her employer and the employer in turn . . .

'It was then that the most terrible thing of all happened. It's something I don't like to think, much less talk about.' Harriet paused, palms to cheeks, staring out ahead of her.

'Oh, please!'

Visibly, Harriet gathered herself. 'You never really knew your grandfather. By the time that you were born, everything had softened – his brain, his body, his character. Before that – he could be terrible. He was terrible to Addy.' She paused and shook her head as though to empty it of an intolerable memory. 'Having at least realized what was going on, he first sacked the man and then decided that poor Addy was sick, dangerously sick. He had heard of this doctor. In England. He performed this – this operation. He took Addy over to London, he had her – had her . . . Oh, don't let's talk about it, think about it!'

'What happened?'

'No, no!'

'Tell me! What was the operation?'

'No, I can't. I can't! No one in the civilized world now does that operation. But that's why – that's why she is what she is.'

'And what has all this to do with me?'

'Well, don't, please don't be stupid like her. Take care! Take care!'

In the years ahead, Alexine would from time to time again press her mother to speak about the operation. But Harriet's response was always the same: Too awful. She could not even to think of it, let alone talk of it. No, no. Please, please, please.

⌇

During Adolph's absence at the wedding, the days dragged bleakly.

The Thierrys threw an eighteenth birthday ball for Sophie; but, having long ago accepted an invitation, Alexine then had no heart for it and merely sent an extravagant present of a gold necklace set with oval and round rose-cut, foiled garnets. Sophie was not appeased by this generosity. Their friendship briefly faltered.

Every day, in a vain effort to still her restlessness, Alexine would go for long walks with the ever increasing pack of dogs around her, or for even longer rides. That people continued to comment adversely on her doing these things alone, in no way worried either her or Harriet. Every morning she would awake thinking despairingly, 'Yet another day.' Then she would await the letter that he had promised but that never came. She herself had been writing daily to him, hastily scribbled letters filled with her love and her longing to see him soon, soon, soon.

One morning, as she, her mother and Addy were finishing their breakfast, old Daan entered carrying a package on a salver. 'The post, madam.'

Alexine let out an inarticulate cry of joy, leapt to her feet and rushed over to him. She grabbed the packet, not noticing that it was addressed to Harriet, not to her, and tore it open with clumsily trembling fingers.

'Oh!' Suddenly she drooped. 'It's for you, Mama.'

'For me?'

'Yes. From Prussia but for you. Oh, it's so unfair. What can have happened to him?' She threw down the packet beside Harriet's place. Frowning, Harriet picked it up. It contained a pile of photographs, some frayed and dented at the edges and badly foxed, others in pristine condition.

The letter was from the Baroness. Her husband had died in Sicily – where, she explained, he had taken up residence for the sake of his failing health – and, among his effects there, she had found these photographs in which Philip appeared. Perhaps Madame Thinne would like to have them as a memorial? He and her husband had been such close friends.

Harriet raised her lorgnette and through it began to examine the photographs one after the other. Alexine bent over her shoulder, examining them with her. Addy went on methodically eating some cheese, totally uninterested even when Harriet explained: 'That Baron's widow has sent some photographs of Philip.'

For both Harriet and Alexine there was something eerie about these representations of the man who would once have been sitting at this table eating his breakfast with them and who was now dead. The art was too new and therefore seemed to them to be too close to sorcery; and there was such a profusion of these images, which showed Philip doing such an extraordinary diversity of everyday things – reading a newspaper, raising a glass of wine, buttoning up his jacket – each action frozen forever.

'That must be the Baron,' Harriet said, pointing to a marmoset of a man, with a bedraggled beard and a hat tipped rakishly over an eye, leaning on a cane, while Philip, standing behind and a little to the left, towered over him. 'Someone else must have taken that. I wonder who?'

'Perhaps one of the servants.'

'Possibly.' But would a servant be capable of working such magic?

Then Harriet came on a scene of Philip dressed as she had never before seen him, not in a formal, black or dark-grey suit, with fastidiously starched and ironed shirt, and a stiff detachable collar and cravat, but what looked like a pair of baggy fisherman's trousers, ending several inches above his bare feet, and an open-necked shirt of roughly woven wool. Beside him, staring intently into the lens with what might be terror, was a boy of fourteen and fifteen in a sailor's cap, his feet also bare.

Harriet examined that photograph with extreme care, holding it up the light from the window. 'Who can that be? The Baron's son?'

'Has he got a son?'

Harriet shrugged. Again she held the photograph up to the light. Her small eyes narrowed, she bunched her mouth. No, the boy was all too obviously an Italian peasant. His feet were grimy, there was a faint down where a beard was already beginning to grow.

Eventually, having thumbed through all the photographs, Harriet put them down with a sigh. She felt a vague bewilderment, even alarm, but she could not have said why. 'Well, it was good of her to send them to us. I must write to thank her. I didn't know that the Baron had died. Well, I never met him. And the odd thing is that your father never spoke about him. They must – they must have been close.' She sighed. 'It all seems to be so long ago now.'

∽

That evening, when Harriet and Addy had gone out on a visit, Alexine, who had refused to accompany them, went into the little room that her mother now used as her study and crossed over to her desk. There was a drawer in which she kept all correspondence that awaited an answer. The Baroness's letter and the photographs would probably be there. Harriet, unlike Alexine, was obsessively tidy, and already the letter and the photographs had been tied into a neat bundle with the same blue tape with which Philip used once to secure his correspondence.

Alexine did not bother to reread the letter, written in an erratic French with many mistakes of spelling. She sat down in her mother's chair, and began to go through the photographs, staring at each for several seconds on end. Suddenly, as one image after another of her father miraculously flashed up at her from the cardboard rectangles, she realized that she had never really known him. With her and everyone else at The Hague, he had always been so tense, forceful, formidable, correct. But here – here in these photographs, taken over what was clearly a period of years – he was totally relaxed, always smiling, untroubled, untidy, happy. The man depicted might be an identical twin, born with none of his own strength of will and fervour of ambition. Again she thought with a mixture of wonder and regret: She had never known him.

Photography could do that, she realized. Yes, it was a kind of sorcery, revealing what was hidden, reviving what was dead, interpreting what was foreign. Repeatedly she went back to the photographs, whenever her mother was out, and repeatedly, with infinite slowness and sadness, she would look at each of the photographs in turn, as though there still remained secrets that they had yet to yield up. Perhaps, if she could only be granted a similar number of photographs of Adolph, she would also be able to approach a step or two closer to the heart of the mystery that he, like everyone else, posed for her.

It was then she made her decision: she would learn how to take such photographs herself.

∽

Alexine, Harriet and Addy had once visited what its owner, an Englishman called Robert Laycock, called his 'Daguerrian Gallery'. Having married a Dutch woman, he had first settled in The Hague as a painter of miniatures. But with the advent of photography that trade had dwindled and, reluctantly and sadly, he had at last decided that he would have to abandon it for this new one. His wife was his assistant.

He worked in a tall, narrow building in which he and his wife – they had no children – also lived. On the ground floor there was an overfurnished, overheated reception area and office, behind which there was a staircase only just wide enough to allow passage for his female clients in their ample skirts. The staircase wound up past the living quarters and finally emerged onto the flat roof of the building, where he had had constructed what was in effect a glasshouse. On a dais stood an upright chair and a table; behind the chair there was tripod supporting a claw-like metal clamp to grip his sitters' heads.

Saying nothing of her plan to her mother and her aunt, Alexine now called on Laycock. A small, balding, middle-aged man, perpetually on the dithering move as he posed and reposed his sitters, he was taken aback by her request. 'Oh, I don't know. My wife assists me, of course, but it's highly unusual for a lady . . .'

'I'm not proposing to set up as your rival in business, Mr Laycock.'

'Of course, of course. I know that, madam. You – you are aware, of course, that the chemicals will stain your fingernails?' He held out a small hand, the long nails of which were dyed with the autumnal tints of an unripe orange. 'I'm afraid, however much care one takes . . . Even my wife . . .'

'Oh, I don't mind about that.' Nor did she. 'I want to learn, and I want to learn quickly.'

He was still dubious. 'Photography isn't easy,' he warned her. He drew in his fleshy, moist lips and sucked on them. 'When I decided to move from portraits to likenesses, it was far from easy for me. Fortunately my wife showed an unexpected aptitude for the scientific side of the business. It was amazing, yes, quite amazing. But for her I could never have made the change.'

'Well, if she showed that aptitude, why shouldn't I? I've always been a quick learner.' Alexine strode over to examine a portrait of a stout, flabby-faced man, forearms resting on the arms of the chair and eyes staring unblinkingly into the lens, that was hanging, among many others, on one of the walls. 'It's extraordinary,' she said of it, in renewed enthralment to this new art. She turned back. 'I'll make it worth your while, Mr Laycock. I'll be your apprentice – but an apprentice who pays. What's wrong with that?'

Laycock saw nothing wrong with it. He knew of the vast Thinne fortune, as did everyone in the country. He was already making far more money than he had ever done as a painter of miniatures, but he had no aversion to making even more. In any case, his flustered, fluttery nature responded, albeit reluctantly, to her forceful one. He realized that he would enjoy teaching her.

'Let us sit for a moment.' He pointed to a chair. 'I have seen my last client for the day.'

At that moment, his wife came bouncing down the stairs, hair plaited in wickerwork fashion above her round, firm, good-natured face, a feather-duster in one hand. She slackened her pace when she saw that her husband was not alone and hurriedly concealed the duster behind her back.

'My dear, this is Mademoiselle Thinne. You may remember her from the time that she, her mother and her aunt came here to have their likenesses made.'

Mrs Laycock withdrew the duster from behind her back and set it down on the table in the centre of the room.

'What are you doing with that?'

'Those frames need a dusting.' She pointed at a wall. 'I noticed it this morning. That girl never sees a thing.'

'Can't you leave it for her?'

'No time like the present. She's gone out to get some bread.'

Alexine and Laycock sat, facing each other, while Mrs Laycock, plump arms akimbo, stood by her husband's chair.

Laycock began to explain that, at first, he had confined himself to the daguerreotype process, but that now he had begun to experiment with another process, invented by a fellow countryman of his, a Mr Henry Fox Talbot. He had had remarkable results from this calotype process, as it was called, since it had the advantage of enabling several positives to be made from a single negative. But he thought that it would be best if Alexine were to confine herself to the daguerreotype.

'Why?'

It was Mrs Laycock who answered, while her husband was hesitating. 'My husband thinks that the calotype process would be too troublesome and difficult for you.'

'But the results are better?'

'On balance, yes, madame.' Again it was Mrs Laycock who answered. 'The final likeness is not reversed, and you can retouch the negatives.'

'Then that is the process I want to learn.'

'There is also another process,' Mrs Layock said. 'There's been a lot of talk about it. It's called the wet plate process. But it sounds even more troublesome than the calotype process.'

'I want to learn the latest process. If it is the best,' Alexine said firmly.

Mrs Laycock approved. She smiled. 'I've been trying to get my husband to investigate its possibilities, but he's been reluctant to do so.'

'Well, we'll investigate it.'

Did 'we' mean the three of them, Laycock wondered, or only the two women?

It meant only the two women.

∽

Excitedly preoccupied with the creation of a camera room in an attic of the house, Alexine only intermittently thought of Adolph. A letter at long last arrived from him, at first full of silly endearments but then containing the dire news that, before his return to The Hague, he had to accompany the Foreign Minister on a diplomatic mission to Constantinople. Alexine was plunged into a state of fury and despair; but soon after the delivery of the letter the builders arrived, followed by Mrs Layock, and in deciding with them how precisely the roof of the attic was to be opened up and glassed over, she forgot these emotions.

Soon, she was not merely buying equipment in the Netherlands but also ordering it from England and France. 'This is all going to be horribly expensive,' Mrs Laycock demurred, for Alexine to tell her firmly: 'Oh, don't worry about expense. In the long run it's never an economy to buy things on the cheap.'

Eventually Adolph returned. He had been sailing the Bosphorus, and the sun and wind had given his neck and forehead a raw flush that, for Alexine, only added to his attraction, even though he himself was embarrassed by it. He had brought her two presents: a necklace of Wedgwood blue cameos illustrating the signs of the zodiac, and, bought in a Constantinople bazaar, a butterfly, constructed from the lightest of balsa wood and filmy, painted gauze, which agitated its four wings if one pulled on a string. The butterfly rested on cotton-wool in an ill-made wooden box, painted vermilion. Under it was a card with a lace edge and a centre of painted lilies of the valley. Beneath each lily of the valley Adolph had inscribed a character so tiny that she had to screw up her eyes to make it out. In sequence, the characters read: 'You talk of constancy – But what does a butterfly know of constancy?'

She blushed with pleasure as she unwrapped first the necklace and then the butterfly. With brilliant eyes, she gazed at him. 'Do you know which of these presents I shall treasure most?'

'No. Which? I know which cost the most.'

'This! This of course!' She held out the butterfly to him and then pulled the thread back and forth so that its wings fluttered as though it were in its death throes. 'Oh, I love it! I shall treasure it always.'

Without saying anything, Harriet now made a point of leaving the pair constantly alone together. 'Come with me for a little stroll,' she would say to Addy. Or: 'I must go to see the milliner about that hat. Why not come too?' Nanny Rose knew precisely what was happening, as her constant sniffing and scowling when Adolph and Alexine were closeted together without any chaperon, made amply clear.

∽

With Mrs Laycock as her assistant, Alexine was at last sufficiently knowledgeable to begin to take photographs. At first, she had to leave to the older woman the tricky task of spreading an absolutely smooth, even coating of a solution of collodion, in which potassium iodide had been dissolved, over each scrupulously cleaned and polished piece of glass. But she was, as always, a rapid learner, so that within a matter of days she had mastered the process. Unlike Mrs Laycock, she did not care if her fingers got stained, even when Adolph remarked, with a grimace, on the discoloration.

Her first sitters were Harriet, Addy and Nanny Rose. The last of these kept protesting 'Oh, do hurry up!' as her hands, now deformed by arthritis, fidgeted on the arms of the chair. At first she had refused to have the clamp put on her neck – 'What are you trying to do? Do you want to throttle me?' But when the exposed print had been rinsed, toned in gold chloride to turn its image dark brown, fixed in hypo and washed and dried, she could not conceal her wonder at it, peering down at it repeatedly, with an entranced, bemused expression.

Next it was the turn of Adolph. Alexine experienced a fluttering, erotic thrill as she posed him in the chair, putting out a hand to rearrange his long, golden hair, so that it fell uniformly round his handsome face, adjusting one foot, spreading his fingers on his knees, tightening the clamp. 'No, don't move, don't dare to move! No! You'll spoil it. Don't move, don't blink. Look into the lens. Here, here!' He soon wearied as she inserted plate after plate. But she herself never did so.

Later, she would look at these images of him for seconds on end, while he grew impatient.

'Why don't you look at *me?*' he demanded.

'I seem to know you better when I look at your likeness.'

'What are you talking about? What nonsense is that?'

Alexine began to experiment with lighting her subjects only from above or only from the right or the left. The Layocks remonstrated with her when they saw the results. Laycock later told his wife that he found these likenesses 'wilful', 'amateurish', 'crude'. By then he was jealous that she should be Alexine's tutor and assistant, not he.

Mrs Layock laughed: 'She says she wants to do with the camera what Rembrandt did with the brush.'

'She's no Rembrandt! That's for sure.'

Mrs Layock admired and liked Alexine. 'She's become like a sister to me,' she told her husband.

'Don't be so foolish. How can a woman of her social standing be like a sister to a woman of yours?'

When, as a young man in England, he had been an itinerant painter of miniatures, Laycock's aristocratic patrons never treated him as a brother and all too often as a servant.

∽

On a whim, Alexine decided to have some more dresses made for the winter season. Her wardrobes and cupboards were full of clothes never worn, sheathed in tissue paper and smelling vaguely of camphor, but an irresistible extravagance constantly urged her on.

Harriet told her, 'It's just a waste of money.'

'I enjoy wasting money.'

'It's wicked.'

'I enjoy being wicked.'

In her feverish attempts to diminish assets that, under John's skilful management, merely went on swelling, Alexine had come to feel her wealth to be not a magic lubricant for her passage through life but an ever growing hindrance. She would see a beggar in the street and, on an impulse, would at once press into his hand as much money as one of the housemaids earned in a week. Before she and Adolph entered a restaurant, she would insist on passing to him the cash to pay for their meal. It was always at least twice as much as was required, but when, the bill settled, he attempted to give her back the difference, she was adamant in refusing to accept it.

'I feel like a kept man.'

'What's wrong with that? If one treasures something, one keeps it. I treasure you, I'm happy to keep you.'

'It's not right.'

'Who cares whether things are right or not? Anyway, what do you mean by *right*? You're not talking about morality, but only about convention. I have no use for convention.'

He laughed. But such a conversation made him feel uncomfortable.

'This is what would make life difficult if we were to marry,' he said on one occasion.

'Why *would*? Why *if*? Why not say "This is what *will* make life difficult *when* we are married"? Anyway – the world is full of men spending the money of their wives, just as it is full of women spending the money of their husbands. What does it matter? Who cares?'

'You're such a rebel,' he said with a sigh, as he had often said. That she was such a rebel was part of her attraction; but it was also what made him, naturally cautious by nature, shrink from committing himself.

∽

Madame Molnar had a cough. She raised a small hand to her mouth and coughed discreetly behind it, as she circled Alexine, examining the blue and white striped dress with its Brussels lace collar, its pleated bodice and billowing skirt. 'I suggest a bright blue ribbon with a black edge for the belt and sleeve bands. What does madame think about that?'

Alexine turned first to right and then to left to examine her image in the glass. She raised an arm. 'Aren't these sleeves too full?' she said. 'At the wrists, I mean.'

Head on one side, Madame Molnar stared at the sleeve. 'No, madame. No, I don't think so. Not at all. That's the way they're now being worn in Paris.'

Once again Alexine held up the arm and then dropped it. 'Perhaps you're right.'

Madame Molnar knew that she was right. She always was about fashion.

'I also need an evening dress.'

Madame Molnar thought: You don't need it, you want it. 'Yes, madame. What exactly did you have in mind?'

'I was thinking of a silver-grey silk. Trimmed – trimmed with red roses. Large double pleats for the skirt. Bodice laced at the back.' As Alexine extemporized, Madame Molnar frowned in thought.

'I have a silver-grey silk,' she said. 'By a coincidence, a bale came in only a few days ago from Lyons. Would you like to see it?'

'Yes. Why not?'

'It's down in the storeroom. I'll get one of the girls to give me a hand with it.' Again she coughed.

'You must take care of that cough,' Alexine said.

'I wish I could. I don't seem able to shake it off. The problem is that I'm always so busy, no rest at all. The new girl who looks after the children isn't all that reliable, and so I must always be looking in to see how they're getting on.'

'Well, it's lucky that you also live in the house in which you work.'

'Well, yes and no,' Madame Molnar said dubiously.

Alone, Alexine wandered about the room, examining the half-finished dresses ranged around it. She recognized a black mantle, rich but austere, that her mother had ordered. Yes, it would suit her, just right. Then she found herself at the chimney-piece, looking down in amazement at an object resting on it, so lightly that it might have been about to flutter away in an instant. The butterfly, fragile and iridescent, was the twin of the one given to her by Adolph. She put out a hand, touched it, took it up, and then replaced it.

She moved away, turned back. On an impulse she once more took up the butterfly, to examine it even more carefully. On the chimney-piece, she suddenly noticed, a card had been propped against the wall. She herself had received exactly such a card, decorated with lily of the valley. Beneath each lily of the valley, inscribed in minuscule characters, she now read – as, filled with totally different but no less tumultuous emotions, she had already read only a few weeks before – 'You talk of constancy – But what does a butterfly know of constancy?'

Hearing Madame Molnar's footsteps on the stairs, she put the butterfly back on the chimney-piece, with such haste that it tipped over on to one side. She felt a sudden heat surge through her, bringing a flush to her cheeks, and then a glacial chill.

'This is it.' Madame Molnar extended the bale of silk. 'What do you think?'

Mechanically, Alexine fingered the cloth. She stared down at it. She said nothing.

'Are you all right, madame?'

'Yes. Yes, of course. Why?' Her tone was irritable.

'You look –'

'I never like to be told how I look,' Alexine snapped.

'I'm sorry, madame.'

'We can talk about the silk another time. Let me get out of this.' She indicated the half-finished dress that she was wearing. Then, with an effort, she forced herself to go on: 'I like it, I like it a lot. I can always rely on you. Perfect.' She gave an artificial smile, her eyes not meeting the dressmaker's.

'Thank you, madame.'

∽

'She's not important. You know how it is.'

'I don't know how it is.'

'Oh, come on! From time to time a man amuses himself. That's how men are made. It means nothing, nothing. You're the only person who means anything to me. It was just...' Adolph made a wide, sweeping gesture with an arm, then shrugged his muscular shoulders. 'She has many lovers. They mean nothing to her, she means nothing to them.'

'Then why did you give her the butterfly?'

'It was a nice present. And cheap,' he added. 'I found those butterflies on a stall in the bazaar. I told you that. On a stall. They cost almost nothing.'

'And did you buy all of them?'

'All of them? Why should I buy all of them?' He laughed.

'For all your other women as well.'

'I don't have other women.'

'You even wrote the same thing for her as you wrote for me,' she pursued implacably. 'On the card. On exactly the same sort of card. Did you also find the cards in the bazaar?'

'It was – fun. Why not?'

'And which did you write first?'

'What do you mean?'

'Her inscription or mine?'

'Yours. Yours of course!'

'And did you also give her the same sort of necklace?'

'I didn't give her any sort of necklace.' He had, in fact, given her a bracelet, pinchbeck studded with tiny rubies. He shook his head. 'No necklace. Never. The butterfly was just a toy – the sort of thing one gives to a child.'

'But she's not a child.'

For a long time they argued. As she grew colder and colder, so he became more and more heated. She did not understand men, he told her. Every man, he repeated – every man who was really a man – liked to fool around from time to time. That was his nature. It meant nothing, well, nothing important. Women learned to accept these little infidelities. Probably her own father . . .

'Don't speak about my father! He was a far better man than you!' Suddenly, her anger flared out.

'No doubt.' Now it was he who was cold and calm. 'But how can you know? How can you possibly know? Even your mother couldn't know. I bet your father often said that he was going to the club or to a business meeting when in fact –'

'Stop it!' She got to her feet, her chin trembling. 'That's enough.' She went over to the bell-pull and gave it a vigorous tug. 'Daan will see you out.' She faced him. 'Goodbye, Adolph.'

'What do you mean?'

'I don't wish to see you again. That's what I mean.'

With a rustle of her voluminous skirts, she swept out of the room.

∽

'Oh, forget about it!' Harriet said.

'How can one forget about such things? He betrayed me. And I'm sure that she left the butterfly and the card out on purpose. She must have done.'

'Oh, no. No! Why should she do that? She probably doesn't even know that you and he –'

'She knows. She knows all right. She hears all the gossip from her clients. She knows everything.'

'I'm sure he was telling you the truth. She means nothing to him. That sort of woman – ready for anything with any man willing and able to be generous to her – is little more than a prostitute. That's how he looked on her. Every wife has to face the fact – there are times when a man would rather go with a prostitute than with a decent woman.'

'It's disgusting!'

'Life is often disgusting. But that isn't a reason to break with him. You love him, don't you? Forget all about Madame Molnar! Forget her! It's not worth wrecking your life for her.'

'I'm not wrecking my life. I have all sorts of plans. All sorts.' She got up and went to the window, looking out on to the snow dithering down out of a leaden sky. 'Oh, if only this winter were over. I want sun, sun!'

'Be sensible. Forgive him. Forget.'

Alexine turned. 'No. Never. Never!'

Flowers arrived, bunches and bunches of them. Nanny Rose said that Adolph must be spending a fortune. Where did the money come from? He wasn't rich, she said. Alexine shrugged and proffered her the latest bunch of flowers. 'You can have these for your room. If there are any over, put them in the drawing-room.' Letters also arrived, full of apologies, excuses, self-castigation and extravagant endearments. He had not seen Madame Molnar again, he would never see her. He belonged to Alexine, to Alexine only. Alexine eventually tore up all the letters that she had so far received, stuffed them into an envelope and sent them back to him not at his rooms but at the Prussian Embassy. Two or three more letters followed, shorter, less ardent in tone. Then there was silence.

Word went round that he had broken with her. It was hardly surprising, people said, when she behaved so wildly and peculiarly. Harriet and Addy were furious – how could anyone think that it was she who had been abandoned? But Alexine said that she did not care, let them think what they wanted. It didn't matter.

Secretly, however, in the recesses of her heart, it did matter. She would go up to her bedroom, open the top drawer of her dressing-table, and take out the butterfly. She would pull on the string, to agitate its iridescent wings in what seemed to be its death throes. Pull, pull, pull. The wings fluttered more and more frenetically. She would think with a passionate longing and despair of that tumultuous love-making in that horrible little attic under the eaves. Pull, pull, pull. The string would bite into thumb and forefinger, leaving a red and raw indentation in the flesh. Pull, pull, pull.

Then, one early morning – she had not been able to sleep for thinking of him – the string snapped off and the butterfly was still.

Later one of the maids found it in the wastepaper basket. Though it was broken, she took it up to her attic room. She might be able to mend it, she thought. But she never got round to attempting to do so, and eventually she too threw it away.

∽

Addy walked over to the piano and, having untied her bonnet, threw it across its closed, shimmering lid. She sighed. Harriet, who had broken off in the middle of a Chopin Étude, looked up. 'A bad day?'

'*Bad?* The end. I mean, I really mean, the end. I'm finished.'

'What is all this?' Harriet rose to her feet.

'I've just spent my last day at the palace.'

'What?'

'It's over. It's all over. Twenty-three, no, twenty-four years, and now it's over.'

'What happened?'

'She's been giving me the cold shoulder for months and months. I told you that.' Addy always referred to the Queen as 'she'. When she did so, Harriet always knew whom she meant. 'Juliana is now the favoured one. She's the one who gets all the confidences – and the plums.'

'Oh, I don't think so.'

'Yes, yes,' Addy snapped irritably. 'That's the way things have been going for a long, long time. She's bored with me, she's been bored with me for an age. She gives herself all those intellectual and spiritual airs and graces and she thinks that I'm not up to them. No wonder the King has so little to do with her. Well, my relationship with her has come to resemble his. The partners hardly speak to each other, but each lacks the courage – or energy – to do anything decisive about it. So today I decided to do something. I told her.' Suddenly her voice, previously so low and weary, took on a triumphant ring.

'Told her what?'

'That I wanted it to come to an end. That I'd had enough. That I wanted my freedom.'

'Oh, Addy! No!'

'Yes, Harriet! Yes! It's the best thing I've done for a long, long time. I'm free. At last I'm free.'

'But what are you going to do with yourself?'

'Read. To begin with, the whole of the *Comédie Humaine*. All of it, from beginning to end. Then ... Then I'll have to think what to do next.'

'You can't spend your whole life *reading*!' Harriet, who rarely read anything other than letters and the newspapers, was appalled.

'Why not? What happens in books is usually far more interesting than what happens in life.'

Addy leaned across the piano and picked up her bonnet. She began to dust it off on one of the billowing sleeves of her dress. She was smiling, not across at her sister but, head lowered, to herself.

3 'AREN'T YOU WELL?'

Addy had not appeared at breakfast, merely sending one of the maids to bring her a cup of coffee. The curtains of her bedroom were closed, and she lay curled up in one corner of her four-poster bed, knees almost to chin and a hand under a cheek. There was a frowsty, vinegary smell in the air, familiar to Harriet from those days when, often accompanied by Alexine or Nanny Rose, she visited some slum tenement on one of her numerous charitable errands. She did not expect to smell that smell in her own house, where, under her exacting supervision, the staff were constantly sweeping, scrubbing and polishing.

When there was no answer, not even a lifting of the head from the bolster in which it was half-buried, Harriet repeated her question. 'Aren't you well?'

The voice emerged dull and muffled. 'No. I'm sick.'

'What's the matter?' Harriet now approached the bed and, after a moment of hesitation, lowered her by now substantial body down on to it. The bed shuddered and creaked. An inarticulate sound of exasperation emerged from Addy.

'I've told you, I'm sick.' Suddenly Addy raised herself on an elbow. Her hair, falling around her gaunt shoulder, was as dull as her voice. 'Sick of life. Of everything.'

'Oh, don't be so silly. What you need is to *do* something. Your problem is that you've nothing to occupy you.'

Rarely ill herself, Harriet was always impatient with illness in others. Addy's mental collapse left her baffled and exasperated. Of course, she had been through a terrible time in the past, with first that lost child and then that horrendous operation, no one could deny that; but it was pointless to continue to brood on such things when all that was necessary was to ask Alexine or even herself for the money to do anything – travel, buy clothes, buy books, entertain – that she wanted. If she would accompany Harriet on even one of her charitable errands, she would at once see how fortunate she was.

'I have plenty to occupy me. My thoughts. And they're far from pleasant.'

The self-pity of it! Harriet had to restrain herself from showing her anger. 'Why not pay another visit to Paris?'

'To *Paris*? What for?'

'You could have another consultation with that man. He did you so much good. Didn't he?'

'Yes, yes, those drops were fine. For a while. But then they began to make me feel confused … constantly tired … nauseous. Oh, you know all that!'

'Well, their effect was probably wearing off. But he might have some other ideas. Doesn't he also use mesmerism with his patients? That might help.'

'Oh, do stop talking about him!'

'I'm only trying to help. I could go with you to Paris. I need some new clothes. Everything I have is getting so shabby. Fashions change so fast these days.' Harriet no longer went to Madame Molnar for clothes, and she had found no one as good to replace her in The Hague.

'We're too old to worry ourselves about fashion,' Addy retorted morosely.

'Too old! I'll be worrying about fashion until my dying day. Come on! Get out of bed! It's a beautiful day!'

Harriet crossed over to the windows and decisively pulled back the curtains. Addy let out a inarticulate wail and put the back of her right hand across her eyes. The sunshine, bright and hot, flooded in. Harriet experienced an upsurge of joy as she felt it on her face. Like Alexine, she loved glare and heat, often saying, 'The thought of hell-fire doesn't frighten me in the least. Now if one froze in hell, that would be another matter.'

'Close them! Close them!'

Harriet shook her head. 'Get out of bed!' she ordered. She might have been speaking to a disobedient child. 'A parcel of books has arrived for you,' she added, hoping that that would tempt her. 'From England. It must be those two Dickens novels you asked John to send you. Addy!'

But, with a groan, Addy had turned away, drawn up her knees, and once again half-buried her face in the bolster.

'You're impossible,' Harriet said.

∽

Later that day, Harriet wrote one of her fluent, businesslike letters to the Russian doctor. Her sister was too ill to visit him in Paris, she told him, and she did not trust any of the Dutch doctors whom they had consulted. She was clearly suffering from some form of neurasthenia; but she refused any of the treatments – rustication by the sea or in the mountains, diet, exercise in a variety of forms, sedatives and tonics – that had been prescribed. It was almost, she wrote, as though she *wanted* to be ill. But who would want that?

A few days later an answer arrived, not from the Russian himself but from his nephew. The nephew wrote that his uncle had retired after marrying a French widow with an estate in Provence. The implication was clear to Harriet – the widow, whom the nephew named and who had a title, was so rich that there was no longer any need for the doctor to work. The nephew, himself a doctor, had taken over his uncle's practice, and was now forwarding, along with his letter, some sachets which the patient might find helpful. Ideally, of course, he would have preferred her to come to Paris for a consultation first; but, since she was not prepared to do that, this was the best that he could do.

The sachets, which were extremely expensive, were of different colours – pale pink for the morning, pale blue for the evening. Addy's daily dose was one of each, its powder dissolved in water. When Harriet first took them in to her, Addy made a wry joke: 'Well, those colours seem appropriate. I am usually in the pink in the morning and blue by the time that evening comes.'

Soon there was some improvement. From time to time Addy would now accompany Harriet or Alexine on a stroll along the canal, her pace so lethargic that it would fill them with ill-concealed exasperation; on one of their frequent and wildly extravagant shopping expeditions; or to a restaurant or café. But there were still many occasions when one or other of them would come on her seated in a chair, no longer reading, the book on her knees or even on the floor beside her, while she stared out ahead of her with puzzled, woebegone eyes, or even cried silently to herself, a handkerchief pressed to her lips, while the large tears rolled down her sunken cheeks.

'Do you really think that medicine is doing her any good?' Alexine asked.

'Yes, of course it is.'

Harriet had the superstitious dread that, if one doubted for even a moment that Addy was improving, then she would at once relapse into her previous state of unrelieved despair.

A Viennese newspaper, left behind by a dog-breeder with whom Alexine was negotiating to buy a mastiff, suddenly and amazingly galvanized Addy. She had laid aside her knitting with a sigh, picked up the crumpled sheets off the table beside her, and begun to leaf through them in desultory fashion. Then something caught her attention. Her eyes narrowed and she jerked up in her chair. She read the item once, at speed, and then a second time, slowly.

A seventeen-year-old niece of the Austrian emperor had returned from a visit to a sanatorium run by a Swiss doctor in a remote corner of Slovenia, totally cured of the decline in which she had seemed to be sliding inexorably to her death. She had recovered her appetite, she had returned to her normal weight, and every one of her symptoms had vanished. The doctor described himself as a 'naturian', since he believed that, if only patients could achieve a total harmony with nature, then they had within them the power to cure themselves, without any drugs. His one imperative was that all his patients must show total obedience to his commands, however irrational or disagreeable they might seem. If they could not undertake to do this, then it was pointless for them to come to his sanatorium.

'Read this!' Addy told Alexine, who had happened to come into the drawing-room in search of a lead for one of the dogs. She thrust the paper out at her. 'Go on!' It was months since she had displayed such peremptoriness. 'What do you think?'

Alexine sat down on the settee opposite Addy's chair, and tilted the paper upwards so that the flare of the recently installed gas lamp fully illuminated it.

'What do you think?'

'Wait just a moment. I haven't had time to read it.'

Impatiently, her hollow eyes fixed on Alexine, Addy waited. 'Well?' she could not resist asking after a few moments.

'Wait! Please!'

At last Alexine had finished her reading. She lowered the paper.

'Well?'

'He sounds like a crackpot to me. Or a crook. Both probably.'

'The Emperor would hardly have allowed his niece to be treated by a crackpot or crook.'

'Every court contains innumerable crackpots and crooks,' Alexine retorted drily. 'You must know that from your own experience. So – it's not so odd to opt for a crackpot and crook as doctor.'

'He cured her – cured her completely. It says that.'

Alexine nodded. She brooded for a while. 'What's interesting is that "imperative" of his. People like imperatives. For some people they're essential, if they're to he happy. Or, at least, contented.'

'I don't know what you mean.'

'People like ourselves have too much freedom. Money and position give us that. We're constantly telling others what to do. It may be that secretly we want ourselves to be told what to do.'

'I don't want anyone to tell me what to do,' Addy objected. But there was a note of uncertainty in her voice.

'No?'

'No.'

‌⁓

Within a few days, the three women were setting off for Lake Bled, with an entourage of Nanny Rose, three maids and old Daan.

'This really is a fool's errand,' Harriet told Alexine.

'Don't tell Aunt Addy that. If she thinks that, then the cure won't work.'

4 HARRIET REMARKED that he looked vulgar.

Nanny Rose said that, if one saw him in the street, one might mistake him for a prosperous bookie.

Harriet laughed: 'Perhaps he is a bookie.'

In the restaurant, the three women had been allocated the best table, in the bow of a tall window overlooking the lake, just as they had also been allocated the best accommodation, a series of suites on the first floor. Away from home, Nanny Rose was now more of a companion than an employee, and ate all her meals with Alexine and Harriet.

The middle-aged man, with the luxuriant moustache that cascaded over either end of the thin, rigid line of his mouth, sat alone at a small table in an alcove by the entrance. If theirs was the best table, his was the worst. It was his clothes that first drew their attention to him. His tight-fitting black trousers, jacket, elastic-sided boots and close-cropped hair all had a uniform gloss; his neckerchief was gaudily coloured; there was a large hot-house red carnation in his button-hole, and a thick, ornate gold ring on his little finger. He devoured his food as though faced with some chore that he was eager to complete as quickly and efficiently as possible, never looking around him and so never noticing that the three women, fascinated by his air of strength, purpose and force, were spending so much of their time surreptitiously glancing at him. Eventually, having risen to his feet, wiped his lips on his napkin and then thrown the napkin down on to his chair, he hurried out.

While awaiting their next course, Alexine became aware that, shoulders hunched and hands clasped behind his back, he was striding restlessly up and down the terrace beyond the dining-room, a huge cigar clamped between his nicotine-stained teeth. The lamps on the terrace, swaying in the wind that so often roused itself at that hour, made his shadow leap hither and thither, now in front of him and now behind him. He struck her as much taller than when she had seen him at the table. His air of crude, brutal vigour both repelled and fascinated her.

Many months later, in a letter that he either never received or could not be bothered to answer, she wrote: 'Little did I then realize that you were the angel of the annunciation – the bringer of my destiny.'

～

Waking early, as she so often did since she had arrived in Bled, she went out on to her balcony and looked out over the lake shimmering mistily in the first light of dawn. A fishing boat, propelled by a single oar manipulated by a man standing in the bows, incised a black line across its grey surface. The air, carrying with it a smell of pine-needles, was cool on her bare arms and forehead. With a sigh of contentment, she went back into the room and began to dress, not with her usual speed but as though every humdrum movement needed to be prolonged for the unexpected pleasure that it brought.

The walk around the lake took about an hour. Shaking her head in refusal when a solitary, somnolent coachman, slumped on a low wall beside his fiacre outside the hotel, scrambled to his feet and called out '*Oui, madame, oui, oui!*' she set off, parasol resting over shoulder, at a leisurely pace. There were only a few people even in the streets at this end of lake, where most of the hotels, restaurants and shops clustered together up the hillside, and scarcely any on the narrow path encircling it. Two young boys, engrossed in fishing, looked up as she passed and one gave her a dubious '*Guten morgen.*' An elderly couple, English surely, he in an old-fashioned blue frock-coat, white drill trousers and white stock, and she in a no less old-fashioned poke bonnet and pearl-grey mantle long enough to sweep the ground, approached, arm in arm, at a snail's pace. They eyed her as though amazed that anyone else should be up as early as they were. Then the man nodded, cleared his throat with a noisy rattle of catarrh, and muttered something inarticulate.

It was at the farthest end of the lake, devoid of any other habitation, that Dr Weiss, the 'naturian', had established what he called now his sanatorium and now his colony. After they had left Addy there, Alexine, Harriet and Nanny Rose had had no further contact with her, even by letter, on Dr Weiss's strict instruction. In the hotel they had met other people who had similarly abandoned a relative or a friend, and had similarly been forbidden to see or get in touch with them. No doubt it was for the best, these people would tell each other dubiously, that was the way the cure worked, Dr Weiss seemed to be sure of what he was doing.

The colony had once been a farm. A long, single-storey, thatched house stood at its centre, with a white-painted front-door, oddly askew, on either side of which were two white-painted rain-butts. The patients were allowed to wash only in rain-water, collected in these and other butts, and never in water from the lake or from the many springs trickling down the surrounding hillsides. Dotted around the main house, in what had once been a pasture, there were a number of what appeared to be sheds for animals, thatched and connected by winding footpaths, always muddy after even the mildest shower. Each of these sheds housed two, three or even four patients. Capriciously – or did he have some subtle plan? – Dr Weiss would decide who would share with whom. His only discernible rule was that the sexes, even husbands and wives, should be separated.

Set some distance away from these primitive habitations, were two rows of earth privies, one for men and one for women. A former stable provided the washrooms. In them there were no tubs but merely enamel basins and ewers containing cold water, on the top of which floated a detritus of leaves, grass and even dead insects.

Alexine, Harriet and Nanny Rose had been appalled by the conditions in which Addy had doomed herself to live. 'Oh, no, madame!' Nanny Rose had protested, wrinkling up her nose and looking around her in distaste, even though Dr Weiss, a tiny, imperious man, with a tuft of ginger hair on his pointed chin and an oddly metallic voice, was standing with them. 'This isn't for you. You can't possibly live here. Miss Alexine would think twice about allowing one of her dogs to live in a place like this. It's worse than a kennel.'

Addy, amazing them by her calm, shook her head and smiled. 'This will be fine for me.' She looked around the little room, with its three bedsteads covered in straw pallets, at the bottom of each of which there stood a roughly carpentered chest. She laughed. 'What a change! I'll be happy here. Yes, I feel it.'

'If you have any valuable belongings, my dear wife – up at the main house – will take care of them. Also of your clothes.'

They had already seen that the other patients were all dressed uniformly, men and women, in what looked like long, grey nightshirts made from a rough cotton, with straw sandals on their feet. On their arrival, some of these patients had been seated out on wooden benches, silent for the most part, either reading, drowsing or staring out at the lake. Others had been working at three asymmetrical vegetable patches, hoeing, digging or planting out seedlings.

'Now I think it would be best if you would leave the patient to my care,' Dr Weiss had said in his guttural but accurate French. 'No visits until her departure, no visits at all. You understand that? I have made myself clear?'

'Perfectly,' Alexine had said.

Harriet had suddenly rushed to Addy and thrown her arms around her. 'Oh, Addy, Addy! Do you really want to go through with this? It's not too late to change your mind. Why not come back with us to the hotel?'

'Of course I want to go through with it.' Addy had disengaged herself and then given her sister a little push, hand to shoulder. 'I'll see you in three weeks.'

Alexine now stood out on a tottery little jetty, and from there gazed out at the cone-shaped island in the centre of the lake. There had been a

Roman shrine there in the past, dedicated to Venus, so she had been told. Now there was a church, dedicated to Mary Magdalene. The day before, she, Harriet and Nanny Rose had taken a boat out to the island. Nanny Rose had sat contentedly in the bows, from time to time addressing the totally uncomprehending boatman in English, while the two other women had climbed up the sheer steps to the church. 'Why do we wear these ridiculous clothes?' Alexine had asked, lifting her skirts high in one hand. 'They're only good for staying indoors and doing nothing.'

'I suppose we should be grateful that our feet were not bound when we were young,' Harriet turned back to say. On such climbs, although so much older, she never had any difficulty in keeping ahead.

Leaving the jetty, Alexine saw that already the patients were up and about. Like drones leaving and entering a hive, the distant, grey-garbed figures hurried in and out of the main house as though on some urgent errand. Then, some of them carrying walking-sticks, they all assembled, a ragged army, on the slope of yellowing grass before the front door. Eventually Dr Weiss also emerged. He was not wearing one of the shifts, but knickerbockers and mountain boots, with a Tyrolean hat jauntily perched on one side of his head. Alexine hurried nearer. '*Meine Damen, meine Herren . . .*' The metallic voice had a penetrating power. He began to give his instructions now in German and now in French. They were to climb that hill, that hill over there. He pointed with his alpenstock. He hoped that they had all observed his instructions not to eat anything since their evening meal. Yes? There was a general assent. Good! In that case, they might as well set off before the day hotted up. He himself would lead and his dear daughter would bring up the rear. There was no need, absolutely no need to hurry. People must climb at the pace that suited them. But one thing he must make clear. There must be no halting. Absolutely no halting.

From where she now stood, half-hidden by a tree, on the path below the colony, Alexine had been able to hear every word that he said.

The group set off. Two women were marching along on either side of Dr Weiss, their unfastened grey hair falling to their shoulders. Behind them were a trio of men, the oldest of whom was frenetically hobbling along, dragging a leg, and then a whole crowd of other people, men and women arbitrarily mingled. Dr Weiss suddenly turned. 'No talking, please! No talking!'

At that moment, Alexine realized with astonishment that one of the two women on either side of Dr Weiss was Addy. She was holding her head erect, chin high, and taking long, firm strides such as Alexine had rarely seen her take before. Her forehead and cheeks, having caught the sun on the previous day, were shiny and flushed. On their arrival in the little town, her complexion had been unattractively sallow. Clearly she was already getting better.

Later Addy described to Harriet and Alexine what happened each morning after the party had reached the summit of the hill. Awaiting them there, set out on a trestle table outside a small hut, were tall earthenware beakers of milk, still warm from the cow, hunks of rough peasant bread, and vast slices of the hard, extremely salty goat's cheese of the area. Parched and ravenous from their climb, the patients would snatch at drink and food, pushing each other unceremoniously, all manners forgotten. Sometimes acrimonious arguments broke out, to be severely terminated by Dr Weiss.

Alexine strolled on. Then, coming on a bench, she sat down on it and once more stared across the tranquil water at the church. From it, a bell had begun to toll, on two reiterated notes, a semitone apart. Some boats were approaching the island, laden with men, women and children, all in their Sunday best although it was not Sunday. Their voices drifted across the water and then echoed back, a vague susurration, from the hills behind her. Clearly some ceremony was about to take place. As she was wondering whether it was a confirmation, a baptism or something else, a capricious gust of wind snatched at her wide-brimmed straw hat and blew it into the water. She waved and shouted to the far-off boatmen but, absorbed in helping the older of their passengers to step ashore, they neither saw nor heard her.

Then, all at once, the stranger from the dining-room was hurrying down the grassy incline from the path to the bench. Without a word to her, he stretched out an arm and grabbed at the lowest branch, clearly dead, of one of the many willows leaning over the water. He struggled with it for a few seconds, swaying from side to side, until there was a pistol-like crack and the branch came away in his hand. He hurried to the water's edge and, bending forward, extended the branch across it. The end of the branch touched the hat, which at once began to dance round in a circle. Again he bent forward. Gently he coaxed the hat towards him. Twice it eluded him, then veered closer and closer.

'There you are!' He held out the dripping hat. 'I hope it's not damaged.'

Alexine laughed. 'No, I'm sure it's all right. That was quick of you. And kind.'

'You're out very early.'

'And so are you.'

'I can never sleep after five or so. I've got used to waking at that hour. Are you English?'

She shook her head. 'Dutch.'

'You speak perfect English.'

'And you're American?' She had assumed that from his accent.

He shook his head. 'No. I was born in Wales. But I emigrated to America. There was nothing else for a poor orphan to do.' He laughed, neither embarrassed nor self-pitying.

As though by mutual consent, they began to walk together round the lake back to the hotel.

It was only when they had reached the entrance that he said to her: 'I'm still ignorant of your name, mademoiselle. May I know it?'

'I'm Alexine Thinne.'

He took her hand and bowed over it, as though they had now, at this very moment, been introduced to each other. His hand in hers was slithery with sweat. There was also sweat on his forehead. It was not yet all that hot, their pace had been leisurely. Already she had noticed the yellowness not merely of his skin but at the corners of his eyes. Was he ill?

'And you?' she prompted.

He hesitated. 'Scott. Mark Scott. Colonel Mark Scott. At your service, mademoiselle.'

He gave her a deep bow.

∽

Abruptly he would accost her, as she sat reading on a bench by the lake, as she played with a litter of mongrel puppies in the dusty and usually deserted public garden, or as she once again took her leisurely, early morning walk round the lake. No less abruptly he would leave her, with no reason given, sometimes even without a goodbye.

He was here to recuperate, he told her, taking the waters which bubbled up, ammoniac and brackish, from a spring in the basement of the hotel. The cure was doing him so little good that perhaps he ought to become one of Dr Weiss's patients. But he hated to obey other people's orders. He liked people to obey his.

What was he recuperating from?

'Oh, a multitude of things. Africa has done for me, I'm afraid.'

'Africa?'

They were seated by the lake. He nodded moodily. 'A terrible place. Far worse than you can ever imagine. And yet – fascinating.'

There was a long silence. Then suddenly he turned to her and demanded: 'Can you imagine people eating worms, living worms – amphistomoid worms they're called – which they've grubbed for among the half-digested contents of the stomachs of cattle they have slaughtered? How about that? Or rats? Or termites? Snakes?'

He had hoped to shock her. He admired her coolness, as she replied: 'Well, if there's nothing else to eat . . .'

Soon, when they met, it was seldom of any subject other than Africa that they spoke. He described how, dying of cerebral malaria, his most trusted black servant had barked like a mad dog, endlessly for hours and then days on end; how, tormented by tooth-ache, he had himself eventually gouged out one of his wisdom teeth with a penknife, since none of his companions had had the courage to do that for him; how he had handed a tribal chieftain a gun as a present and the chieftain, having told him to load it, had then laughingly passed it to his son, a child of five or six, and ordered him to go out into the courtyard and shoot somebody – which the boy had promptly done, killing another child.

'Does nothing shock you or surprise you?'

She shook her head.

'Then you're the right person for Africa. Perhaps I should take you with me when – if – I ever go back.'

He was joking, but she took him seriously. 'Oh, do! Please! I can be your photographer. And I know a lot about botany and biology.'

'I think your mother would have something to say about that.'

'Oh, she could come too. She's strong, very strong. Far stronger than I am.'

ꙟ

For a while that afternoon Alexine sat with a handful of other residents in the music-room of the hotel and listened to Harriet playing on a piano that, because of the damp from the lake, from time to time produced a disagreeably rancid note. Harriet frowned each time that it did so, but none of her audience seemed to notice. Then overcome by the restlessness from which she had been suffering all that day, Alexine got to her feet when a round of applause greeted the end of a Chopin Berceuse, and slipped out. As a variation to her early morning circling of the lake, she instead took a narrow path up the hillside at the back of the hotel. She was wearing no hat and she did not have her parasol with her; but she welcomed the blaze of the sun on her face, even though she knew that her usually pale complexion, so often an object of admiring comment, would have an unfashionable glow that evening.

The path led into a wood, zigzagging erratically between high ferns, brambles and saplings. It was cool now, since the sun hardly penetrated the thick vegetation. She began to think of how to realize the plan that was already coalescing in her mind. Soon she would have to tell her mother. She would have to set about reading what others had written. She would have to learn Arabic, and the rudiments of medicine. She would also have to discuss money – something which she had never understood and which, since her father's death, her two half-brothers had handled for her – with John, preferably, since of the two he was the more capable, likeable and accessible.

A shot, its sound ricocheting back and forth between the hill up which she was trudging and the one opposite to it, roused her from her reverie. It was followed by a loud beating of wings, as startled birds bounced up into a sky visible to her only in rare patches between the thickly planted trees. Again a shot reverberated and again there was that tumultuous beating of wings. She felt a momentary panic. Might not a stray shot hit her? Then, as she rounded a clump of bushes, she saw Scott, rifle in hand, with his constantly scurrying, gabbling Cockney manservant, Jennings, in attendance.

He stared at her, amazed, clearly not pleased. 'How did you find me here?'

'By accident. I decided to vary my usual walk. What are you shooting?'

'Wood pigeon. Or anything else that moves.' He laughed. 'I might have shot you. You were moving.'

He raised the rifle that he was holding and fired it off twice in rapid succession. At the first shot, a cloud of birds clattered up into the sky and then began to whirl away at a tangent. At the second, a single bird plummeted downward. Like an eager retriever, Jennings at once plunged into the undergrowth and, except for a distant rustling, was lost. 'He has the nose of a dog. Remarkable. You'll see. He'll find it.'

Eventually, grinning at his master but never gazing in the direction of Alexine much less looking her in the face, Jennings emerged from the undergrowth clutching the pigeon. There was a dark red stain on his white shirt. He held the bird out to his master. 'Nice,' he said. 'Plump. Just feel that breast.'

Scott inspected the pigeon without touching it. 'Take it with the others to the kitchens.' He turned to Alexine. 'I've never much cared for pigeon. On my travels, I'd eat anything. But now that I'm back in civilization, it's odd how my civilized preferences have begun to return.'

She extended a hand. 'I've never seen a gun like that.'

He held it out to her. 'New. It's what called a revolving rifle. Made by a famous English gunmaker. G. William Tranter. Ever heard of him?' She shook her head. 'No, of course not. Why should a woman have heard of him? Basically it has the same action as a percussion revolver. The difference lies in the butt and the long barrel. On pressing the lower trigger' – he demonstrated – 'I rotate the five-shot cylinder and the action is cocked. If I press the top trigger – here – inside the trigger guard' – he indicated but did not press the trigger – 'then the shot is fired.'

She was listening and watching intently. 'May I try?'

Reluctantly he handed the rifle to her. 'Take care,' he said.

Her fingers moved over the butt and then the barrel. Suddenly she was thinking of that time when she had hesitantly taken Adolph's bow from him and decisively inserted an arrow. Like Scott now, Adolph had been at first vaguely disapproving, then grudgingly admiring.

'I've only once before met a woman with any interest in guns. That was in Oregon. The woman in that case was only interested in guns because she used one to shoot her husband.'

'May I?'

She raised the rifle, looking over at him.

He nodded.

She fired up into the empty sky, with no intention of hitting anything. She listened intently to the sound reverberating first in her ears and then, so it seemed, at the central core of her being.

'I hope the kick wasn't too much for you?'

She shook her head, smiled. Back at home, the gun-room still contained all her father's guns, regularly cleaned and polished by old Daan, who was the only person now to enter it. On her return, she would go into the gun-room, she would inspect the guns, she would learn to use them. Daan would teach her.

'This may interest you.' He stooped with difficulty, a hand to knee, and picked up a revolver that had been lying on the ground. 'A percussion revolver. Made in the States. Robert Adams made it. Its beauty is that it can be cocked either by the thumb or by pressure on the trigger. Lovely.' He weighed it in his hand.

'May I?'

It felt cold and hard on her palm.

'Death in such a small thing,' she said.

'Death can be in even smaller things than that. An insect-bite. A snake-bite. Even a thorn. I've seen it.'

Again she hefted the revolver. 'I want one of these. I must get one.'

She stroked the barrel, smiling, then handed the revolver back to him.

∽

Sometimes he was limping. Sometimes he was hardly able to walk. Sometimes Jennings, with his quiff of heavily pomaded hair sticking up above his high, shiny forehead, would push him out around the lake in a basket-work chair borrowed from the hotel. On those last occasions, she would adapt her pace to that of the manservant, who, she sensed from his manner of constantly sniffing and turning his head away from her before answering anything she said to him, resented her presence.

'He seems devoted to you,' she remarked on one occasion, in Jennings's absence to fetch a handkerchief for his master. She hoped to learn more. The relationship between the two men, though deferential on the one side and commanding on the other, nonetheless was puzzlingly close.

'Yes, he must be. To have accompanied me on all my travels. And now to look after me when I'm such a crock, instead of going back to his wife and children. He hasn't seen them for, oh, at least two years.'

Soon he was telling her the story of how he and Jennings had first met. He had been staying in a cheap Bloomsbury hotel – 'all that I could afford at that time' – and had encountered this youth of about fourteen or fifteen, who worked there as a general factotum. Nothing was too much trouble for him, nothing beneath him. An orphan, the boy had been brought up in a workhouse, from which he had escaped – 'his early years were not all that different from mine.' When the time had come for Scott to leave the hotel for a journalistic assignment in Turkey, Jennings had asked, simply, as though it were the most ordinary thing in the world, if he might come too. 'I told him I didn't know how I could pay him, and he said he didn't care about pay. All he asked was that I should meet his expenses. Then he said to me: "I feel that you are my fate." An odd thing for a boy like that to come out with, don't you think? Disturbing, too. But' – he shrugged – 'that clinched it for me. We've been together ever since. He's a rogue, a scallywag – pinching things not merely from others but from time to time from me. But he's been through horrific experiences with me and never once complained. Over trivial things he constantly lets me down. But over anything big – well, I know by now that he would stick with me to the death.'

Scott went on to reveal to her the reason for his gammy leg. As his straggling, famished party had approached a jungle settlement, a dog had rushed out and fastened its teeth in his calf. Fortunately the dog had not been rabid – or he would not be with her now on this hillside, Scott added with a laugh. But the jagged wound had become infected, and the infection often still flared up. 'I suppose I was lucky not to die of it. If those ninnies wouldn't pull out a tooth for me, then they'd hardly have been willing to amputate a leg.'

'What happened to the dog?'

'Oh, the dog it was that died. Jenkins shot it' – he raised a hand, miming the holding of a revolver – 'bang, bang, just like that. The headman was furious. Only an unusually large handful of beads appeased him.'

✧

They walked out of the hotel, where a dance was in progress, and began to stroll through the gardens bordering the lake. Behind them, gradually fading, they could hear the music of a waltz. It was the first waltz to which Alexine had danced with Adolph. She now rarely thought of him, and never with the rage and anguish of the past. But the voluptuous triple time, over-accentuated by the indifferent little band of elderly musicians, brought back a recollection, momentarily piercing and then swiftly fading, of his smooth cheek gleaming under a flaring gasolier, the firm hand at her waist, and the amazingly pale blue eyes looking down into hers.

'Don't you want to dance?'

She shook her head, slipping her arm through his.

'I feel bad about monopolizing you like this. All those young men who asked you must be furious with me. An old crock has no business to keep a beautiful young girl from dancing. Certainly not with a lot of handsome and no doubt rich young men like those.' There was something clumsy and forced, as always, in his banter.

'Oh, I'm not interested in that crowd. They're all so feeble. They have absolutely nothing of interest to say. They've never *done* anything.'

'You want to be a doer?'

'Yes, yes. I only respect people who are doers. Like my father. But how can I become a doer? Not easy for a woman.'

'Not easy, no. But – you'll manage it.'

'You think so?'

He nodded.

'Do you think that only because I'm rich?'

'I'd no idea whether you were rich or not – not until now. But I see in you...' He halted and turned to her, searching for a word. 'Determination. A determination to do – and get – what you want. We're alike in that.'

'Ever since I was a child, my aunt has been telling me that I'm the girl who always gets what she wants.'

'Yes. She's right. You always will.'

His limp was becoming more pronounced, and she could hear a wheezing, like a kettle coming to the boil, from his barrel-like chest. He pointed to a bench. 'Let's sit here for a moment.'

As, with a rustle of the last of all the many evening gowns that Madame Molnar had made for her, Alexine seated herself, she suddenly heard, now from far off, the accelerating close to the waltz. It was followed by the distant sound of clapping.

'What a ludicrous occupation – to hop round a room attached to someone else!'

Was he being serious? 'Oh, it can be fun.'

'I've never danced from choice. Only from duty. Now' – he tapped his leg – 'I have the perfect excuse for not doing so.'

For a while they sat in silence, staring out at the lake.

Then Alexine turned abruptly to him: 'Why did you do it?'

He stared at her without answering. There was a flutter of alarm in his eyes.

'Why did you first decide to go to Africa?'

He shrugged. Was he going to respond or not? Then, at last, he did so. 'It's a question I've often asked myself. And there are so many answers. Even as a boy, I felt that I had to be somewhere else – it didn't matter where – just, just somewhere else. The goal has never been all that important to me – though of course I've had to make others believe it to be important, since otherwise I'd never have been able to raise the cash!' He laughed, stretching out his long, powerful legs ahead of him. 'What is odd is that, whenever I've set off on an expedition, I've felt this tremendous excitement. And then, when I've returned – however successful the expedition may have been – I've felt this profound depression. Success for me is even more disappointing than failure.'

He brooded for a while. Then he continued: 'And I love the sense of freedom. I hate all the silly conventions – the constraints – the hypocrisies – the petty ambitions represented by what is now going on over there.' He indicated the hotel with a jerk of his head. 'And I hate domesticity. Dreadful. I don't want a little woman to put on my slippers for me when I come home from the business of the world – or a crowd of children to fondle on my knee. Ugh!' He pulled a face, teeth clenched and eyes almost shut.

She felt an extraordinary relief. Here was someone who felt as she had done ever since her childhood.

With difficulty, as though he were wrestling with himself to reach the truth, he went on: 'But of course there's always been a discreditable side to my motives. There has to have been. Motives almost always have a discreditable side – as, no doubt, you'll eventually learn. I like to be a Prospero, with no Ariel in attendance but only a host of Calibans, to be cajoled, bullied and bent to my will. I like to have that almost superhuman power.' He laughed. 'And now that almost superhuman power has been taken from me. The only person on whom I can rely to obey *all* my orders, no matter how foolish or repugnant they seem to him, is my little Cockney sparrow. I'm no longer emperor in my own little kingdom but merely a subject in this much larger, safer and drabber one.' He laughed. 'I can't even get myself a decent table in the dining-room or a bedroom with a view of the lake.'

She stared out at the calm water, across which a solitary black swan was gliding, seemingly without any effort.

'I'm going to go to Africa.'

'Oh, no, my dear. That's not the place for you. It's not the place for any woman, and certainly not for a woman who has – I should guess – never lived even for a day in anything but the utmost comfort.'

'That's why I want to go.'

He turned his head and stared at her. Then he smiled, revealing those nicotine-yellow teeth of his, and nodded. 'And I think that you'll get what you want. Somehow, some time you'll get it. Didn't you say that your aunt called you the girl who always got what she wanted?'

Boldly, defiantly, she now did something that she had been taught that no decent girl ever did. She extended her hand along the back of the bench, the full, cobweb-fine sleeve of her dress falling away to reveal her arm gleaming in the moonlight, and placed it on the back of his neck. She caressed the neck and then drew his head towards her. 'Please.' When he resisted her, she repeated it: 'Please. I want it.'

He gave a sigh. Then he leaned towards her and put his lips first to her cheek and then, feather-light, to her mouth. She responded by swivelling round her body and putting her other arm about his shoulder.

Abruptly he jerked away. 'No. No. This won't do. I'm sorry. I'm just not up to it.'

She was stunned by the oddity of what he had just said. His lips had been dry and granular, his clothes, perhaps even his body, had smelled strongly of cigar smoke. 'But why . . . ?'

He got to his feet, staggered momentarily, and gave a jerky laugh. 'My health. I'm an old crock. Past it. Let's forget about all this.'

They walked in silence back to the hotel. As they approached it, he began to hum tunelessly to the loudening music. Then he put out an arm and touched her elbow.

'No hard feelings?' His voice was thick. He opened his mouth to gulp in air, and once again she heard that wheezing.

'None. Oh, none at all.'

∽

It took her a long time to get to sleep. Was it unusually sultry or did she have a fever? When she did at last drop off, it was to experience a series of confused dreams of wandering alone through a jungle, the birds and animals raucous all around her and sticky lianas trailing over her face and bare arms. He was somewhere deep in the jungle, lying ill, perhaps even dying, and she was unable to find him. She called his name, more and more frantically – first 'Colonel Scott! Colonel Scott!' since that was how she had always addressed him, just as he had always addressed her as either 'Mademoiselle' or 'Mademoiselle Thinne' – and then, 'Mark! Mark! Mark!' Repeatedly she awoke and repeatedly she dreamed the same dream.

Then the dream changed. She was rowing herself in a boat along the tranquil canal beyond the garden of her home, with no one for company other than the mongrel Flopsy. He sat in the stern of the boat, unmoving, ears pricked, his bright eyes fixed on her. The canal kept narrowing; and simultaneously the sky grew darker and darker, and descended lower and lower. Now there was vegetation springing up on either side, black and furry, unlike any vegetation that she had ever known, and she said to herself 'Mangrove', having heard him use that word in describing his odysseys. *Mangrove.* She repeated it. Soon the vegetation was so close that, if she raised and thrust out an oar, she would be able to sweep the oar along it.

Flopsie stiffened, let out a yelp and leapt out from the boat, towards the encroaching land. She heard a sound of scrabbling paws against those black, hairy leaves, and then a series of high-pitched squeals. She stopped rowing, aghast, but now propelled forward not by her rowing but by an irresistible current, the boat did not slow but, instead, merely sped on the faster. The leaves were brushing her face. The channel was constantly narrowing. Soon it would be impassable. She could feel that encroaching fur, dry and suffocating, on her face and even in her mouth. But, after a few moments of panic, she felt totally relaxed. She let her body slip sideways and back in the boat, she let the oars fall from her hands. She closed her eyes. The fur cocooned her. 'Death,' she thought. 'This is death.' She felt no terror. She welcomed it.

At that moment, she was roused by a knocking at her door. 'Aren't you awake yet? Didn't Liliane call you?' It was Harriet.

'No. I told her not to call me.'

'I'm just going down to breakfast.' Harriet stared at Alexine. 'What's the matter? Aren't you feeling well.'

'I'm fine. Fine. I'll be down in a moment.'

∽

Without going to the dining-room for breakfast, she hurried out, eager, however belatedly, once again to take her by now regular morning stroll round the lake. Seated on a bench not far from the hotel, he was waiting for her.

'I overslept. It was a night of strange dreams.'

He nodded. 'For me too. In Africa I could sleep in atrocious heat and discomfort. But here ... Do you know – this is very odd – in Africa Jennings and I would have almost identical dreams? Once on the same night each of us dreamed that he was using a spear to kill a charging rhinoceros that was about to gore him. Perhaps you and I dreamed the same thing last night?'

She could not tell him of the ever-encroaching mangroves, she did not know why. 'I don't think so. I was dreaming that I was rowing on a canal back in The Hague. I tried to stop dreaming the dream but it wouldn't let me.'

'Yes, I know those dreams. I often have them. It's as though one were being dreamed by the dream, not the other way around ... Forgive me if I don't accompany you on your walk. I'm off later today and I have a number of things to see to.'

'*Off!*' She was amazed. 'I'd no idea. You never said ...'

'I decided only late last night. Between one dream and another. I suddenly realized there was no point in my staying on here. The waters have done nothing for me – other than giving me diarrhoea. I had enough of that in Africa. I suppose I could entrust myself to Dr Weiss, but somehow I don't think I'd fall for his sort of charlatanry. And to fall for charlatanry is the only way to be cured by it. Besides, I really must get to London, where I must see to the publication of my book, and give a lecture at the Royal Geographical Society and, oh, deal with a host of other things.'

'Well, then...' She tried to conceal her desolation that he should not merely be leaving but should also be leaving so abruptly, without any apparent qualm. Was that all that their friendship had meant to him? 'I hope that we meet again one day.'

She held out her hand, but he seemed not to see it.

'I hope so too. Who knows? At all events, thank you for your entertaining – and stimulating – company. I have a feeling that your mother didn't really approve of me. It was good of her to allow us to see so much of each other.'

'My mother doesn't tell me whom I see and don't see.'

He laughed. 'Good. You're clearly a woman not merely of independent means but also of independent mind. You're prepared to take risks. Not to be prepared to take risks is the greatest risk of all in life. I can see you'll go far.'

'Even to Africa?'

'Wherever you want to go.'

Again she held out her hand. 'Goodbye, Colonel Scott.'

'Goodbye, Mademoiselle Thinne.' This time he took the hand.

Slowly, without once gazing round, she began her circle of the lake. Yes, it was much sultrier today. It even looked as if a storm were brewing. Clouds were bulging grey-green above the darker green of the mountains ringing the lake. But she neither turned back nor hurried. At first she had been nauseated by the smell of his cigars, just as she had been nauseated by once boldly trying to smoke one of her father's. But now the smell came back to her with a hallucinatory vividness, as though it were an emanation of his whole being. It was far stronger than the smell of the lush grass beneath her shoes as she skirted a puddle brimming with water, of the trailing wild roses under which she was constantly obliged to stoop, or of the eau-de-Cologne on the handkerchief that she drew from a pocket and pressed first against her forehead and then against a cheek.

She knew that she would never see him again. Perhaps that was the reason for that at first terrible and eventually strangely comforting dream that had ended in death. They were now dead to each other. But she, if not he, was like a butterfly about to emerge from its chrysalis into an existence totally different from what it had so far known. Death for her was also life.

∽

That evening, one of the hotel servants came over to her in one of the hotel drawing-rooms with an envelope on a silver salver. He bowed and said: 'The American gentleman left this for mademoiselle.' Harriet watched, eyes narrowed, as Alexine took the envelope off the salver and, with trembling hands, opened it.

All that the envelope contained was a stained, tattered map. The map was of Africa, and for that reason whole areas of it were blank. Across the top, in bold, irregular capital letters, he had written: Here be monsters. Zigzagging the map were what at first seemed to be the fine, random scratchings of a pen in red ink. Then she saw that, at the place where the map showed Alexandria, there was an arrow, beside which he had scrawled: My journey started here. There were other, smaller arrows, leading her gaze on an erratic, zigzag course, often doubling and redoubling on itself, south and west. An insect might have crawled there, leaving its trail. But this was the trail of a man.

'What is it?' Harriet asked.

'Oh, just an old map. Colonel Scott and I were talking of his travels and he said he'd show me one. He must have forgotten, and so now here it is.'

She attempted to keep her voice flat and indifferent. But she knew that her mother and Nanny Rose were not fooled. Eventually she would show the map to Harriet and tell her of her dreams – not merely that one of the previous night, already half obliterated, but also that other, which would now remain with her forever. But for the present she merely folded up the map and then placed it in her reticule.

'You're crushing it, dear,' Nanny Rose warned, having watched what Alexine was doing. Then she said: 'He was a rum character, that one, and no mistake.'

Alexine laughed. 'Well, for that matter, I'm a rum character too.'

5 AT THE NEWLY BUILT STATION IN VIENNA, they waited in their reserved, first-class carriage for the luncheon basket that ought to have been delivered. Alexine had insisted that not merely Nanny Rose but also Daan travel with them, rather than in a second-class carriage by themselves.

'He'd be far happier on his own,' Harriet had said. 'It'll only embarrass him.'

'People are never happier if they're uncomfortable.'

'Oh, yes, they are,' Addy put in. 'Look at me. I was far happier in the discomfort of that shack – sleeping on straw, devoured by fleas, my stomach rumbling with hunger – than I'd have been in the luxury of your hotel.'

Now Addy was leaning out of the window, scanning the crowded platform. Then she saw the trolley with the wicker baskets piled on them. 'Here! Here!' she shouted in German. The man paid no attention to her as he lethargically pushed the trolley in the opposite direction. With an inarticulate exclamation of annoyance, she flung open the carriage door and jumped out.

'Let Daan go!' Harriet called after her.

But Addy paid no attention. In recent years she had rarely shown such decisiveness and energy.

'If she's not careful she'll miss the train,' Nanny Rose said. She was terrified of this new-fangled contraption. Why couldn't they travel in a civilized way, by coach?

Addy eventually returned, followed by the attendant with the basket, and almost at once there was the long, thin screech of the station master's whistle and the carriage jerked forward, all but toppling her over. The attendant leapt off, clutching the coin, a tip far larger than any he had ever received in all his years in the business, handed to him by Alexine.

'Addy, that was extremely silly of you. You might have missed the train.'

'Well, at least we haven't missed our luncheon.'

'Why didn't you let Daan go?'

'Because I'm much quicker than he is.'

Nanny Rose said nothing, but she pursed her lips and frowned in disapproval. She was by now used to Alexine's unseemly behaviour, but Addy's had surprised her. Had that peculiar doctor put ideas into her head? In the past she had always been every inch the lady.

Harriet had difficulty in persuading Daan to eat any of the contents of the basket. 'Oh, no, madam, thank you very much. I'm not at all peckish. Really.' But Harriet insisted. When he ate, he did so with his head turned aside, away from them, in the direction of the window beside him, so that they could not see him gnawing at a chicken leg held between thumb and forefinger.

'What about some wine?' Alexine asked him, bottle in hand. It must have been chilled before being put in the basket, it was so cold to the touch even on that day of summer heat.

'Oh, no, thank you, no,' he said, flustered. 'Just a little water. That's all I need. I never partake of liquor.'

Daan had the reputation of from time to time helping himself to a glass of sherry or even Dutch gin. About this, Philip had never reproached him; and, after Philip's death, Harriet had carried on the same benevolent tradition.

'Well, it'll be good to get home again,' Nanny Rose said. Home to her had long since become the house in The Hague. She now rarely thought of England, and even more rarely corresponded with anyone there. 'Wouldn't you like to come with us?' Harriet had suggested when she and Alexine had last travelled to Philip's sons in England. 'You could visit your family.' Nanny Rose had considered for a moment. Then she had shaken her head. 'Oh, no, ma'am. It's kind of you to suggest it, but I'd really be happier to stay on here at home. Unless you really *want* me with you,' she added, as always punctilious in her desire to fulfil her duty.

'Yes, it'll be good to get home again,' Harriet echoed, as she bit into a piece of bread liberally spread with butter. She no longer cared that she was getting so fat, her arms cylindrical except at the still tiny wrists, her once shapely neck now disfigured by two sagging dewlaps, so that over recent years she had had to have many of her choker necklaces lengthened.

'Will it?' Addy shook up sharply. 'Oh, I wish I felt that! But I don't. I hate the thought of returning to that place.'

The other three women stared at her in consternation. Then, 'Aren't you happy in the house?' Harriet asked.

'Oh, don't sound so offended! I'm not complaining. You've made me think of it as my home, you've been wonderful to me. But ... but...' She gazed out of the window beside her, lips parted. Then she turned and said: 'Is happiness what one wants?' None of them answered. 'I don't know that it's what *I* want,' she continued. 'I thought it was, but now I'm not sure.'

'Is that a result of your cure?' Harriet's tone was acid.

Addy nodded. 'Yes. In part. I spent a lot of my time thinking –

when I was not doing disagreeable things like digging and weeding and haring up and down hillsides. I don't want life merely to make polite requests of me – which I'm at liberty to refuse, if I want to. I want it to make demands. Yes, demands. That's what it did during those days of the cure. And it *was* a cure. At last I feel well, really well, again. I want to be stretched. Even if it's on a rack.'

Harriet stared at her, frowned and shook her head. This was not a suitable conversation for Nanny Rose and Daan to hear, she was attempting to indicate.

'Oh, I know exactly how you feel!' Alexine suddenly cried out. 'That's why I've reached my decision!'

Harriet jerked round from Addy. 'Your decision? What are you talking about?'

'Soon – very soon – I'm going to travel. The world's so large and I've seen so little of it.'

'You've seen a great deal of it for someone of your age,' Harriet said.

'I don't want to *sit*. I must get moving.'

'And where are you proposing to move?' Again Harriet wished that this conversation could be terminated until the three of them were alone together.

'Africa.'

'Africa!'

Alexine nodded.

'Oh, I can see where this idea's come from! It's from that vulgar man – that bogus colonel.'

'Yes.' Alexine was irritatingly calm. She paused in thought. 'Is he vulgar, is he bogus? What does that matter? He's a hero.'

'A hero!'

'Yes, a hero. He's gone to places where no other white man has gone.'

'Who wants to go to such places?'

'I do.'

'Oh, don't be so silly. A woman can't go off on that sort of journey. It's out of the question.' But even as she spoke, Harriet was suddenly thinking: Why not, why not?

'Most women aren't free to do so. I am. I have that freedom. Father's money has given me that freedom.'

Harriet stared at her with panicky eyes, Addy with a dawning admiration.

'You could go to Cairo,' Nanny Rose said, in an attempt to defuse the situation. 'You remember that Nanny Gilbert went there the winter before last with her family. Mr Van Zwannenberg needed the climate for his lungs and the whole family went with him. You could do that. Nanny Gilbert said it was beautiful, really beautiful. They've recently built this luxury hotel.'

'Oh, I want to go much further than Cairo,' Alexine said. 'But that would certainly be the starting point.'

Suddenly Addy leant forward. 'I'll come with you. May I? Yes?'

Alexine considered it. Then she said: 'Why not?'

At that moment, with a swish and rattle, the train plunged into a long tunnel. In the darkness, they all sat silent.

When at last they emerged into a sudden, punishing glare, Harriet raised a hand to her face. 'And what about me?' she asked. She felt her eyes watering and was not sure whether it was because of the glare or the imminence of tears.

'Well, mother, you could come too! Why not? Oh, do, do! It'll be such fun. Please! *Please!*'

'Fun's the last thing it's likely to be. But – but I can hardly let my only child go off to places like that on her own.'

Again they entered a tunnel, even longer than the previous one. Again they sat in silence in the darkness.

When everything in the carriage was once again glittering in sunlight, Harriet was smiling. 'I've always wanted an adventure,' she said. 'One adventure before I die.'

'You're not going to die,' Addy said. 'None of us is going to die. We're going to have fun and be free.'

6 'WHAT ARE YOU GOING TO DO WITH THE DOGS?' Sophie asked. She had been watching Alexine comb one of them, an asthmatic Pekinese.

'Take them, of course.'

'*All* of them?'

'All of them. We may be away for a year, two years. It would be terrible if I came back and found that, while I was away, one of them had died.'

'In that sort of climate, they may die more quickly than if they stayed here. They won't be used to such heat.'

'Well, at least I'll be with them when that happens.'

Sophie got up from her chair and knelt beside Alexine, as she continued to groom the Pekinese. 'Alexine. I've been thinking. Thinking a lot.' She hesitated.

'Yes?'

'I want to come with you.'

Alexine was at a loss for an answer. She knew that Sophie, so sweet and so soft, lacked the steel for the journey. But she was her closest friend, and what was more natural than to take one's closest friend as one's companion on one's journey of a lifetime?

'Oh, no, Sophie! It's not your sort of thing. You ... you...' How could she say it? *You're not strong enough, stoical enough, resourceful enough* ... 'I mean, I'd love to have you with me, but ... You've no idea what it's going to be like.'

Sophie misunderstood Alexine's reluctance. 'I know that you're afraid I'll want to do things my own way. But I won't, I promise I won't. I'll do exactly what you tell me. You're the leader and of course I'll obey you in everything. I promise – cross my heart and hope to die.' She made the gesture. 'Oh, please, Alexine, please!'

Moved, Alexine thought for a while, the comb poised above the dog, which lay on its back, stumpy legs in air, looking up at her with moist, bulging eyes. Then she said: 'All right. If your parents agree.'

Sophie let out a squeal of pleasure. 'Oh, we're going to have a wonderful time. I know we are! We'll be the first white women that many of those savages have ever seen. They'll think that we're angels – or devils.'

Alexine resumed her combing of the dogs. Sophie felt so much joy, and she herself now felt a leaden depression.

∽

'I've never heard of such nonsense!' Monsieur Thierry got up from the desk at which he had been working, with such violence that he all but knocked over his chair. 'Of course you can't go! Certainly not!'

'But why, papa, why?'

'Well, firstly, because I can't afford it. You know that. You know how short of money we are.'

'But I don't need any money. Alexine has money, lots and lots of it. She's the leader of the expedition, she's financing it. She told me that.'

'You'll need something for your day-to-day expenses. The very rich can be capricious in the way in which they part with their money. But money aside' – he made a gesture with his white, plump hand, the nails carefully manicured, as though he were dismissing an importunate beggar – 'I have to think of your reputation. And your mother's and my reputation,' he added.

Sophie stared at him, bewildered.

'You don't seem to understand, my dear. If Monsieur Thinne were still alive and were going – or if I were going – not that I'd ever dream of doing anything so crazy – it would be an entirely different kettle of fish. But for a group of women to set off alone, unchaperoned ... Already people everywhere – the common sort as well as our friends – are talking about the scandal of it. You must know that.'

'Why should it be a scandal?' Her voice was small; she herself looked diminished.

'You can take my word for it that it is. And a scandal is the last thing in which I want you involved. We have to find a suitable match for you. I've told you that a number of times. We're certainly not going to succeed in doing that if we allow you to be one of this extraordinary party.'

'I want to go,' she pouted, looking down at the floor; her lips quivered.

'No doubt. But we can none of us always have what we want.'

It was the same thing that he had said to her when he had severed all connections between her and her impoverished Turkish prince. For days she had pleaded, for even more days she had been prone to sudden attacks of anguished howling. But she had accepted her father's edict, as she had always done and as she was always to do.

'*Please*, papa!'

'No.'

'Oh, please!'

'No!'

Later, she faced the horrendous task (as she viewed it) of breaking it to her beloved Alexine that she would not, after all, be able to accompany her. That Alexine should be relieved, she had never for a moment imagined.

'What can I do? He says that, if I disobey him, he'll disown me.'

'There's nothing you can do. It's sad, so sad. But there it is.' Alexine tried to convey a regret that she did not feel, and to conceal a relief that she did.

'He never once mentioned all the dangers. I mean, we could drown on the voyage. We could pick up all sorts of horrible diseases. We could be robbed or – or even murdered. All that's nothing to him. The only thing he cares about is whether the expedition will be *respectable* or not.'

'That's the only thing about which most people care. You saw that piece in the newspaper?'

'Yes, I did. And I'm sure that papa saw it, although he said nothing about it.'

'You'd think we were going to Africa to open a brothel.'

'Oh, Alexine.' Sophie put a hand up to her mouth and laughed behind it. 'You're dreadful.'

'Perhaps when you've been married and had children and your husband has conveniently died young, we'll make another expedition and you can come along then. Why not? You'll be like mother then. She doesn't care what anyone says. And nor does Aunt Addy.'

Sophie's eyes filled with tears. 'I can't bear to think of life without you.'

'Oh, you'll soon forget about me,' Alexine said briskly.

'Never! Never! Never!'

∽

That night Sophie lay sleepless in bed. She felt that she had betrayed not merely Alexine but also her own self. If only she had had the courage to defy her father! If only she had continued to argue with him! If only she had threatened to starve herself or poison herself if she did not get her way! When she had acquiesced in never having any further contact with her Turkish prince, she had reproached herself in the same way, with the same self-savaging bitterness. Alexine would not have been so feeble. Alexine would have fought.

Eventually she got out of bed and lit the lamp beside it. Although the night was sultry, she shuddered and shuddered again. Then, from a drawer in the bedside table, she took out the Bible that her former English nanny, a friend of Nanny Rose, had given to her as a farewell present before returning to London. The nanny had been profoundly religious, and she had passed something of that on to her charge.

Her lips moving soundlessly as she sat on the edge of the bed, the Bible on her knees, Sophie read:

> And Ruth said Entreat me not to leave thee, or to return from following after thee: for whither thou goest I will go, and where thou

lodgest I will lodge; thy people shall be my people, and thy God my God; where thou diest will I die, and there will I be buried; the Lord do so to me, and more also, if aught but death part thee and me.

∽

Her knees buckled and the Bible crashed to the floor. She flung herself on to the bed and pressed her face into the pillow, as she let out one stifled wail after another.

7 HARRIET NOW RARELY LEFT THE HOUSE, unless on business to do with the expedition. When she received an invitation, she would either wholly ignore it, thus causing certain offence, or send a few perfunctory words of regret, with often the same result. People once close to the family would ask each other if those three silly women had finally taken complete leave of their senses. Every conversation about them was a mixture of pity, disapproval and derision.

Head bowed over her desk and pince-nez low on her nose, Harriet was making yet another of her lists. About these lists Alexine would tease her that she seemed to believe that, if something were written down on a piece of paper, then that gave it reality.

Harriet wrote:

1) A microscope.
2) An ice machine, with ample stock of powder.
3) Sewing machine, simple kind. Worked by hand, not feet. Thread, extra needles.
4) A reveille matin. One that lights a candle when it wakes one? Possible? Read somewhere of it. Enquire.
5) A large chest of good black tea.
6) Magnifying glass (capable of lighting fires).
7) An appareil photographique Debroni for myself (Alexine has her own). Easy to manage, small. Requires few chemicals.
8) 25 yards of black cloth, ditto red.
9) 24 gaudy cotton handkerchiefs, 24 ditto silk (first quality not necessary).
10) 20 tins Liebigs extract of meat. Not essence of beef only, lamb and chicken also.
11) Tooth powder, brushes. 20 of each?
12) Dr James's fever powders. IMPORTANT.

As she underscored the last word, there was a knock at the door and Nanny Rose entered.

'Oh, Nanny, may we talk another time? I have to concentrate. It's so difficult to remember everything. If we could be certain of what can bought in Cairo and what can't . . .'

'I just want a short word, madam. I won't keep you long.'

Harriet sighed and laid down her pen. By now she knew that, if

Nanny Rose had decided to do something, then it was hopeless to attempt to deflect her.

'Well, what is it?' Nanny Rose remained standing, her hands clasped before her. 'Oh, do sit down! Sit down!' Harriet indicated a chair.

Having begun to suffer from arthritis, Nanny Rose walked stiffly over to it and lowered herself with care. She sighed and began to smooth down her black skirt over her knees. Since her widowhood, many years ago now, she always wore black. Sophie had once gigglingly told Alexine that the shiny black dress, which always seemed to be the same one, and the no less shiny black widow's cap made the humpbacked English-woman look like a giant beetle.

'Well?'

'I've been thinking, madam.' This was Nanny Rose's usual prelude to saying something that might be unwelcome to her employers.

'And what have you been thinking, nanny?'

'I'll have to come with you.'

'Come with me?'

'Come with you, Miss Addy and Miss Alexine. On this madcap jaunt of yours. I'd better come. I've thought about it and that's what I've decided.'

'Oh, but I don't really think...' Harriet broke off. She wanted to say, 'Oh, no, you're far too old for anything so demanding,' but Nanny Rose was in fact younger than Daan, Addy and even herself. Her life, at first impoverished in a small, overcrowded farmhouse and then unremit-tingly strenuous as she had brought up first other people's children and then her own children, while at the same time nursing a husband mor-tally ill with consumption, had aged her prematurely. She had carried an endless succession of burdens, and that bent back of hers seemed to be the physical witness to it. 'I've been counting on you to keep an eye on the house in our absence. There's no one among the servants that I can trust as I can trust you.'

'I'm sure you can trust Mrs Palmel.' Harriet had just appointed this woman to be housekeeper in her absence. 'You told me she had a refer-ence from the Palace.'

'Oh, well, yes, perhaps. But you're the one...'

'I don't really care for travel. When we went to that Bled place, all those train journeys, with their joltings and noise, gave me a constant headache. I could hardly think. And you know what the heat does to me. But I like to do my duty. I feel you'll need me. Particularly as I don't think Eva is going to go with you after all.'

'What makes you think that?' Eva was the plain, perky maid whom the three women were planning to share on their travels.

'Her – her intended told her that he wasn't prepared to wait for her.

Didn't she tell you? It was yesterday evening. They were walking out and he suddenly broke it to her. She was crying and crying when she got back, a real scene. Well, one can understand it. He's impatient to get married now that he's got that job at the butcher's. And she was impatient to get married.'

Harriet considered in silence.

'I've no objection to doing the sort of things that she was going to do for you,' Nanny Rose went on. 'I'm better with an iron than she is, I can tell you that. And I'm not likely to be carrying on with all and sundry,' she added.

'Well . . .'

'I won't be any burden to you.'

'You know of course that this trip of ours could be dangerous, don't you?'

Nanny Rose gave a shrug. 'All my life's been dangerous in one way or another, madam, since I first drew breath. I'm past fifty now. It's too late to worry about danger.'

At that moment Addy rushed into the room, two books in her hand. 'It's really too bad! I told John that what I wanted was *Barry Lyndon* and *Harry Esmond*, and that wretched bookshop has sent me neither of those but these two volumes of *Pendennis* instead. I've read *Pendennis* – and I *hated* it. Now it's highly unlikely that the two others will reach me in time.'

'I've just been having a chat with Nanny Rose. She wants to come with us.'

Addy was appalled. '*What!* Oh, but Nanny Rose – I honestly don't think . . .'

'I've made up my mind, madam. I feel that you'll all need me. I'm not one to shirk my duty.'

Harriet and Addy looked at each other. Mouth pulled down, Addy raised her bony shoulders in despairing resignation. Harriet then did likewise.

8 SLUMPED, LEGS THRUST OUT, at the circular café table out on the quay, Adolph yawned and yawned again. His eyelids were heavy, and his blue eyes had a glazed, drowsy look to them. Dock workers constantly passed, their voices strident and their sabots clattering on the cobbles, as did overloaded drays and an occasional carriage. There was a smell of putrescence in the air from the fruit and vegetable market held in the square at the end of the street. Some ragged, barefoot children were going through the produce jettisoned in the gutters after the close of business for the day. But those eyes, wide open but vacant, took in nothing of all this.

'Adolph! Aren't you coming aboard? You'd better make it snappy. They sail in less than half an hour.'

Adolph stared at the dapper young man, in a white, shiny collar so high that it all but touched his earlobes. It was Franz, who had lent the lovers his garçonnière. He and Adolph were close friends, but anyone seeing them at that moment might have assumed them to be acquaintances, even strangers. He shook his head. 'I've not been invited.'

'Invited!' Franz laughed. 'You don't have to be *invited*, old chap. It's a free for all. Everyone welcome.'

'Everyone?'

A laugh. 'Well, everyone who's anyone.'

Morosely, Adolph leaned forward, picked up his tankard of beer and raised it to his mouth. When he lowered it again there was a line of foam along his upper lip. 'Enjoy yourself,' he said.

Franz frowned, puzzled and disquieted. 'Oh, do come!'

Adolph shook his head.

'Well, I'll tell them that you wished them *bon voyage*.' Gold-knobbed cane in hand, Franz hurried on.

Now Adolph suddenly became aware of the braying of the small German brass band on the upper deck of the ship. When there was a silence between one number and another, it would at once be filled by a din of laughter and chatter. He shut his eyes. It was as if he were lying on a beach and, wave on wave, the tumult of the ocean, vast and perilous, swept over him. The tumult increased, became deafening, was like a physical assault. He shut his eyes, he succumbed to its battering, he even came to welcome it. He had been an idiot, he had ruined his life. But for that crazy business with that Molnar woman, he might himself be travelling with them.

He picked up the tankard, and this time he drained it.

'It's quite extraordinary. And rather magnificent.' Juliana, who had supplanted Addy at the Court, was talking in her loud, plummy voice to Monsieur Thierry. She agitated her fan. Even though it was now October, the unprecedentedly hot summer still flared on. 'Do you know that they've taken over the *entire* first-class section?'

'Well, it's a small ship.'

'But even so. Imagine! The entire first-class section, all the way to Alexandria. You can guess what that must have cost them.'

Madame Thierry, accompanied by Sophie, approached. 'Thirty-six pieces of luggage,' she said. 'That's not including all that's been put in the hold. Someone said there's a piano.'

'Oh, no, mama, that's not true. Alexine told me that Madame Thinne is planning to buy a piano in Cairo.'

'Well, that's what I overheard someone saying. He must have got it wrong. People exaggerate so.'

'They *are* taking five dogs with them,' Sophie said.

'Five dogs! Egypt is full of stray dogs! Why take more dogs?' Juliana rolled her eyes. 'Mercy! What it is to be rich beyond the dreams of avarice!'

Sophie wandered off. She heard her mother calling, 'Sophie! Sophie! Where are you going? Come back here!' But without glancing round, she continued to thread her way through the people crowding the deck.

At last she saw Alexine, the centre of at least a dozen people, male and female. She wanted to push through them all and stand close to her, but lacked the boldness to do so.

'You must be terribly excited,' a woman said.

Head on one side, Alexine considered. 'No. Strangely not. I *was* terribly excited, until this morning. And now ...' She laughed. 'I might be going off on a holiday visit to Knokke or somewhere equally dreary.'

'I must say, I think you're all amazingly brave,' an elderly man, one of the richest landowners in the country, announced in his loud, gruff voice. Only the evening before he had been telling friends at his club that he thought the three women so dotty that the place for them was a madhouse.

'If one wants to do something strongly enough, bravery doesn't come into it.'

'It would for me,' the old man said. 'But I've always maintained that women have more courage than men. If men had to bear children, instead of the so-called weaker sex, the human race would die out in no time at all. And I'm talking as a man who fathered eleven children in his day.'

'Oh, I do wish that band would give us a moment's peace!' a woman complained. 'One can't hear oneself speak.'

'It all adds to the jollity,' her husband told her.

'But is it so jolly – to say goodbye to three of our oldest and dearest friends for who knows how long?'

The words pierced Sophie, since they confirmed all that she had been feeling. Why was everyone laughing and drinking champagne? Why was that band blaring out all those marches and polkas? It was beastly. She put both hands to her lips, pressing fingertips against them, and stared imploringly at Alexine, willing her to look in her direction.

The band broke off abruptly. The ship's siren sounded, a melancholy wail, followed by two more. A moment later an officer, megaphone in hand, was pushing between one group of people and another. 'Would all people who are not passengers please leave the ship!' he shouted. 'Please! Ladies and gentlemen! Please, please! We are about to sail!'

The imminence of the separation at last gave Sophie the courage to fight her way through. 'Oh, Alexine ... Alexine ... I just wanted to say – to wish you ... Write to me if it's possible to write.' She was looking up at Alexine, her eyes brimming with tears, and Alexine, still smiling from her previous conversation, was looking down at her. 'Come back soon. Oh, I shall miss you. I'll miss you so much. I wish, wish, wish I could have come with you.'

Perfunctorily Alexine was kissing her. But her eyes were elsewhere. As Franz approached, she broke away. 'Franz!'

'Alexine. I'm late. My horse went lame and – oh, well, it's too long a story. I saw Adolph. On the quay, drinking beer. He wouldn't come with me. He said he didn't have an invitation. But I told him . . .'

She was staring over his shoulder. Her mouth was drawn into a hard line, a muscle twitched in one of her cheeks.

'He was right not to come. He wouldn't have been welcome.' Her gaze returned to his. 'Tell him that, if you like. Tell him. He wouldn't have been welcome.'

Book 3

1 NANNY ROSE WAS HELPING ALEXINE to dress for a dinner-party given in honour of the three women travellers by the Italian Minister, Alessandro Rossetti, and his second and much younger wife, Maria. The Italian legation acted for the Dutch government, which as yet had no representation in Egypt.

Nanny Rose, aided by two diminutive Egyptian maids, had helped Alexine to have a bath – 'No, no, not so much hot water,' Alexine had repeatedly protested, as Nanny Rose had yet again ordered one or other of the maids to fetch another ewer – and now, while the maids watched in silent awe, Nanny Rose was helping her to dress.

Nanny Rose held a pair of long, lace-trimmed drawers up to the light from the window, and then effortfully stooped with them, for Alexine to insert her legs. 'This under-petticoat has been badly ironed.' She showed it to the girls and repeated the words. Understanding nothing, they both began to giggle. There followed a petticoat wadded at the knees and, in its upper part, stiffened with whalebone. Alexine drew in her breath as Nanny Rose helped her into it and then let out a groan. Nanny Rose made a sign to one of the two maids and then exclaimed: 'Oh, come on, come on!' The girl at last understood what was expected of her and fetched a white, starched petticoat, with three stiff flounces, off the bed. A muslin petticoat followed, so diaphanous that, as Nanny held it, her hand, red and gnarled with arthritis, could be seen through it. Finally, between them, the two maids brought over the heavy brocade dress, carrying it as though it were a living thing.

'Wasn't this the dress that Madame Molnar made for the last palace ball?'

Alexine nodded.

'It suits you. That green is just right for you. She always knew what she was doing, I'll say that for her. Perfect taste.'

Alexine gazed down at the dress. Then she exclaimed: 'Oh, this is ridiculous. How can one wear all these clothes in this heat?'

'Well, you want to dress properly for the ambassador, don't you?'

'Minister, minister,' Alexine corrected irritably.

∽

Alexine sat on a sofa with the Minister's wife, while Harriet sat on another sofa with the Minister.

It was Harriet's task to enlist the help of Rossetti, who had lived for many years in Egypt and who was said to have innumerable influential contacts, to procure one of the few paddle-steamers available to people

147

not members of the government. A tiny, desiccated man, with a stiff kiss-curl stuck, as though with glue, on to his wrinkled, dark-brown forehead, he was dressed in clothes such as she remembered her father, then a mere Lieutenant, wearing for evening events in her childhood: stockinet pantaloons reaching down to his bony ankles, patent-leather pumps below them, and a coat with high collar and spreading lapels above. He smelled strongly of patchouli. At one moment, she peered at his hair. Yes, she was sure that, lustrous black with an orange glint to it, it was dyed, it must be.

He responded delightedly to her flirtatious manner, constantly assuring her, in a French as old-fashioned as his dress, that her word was his command, that he would be only too pleased to help her in any way he could, that she must not hesitate to ask for anything she needed. But when she spoke of the paddle-steamer, he became evasive.

'I can find you as many dahabiahs as you need. All comfortable, some, yes, luxurious – perhaps not by your standards but by the standard of this country. That poses no problem, no problem at all. But a steamer... Occasionally, very occasionally, one becomes available. Last winter our Minister for Home Affairs and his wife came here – she for her health – and for them I did manage... But it took a lot of time and effort.'

'I see.'

'Of course, dear madame, I am also prepared to devote endless time and effort to find such a steamer for you. But' – he shrugged and gave a rueful smile – 'whether I shall be successful – that's another matter.'

'What we need is the steamer and then, in addition, well, three or perhaps four dahabiahs, which the steamer can tow. Is that feasible?'

He looked amazed, his mouth opening and shutting to reveal teeth almost all of which were capped with gold. 'Feasible, yes, madame, of course, if we can find the steamer. But hugely expensive. Most parties manage with one dahabiah. Perhaps two if there are many people and also many servants.'

'Ours is likely to be a very large party. And there are also five dogs.'

'Five *dogs!* I am not sure...'

'We travel everywhere with our dogs. We couldn't be separated from them.'

Meantime, Alexine was asking the Minister's sprightly, swarthy wife, her full cheeks hectic with rouge and her magnificent bare shoulders floury with powder, how she managed in such heat.

'Oh, I'm used to it. It's often very hot in my native Sicily. And in any case, one gets used to everything in the end.' Despite this declaration, she had been fanning herself vigorously throughout the conversation. Small beads of sweat were glistening under her heavily mascaraed eyes and in the creases of her neck.

As though she and Alexine were already close friends, she now began to speak of the absolute necessity of mosquito nets. Her only child, a little boy, had died two years ago of malaria. No, the Good Lord had given her no other child and now perhaps – perhaps it was too late to have any hope of one. She had her step-children but they were all older than she was and they were in Italy. She hardly knew them.

This frankness persuaded Alexine to be frank in her turn. Wasn't it crazy, she asked, to dress as they were dressed – she indicated her own elaborate costume, layer on layer – in such a climate?

'Yes. So it may seem. But it's necessary to keep up standards. Surely? Otherwise – we become just like the natives.'

'But these stays! They're suffocating me. I can hardly breathe.' Both women laughed, as Alexine pressed a hand to her midriff. 'I'm not going to wear them again. I can't. They'll kill me.'

'You're not being serious?'

'Of course. How can you bear to wear them yourself?'

Signora Rossetti thought for a moment. 'They represent something. Small but important.'

'And what's that?'

Again Signora Rossetti paused in thought. 'Discipline. The people here don't know what it means. No discipline! You will learn that. Lazy, unreliable, dishonest. Oh, charming, charming, yes. But . . . If I didn't wear stays, it would be the same as receiving my guests in curling-pins!' Alexine laughed; but Signora Rossetti shook her head in admonition: 'No, no. No joke. I'm being serious. Please – believe me. It's the same with your skin.' She put out her hand and tentatively touched Alexine's cheek. 'Beautiful. So white, smooth. You must keep that. Remember – always wear a hat, carry a parasol. My skin' – now she touched her own cheek – 'is born this way. Brown, coarse. But you – you must stay white, white. Fragile. Pure. Beautiful. European.'

Later Signor Rossetti led Addy down a long corridor, its once uniformly pink distemper peeling in grey and brown shreds from its walls, to show her his library. 'I love books, but Egypt's not the place for them. The insects eat them, and when it rains . . .' Shelves reached up to the ceiling of the cavernous room, with only two skylights for windows. The colza oil lamp in his hand threw off huge, erratic shadows, as he walked from shelf to shelf to show her his treasures.

'You've a wonderful collection.' Then Addy's often embarrassing devotion to the truth made her add: 'But, to be frank with you, the age and physical condition of a book means nothing to me. I love books but only for what is printed on the page.'

He sighed. 'You miss a lot. This is the collection of a lifetime. My first wife used to complain that I was wasting my money. And now my

Maria does the same. A new frock from Paris is one thing, but a book . . . !'

He put down the lamp, fetched some library steps and, swaying perilously from side to side, mounted them. 'Take a look at this. Machiavelli. *Il Principe*. I know of no similar copy in existence.'

Gingerly, Addy took the book from the hand that he extended downward. There were tiny perforations in the stiff pages.

'These pages . . .'

'Yes, the insects have been at them.' He gave a high-pitched laugh. 'They like printer's ink even more than human blood.'

She handed the book back to him. When he had replaced it, she put out a hand to help him down from the ladder. He took her hand, swayed, and finally jumped, all but toppling over as he landed. He laughed and began to brush the dust off the front of his jacket. 'You should stay in Cairo for the winter, not go on this journey. Life here in the next few months will be truly diverting. We call it the season. People from all over the world, even from America. All sorts. Tourists, artists, botanists, archaeologists, sportsmen. A wonderful opportunity for a young girl to find a husband.' His left eyelid flickered. It was almost a wink.

'I'm afraid my niece has set her heart not on a husband but on a voyage of discovery. She's a girl who always gets what she wants.'

'Always to get what one wants is not good for anyone.' Again he gave his high-pitched laugh. 'Why not rent a house here? I know of a beautiful one, in Ezbekiya Square. Near your hotel. I can get it for you at a bargain price. One of the finest houses in the city.'

Addy shook her head. 'Bargains never appeal to my niece. She's one of the most extravagant people in the world.'

'But surely you and Madame Thinne must . . . ?'

Addy smiled. 'We have absolutely no control over her. We merely do her bidding. The money is hers,' she added. 'And money, as you will know, is power.'

∽

In the drawing-room, a middle-aged man carried a stool over to where Alexine was sitting. 'May I, mademoiselle?' he asked in English, still holding the stool in both hands.

'Please.' Alexine turned away from Signora Rossetti to look up at the newcomer. With his heavy eyelids, lumbering walk, and slow, deep voice, he gave an impression of sated languor; but it was the languor of a tiger or panther, which at any moment can stir from its somnolence to leap on to its prey. His grey, untidy hair cascaded down from a head too large even for a body as powerful as his, to reach almost to his shoulders; his beard needed trimming; one of the sleeves of his jacket was frayed.

'We were introduced, but we haven't yet had the opportunity of talking.' He bowed: 'Tim Fielding. At your service, mademoiselle.' There was something mocking in the formality of it.

She nodded. Earlier, Signora Rossetti, telling her about the other guests, had pointed out this man and then spoken at length about him. He clearly fascinated her. The youngest of eleven children of an Irish peer, who had gambled away most of the ancestral estates, he had arrived in Africa, virtually penniless, at the age of sixteen. Now, in his mid-forties, he was one of the richest men in Cairo. How had he made his money? In answer to Alexine's question, Signora Rossetti had given a knowing smile: 'Who knows? Doing many things. Trading in ivory and gold. Perhaps also in human bodies,' she had added in a whisper. 'He has many Arab friends. They – work together.'

'Do you mean he's a slave-trader?'

Signora Rossetti had put a finger to her lips, screwed up her eyes, and then slowly nodded. Then, again in a whisper, a flush spreading up her neck, she had leaned forward to confide: 'He has a terrible reputation. He once told my husband that the only way to understand Africa was to sleep with as many African women as possible. You know, in Cairo he has two houses. One, charming but modest, is for his European and American friends, gentlemen and ladies. The other . . . a palace. Out in Ghiza, near the Pyramids. People say he keeps many women there. All nationalities. Sometimes he invites his gentlemen friends. My husband says he was never invited. But even a girl as young as you knows that men are liars. Can I believe him?'

Having seated himself on the stool, Fielding leaned forward and asked: 'You are one of the three ladies hell-bent on adventure. Am I right?'

Alexine nodded. 'I don't know why everyone's so surprised. We're only planning to do what many men have done before us.'

'But I gather that you differ from your male predecessors in that no expense is to be spared?'

'No reasonable expense.'

He again leaned forward. Fanatical about cleanliness as she was, she noticed, with distaste, that the overlong fingernails of his strong, sunburned hands had grime beneath them, and that there was a yellowish stain on his collar. 'And what is the purpose of your – your *exploration*?' He gave the last word a derisory emphasis. 'Am I permitted to ask that?'

'I don't see why not. The truth is – I'm not yet sure of the purpose. Does that seem very naïve to you? Yes, I can see that it does. This is a case of not knowing what one is setting out to find until one has begun to find it.'

He shook his head in amazement, then laughed out loud.

'Yes, you're right to laugh at us. What do *you* think should be our objective?'

He hesitated, head tilted to one side. 'Well, I suppose you could undertake what every explorer is undertaking now. You could venture up the White Nile. To find its source. That would be something. But I hardly think that for three ladies – without any gentlemen – however much money they are willing to spend . . .'

'We have a Dutch male servant with us. And we're going to engage a number of men here.'

'I said, "Without any *gentle*men." Servants and Africans – and even Arabs – are something rather different.' He leaned forward again, hands clasped. 'Have you heard of the Dinka? You'll have to travel among them.'

She nodded. 'Of course.'

'Well, all of them go around as naked as on the day they were born.'

'That's not going to upset us. If it doesn't upset white men to see naked black women, why should it upset white women to see naked black men?'

'Good for you! That's the spirit! . . . And when do you start out?'

'In another two months or so. When it's cooler. And when I've learned some more Arabic. We plan to sail down to Khartoum. Then . . . we'll see.'

'Arabic! You're learning Arabic?' Once again he was astonished. 'There are women who've lived here for years and years and who speak hardly a word. Like our hostess.'

'I started to learn in the Netherlands. Now Mr Shepheard of our hotel has recommended someone to teach me here.'

'I bet it's old Mahfouz.'

'Yes. That's the man.'

'He taught me. An old scoundrel. But you couldn't do better.'

'Really? That's good news. I start tomorrow.'

'Oh, I wish I could come with you, to share your adventure! How I wish it! But I'm sure you wouldn't want me. And in any case I have so much unfinished business here in Cairo – and elsewhere. But I feel certain that in the course of our travels we're going to meet again. Africa is such a huge place and yet people keep bumping into each other.'

She smiled. 'Yes, I'd like to bump into you.'

'Who knows? We might even one day meet in the same cooking pot. Boiling away happily to make a cannibal stew.'

2 AT HARRIET'S INSISTENCE, Daan accompanied Alexine to her first Arabic lesson. In thick black woollen trousers and jacket and a stove-pipe hat, all of which Alexine recognized as once having belonged to her father, he was sweating profusely as he sat opposite to her in the carriage. They had rented this vehicle, its leather hood cracked here and there to admit lances of brilliant sunlight, for their sole use during their stay. He kept his eyes lowered and his knees drawn in, as though embarrassed by such a close proximity. From time to time he raised a bony hand to wipe off a drop of sweat from the tip of his long, beaky nose, or gave a nervous little cough.

Because of the crowds which, heedless of the carriage, constantly blocked their progress, their journey took an age.

'It would have been quicker to walk.'

'Oh, no, miss! You couldn't do that! Anything might happen.'

'Anything? What would that be?' She laughed, but, instead of joining in, he merely gazed out into the street, his mouth pursed.

At last they arrived at a grim, four-square house built of grey-brown stone. Tall, dusty, straggling trees surrounded it, their silvery leaves looking like shards of metal in the sun glinting off them. Alexine reached to open her parasol, as she prepared to step down from the carriage. The coachman put up a grimy hand to help her, but Daan, who had already scrambled out, forestalled him. 'Please, miss! Please!'

Some elderly men were squatting round the entrance. They stopped their conversation when they saw this elaborately dressed white woman under her lace-fringed parasol, and stared at her. One of them addressed Daan, who shook his head and said: 'Sorry. No understand. No speakee.' The coachman hurried over and said something, which caused everyone to laugh. Then the coachman accompanied Alexine and Daan up a flight of stone stairs to the quarters at the top of the building. Daan, stove-pipe hat in hand, became breathless with the climb. From time to time he would pause between one flight of stairs and the next, gulp for air and give his nervous little cough. 'Oh, lordy, lordy! Forgive me, miss. Old age,' he apologized on the first of these occasions, to be reassured by Alexine: 'No hurry. Everyone says the Egyptians have no idea of time.'

The door to the apartment was ajar. The coachman strode up to it and shouted out something. Someone within shouted back. Then there was the sound of bare feet slapping over stone, and an enormously fat man in a shabby, dirt-blotched jellaba came into view, swaying from side to side. 'Mademoiselle Thinne?'

'Yes. Good morning. I've come for my lesson.'

He bowed. He had a number of ornate rings on his fingers. A thick gold chain hung round his neck, with, at the end of it, an elaborate amulet which nestled in the hair between vast breasts.

'I'm delighted. Please. Come in.' He spoke in good French. Then he turned and said a few peremptory words to dismiss the coachman, who retreated down the stairs.

Books were piled everywhere, in tottering cairns. An enamel tray rested on a low table, with an empty coffee pot and cup on it. A long, narrow, orange-and-white striped cat, sleeping on the same table, opened its eyes briefly as Alexine walked past it to the chair indicated to her.

'This is our manservant, Daan.' She pointed. 'My mother thought he ought to accompany me.'

'When a lady's so young and beautiful, that's a sensible precaution. Please, sir, come, come, sit here.' Mahfouz indicated a straight-backed chair against a wall. Daan reluctantly crossed over to it and, back rigid and knees close together, sat down.

Mahfouz offered Alexine some coffee or tea. She refused either, but suggested that Daan might like some. 'Oh, no, miss,' he said in a startled, affronted tone.

The lesson began, pupil facing teacher across a table piled high, like the floor, with books. Mahfouz was amazed by how much Arabic she had already managed to learn. He was even more amazed by the speed with which she picked up everything he told her.

'I've never had a pupil like you,' he at last confessed in grudging admiration.

'You mean you've never had a woman pupil?'

He shook his head. 'I've had a few women pupils. But I've never had a man or a woman who learned so quickly.' Then he corrected himself: 'No, there was one man. An Englishman. Many years ago.'

'Mr Fielding?' she asked, in a flash of intuition.

'Yes. How do you know?'

'I guessed. I met him last night. At the house of the Italian minister.'

'Mr Rossetti? He was also my pupil. He was a dunce, a real dunce. His wife – beautiful lady!' He laughed joyfully at the recollection of her.

Suddenly, as they were conversing in rudimentary Arabic, Mahfouz jumped up to take the cat in his arms. It let out a protesting squawk and then began to purr loudly. 'I heard that you have five dogs with you,' he said, gently running his forefinger up and down under the cat's chin.

How, in a city so large, could he possibly have heard that? 'Yes. Mr

Shepheard told me it's the first time the hotel has had so many animal guests.'

'I hope you don't have to pay for an animal guest what you pay for a human one.'

'Almost as much.' She laughed.

'In Egypt we love cats. Dogs – we think dogs unclean.' He pulled a face.

'My dogs aren't. We wash them almost every day.'

When the lesson ended, Mahfouz followed them down the stairs. He had now thrust his tiny, bare feet, so out of scale with his mountainous body, into brocaded slippers. 'Oh, you don't have to come all the way down with us!' Alexine protested. But he insisted on doing so. As they approached the carriage, he touched her arms. 'Excuse me, mademoiselle. How much do you pay this man?' He indicated the coachman with a jerk of his head.

'I'm not sure. He's on a retainer from us. Mr Shepheard arranged it.'

'I'm sure you're paying too much. Mr Shepheard sees to it that everyone at his hotel pays too much. And this carriage is old. Not elegant enough for a fashionable and rich lady like yourself. I can find you a better – and cheaper – carriage.'

'Oh, that's very kind of you. But ... well, we've now fixed things this way.'

His face darkened momentarily, then once again lightened. 'Then that is all right, mademoiselle. But if you change your mind – or if you require assistance in any other matter ... Many people – Mr Fielding among them, I'm sure – will tell you that I'm entirely honest and that I can do all kinds of things that others are less able to do.' He bowed. 'Once again, I must congratulate you on your natural gift for our language. You have' – he tapped one of his large ears, out of which black hair sprouted profusely – 'a true ear. That's rare, mademoiselle. I have such an ear, you have such an ear. We're lucky.'

The carriage began to move off.

'It was so hot there, under the roof. I should have asked if we might sit out on his terrace.'

'I glimpsed some women out there, miss. Just a glimpse. Through the window. They were preparing food. Perhaps in such circumstances...'

'Oh, I'd have been only too happy to meet them, whatever they were doing – and even to help them.'

'But since I was there, a foreign man, miss...'

A silence followed. Alexine shifted uncomfortably in her heavy, voluminous clothes. Then she shifted again. 'Can you remember the name of that dressmaker my mother went to?'

'You mean yesterday? When I went with her?'

'Yes.'

Daan thought for a while. 'I don't remember her name but it was in the Coptic quarter. I think I'd remember the way.'

'Well, tell me and I'll tell the coachman.'

The dressmaker's establishment was very different from Madame Molnar's. There was a single large, airy, curtainless room, almost bare of furniture, with magazine illustrations of women in elegant clothes pinned up haphazard on its walls. A treadle sewing machine, operated by a pale, bright-eyed girl who looked as if she were no older than eight or nine, stood in its middle. A tailor's dummy stood beside it.

The dressmaker was astounded when Alexine told her what she wanted. Her speciality was to make exact copies of gowns brought from Europe, usually Paris, by her clientele. 'I don't understand, mademoiselle. You wish for an *Egyptian* costume?'

'Yes. Something loose. Light. Something suitable for this heat.'

The woman shook her head, frowning. Then she said reluctantly: 'Well, I suppose it's possible.'

'Good. Now what material do you have? Something gauzy, filmy. I don't mind if it's a European material.'

The woman stooped and picked up a bale off the floor. 'This is a silk. But it's very expensive, I'm afraid.'

Alexine felt the sheer, grey material. 'Perfect! But I don't want just one robe. I want a number. What other cloth have you got?'

∽

Harriet was appalled when she saw Alexine setting off for her next lesson in one of the dresses made for her by the dressmaker within a mere two days. 'You can't possibly go out in that! It looks like a nightdress.'

'It's as comfortable as a nightdress. And as cool. What's wrong with it?'

'But what will people say? No stockings, slippers, that – that robe thing. You'll only make a spectacle of yourself.'

'Oh, by now, I'm used to doing that.'

∽

Soon Alexine had made enough progress in Arabic to be able to carry on conversations with Mahfouz. When they discussed the crew necessary for the voyage, he at once volunteered to put her in touch with a *reis* or captain – he knew just the man, totally efficient and honest – and a cook, who had worked at the French legation until he had quarrelled with the over-exacting wife of the new minister. Then there was the son of one of his brothers, who was learning to be a waiter. He would not expect to receive the sort of wages paid to someone with experience. He was a healthy, strong, willing boy, ideal for an expedition.

At first Alexine was distrustful of Mahfouz's eagerness to help. But eventually he won her over. He joked with her, even flirted with her, paying her extravagant compliments, at which she only laughed. She admired both his teaching abilities, so much superior to those of the former missionary who had tutored her in The Hague, and his eagerness to improve his own French. Soon, instead of taking Daan upstairs with her, she would slip him some money and tell him to return in two hours. On the first occasion that she did this, he protested: 'Oh, no, miss. Madam wouldn't at all like me to leave you here all by yourself'; but eventually he became grateful for the opportunity to slip around the corner to a café, instead of having to sit listening to all that chatter in unintelligible Arabic and French.

One morning, Mahfouz was smoking a hookah on her arrival. The previous day he had surprised her by smoking a small cigarette, little more than a pinched roll of paper containing a few shreds of black tobacco, without first asking her permission. This time she was even more surprised.

'I've never seen you smoke that before.'

As often now, he had failed to get to his feet at her entry. He put his lips to the mouthpiece and there was a gurgling sound as he drew on it. He smiled up at her with his small, mica-bright eyes. 'Better than cigarettes.'

She flopped down on the floor beside him. 'May I try?'

He shook his head. Smiled. 'Not for a lady. No.'

'Please! I've smoked cigarettes, you know.'

He hesitated. Then he removed the ivory mouth-piece from the tube and wiped it on a corner of his soiled djellaba. He reattached it and then held it out to her.

She drew on it. 'Good. Very good. What is it? Tobacco?'

'Partly,' he replied evasively. 'Other things too. Herbs. Good for the health.'

She nodded. Soon, she felt euphoria, an irresistible tide, sweep through her. She had no wish to have her lesson. She just wanted to squat here beside him, sucking happiness in through the yellowing ivory mouthpiece already soiled with his saliva and the saliva of no doubt innumerable other people.

'Do your women also smoke?'

He shook his head and laughed. Then he put out a hand and gently prised the mouthpiece away from hers. 'Enough,' he said. 'Too much the first time isn't good.'

'Oh, please!'

'No, no. Enough.'

It was later that morning that she began to talk about the impossibility of chartering a steamer. The Italian minister had achieved nothing and, after extravagant promises, the French minister had been equally unsuccessful.

'Maybe I can help.'

'You?'

'Maybe. I'm lucky to have many relatives in the government. Also many friends. Do you wish me to try?'

'Oh, please! It'll make our whole journey so much quicker and easier.'

'But it'll cost you a lot of money. You realize that? In this country, miracles are never cheap.'

'Oh, I don't care about money. If it'll buy me a miracle, then I'm perfectly happy to spend all the money in the world. How much did you have in mind?'

When he mentioned the sum, she was briefly aghast. 'You mean that's just to get the steamer? It doesn't include its actual hire?'

He nodded, drawing deeply on the hookah. 'That's right. An expensive – a very expensive – miracle.'

Briefly she thought, one hand playing with her bare toes. Then she nodded. 'All right! Fine! Done! I'll bring you the money tomorrow.'

3 SEATED AT THE LARGE BUREAU which she had demanded to replace the elegant little escritoire in the sitting-room of her suite, Harriet was drawing up yet another of her lists:

STEAMER

Self
Addy
Daan
1 reis
1 pilot
12 sailors
8 chasseurs
1 cook
1 waiter
2 maids

DAHABIAH 1

Alexine
Nanny R.
1 reis
1 pilot
10 soldiers
12 sailors
1 carpenter

At that point she broke off. They had still to find a dragoman. Mr Shepheard had suggested a man, half Arab and half Greek, but the French minister had warned them against him: he was a drunk and a pilferer of any small objects left lying around. Mahfouz had said that he knew of an ideal candidate, someone called Osman Aga, but he had still to return from escorting two effete and demanding young Americans, heirs to fortunes almost as large as Alexine's, up the Nile to Luxor.

At first Harriet had been happy to be, as she saw it, chief of staff to Alexine's commander. But now all these trivial arrangements weighed on her. If only Alexine would stop exploring the city either on the horse that she had insisted on buying or in the rented carriage! If only Addy would stop accepting every invitation sent to her, and endlessly reading all those novels!

Eventually Harriet decided that she had had enough for a day. The sun was sinking, the air was beginning to cool. She would do what she was constantly telling Alexine not to do: go out for a walk on her own.

Once she was down in the hot, smelly, overcrowded street, she regretted her decision. But obstinately she pressed on. 'Madame! Madame! Here! Over here! Real bargain! Please! Come!' On all sides the voices assailed her, in French, in English, even in German. From time to time someone particularly importunate would grab at her arm or her dress. Her parasol, bobbing above the heads of the crowd, made her particularly conspicuous.

She was halted by a strong smell of scent. Ranged on a table outside a timber shack, there were innumerable bottles of every shape and size. 'Yes, madame, yes!' a bald man rushed out from the shack to greet her in French. 'Try, madame, try! Come, come!' He picked up a bottle, pulled out its stopper, and then held it under her nose. She jerked her head away. There was something disgusting about the smell, so sickly and penetrating. Essence of vomit, she thought. She hurried on, the man pursuing her, bottle in hand.

At another stall, a man was selling caged birds. The sun glinting on their brilliant plumage might have been reflected off glass, so dazzling was it. Seeing this foreign woman, a potential purchaser, the man grinned at her, revealing a mouth almost empty of teeth, and then put a hand to one of the cages to open it. At once, with a creak of wings, a green and yellow bird poised itself for flight and, with disconcerting clumsiness, wheeled up into the air and landed in the branches of a dusty tree. Harriet looked up at it, both rejoicing in its freedom and wondering why the man had let it loose. Then she saw the slim, red cord fastened round one of the bird's legs, to tether it to the wicker-work cage. Disappointment and anger overwhelmed her and she at once turned away.

It was at that moment that she saw the two figures in black: the woman, head lowered, back humped, and the man as erect as a soldier on parade. Her arm was linked in his. It was Nanny Rose and Daan. They might have been mistaken for some elderly married couple who had escaped to Cairo from Northern Europe for their health. Harriet followed behind them, adapting her pace to the leisurely one set by Nanny Rose.

The pair eventually halted at a stall selling what were clearly fake antiques. Ignoring the shopkeeper, they examined inexpertly manufactured object after object, from time to time setting one aside. Daan would pass an object to her or she to him. They would then nod in agreement or one of them would shake a head. Finally, they began their bargaining for the dozen or so pieces that they had singled out. Harriet continued to watch them from under the shade of the tree in which the tethered bird had alighted. The bargaining went on for a long, long time. They were surprisingly persistent. A sum having been finally agreed, the shop owner produced an osier basket and, having first wrapped each object in scraps of newspaper, placed one after another carefully in it. 'Well, that was a good day's work,' Harriet heard Daan say, as he hefted the basket.

She decided to reveal herself. 'Nanny Rose!'

'Oh, it's you, madam!' Nanny Rose cried it out not in pleasure, but dismay.

Daan turned and bowed, the basket in one hand.

'What a lot you've been buying!'

Nanny Rose became flustered. 'Just some souvenirs, madam. Presents for when we get home. Daan came out with me to help me. I could never have managed on my own.'

'Are you going back to the hotel now?'

The two looked at each other, undecided. Then Nanny Rose said: 'Yes, I think so, madam. Yes.'

The three walked back in silence, Harriet in the middle.

ᔈ

It was two days later that the mystery of the purchases was solved.

At breakfast, which she was eating late and therefore alone, Addy fell into conversation with a sunny young Swedish couple, in Cairo on their honeymoon. At one point, they told her of their extraordinary good fortune. They had wanted to take back with them some archaeological souvenirs of their visit, but had feared that they would be unable to discriminate between what was genuine and what was fake. By a happy chance, they had run into this dear old man and his wife in the lobby and had got into conversation with them. The man spoke little of any language other than Dutch, but the woman's English was excellent. He was engaged in some sort of archaeological work and was, they discovered, selling some of his finds after having had a large sum of money stolen from him in the street. They had acquired from him three quite beautiful objects for what they were sure was a knock-down price. Addy must see them for herself.

When Addy had told Harriet and Alexine the story, she asked: 'Do you think that we should do anything about it?'

'*Do* anything?' Alexine laughed. 'No, of course not. Good luck to them. They're only doing what everyone does in this place – turning a dishonest penny.'

'But what about the couple?'

'If they can afford a honeymoon in Cairo, then they can afford to be cheated.'

'Have you no sense of morality?' Harriet asked, in pretended shock.

'None at all.'

Then all three women laughed.

∽

'You know, we're just racing through money.'

'Are we?' Alexine was indifferent, as she turned over the pages of the French-language Cairo newspaper.

'I'm being serious. In the past seven weeks, the Bank of Egypt has given us two hundred pounds in gold, ninety pounds in silver dollars, a banker's note for another two hundred to pay for the steamer, and a credit of five hundred pounds more.' Harriet looked down at the ledger open before her. 'We have to pay ten percent – ten percent! – on any credit.'

'Oh, please! This is all so boring.'

'Boring or not – we have to think about these things. I've had to write to Glyn's for another two thousand pounds. And, oh yes' – once again she consulted the ledger – 'the bank in The Hague is in the process of transferring ten thousand florins.'

'Good.' Again Alexine laughed.

'That horse cost far too much. Seventy pounds! I ask you!'

'It's an Arab, mama.'

'Well, if you have an Arab, do you really need a white donkey as well?'

'That's for the trip.'

Harriet sighed and pushed the ledger away from her.

'Your father wanted only to make money, and you want only to spend it.'

Alexine went over to the desk and bent down to kiss Harriet on the cheek.

'You only live once,' she said.

'No doubt. And you're going to be the death of me.'

4 ADDY LAY OUT IN A HAMMOCK in a shady corner of the deck. Pince-nez low on her nose, she was reading *Cousine Bette* for the third time.

'Doesn't that French provincial world seem terribly far away?' Harriet had asked her.

'Yes, terribly. I never thought that such a world – small, ingrown, and riddled with envy and hate – would seem preferable to the one in which I was living.'

'Oh, we're not having so bad a time. It's fun.'

The wind had changed direction and, instead of being cool, was now hot. That morning Nanny Rose had carefully washed Addy's hair and curled it for her, but already it felt sticky and limp. From time to time she pressed a handkerchief to her forehead, her cheeks, or the side of her neck. From below, in the saloon, she could hear Harriet at the piano. 'It's surprisingly good,' Harriet had said, running her hands up and down the keys in one fluent arpeggio after another, when two huge, sweating, grunting Egyptians had carried it aboard and placed it where, after a lot of deliberation, she had decided that it should go. The endless noise from the crowds on the banks and from the servants and soldiers not merely on the steamer but on the two dahabias towed behind, was bad enough without that endless strumming. How was one expected to concentrate?

Now, with a veering of the wind, Addy became increasingly aware of the smoke blown towards her from the monotonously thumping engine. She coughed, handkerchief to mouth, and then tasted the sulphur on her tongue. With an exclamation of annoyance she lowered her long, narrow feet in their morocco slippers down on to the deck and swung herself out of the hammock. There was nothing for it. She would have to go below, to read on her berth.

At that moment, with a series of judders and a bump, the steamer moved alongside a rickety jetty. Why were they stopping yet again? It was pointless to ask. When they did so, their handsome, vain young Nubian janizary, Osman Aga, would strike yet another of his heroic poses, arms crossed over massive chest or heavily jewelled hand resting on one of the three revolvers that he carried at his slim waist, and would give a variety of reasons: they had to take aboard fresh provisions for the crew; one of the dahabiahs was leaking; the engine had developed some defect; someone sick must be put ashore; they had to bake more bread; two servants had been left behind at their last port of call.

Having finished his weeks of service with the two Americans, Osman had been delighted to take on the three women at a salary proposed by Mahfouz, who of course received a percentage of it, even higher than that exacted from his previous employers. Addy led the others in making fun of his conceit; but, as she remarked, he had so much to be conceited about – his physique, his excellent English and French, his aquiline nose, and above all a skin, the colour of a ripe aubergine, that glowed with health.

On her way down to her cabin, Addy passed Alexine, who was leaning over the taffrail, her hair hanging untidily loose down the back of one of those ridiculous and embarrassing garments made for her in Cairo, her feet bare. Why did the girl have to let all standards slip? Not even a self-respecting Egyptian woman would go around like that.

Crowding the jetty were a host of small boys, all totally naked. They were calling out to Alexine, and she was shouting back to them. Since their Arabic was so different from hers, misunderstandings were clearly taking place. When they did, laughter rang out.

At the prompting of one of the boys, Alexine reached into the bag, purchased in one of the Cairo bazaars, that she wore slung around her neck and brought out some coins. She flicked one into the water and at once all the boys flung themselves off the jetty. For a moment, Addy saw the skinny, lithe bodies twisting and turning, like a shoal of giant fish. Then they vanished, so murkily brown was the water. Finally, one emerged, a silver dollar glinting between his teeth. A dollar! Was Alexine crazy? Now all the boys, the water dripping off them, began to shout out for more, more, more. Alexine placed another coin between forefinger and thumb and flicked it outward. Again there was that seething shoal of human fish, just below the iridescent surface of the water.

Addy approached Alexine from behind, as she still leaned over the taffrail. 'Throwing money away once again?'

Alexine turned to face her. Then, saying nothing, she turned away.

The two women had already begun to get on each other's nerves.

∽

When not playing the piano, working at her ledgers or, with the assistance of Daan, Nanny Rose and a reluctant Osman, supervising the domestic staff, Harriet was happy merely to sit out on the deck, usually at a distance from Addy and Alexine, and watch the sometimes changing but usually unvarying scene. When passengers on other dahabiahs, amazed by the size of their party, shouted out their greetings, it always irritated her. But out of a natural courtesy, she would greet them in return, wave, and even go to the rail for the conversation that they so obviously wanted.

These slow, uneventful days, when the chief excitements were the temporary disappearance during a walk ashore of one of the dogs in pursuit of a pariah bitch on heat, a quarrel with knives drawn but never actually used between two of the soldiers, and the firing off of a gun in warning by a Russian boat whenever it passed or was passed, ended when they arrived at Aswan. Their party alone was proceeding up the cataracts. The others, daunted by the expense of hiring scores of men to tow their boats for four miles up and up over a forest of boulders sticking out of the churning, frothing water, were turning back.

Addy retreated with Nanny Rose to the newly opened hotel in Aswan as soon as they had arrived at the cataracts.

'Well, it's a relief to be back in civilization again!' she exclaimed, as she began to remove her clothes, preparatory to taking a bath.

'Civilization, madam! Do you call this civilization? Just take a look under that bed. It looks as though there'd been a duststorm.' Nanny Rose bustled over to the bell-pull and tugged on it, even though she had already ordered a maid to bring water for the tub. 'Someone will have to see to that.'

'Well, I don't want anyone to see to it until I've had my bath.'

Harriet, accompanied by Daan, Osman Aga and three of the Russian tourists, all men and all painters, who were not leaving until the next day, first scrupulously supervised the unloading of most of the luggage and the animals to lighten the boats – she had been warned of frequent thefts – and then, as the day began to wane, led the party to a cluster of jagged rocks, from which they could watch the arduous passage. Alexine, despite Harriet's protests, had insisted on remaining on board with Flopsy and the crew.

'I can see how the pyramids got themselves built,' one of the Russians remarked, as the near-naked men, straining, sweating, shouting, grimacing and constantly drenched with spray, hauled on the tow-ropes.

'Oh, I do hope my daughter will be safe.'

'Your daughter is the sort of person who can survive anything,' the Russian said. He had had an argument with Alexine about the dogs, telling her that it was cruel to confine them to a boat. Refusing to be cowed, she had at once retaliated that the Russian boat looked filthy and that it was even more cruel to confine anyone human to it.

When night fell with extraordinary abruptness, only the first of the four cataracts had so far been negotiated. Once more aboard the steamer, Harriet slept fitfully, seeming still to hear the thunder of the water, the shouts of the men, and the shrill dissonance of the innumerable birds startled by so much unaccustomed activity. Alexine declined to sleep, sitting up on deck with Flopsy in her lap while she talked to Osman, now in Arabic, now in English and now in French.

Aroused yet again by their voices above her cabin, Harriet descended from her bunk and made her stiff, weary way up on deck.

'Oughtn't you to try to get some sleep?'

It had particularly irritated her that, at her approach, Osman should have bared his teeth, gleaming in the moonlight, in an impudent grin; and now it irritated her even more to see, from close quarters, that he had stripped off most of his clothes, no doubt because it was a night of exceptional heat and humidity for that time of year.

'Oh, no, mama! I couldn't possibly sleep after all that excitement. There were times when I really thought we were about to capsize.'

'I was burned to a cinder on those rocks.'

'You should have gone to the hotel with Aunt Addy and Nanny Rose.'

'No. I had so much to see to here.' Harriet turned her head aside, frowning. Then, all at once, her bad humour evaporated. 'It was worth it. Quite extraordinary.' She repeated what the Russian had remarked about the Pyramids.

'Yes, those poor men! I heard that the last time they dragged that steamer up the cataracts two of them drowned.'

'Do you remember the Schaffhausen? And the fjords? They were nothing compared to this.'

Harriet moved off along the deck, sniffing the smoke from Osman's cigarette. Then she paused. From the dahabia immediately behind the steamer, she could hear someone singing. A man or a woman? From the voice, high-pitched and nasal, it was impossible to say. She imagined some song of love and loss. Tomorrow she would try to pick out the melody on the piano. She hummed it over to herself, as a sudden gust of wind, surprisingly cool, wafted through the hair hanging down her back to her waist. She and Addy had always been proud of their hair. But, since she had arrived in Africa, hers had become increasingly thin and grey.

∽

At Korosko, the party learned that the waters of the river were now so unusually low that they would either have to wait, perhaps for many weeks, or else abandon the steamer and the dahabias and make their way by land across the great U-bend of the Nile to rejoin the river again at Abu Hamad.

Addy became almost hysterical at the news. 'But why did no one warn us of this before? Why? Why?'

'Because no one knew.' Alexine struggled to conceal her growing exasperation with her aunt.

'Well, why didn't they know? Why? Why?'

Harriet was as appalled by the prospect as her sister. But, unlike her, she had not forgotten the stoicism inculcated in them in their youth by their stern father and their even sterner mother. Wearily, with aching head and eyes unaccountably red and itching, pad of paper and pencil at the ready, she once more made an inventory of the immense quantities of provisions that, over the next two days, had to be unloaded from the boats and then loaded on to camels.

During that interminable process, she constantly watched, ticking off item after item, as all these things, followed by innumerable trunks, hatboxes and packing-cases, were brought down the gangway, to be first stacked as she directed and then covered in tarpaulin. The men groaned more loudly than ever when they had to lift the piano and the two tea-chests containing Addy's library of books.

On the first night away from the steamer, seated in a tent with a lamp flickering beside, Harriet again laboured at her notes, while, at the farthest end of the encampment, the others watched the performance of some clumsy, barely pubescent dancing girls from the nearby town. She wrote:

> Dogs to be carried in panniers.
> Ditto sheep, fowls, turkeys (for consumption on
>   journey).
> Daan on donkey.
> A, NR and self on camels.
> Water. How many goatskins? Consult Osman Aga.

She put a hand to her throbbing forehead. There was too much to remember. What else? What else?

Frantically, she riffled through the pages of the ledger, one after another covered with her handwriting, until, at long last, she found a clean one. Again she took up the pen.

> 102 camels
> 6 guides
> 30 camelmen

∽

'Why don't you try to get some sleep? It's a long journey tomorrow.' It was Nanny Rose, dressed in her customary widow's cap and thick black dress. She had lost weight on the journey, her pocked cheeks fallen in and the dress sagging on her.

'It's all too big, too big for me!' Harriet cried out in despair. 'All these people, all these animals depending on us – not just for their food and their safety but for their lives. And the camels! How are we to find more camels? I'm not a Napoleon. I leave that to Alexine. I'm just an ordinary woman.'

Nanny Rose waddled up to her. She put her hand on her shoulder. Then she did something that she would never have done in The Hague: she bent her crooked body forward and put both arms around Harriet, from behind, and laid her cheek against hers. She might have been comforting Alexine when she was young.

'You're not an ordinary woman, dear. You're an extraordinary one. Don't worry about it. It'll all work out. You'll see. We'll be fine. Yes, yes! I'm sure of it.'

Impulsively Harriet swivelled round in her chair and now put her own arm around Nanny Rose's neck. 'Oh, Nanny, Nanny! What would I do without you?'

'I expect you'd get on much as you do now,' Nanny Rose replied drily. She released herself and made to leave the tent. 'Well, goodnight, madam. If you need me, I'm just in the next tent, as you know.'

Harriet got up from the chair, fetched a bottle of laudanum from her medicine case and poured some drops into a glass, which she then filled with water from a carafe. The water looked cloudy and had a salty taste to it. She thought of the sparkling, clean water of the spring at Bled with a sudden longing and despair. Then she stretched herself out on the narrow camp bed and tried to sleep. Somewhere, far off, one of the dogs was howling.

Eventually she fell asleep but only for a brief time. She fell asleep again, woke again. When she awoke, it was always to a throbbing of her head and to a feeling that every bone in her body was simultaneously aching and shaking.

'Mabel!' She heard the whisper between one dream and another.

Mabel? Who was Mabel? Of course. That was Nanny Rose's Christian name.

'Mabel!' The name was repeated, with greater urgency. She recognized the voice. It was Daan's.

Why should he want Nanny Rose at this hour? And why should he be calling her by the Christian name that no one ever used?

Head propped on elbow, she listened intently for more. But she heard nothing. Eventually she fell asleep again.

5 'NO, I REFUSE, I ABSOLUTELY REFUSE to travel on one of those brutes.'

Wrapped in white muslin, so that only her eyes and nose were visible, a wide-brimmed straw hat tied under her chin, Addy stood beside the camel, a book in one hand, while the other held the lead of her favourite dog, a tiny white Spitz called Mister. The dog was scratching himself, indifferent to what was going on.

'Well, there's nothing else on which you can travel,' Alexine said in the sharp tone that she now constantly used to her aunt. 'Unless you'd like to have the donkey. You can't possibly walk.'

'But how am I to stay up there? And it might bite me. They say camels bite. And the bite can be poisonous.'

The argument prolonged itself. 'Well, I'm going to get up on one, willy nilly,' Nanny Rose proclaimed; but Addy remained unpersuaded even by that.

'I can't, can't, can't!'

'Well, in that case you'd better return to Cairo.'

'How can I do that? The boats have all gone. And anyway what would I do there?'

'Well, you'd just have to wait for us, wouldn't you?'

It was Daan who eventually proposed a solution. Would it not be possible to make a, well, a kind of bed on top of the camel with cushions and a mattress? Everyone was dubious, until Osman began to issue commands for this to be done. Soon the camelmen were laughing among themselves as they busied themselves with first hoisting up the horsehair mattress and then strapping it with ropes to the camel. They had never before seen anything so odd.

'And how am I suppose to get *up*?' Addy demanded, when the cushions had also been secured.

'They'll lift you,' Alexine said.

'Who are going to lift me?'

'The camelmen. You're far too heavy for me.'

'Couldn't Daan and Nanny Rose lift me?'

'You're far too heavy for them.'

Addy let out a shrill scream as the men hoisted her aloft. Then, as she settled herself, she shouted down: 'It's really not at all bad. Can you pass me up my book? Oh, and Mister!'

After innumerable false starts – one of the dogs jumped out of his pannier and raced off into some scrub, a packing-case had not been properly loaded and fell off a camel spilling its contents, Addy demanded some water – they finally got moving. Harriet and Nanny Rose were also each on a camel, with a camel boy striding out beside it. Daan was on the white donkey, Alexine on the Arab. Osman also rode.

∽

Alexine was amazed by the variety of the countryside through which their huge caravan wound its way for days and days on end. At one point, as they proceeded up a grass road between low rocks, she called out to her mother: 'We might be in Scotland! It's so green, green! This isn't a desert! Why do they call it a desert?' Only a few hours later, she was overawed by the distant mountains which, in the clear light of evening, suddenly rose up before them.

The next day, they reached the foothills of these mountains and took the path that Osman indicated, through a narrow cleft. The white sand of the path shone with fragments of marble and granite; the rock face on either side was streaked with what looked like rusty iron. Later, as they encamped, the moonlight seemed to have dusted everything with snow.

'Oh, I'm so stiff!' Addy groaned. 'That camel! It's like travelling on the high seas. And it stinks!'

They all laughed. Addy looked hurt. Then she too began to laugh.

∽

The next morning, Addy had succumbed to a violent diarrhoea. Time after time she had to be helped down from the camel and hoisted up again. Desolately she would totter off to where some bushes or rocks provided cover for her. At first, Daan had attempted to escort her but she had angrily waved him away. On his donkey, he had ridden with his trouser legs rolled up, and in consequence his calves were now raw from sunburn. Harriet noticed how solicitous he was for Nanny Rose, far more than for Alexine, Addy or herself.

Alexine briskly dosed Addy with laudanum. She had with her a German medical encyclopaedia recommended to her, so long ago it now seemed, by Colonel Scott in Bled. It described laudanum as a panacea for tropical illnesses. As a result of the massive doses pressed on her, Addy spent most of the time sleeping, when not yet again being helped down from the camel and tottering out of sight.

One evening, Addy was particularly fractious over dinner. 'When is this ghastly journey to end? When, when? I'm worn out. It's going to be the death of me.' She turned on Alexine. 'Why on earth did you persuade me to come?'

Alexine controlled herself with difficulty and said nothing.

'When it's all over, you'll be pleased and proud to have done it,' Harriet said placatingly.

On the following morning Addy had a high fever. She lay out on her camp bed, her shift, drenched in sweat, clinging to her body. She alternated between restlessly twisting and turning from side to side, and lying totally motionless, eyes closed. From time to time, supported by Harriet or Nanny Rose, she would stagger to the commode which had been placed, surrounded by wicker screens, near to her tent. It was the task of one of the Egyptian servants repeatedly to carry its contents to a pit dug some distance from the encampment. Clearly, Harriet said, they would all have to wait to continue their journey until she was better.

Alexine was consumed by impatience at the delay. Because of the size of their party and the time that it took to set up camp each night and then to strike it each morning, they were merely inching their way insect-like to their destination, whereas the parties of Arabs who from time to time rode triumphantly past them, were galloping to theirs. She had until now enjoyed the grandeur and luxury of their progress, so much envied by the other foreign travellers on the Nile. But now she began to rage inwardly against this ridiculous, constantly hampering superfluity of companions, servants, animals, tents, furniture, and provisions.

On the second morning, three of the soldiers were found to have deserted. They came from a settlement only a few miles away and Osman said that they must have decided to make for their homes rather than continue with a journey far more arduous and lengthy than they had expected. On hearing a rumour from one of the Egyptian maids that, before going, they had pilfered some provisions, Harriet, inventory in hand, at once began to carry out a check. But, stacked as they were, it was impossible to do so properly. She ordered the tarpaulin to be pulled off a pile of bags of flour and sugar, and then began laboriously to count them. As the sun beat down on her, she began to feel nauseous and dizzy.

Alexine, followed by Flopsy, whom she had yet again been combing for the fleas that devoured all the animals, came up: 'What are you doing?'

Harriet explained.

'But what's the point?'

'Well, I must see what's missing. Mustn't I?'

Alexine was stricken with the pathos of this dumpy, middle-aged woman, strands of hair sticking to her flushed neck and forehead, stooping to count sacks in the glare of the midday sun.

'Why? Why must you?'

'If things get stolen . . .'

'So? They get stolen.'

'But they may have taken things vital to us.'

'With luck, we can replace them in Khartoum.'

'If we ever get there.'

'Of course we'll get there.' Alexine spoke with growing irritation. 'What was the guard doing? I told Osman that there must always be a guard.'

'Sleeping, I suppose.'

'Oh, if only one could rely on someone!'

'You can rely on me. Do stop all this fussing and complaining!'

Then, remorseful, Alexine rushed over to her mother and put her arms around her. 'Don't become discouraged now. Darling! Please! You've been such a rock to us all. Without you, we'd never have got even as far as this. Please!'

She began to coax her mother to the largest of the tents, used as a makeshift living-room. 'Sit down. I'm going to get you some water. Sit!' Her voice ceased to be tender and acquired an imperious sharpness. She pointed to a chair. She might have been commanding one of the dogs.

Sipping at the water, Harriet said: 'You haven't been to see Addy.'

'Oh, Addy!'

'Be patient with her, darling. It's hardly her fault that she's holding us up. I'm terribly worried about her. There's blood in her stool.'

Alexine, who was now squatting on a rolled-up carpet, put a hand up over her eyes. 'Oh, please! Spare me the details!' Never ill herself, she shrank even from talk of illness.

'Look in on her. She's devoted to you.'

'I'll see.'

Alexine did not at once go to Addy's tent. Instead, as soon as the heat of the afternoon was beginning to cool, she took herself off, with all five of the dogs, in search of plants. Before leaving The Hague, she had begun to study botany, in addition to Arabic, and she had subsequently included some books on the subject in Addy's library. Harriet had come to share this interest, tenderly pressing and then mounting each exotic flower, but on this occasion, wishing to be alone, Alexine did not ask her to accompany her.

The sun was already plunging towards the horizon when she got back. Well, she'd better get it over with. Flopsy faithfully trailing with lolling tongue behind her, she approached Addy's tent. At once Mister set up a shrill yapping. 'Quiet! Quiet! Stop that!' she could hear Nanny Rose shout.

Alexine raised the tent-flap and went in. At the sight of her, the Spitz at once fell silent and began to wag his tail. Since it was she who always insisted on feeding and exercising the dogs, they looked on her as their mistress. Nanny Rose got to her feet and tiptoed over. Addy lay out, eyes shut, her mouth twisted at one corner, and a hand resting up against a flushed cheek. 'She's been delirious, poor darling,' she whispered. 'Saying the oddest things. One can't reason with her.'

Alexine gave a small, involuntary shudder. Since they had arrived in Egypt, she had grown used to nauseating smells; but this was particularly horrible, even though it was overlaid by the clean pungency of the eau-de-Cologne that Nanny Rose had been liberally splashing over the damp sheets and pillows and, from time to time, patting on to Addy's sweating forehead and neck. She edged towards the bed.

'Take my chair.'

'No, I'm all right standing.'

'Take it, dear.' Nanny Rose was insistent. The poor girl looked as if she were about to faint, she thought.

Alexine sank on to the chair and then remained motionless for several seconds, staring intently at Addy, as though willing her to get off the bed and walk.

'She hasn't eaten a thing for more than twenty-four hours. She just drinks glass after glass of water.'

'That's probably best.'

Addy's eyes opened. They squinted up at Alexine with an extraordinary intensity. With the hands that Nanny Rose manicured for her with so much care and skill, she jerked the sheet up from her midriff to the tip of her chin, as though in inadequate protection against this intruder.

'Alexine.' She croaked the word, with no welcome, much less pleasure.

'How are you?'

'Dying.'

'Don't be silly. Of course you're not dying. You're going to be perfectly well in a day or two. Are you taking that Dr James's mixture? And the laudanum?'

The eyes still squinted up at her, with a dazed malevolence.

Nanny Rose answered: 'Yes, dear. I've been following your instructions to the letter.'

'We all follow your instructions.' Addy spoke again from the bed. 'What are you?'

'What am I? What do you mean? I'm your niece.'

Addy closed her eyes. Mouth open, she began to breathe stertorously.

Nanny Rose touched Alexine's shoulder. 'Don't pay any attention. She doesn't know what she's saying. She's delirious. She's been talking nonsense to me off and on for most of the day.'

Alexine leaned forward and attempted to take one of Addy's hands in hers. But with a whimper Addy jerked it away. Nanny Rose picked up the bottle of eau-de-Cologne and shook some of it on to the handkerchief that she had already used for this purpose. She stooped and patted Addy's forehead with it.

Addy opened her eyes and smiled at Nanny Rose in gratitude. Then the eyes swivelled, her gaze settled on Alexine. 'Did Nanny tell you about it? Did you go and look?'

'Tell me about what?'

'Go and look! Look! The snake.'

'Snake?'

Nanny Rose shook her head at Alexine. 'Pay no attention,' she whispered. 'It's the fever. That's all. There's no snake.' Nanny Rose leaned over Addy. 'There's no snake. I looked, I got Daan to look. No snake,' she repeated, loudly now, separating the two words.

'It was in the commode. I saw it. This snake. Huge. Shiny. Yellow. With red, red patches. I saw it.' Her face screwed up. She began to whimper. 'I saw it. Why don't you believe me? I saw it, saw it!'

Nanny Rose looked down at Addy and Addy in turn looked up at her, mouth open and brows puckered in a frown.

Again there was a silence. Then, eyes closed, Addy twisted her head convulsively from side to side. She began to mutter. What was she saying? Half of Alexine did not wish to know, the other half was morbidly avid to do so. 'Why do we always do what you want? Why, why?' Again the eyes opened. She stared up at Alexine. 'Have you put a spell on us? Is that it? Even Nanny, even poor old Daan? Is it?' She rolled her body away and once more drew the sweat-saturated sheet up to her chin. Alexine could still hear her muttering: 'You're a witch. That's what you are. The witch who always gets what she wants.' At that she relapsed, eyes once more shut, into immobility and silence.

Alexine forced herself to sit on and on, though she longed to get away into the fresh, dry air, out of this miasma. At a gesture from her, Nanny Rose brought up a camp stool. She was about to lower herself on to it when Alexine insisted on herself taking the stool, so that Nanny Rose could once more have the chair in which she had been sitting. 'No, no,' Nanny Rose protested, but Alexine got her way. *She got her way*. She thought about that: I always get my way. Perhaps that was dangerous not merely for others but also for herself? She forced herself once again to take Addy's hand and to hold it in hers. This time, still apparently sleeping, Addy made no attempt to withdraw it.

The hand grew hotter and hotter and stickier and stickier in her grasp. Then she saw the large beads of sweat pricking through the tall, narrow body, and drenching the sheets. How could one person contain so much fluid? Nanny Rose reached for a cloth and, pulling back the top sheet and jerking up the shift beneath it, began to mop Addy's small, pointed breasts – they were like those of a pubescent girl, Alexine thought, now seeing them for the first time – and belly. 'This must be the fever breaking,' Nanny Rose said. 'Poor dear. Poor, poor dear.'

Suddenly Harriet appeared. 'Oh, here you are!' she greeted Alexine. 'Do you know – I've just discovered – those scoundrels made off with three tins of biscuits. They can't have eaten a biscuit in their whole lives.'

'Please, mama, please. Can't you see . . . ?'

Now Harriet approached the bed, full of remorse. She stared down. She almost said: 'She's dying.' Tears began to gather in her eyes.

'It's all right, madam. I think it's all right. One of my little ones – it was just like this when the fever broke.'

∽

The next day Addy was better, sitting up in bed, propped on pillows, to continue with her reading, and even taking some of the gruel that Nanny Rose had prepared for her and now, with tender caution, spooned into her mouth. She seemed to have little recollection of her illness and never again mentioned the snake.

Alexine's restlessness intensified. She wanted to get moving, push on. Once again she went for a walk accompanied by only the dogs, and once again she stooped to examine the tiny, brilliant flowers, embedded in the crevices of rocks or scattered in the undergrowth on either side of the zigzag pathway.

At one moment, silhouetted against the dark blue sky on a yellow-white rock streaked with brown and orange that soared up like a huge decaying molar, she was delighted to see a gazelle motionless, head raised. In a moment, however, the dogs had raced off, barking wildly, in futile pursuit of it. Leaping sideways and away, it was at once lost to sight.

Later, an ancient, bearded man had leapt towards her from rock to rock. White hair flowing to his emaciated shoulders and stick-like legs covered in ulcers, he had some of the uninhibited, graceful agility of the gazelle. The dogs barked and snarled at him, teeth bared. But he paid no attention either to them or to her, continuing his rapid progress downward, the wind and his precipitate descent making his long white hair swirl like foam about him.

After he had passed her, Alexine turned round to follow his progress. But in what seemed a moment, he had vanished behind a particularly tall rock, never to reappear. She felt an unease far more intense than she would have felt had he accosted her. Who was he? Where was he going? Where had he come from? He was carrying nothing, he was almost naked. Had he been a delusion, like Addy's snake in the commode?

175

She began to hasten back to the camp, whistling or calling to the dogs if they attempted to stray.

∽

Late that afternoon Osman asked Alexine whether she would like to see something.

'See something? See what?'

He smiled. 'A market. A market unlike any you have seen. Interesting. Yes? Why not? Few white people see such a market. Not far.' He made a wide gesture, the full sleeve falling away from his muscular, coal-black arm, to indicate that the market took place behind a low range of hills to their left.

'All right.' She was bored, she was restless. Yes, why not? Perhaps that mysterious old man had been going to this same market. 'Let's go.'

'But tell no one else – not mama, not auntie.'

She laughed. 'I don't think either of them is in any state to come with us.'

They rode out side by side. Conversation between them was always sporadic, each talking, either in Arabic or in English, only when there was something that needed to be said. On this occasion both of them were silent.

Seeing them leaving the camp, Nanny Rose had said to Daan, 'I don't think she should go off with him alone. Anything could happen. I don't trust him. A rogue.' Daan had then laughed, as, seated on one of Addy's crates of books, he dabbed camomile on to his still inflamed calves. 'Oh, that one can look after herself. Don't you worry!'

Alexine rarely felt tired but she did now. The wait to resume their journey had been so long, and waiting to do something, she told herself, was often more exhausting than actually doing it. She felt like one of the plants that, picked on her walks, drooped, as though already dead, in the ferocious midday heat. Perhaps, like them, she would revive when the sun began to sink.

'Look!' Osman roused her from a near-sleep, pointing at a wide swathe in the sand beside them. She peered at it. It was as though someone with a huge flail had swept it across the low dune in an arc. 'Snake!' he said, and laughed. He let go of his reins and extended his arms to their full extent. 'Big, big. Swallow you, swallow all of you, and then, slow, slow, you disappear.' Again he laughed. A boa constrictor? That must be what he meant.

Suddenly, as they passed through another cleft between two jagged rocks covered in a lichen emerald in some places and so brown in others that it appeared to be dead, Alexine saw a green, grassy expanse ahead of them. 'An oasis!' she cried out.

Osman nodded. 'Oasis.' He grinned.

'Why didn't we come here to camp?'

He shook his head. 'Not good.'

'Why not good?'

Again he grinned, again shook his head.

Totally naked children soon surrounded them, appearing from nowhere, so it seemed. They ran along beside the two horses, holding out skinny, often ulcerated arms and shouting. Alexine searched in her saddle-bag and scattered a handful of coins. The children rushed to pick them up, pushing and even hitting and kicking out at each other. Was there nowhere on this continent that people did not fight over money? Alexine wondered. Then she reminded herself that, albeit often more formally and gracefully, people fought over money everywhere in the world.

They were approaching a village, its neat straw beehive huts set out in orderly rows, with an oval pool in the foreground surrounded by grazing buffaloes, palm-trees and a plant, its bulky stems surmounted by feathery, amazingly delicate foliage; she had learned from an illustration in one of her botanical books that the plant was ambatch. Osman now explained to her that the people used its spongy wood to make their narrow boats.

When they were some hundred yards from the village, shots rang out, the sound ricocheting back and forth among the surrounding hills and causing Alexine's Arab to rear repeatedly, so that, had she been riding side-saddle, she would certainly have been thrown. Were they about to be killed? As she struggled to control the horse she felt, amazingly, no terror at the prospect.

Osman's horse, a bay, had done no more than curvet from side to side. Now he pulled out two revolvers from his belt and raising one in each hand, fired them repeatedly up into the sky. He smiled at her, then called out: 'No worry, no worry! Greeting!'

A straggling group of some dozen or so soldiers emerged, their uniforms stained and ragged. Some of them carried antiquated rifles or pistols, some merely cudgels or sticks. Two or three wore red, gold-braided tarbooshes. All were barefoot, their toes widely splayed. At first, since she was riding astride and had covered most of her face with a white linen scarf to protect it from the sand-laden wind, they assumed Alexine to be both an Arab and a man. But then, when she began to speak English to Osman, they realized their error and at once crowded round her horse, pointing at her, while jabbering excitedly. One of them even put out a hand to touch her leg in its stirrup, only hurriedly to withdraw it, as though it had been burned by the contact. His companions all burst into laughter.

Osman greeted the soldiers and they waved their weapons in the air and shouted their greetings back.

Surrounded by this escort, they trotted up to a long, low-lying thatched house, with a wattle fence around it. Standing in the doorway was a tall Arab, Mohammed Kher, a fly-whisk in one hand and an expression of disdain on his face. Osman at once jumped off his horse and, handing the reins to one of the entourage, rushed up to Kher to enfold him in an extravagant embrace. A vivacious conversation followed, with a lot of slapping of backs and laughter. Alexine slipped off her horse but remained with it. When Osman at last indicated her presence, Kher at first merely peered at her, with a frown and a pursing of the lips. He later told Osman that she was the first white woman ever to have visited the place. He had also added (though Osman did not also report this to Alexine) that she was far too narrow-hipped and flat-chested to be in the least attractive.

Having peered at her from afar, Kher then strode over and, circling her, haughtily examined her, as though he were wondering whether to purchase an inferior mare or cow. Then he nodded and returned to Osman. The two men once again took up their conversation, but this time the tone was clearly serious.

Having tethered her horse to a tree, Alexine went and sat down on a rickety bamboo stool that stood by itself, as though abandoned, among recently watered beds of tomato and aubergine plants. The flies constantly settling on her arms and on her lips and even in her nostrils, she waited with ebbing patience.

Osman approached her. 'He wants money,' he said in English.

'Money? What for? Does anyone in this country not want money?'

He laughed. 'Everyone wants money. He wants money if you wish to see market.'

'What's so special about the market?'

'You will see.'

'How much money?'

He hesitated. Then he named a sum. She knew that the sum was larger than that demanded by Mohammed Kher, but by now she no longer felt any resentment when people whom she thought that she trusted played such tricks on her.

'I haven't got that sort of money with me.'

'How much money?'

She told him.

He shook his head. Then, in a moment of inspiration, he pointed at the bracelet on her wrist. It was one that, so many years before, Adolph had given her after they had made love for the first time in the squalid *garçonnière*. 'That,' he said. 'Give that. Good.'

'Oh, no!'

'Yes, yes.' He was insistent, nodding his fine head. He put out a hand and touched it. 'Gold. Diamonds. Good.'

Suddenly, on a whim, she wanted to be rid of the bracelet, just as, still intermittently thinking of him against her will, she wanted to be rid of Adolph's memory. She began to unfasten the bracelet. 'All right.'

He took the bracelet and, holding it out ahead of him, returned to Mohammad Kher. Kher was delighted with the gift, but at first he put on a half-hearted show of not being so, frowning, shaking his head and refusing to take it from Osman's grasp. When he did so, he at once fastened it around his own wrist. There were two other chunky silver bracelets there already. He held out the wrist and twisted it from side to side, smiling down at his new acquisition.

'Now we can go to the market. It will begin soon, soon.'

With Kher, Osman, the entourage of soldiers and some other Arabs who had suddenly emerged from the house all ahead of her, Alexine found herself walking alone through the village. The horses had been left behind. Dogs, fortunately tethered, barked and threw themselves in her direction, incensed by her alien smell. Children kept crowding around her, jabbering and laughing, and then, for no apparent reason, racing off with squeals of what might have been either terror or derision. Some women, carrying pitchers on their heads, halted and stood motionless, staring at her in silence.

Beyond the village, there was a zaraba: an enclosure made of high poles, sharpened at the tops, so thickly intertwined with brushwood that it was impossible to see between them. Long before they neared it, Alexine was assailed by a stench reminiscent of the time when, a small child, she had been taken by her mother and father to stay at John's country estate in Derbyshire, and, wandering about the grounds alone, had inadvertently approached the pigsties. She pulled a handkerchief out of the pocket of the breeches that she had taken, despite Harriet's and Addy's protests, to wearing for riding, and held it to her nose.

There was a makeshift gate, fastened with string. One of the soldiers, presumably the man in command, ran forward and, having fumbled for a time with the knot of the string, dragged the gate open. Osman now turned and beckoned to her.

Sulkily she went forward. 'You shouldn't have left me like that. On my own. In a place like this.'

'What can happen to you? You are now Mohammed Kher's guest. Nothing can happen to his guest.'

What sort of market was this? She had expected to see stalls laden with fruit and vegetables, with garishly coloured clothes, and with no less garishly coloured bottles of scent, like the ones visited by her,

Harriet and Addy in Cairo. Stretching ahead of her were closely huddled clumps of bodies, all motionless, the once black skin almost ashen with dust, the faces devoid of any sign of emotion, the eyes like the artificial ones, lambent and expressionless, in the masks of the stuffed animals in the hall of John's country mansion. Fascinated and appalled, she moved her gaze hurriedly from one of these groups to another. Men, women and children were indiscriminately tethered together by straw ropes linking their wrists and ankles. They waited, almost totally naked and totally apathetic, under the slanting afternoon sunlight. The presence of a white woman, something wholly new to them, aroused absolutely no interest.

It was then that Alexine saw, under a tree devoid of any leaves, what it took her some seconds to identify as the swollen body of a woman whose sagging breasts and greying hair indicated that she was approaching old age. A straw rope had been pulled so tight around her neck, biting deep into it, that she must have been garroted. There were livid weals on her round, upturned buttocks and on her back. Flies were clustered on these wounds, on her bulging eyes, around her nostrils and in her raw, exposed vagina. Alexine put both hands over her mouth and gasped in horror.

'What is this?' She turned on Osman. 'What sort of market is this?'

But she already knew the answer to her questions.

'It is good for you to see,' he said in the easy, half-mocking tone that he so often used to her.

'*Good!*' She was furious. It was only later that she thought that perhaps he was right. It was good for someone as privileged as herself to witness the horrors that so many people in this continent were inexorably doomed to undergo.

Now she noticed the plump, well-groomed Arabs in their flowing robes, wandering in twos and threes from group to group. One put out a hand and, as though he were assessing some livestock, first pinched the skin of a woman's belly between finger and thumb, and then prised open the mouth of the child huddling against her. Having turned away from this couple, he began a discussion with the Arab next to him. Later, Osman told her that the Arabs were constantly selling and reselling the slaves among themselves, each time with the aim of further profit. It was, Alexine thought, a macabre parody of the commercial transactions conducted on the bourse by her father and John, with human beings taking the place of stocks and shares.

'It's disgusting!'

Osman enjoyed her repugnance. He threw back his head and laughed. Then he beckoned: 'Come. Come! The best are over there. There!' He pointed to the farthest end of the enclosure.

She forced herself to go with him, though her first impulse had been to turn away and quit the place. She must plumb this midden to its depths, she told herself. She must submit to having her civilized sensibilities ravished, just as these uncivilized bodies had been ravished. She owed that to them and the humanity that she shared with them. But, her gorge rising as the stench of the naked flesh arose about her, it was only by an exertion of her formidable will that she kept herself from vomiting.

Two of the Arabs were haggling with Kher, raising their voices and making sweeping gestures. One of them, the more vociferous and the younger, had a pock-marked face and a wall-eye. The other had a vast, high belly protruding before him, as though he were pregnant. What was the object of such vigorous bargaining? She could not yet see. As Osman thrust his way between the shackled people now jammed closer and closer together in his path, she trailed after him, eager to discover. From time to time he would put out a hand to shove away, or a foot to kick aside, one of these human obstacles. Later, he was to tell her that all the merchandise at this end of the enclosure belonged to Kher.

Now, at last, she and Osman had managed to reach the three Arabs. Their voices, raised in increasingly vehement argument, might in their shrillness have been mistaken for women's. Between them, his overlarge feet and hands bound, stood a skinny little boy with huge, thickly lashed eyes; cracked, half-open lips revealed that one of his front-teeth, the gum raw, must have been recently knocked out. The pregnant-looking Arab waddled around him, examining him as a connoisseur might examine some dubiously authenticated piece of sculpture in a gallery. He pointed to one of the boy's almost non-existent calves, and remarked in Arabic: 'No muscle there.' From time to time shifting from foot to foot or, lizard-like, flicking a tongue in a usually futile attempt to frighten away the flies settling on his nostrils, the boy remained totally indifferent to this scrutiny.

Amazing the men with her knowledge of Arabic, Alexine asked, 'Why don't you untie him?'

'Why? Why?' All three stared at her, as Kher rapped out the words, his hands hidden in his sleeves and his huge chest thrust out. 'Because this boy has already run away once. We caught him. He ran away with his mother. We caught both. She died. Luckily he's still alive. You can see, he's not very strong but he's healthy. Perhaps I can sell him to one or other of these men.'

Was it the mother's body that she had seen, bloated by heat, under the tree? It had looked elderly but perhaps she had been wrong in assuming it to be so. If it was indeed the mother's body, then the boy showed no sorrow for her death or fear for his own future.

The Arab with the pock-marked face now also circled the boy, examining him scrupulously. Then he held up three fingers, indicating the highest price to which he would go. Kher shook his head and laughed. The other man said something, and Kher shook his head again.

Suddenly Alexine was aware that the boy, as fragile and beautiful as a marmoset, was gazing at her. There was no surprise, curiosity or appeal in his eyes. They were totally blank. She remembered Sammy, plump, smiling, clean, dressed in the extremely expensive suit that Philip's tailor had, after three protracted fittings, completed for him; this recollection stung her like the hornet that, only two or three days before, had alighted on her forearm and then, before she could do anything about it, had driven deep its poisonous barb.

She gazed back into those unfathomable eyes. Like all the other crowded bodies, his pitifully meagre one looked as if it had been dusted with ash. It was only at the crotch, between his stick-like legs, that the skin still glowed ebony black, as it must have done before he had started on the unending trek up from the heart of Africa.

'How much?'

'How much?' Kher drew in his chin and then turned his head to one side. 'How much?' Now he repeated the words not to Alexine but to Osman, as though to ask: 'What does this crazy white woman want?'

Osman looked over to Alexine. 'Do you want to buy him?' he asked in Arabic, not in the English they had so far been using between them during the excursion.

'Yes. I want to buy him.'

The younger of the Arabs began to protest: he and his partner had already made an offer for the boy, it was too late for this woman to make one.

Kher, amused, smiled and shook his head. No, it was not too late, not at all. The sum offered by his two friends – he indicated them with a pliant hand, palm upwards – was too small. If they wished to increase it, then that was another matter. Otherwise . . .

'How much are you willing to pay?' Osman asked Alexine, again in Arabic. She knew that he was yet again sniffing out a commission.

'How much does he want?'

'How much do you want?' Osman asked Kher.

Kher considered. His two friends here had offered so much – he named the sum. It was far too little for a healthy boy with many, many years of work ahead of him. She would have to double it at least.

'Why do you want him?' the older Arab asked her.

'To free him.'

All four men burst into laughter. The boy's eyes were still constantly fixed on her, never on them.

'You can't free every slave in Africa,' Osman said. 'It would be as difficult as catching every fly.'

'No. But I can make a start with one. I want to free him. Then – free – he can come with us if he wishes, or he can go home.'

'Go home! He'll be captured again. And, anyway, how can he travel all those miles without any food or money?' Osman spoke with indulgent mockery. The idea was preposterous, but since it came from a woman and a white one at that, he was prepared to make allowances.

Unlike Harriet, Addy, Nanny Rose and Daan, Alexine had so far never bargained. A price was asked and, however preposterous, she paid it. When the others remonstrated with her, she would reply: 'Why waste time arguing about a penny or two in this heat?' But now she bargained implacably. When Kher again reminded her that, since the boy was so young, she would probably get years and years of service out of him, she pointed to a crescent-shaped scar on his right shoulder-blade. When Kher claimed that, though so skinny, the boy's arms were muscular, she indicated that one of his toes overlapped the other, as though it were deformed.

Finally, they agreed a price. It was far higher than it would have been for an Arab purchaser but far lower than the one first quoted. The next question was how she was to pay. She would, she said, have to return the way she had come and then send the money back by Osman or someone else whom she could trust. Kher was dubious. He could not let the boy go until he had the cash in his hand. He held out the hand, cupped, to indicate this.

The two other would-be purchasers stood mutely listening to the argument. Neither bore Alexine or Kher any ill will for having cheated them of their purchase. In similar circumstances, they would have acted precisely as Kher had done. Suddenly one of them pointed at the gold chain around Alexine's neck. The ivory crucifix at the end of it, hidden by her robe, had been a christening present from Queen Sophia; the chain itself she had bought in Cairo, since the original chain had been too heavy. Why did she not pay with that? the Arab asked.

Yes, why not? The others, having examined the chain – she shrank as the pock-marked Arab put out a filthy hand and lifted it up close enough for his purblind eyes to focus on it – agreed. That would be the best solution. Then the boy could return with her at once.

She hesitated. The gold chain had cost considerably more than the sum agreed for the boy. Oh, never mind! She raised her arms and undid the clasp. Deftly, she removed the crucifix, placing it in a pocket of her breeches. She held out the chain. 'You've won yourself a bargain,' she told Kher.

He gave an impudent laugh, his narrow eyes widening. Yes, he had won himself a bargain, he knew that, as did his companions. Turning, he shouted out a name, and at once one of his soldiers came running. He pointed at the boy, and the soldier then drew a large, curved knife from his belt. When he approached the boy with it, the boy never flinched. The soldier cut first the rope round the boy's ankles and then the one binding his wrists together. The boy rubbed his left wrist, where the rope had bitten deep, with the palm of his right hand. He showed no emotion. Perhaps Alexine thought, he did not realize that now he was free not merely from his bonds but from his captors.

Kher put out a hand to the boy's shoulder and gave him what was almost an affectionate shove in Alexine's direction. 'Now he's yours,' he said. It was as though he were a breeder handing over a newly purchased dog.

Alexine felt a surge of triumph and relief, such as she had once experienced at an auctioneers in Bond Street, after having at last succeeded in outbidding an elderly, eventually furious old man for a compass that had once belonged to Mungo Park. Somehow, in Cairo, the compass had disappeared, either stolen or stowed away in some forgotten place from which she hoped that it would eventually emerge. 'We'd better get moving,' Alexine told Osman. The sun was sinking in the cleft between the hills. The straggly trees, once silvery, were now a charred black, flecked here and there with molten gold.

'How's he to travel?' Osman asked. 'Do you want to buy a donkey for him? I'm sure someone will sell one.' He was thinking of yet another commission. 'He can't walk.'

'He can ride in front of me on the horse.'

'Impossible!'

She shook her head. 'We'll try.'

Silent and naked, the boy remained close to Alexine as they made their way back to Kher's house and the horses. She found a searing pathos in his continued indifference to what might happen to him. He could not have understood any part of their conversation and so could not now know that he was free. Unless, she thought, by some miracle he had intuited it. That would explain his closeness to her, his face constantly upturned to gaze at her, as though she alone, of all the people around him, were someone to be trusted.

'We must find something for him to wear.'

'He's used to being naked.'

'Yes. That may be. But it's not what we're used to. Can't we buy him some clothes?'

'Here?' Osman laughed in incredulity. 'You can see . . .'

Suddenly she pulled off the linen scarf wrapped around her head. As she dangled it from one hand, the cool wind that so often arose at this hour tugged it away, to make it flutter out from her like a streamer. 'Have you got a knife with you?'

Osman fumbled in his belt and eventually produced a dagger.

She held up the scarf and then plunged the blade into it. Having cut a hole, she turned towards the boy and slipped the hole over his neck. He made no attempt to resist, merely staring down at the newly created garment. The men all began to laugh. On an impulse she put out an arm and drew the boy to her. There was a pungent odour to his body, which all at once revived that previous memory, so piercing in its unexpected advent, of Sammy.

The boy huddled up to her, as an animal might to its dam for protection. Then, as though suspecting some subterfuge that might destroy him, he jerked his pitifully thin body away from her and let out a single, abrupt wail.

∽

Precipitately, the night fell before they reached the camp. With one hand, Alexine held the reins. The other hand was against the boy's midriff, the taut skin of which was hot to the touch even at this hour and even through the linen scarf, as her arms encircled him. Totally limp, eyes closed, he might have been one of the dolls that her father used to bring her back from his travels. Reluctant to move for fear of awaking or even dislodging him, she felt an increasing discomfort. But, oddly, this discomfort, so far from bringing any exasperation with it, as it would have done on any other occasion, merely filled her with contentment.

She leaned forward to rest her cheek on the boy's hair. Her nostrils filled with the smell that emanated from the fur of the cats that, now kept in wicker cages for fear that they might escape, she would from time to time release and hold in turn, some wriggling furiously and others contentedly purring, up against her face, before she put out their food for them.

'You all right, mademoiselle?'

'Yes. Fine. Thank you.'

'You wish me to take boy?'

'No, no. It's fine. Fine.'

Her arm around the small body was aching. Her back was aching. But she was filled with an emotion that she had rarely felt since Sammy's abrupt disappearance: tenderness. With Adolph she had felt sexual passion, possession, love, contentment, happiness, joy; never this pervading, soothing, almost sorrowful tenderness as she held the body of this creature, so totally unlike herself, close against her own. In moments of annoyance, Harriet or Addy would accuse her of having no deep feelings for creatures other than her animals. Was that how she now regarded her purchase? Was he one with the dogs that she patted and the cats that she stroked? She had, on first seeing him, thought of him as a beautiful, solemn little marmoset. But he was a human, for God's sake he was a human!

∽

That night, as she lay sleepless, he lay sleeping, head supported on crooked arm, on some cushions covered by a rug at the foot of her bed. She had tried to indicate to him that he should sleep with the Egyptian men, already huddled, separated into groups by age or friendship, round a long line of dying fires, but either he had not understood her or, having understood her, had been determined not to comply, having sensed the men's hostility at having this little black savage foisted on to them.

'You can't have him in your tent!' Nanny Rose had protested. 'What a thing! You could catch something from him.'

Alexine had laughed and put an arm round the boy's shoulders.

As the dawn began to break, she sat up in bed and saw, with horror, that he was no longer beside her.

'Monkey! Monkey! Where are you?' Without thinking, never having used it before, she used that name to call him, as she scrambled off the low camp bed.

In her night-shift and slippers, she emerged from her tent. Harriet, aroused by her calling, almost simultaneously emerged from hers. 'You can't call him that,' she said.

'What do you mean?'

'He's not an animal. He's a human being.'

'I'm only being affectionate. I love monkeys. You know that.' Alexine now felt ashamed and that made her tone indignant.

Harriet shook her head. 'No. It's not right. Please, darling. Don't call him that again. I don't like it. And if you think about it, I don't think you'll like it either. Anyway – what's the trouble?'

'He's disappeared. He was asleep on the ground beside me and now...' She turned repeatedly, frantically gazing to now the right and now the left.

'I hope he's not run away. We should have taken greater care.'

'We could hardly have tethered him.'

Harriet shivered, her plump arms – she was the only one of the five Europeans not to have lost weight during the trek – across her breasts as her hands clasped her shoulders. At this hour, it was often chilly. 'Poor little soul.'

Then, suddenly, they saw him. Where had he come from? What had he been doing? A moment before, as Alexine had circled round and round in her search for him, the cluster of rocks had been bare. Now there he was, on the highest of them, gazing down at them, the dawn wind fluttering the makeshift garment around his emaciated body. Nanny Rose had said that, before they struck camp, she was going to run him up a shirt and some trousers.

'Come! Come! Here!' Alexine called. Then she realized that these were precisely the words and precisely the tone, by turns coaxing and commanding, that she used to summon back one of the straying dogs.

He did not respond. He merely stood motionless, the rising sun a vast orange globe on his right and the sky a greenish-grey on his left.

Alexine, Harriet beside her, her arms still clasped around her shivering body, raised a hand. She beckoned.

Still he did not respond.

Alexine held out both her arms. Then, at last, he moved. He began to leap, barefoot, with extraordinary agility and assurance from rock to rock, in a disquieting reminder of the strange old man seen two days before. Once he had completed the descent, he raced towards her. He was smiling. Then he was laughing. It was the first time that she and Harriet had seen him do either.

It was as useless to question him as it had been useless to question Sammy on his first arrival in the house. He threw himself into Alexine's arms and she held him there.

'Perhaps he was hungry,' Harriet said, always practical, though it was impossible that he could have found anything to eat up on the barren rocks.

'Perhaps he had to see to a call of nature.'

'Yes, that was probably it.'

But why had he had to go so far? The night before they had shown him the latrines dug for the Egyptians.

∽

He learned with astonishing quickness. As the endless procession inched once more forwards, he would always be with Alexine, now sitting in front of her on the horse and now walking beside her. When walking with her, he would often unselfconsciously slip his hand into hers. As soon as he heard any word or phrase, whether in English, French or Arabic, he would begin to repeat it over and over to himself, at first in bewilderment and then, nodding his head, in satisfaction that he had succeeded in memorizing it. Later, if the word or phrase were in English or French, he would bring it out again when needed. But they soon noticed that he would never bring out any word in Arabic. They decided that he associated that language with his former captors. But, if he never spoke Arabic, it was soon clear that he could understand simple things said in Arabic in his presence.

Each day, Alexine would no longer devote so much of her time in searching for botanical specimens while waiting for the main party to catch up with her and Osman. Instead, in the skimpy shadow of a tree or the more substantial one of a rock, she would instruct the boy as she used once to instruct Sammy. These lessons now were much less frustrating than those of the past, since there was no longer the continual effort of scrambling over the cruelly spiked railings of Sammy's deafness. She would point, she would say something. Reproducing the sound with an almost comic exactness, he would name the thing for himself.

On the first day no one came up with a name for him, merely referring to him as 'he' or 'the boy'.

'We must give some sort of Christian name,' Nanny Rose said.

'Since he's certainly not a Christian, why should we do that?' Addy asked. Recovered from her illness, she had taken to colouring her prominent cheekbones, still yellow from the days of fever, with far too much rouge.

'You know what I mean!' Nanny Rose was no longer as deferential as when they had started on the journey, so that only the day before Addy had complained to Alexine, 'If you ask me, she's getting a little too big for her boots,' adding: 'And Daan is no better.'

'I wonder if there's any way of finding out his name from him?'

Alexine beckoned the boy over, from where he was squatting on the ground, turning over a tattered and soiled pack of cards that she had given him after he had absorbedly watched her and Addie play a game of piquet. Knowing nothing of any card game, he was merely fascinated by the strange images.

He jumped up, leaving the cards in the dust, and hurried over to her.

She pointed now at Addy, now at Harriet, now at Daan and now at herself, each time repeating the relevant name a number of times. Again she pointed at herself. 'Alexine! Alexine! *Alexine!*'

She pointed at him. He frowned, biting on his lower lip.

Again she pointed at herself. 'Alexine.' Now she said it quietly, with none of the previous emphasis.

'Alexine.' He repeated it. He looked up at her for approbation under lowered lids.

She nodded. 'Good.' She smiled. It was all so like her lessons with Sammy all those years ago.

He smiled back, hesitantly at first, then his mouth widening and his eyes lighting up.

She pointed at him. 'You?'

'You?' The sound was repeated with uncanny accuracy.

She shook her head, pointed at him again. 'You. Name.' With both hands she made a beckoning gesture, which said: 'Come on, come on, try!'

Again he frowned. Then he stooped and scratched at one of his bare legs, where a fly had settled. He looked up again. His mouth opened. From the back of his throat came a guttural series of sounds. What were they? It sounded like 'Abgilgusunni' or 'Abgilgusummi'. Harriet and Addy declared that it was the latter, Alexine was sure that it was the former. Nanny Rose and Daan shook their heads and said that they couldn't make head or tail of it.

'Anyway, that seems to have solved the problem,' Nanny Rose said.

'It's a name but hardly the Christian name you wanted,' Addy retorted.

Alexine tried to say it. 'Ab-gil-gu-sunni.'

'Summy, summy,' Harriet corrected her sharply. It had been a long and particularly bumpy ride on the camel and she was feeling irritable.

'We can't call him all that. Let's just call him Sunny,' Alexine said.

'Sunny doesn't really describe him,' Addy objected, not foreseeing that later it would do so.

'Well, Sunny it is,' Daan said. He was puffing at his pipe, something that he would never have done in their presences in The Hague or even in Cairo.

Alexine pointed at the boy. 'Sunny,' she said. Again she pointed at herself. 'Alexine.' Again she pointed at him. 'Sunny.'

He gazed anxiously at her, shook his head. Then he pointed at himself; 'Sunny?' The tone was interrogative, dubious, wary.

She nodded.

Yet again he pointed at himself. Then, with a surprising assurance, he said: 'Sunny. Sunny.'

But was he Sunny or Sonny? Alexine was never sure.

'You treat that boy as if he were your own child,' Nanny Rose told her on one occasion, irritated that the leader of this vast expedition should jump up to fetch some iodine and a dressing as soon as she saw that the little rascal had cut a finger while slicing some tomatoes. There were often times when Alexine did indeed think of him as her own child, with a protective, yearning tenderness. 'He might be one of your dolls,' Nanny Rose told her on another occasion, as Alexine carefully dressed him in clothes made for him not, on this occasion, by Nanny but by herself. In the past she had never been in the least interested in needlework; but, as with every practical activity, she was soon adept at it.

One day, when calling for him as they were about to resume their journey soon after dawn, Alexine was amazed and disconcerted to hear the name that emerged from between her lips. It was 'Sammy', not 'Sunny'. Thereafter, the same slip was often to recur, particularly when she was in a hurry or tired. To both names he answered with equal alacrity.

6 AT LONG LAST, after eighteen days of travelling, suddenly, at sunset, they saw the Nile, a vast, burnished snake slithering between two ochre sand banks. Sunny cried out in amazement and pointed at it. 'Nile, Nile,' Alexine said, and he repeated 'Nile.' It seemed so near, coiled there in the rapidly diminishing light, but they did not reach it until the following day, since Addy had begun yet again to complain of exhaustion and the heat and one of the dogs had again raced off and got lost.

When they finally reached the river, and prepared to set up camp, Sunny pulled off all his clothes and, with an exultant cry, raced off and plunged into the brown, lethargic waters.

'He'll drown!' Nanny Rose cried out in alarm. She turned to Daan: 'Do something!' But Daan, who had never learned to swim, had no intention of risking his life to save someone to whom he still referred, when out of earshot of his employers, as 'that little savage'.

But there was no real cause for alarm. Whether he had ever before swum, there was no way of knowing; but he certainly managed to keep afloat, splashing round in circles like the straying dog, which, having at last caught up with them, had now jumped in to join him.

'Oh, I'd love to go in,' Alexine said.

'Oh, no, no! It would be the death of you,' Nanny Rose protested. 'You could catch enteric – or something even worse. They do *everything* in that water. You know that. You've seen them.'

Since Addy still looked so frail and since her complaints were becoming more and more clamorous, Osman managed to hire a small boat in which she could travel upstream. Another boat was also hired for the animals. Six men, constantly complaining and constantly persuaded to continue their task by lavish tips from Alexine, pulled the vessels. Indifferent to everything around her, Addy spent day after day stretched out on the sagging bunk in the one stifling little cabin reading *Père Goriot*. From time to time she would get up to inspect her face in the fly-blown mirror hanging askew on the wall beside the bunk and then, having dabbed at it with a handkerchief, would once more apply rouge and powder to the wrinkled, faded skin. 'I look a fright, an absolute fright,' she would mutter aloud to herself. 'A hag. This is crazy, crazy, crazy.'

∽

Now they would often stop at some town or even large village, astounding its inhabitants with the endless procession of camels, donkeys, dogs and porters sweating under vast loads. At the first of these halts, Barbar, some dozen sheiks galloped up to the caravan on camels and told them that the Governor wished to see them.

'We can't go like this,' Harriet said. 'We're filthy. What'll he think?' She turned to Alexine: 'And you'll have to get into a proper frock.'

'Is this an improper one?'

'Frankly, yes. It looks like a nightdress.'

'The Governor might approve of that,' Harriet said.

Eventually, it was agreed that the visit to the Governor should take place in two hours' time. At once, the servants started to put up the tents. Once Harriet's, Addy's and Alexine's were ready, the servants set up folding tables and brought basins and ewers of water. For many days, at the outset of the expedition, they had performed these tasks as though for the first time. But now they had at last become a routine, so that the men rushed around without any pause for thought.

Harriet examined herself in the long mirror, brought from The Hague, that she constantly dreaded that one of the servants would drop and break. 'Well, I must say I don't look too bad.' Each day of the trek, the two laundry maids would patiently wash and iron the women's clothes, supervised by Nanny Rose and sometimes by Harriet herself. These last days the washing had been done with water from the river, and in consequence the clothes had an unpleasantly dank, deadly smell, which their wearers had tried in vain to eradicate by splashing both the clothes and themselves with eau-de-Cologne or lavender water. 'And you look marvellous,' Harriet told Addy, even as she wondered if all that rouge and powder might not create the wrong impression.

'Oh, I don't know that I'll go with you,' Addy suddenly announced.

'Oh, you must come, you must! After you've taken so much trouble to make yourself look so elegant. Why not?'

'It'll be a bore. You know it will. I'd much rather stay here and finish *Père Goriot.*'

'Don't be silly. You must come.'

'Oh, very well.' Addy raised a hand and pulled down the heavy lace veil hitched over the brim of her hat. 'Let's get it over with.'

A carriage, drawn by two emaciated horses, flies clustered in the lacerations on their fallen-in flanks, had already arrived. 'Oh, these horses!' Alexine pulled a face. 'I can't bear to look at them.' When the unshaven coachman began to belabour them, she jumped up from her seat and, to his amazement, cried out in Arabic: 'Don't do that! Don't! Stop it!'

'That's the only way to get them to move,' he told her. From then on, the horses ambled along, from time to time stopping either to crane their necks for leaves from the avenue of trees up which they were travelling or to lower them to champ at some tuft of sere vegetation.

'Something is biting me!' Addy announced. She plunged a hand down the front of her dress. 'This carriage must be full of fleas.'

'It's too late to worry about fleas now.' Harriet laughed. 'I can't count the number of times I've been bitten.'

'The bugs on the steamer were far worse than any fleas. I think they must have been eating that powder recommended by Mr Shepheard, instead of being killed by it.'

'May we talk about something a little more elevated?' Harriet suggested.

'Oh, I'm being bitten to death!' Addy cried out, again plunging her hand down the front of her dress.

Alexine put a hand into her bag and drew out some coins. A group of children, surprisingly well clothed and showing few of the usual signs of malnutrition, were running along beside them. When she flung the coins out in a glittering arc, the children at once left the carriage to scrabble for them.

'I wish you wouldn't do that,' Harriet said.

'Why? What's wrong with it? I'm sure the children are pleased. And it saves me having to give to some children and not to others.'

'I don't know. I find it ugly.'

'I wish I'd brought Sammy with me.' Hastily she corrected herself: 'Sunny.'

'Oh, no,' Addy said. 'That wouldn't really have done.'

'He'd have behaved perfectly. He always does.'

'That's as may be. But it would have been, well, a kind of insult to the Governor to bring someone like that to see him.'

'I don't see why.'

'I'm surprised that you don't.'

The long, low, house, surrounded by a wide veranda and enclosed in a garden, was far larger than they had expected. As the coachman tried to help them down from the carriage – 'No, thank you, thank you, I can manage *perfectly* well, thank you' Addy told him in French, pulling her white-gloved hand away from his outstretched one – a shaggy dog, lying out as though dead under a tree, bestirred itself, gave a single bark followed by a growl, and then resumed its slumber. The two men who had been escorting the carriage jumped down from their horses, and one of them then shouted out that the foreign ladies had arrived.

A slight, youngish man, dressed in western clothes but with a fez on his head, appeared in the doorway of the house, stared at them for a few seconds and then limped towards them, with a smile of greeting. He spoke French. In an ante-room he told them that the Governor had received instructions from both Cairo and Khartoum to ensure that they received everything that they needed during their visit to Barbar. They were '*visiteurs d'une classe unique*', he assured them. Then he pointed down a corridor. 'Please!'

As they walked down the corridor, Addy let out a squeal. A lethargic rat, a curious orange-brown in colour, was nosing at something not far away from them. At the sound of the squeal it scuttled away and vanished. By now Harriet, Alexine and Nanny Rose had become used to rats, since the steamer and the dahabiahs had both been infested with them until the cats and dogs had begun to reduce their numbers. But Addy was always astonished and terrified when one appeared. Her worst moment had been when, raising the lid of one of her valises to get out a dress, she had come on a nest of baby rats, wriggling on the dress, a vivid peacock blue in colour, that lay on the top. There was a gaping hole on one side of the valise, where the teeth of the parent rats had gnawed through the canvas. Her scream had summoned Nanny Rose, who had briskly picked up the dress and baby rats together and flung them out of the porthole. 'My dress, my dress!' Addy had wailed, to be told by Nanny Rose: 'Oh, you couldn't possibly wear it again, oh no, no!'

'Excuse me, excuse me,' the young man said, as he now sidled past them in order to open the door at the end of the corridor. A sweet, powerful scent struck at them from him. With a narrow hand he turned the handle. The door refused to open. He pushed at it and then administered a kick. He gave an exclamation of annoyance, pulling a face. Then he rattled the handle back and forth again, until at long last it yielded. He smiled, bowed. 'Please, ladies. Please.'

The room was vast and almost wholly bare. There were no curtains on the soaring windows but, oddly, what looked like a frayed and stained damask curtain had been tacked, askew to one wall, a travesty of a Gobelin. At the far end there was a throne-like chair, with a high back, upholstered in red velvet, and arms that ended in lions' heads. One of the ears had been chipped off one of these heads, the wood yellow against the heavily varnished brown of the rest. An elderly servant with a long fly-whisk in his hand stood behind the chair. Seated in it was a plump, jolly-looking man, whose low forehead was heavily corrugated above a face otherwise unlined. He was wearing a soiled white silk shirt, a gaudy silk cravat, creased grey cotton trousers and a jacket far too large for him, its sleeves almost concealing his hands. In a corner, behind him, there was a mattress, horsehair protruding from one edge of it, with cushions piled on top of each other at one end. From an indentation in the cushions and from the presence, near to it on the floor, of a dish containing two meatballs glistening with oil, it was clear that the Governor must, on their arrival, have been reclining there.

He got slowly to his feet, shod in Turkish slippers upturned at their toes, to reveal that his plump, powerful body was supported by disproportionately small legs. Since Harriet was clearly the eldest, he approached her first. He, too, spoke French. He raised her hand and lowered his head to it, without actually allowing his lips to touch it. 'Enchanted,' he murmured. Next, he turned to Addy. She gave a small grimace, as she felt his luxuriant beard brush against her trembling fingertips through the thin white cotton glove covering them. Finally, it was the turn of Alexine. He raised his head, her hand still in his, and gazed up at her appreciatively for several seconds.

Down the room, on the right side of his makeshift throne, six chairs, their leather upholstery worn and cracked, had been ranged. Opposite them, there was one other plain straight-backed chair. The young man took this chair; the three women were invited to sit opposite. The young man, the Governor said, was his nephew.

The Governor had prepared a speech in their honour. As the muscular servant behind him lethargically waved the fly-whisk above his head, he told them how delighted he was to receive them, how surprised he was that three ladies should venture on such a trip by themselves, and how he had received a number of requests from important people to do everything in his power to help them. If they wished, he continued, he would be happy to have them to stay in this house. There were many rooms and, as they must already have noticed, it was remarkably cool because of the thick walls and high ceilings.

Addy looked in panic at Alexine, fearful that she might accept this offer. But Alexine graciously declined it. They were all, she said, deeply touched, it showed the hospitality for which this whole region was famed. But they had already set up camp, there were so many of them, and in addition they had a number of dogs and cats of which they personally were accustomed to take care.

The Governor was relieved.

At all events, would the ladies do him the honour of joining him in a meal?

Once again Addy glanced in panic at Alexine. Alexine smiled and nodded: Yes, they would be happy to do so. She fumbled in her bag and produced a curved, ivory-handled penknife wrapped in tissue paper. She had brought this present for His Excellency, she told him.

He smiled, took the package from her, and with large, clumsy hands, began to unwrap it. Disappointment flashed briefly across his face; then, having swiftly handed paper and penknife to his nephew, he smiled and thanked her elaborately. Realizing that the penknife had not been adequate, Alexine removed the yellow silk scarf that she was wearing and told him: 'This is for your wife.'

He laughed. 'Which wife? Which?'

They were taken aback.

'I have eight wives. Eight wives, twenty-two children.' He glanced roguishly not at Alexine but at Harriet: 'Perhaps I may find another wife? I'm not too old?'

None of the women responded to these questions.

He held out the scarf, head tilted appraisingly to one side. Then he stroked it with a hand, smiled with childish pleasure, and laid it against a cheek.

'Please! Come and see my garden. It's beautiful at this hour.'

He was right. The garden into which he led them was not the one, its soil cracked and many of its plants dying or dead for lack of water, that they had already seen at the front, but one, far larger, at the back, with a well at its centre. Harriet breathed in deeply. 'The air is wonderful here,' she said in Dutch. 'Isn't it, isn't it? So cool, so fresh. We might be by the sea.' She suddenly thought of walking the beach at Knokke, as the sun was sinking, just as it was beginning to sink now, and of feeling a breeze on her forehead, cheeks and lips. Another Nanny, not Nanny Rose but her own childhood one, was with her and Addy. That Nanny was telling them not to loiter, to get a move on. They must get back home for supper.

Alexine put up an arm, plucked a rose and held it to her nostrils. She, too, now breathed in deeply.

'You like my garden?'

'Oh, yes, yes!' Addy said. 'It's more beautiful than any of the much larger gardens we saw in Cairo.'

He was delighted, they could see. But in a deprecatory tone he said, 'You think that only because you've had such a long journey through the desert. It's a very simple garden, nothing special. But I love it. And my wives love it.'

Where were these wives? Would they be allowed to see them? Each of the three women silently asked herself the same question. Then they noticed the high fence around this garden. Perhaps it was so high to prevent people looking in on the wives.

They sat in rickety cane chairs in an arbour beyond the well. From somewhere behind the arbour they could hear a staccato tut-tut-tut sound, presumably a bird. Otherwise everything, in the gathering darkness, was extraordinarily still. Servants came out carrying sconces, their flames juddering in the breeze. Then they brought a long trestle table and some small ones made of bamboo. For a while the Governor was silent, a vague smile hovering round his mouth as with one hand, having kicked off a slipper, he scratched at the bare sole of a foot. Meanwhile his nephew chattered away, telling them about his last visit to Khartoum, about the copy of Lemprière's dictionary presented to him by the last party of foreigners, three Frenchmen, that had passed that way, and about his desire one day to travel to France.

Dishes were now brought out piled with food. Addy shook her head when she was the first to be handed a serving.

'You must eat *something*,' Harriet told her in English.

'I can't. The mere sight of it makes me feel sick.'

'Please try. You'll only offend them.'

'Oh, well! I'll have some of that bread then. If I must. And perhaps some of that chicken. That can't do me any harm.'

Later Addy sipped once at the bitter-sweet, sticky cordial handed to her in an ornate brass goblet and then set it down, with a small grimace. It would only make her more thirsty, she decided, and, if there was any unboiled water in it, it would certainly not have been through a purifier such as they had brought with them from the Netherlands.

'This rice is delicious,' Alexine told the Governor in French. She alone of the Europeans had never once suffered any nausea or diarrhoea during the journey. Nanny Rose had repeatedly remarked that she must have a cast-iron stomach.

The Governor inclined his head. 'Thank you, mademoiselle.' He raised his goblet to toast them: '*Santé*!' Then he drained it at one go. Later they were to wonder whether his drink, unlike theirs, might not have contained alcohol. Each time that he drained his goblet, only to have one of the servants rush over to refill it, he talked yet more fluently, and laughed yet more often and more loudly. Eventually, he was telling them about his eight wives. One, the first, was forty-one, no, forty-two years old, and she had born him eleven children, seven of whom had died. The youngest wife was only twelve. She had been given to him only a month or two ago by a Portuguese trader, who had originally bought her for himself.

'*Bought* her?' Alexine demanded.

He nodded, smiled, wholly relaxed. 'That's the custom of our country. Good, bad?' He shrugged.

Suddenly, he shouted out a command to one of the servants, who hurried off, to return with an instrument that looked like a primitive banjo. The Governor tuned the strings, head on one side, his eyes glittering in the light from the sconce on the table beside him. Then he began to play. Addy kept shifting uncomfortably in her chair – really it was excruciating to have to listen to such a cacophony, and how it went on and on! – but Harriet and Alexine were both transfixed. Huge moths were now blundering around the candles. That strange tut-tut-tut sound, almost like a woodpecker, had ceased. Instead, they could now hear water lisping from a height on to other water. Was there a fountain somewhere?

The Governor began to sing, his voice high-pitched and nasal, his eyes half shut. His plump body swayed from side to side, as his long nails now energetically raked and now hesitantly plucked at the strings. Addy drew out a fan and began gently to agitate it before her face, not to cool herself – she was cool enough already – but to keep away the mosquitoes and gnats. From time to time, piercing the music, she would hear a disconcerting whine.

At the close of the song, Alexine clapped, to be eventually joined by Harriet and then, lethargically, by Addy.

'Was that a sad song, do you think?' Harriet asked.

'It was an interminable one,' Addy said.

'Oh, I liked it.' Alexine turned to the Governor to tell him in French: 'You sang beautifully.'

'Yes, my uncle sings beautifully,' the nephew said. 'He's famous in the country all around.' He made an expansive gesture with an arm.

Harriet reached out for the instrument, which the Governor had set down on the table between them. 'May I?'

He nodded. 'Certainly.'

She plucked the strings at random. Then she began to retune them. Everyone watched and listened. At last, she began to play. She had once, as a girl, played the guitar, but this was something wholly different. All she could do was to pluck out a simple melody, single note after note.

'Home, sweet home!' Alexine cried out in recognition.

Again Harriet plucked out a halting, blurred approximation to the melody. Her head lowered over the instrument, she suddenly felt an overwhelming nostalgia for what was certain, clean, comfortable, safe, humdrum, predictable, known. This overwhelming nostalgia eventually communicated itself to Addy, who straightened herself in her chair and gazed out, with hungry, hurt eyes, at the vast moon that was just beginning to appear above the roof of the house.

But Alexine was impervious. The sentimentality of the air merely irritated her.

Later, more candles were brought out and the spent ones carried away. Then there was a sound of girlish laughter from behind the high fence, succeeded by a man's peremptory voice issuing a series of commands. The three women looked at each other. Were they now going to meet the wives?

But the new arrivals were not the Governor's wives but a troupe of some dozen dancing girls, ranging in age from a woman with hennaed fingernails and hair who looked at least fifty, to a pubescent girl, almost a child. With them were three male musicians.

At a gesture from the Governor, the musicians struck up. Soon after, the girls began to dance, first one, then another, and then two or three simultaneously. The sequins in their hair and on their fluttering skirts and stiff bodices glittered in the candlelight, as did their teeth, revealed each time that they smiled.

The oldest of them now began to rotate her huge, wobbling belly in front of the Governor. Then she turned and it was her backside that she was rotating even more frenziedly. Girls began to rotate in a similar manner in front of Harriet, Alexine and eventually Addy. Addy, turning her head aside, refused to look. Harriet and Alexine, leaning forward, mouths half-open, were enthralled.

The wriggling and writhing went on remorselessly. Beads of sweat appeared on the faces and between the breasts of the girls. The oldest began to gulp for air. Addy, her head still turned aside, raised her fan to her mouth as she yawned twice. Harriet picked at a loose thread on her frock. Alexine gazed past the dancers at a cat that sat motionless, eyes gleaming amber, in some nearby bushes.

At long last the performance came to a close. The Governor's nephew clapped and, with less enthusiasm, the Governor joined in. Then the Governor fumbled in a pocket of his creased trousers and drew out some coins. Knowing what was to follow, the woman with the hennaed hair and nails leaned forward, smiling and proffering her huge breasts. He dropped the coins between them. She muttered something, smiled even more broadly, and whirled away. Alexine searched for some coins in her bag. The girl who had danced in front of her had already retreated. Alexine beckoned to her and the girl eagerly ran up. She too leaned forward and Alexine dropped the coins between her breasts, as the Governor had done with the older woman. The girl, realizing the size of the tip, let out a squeal of delight.

'I'm sure it wasn't necessary to do that,' Addy said. 'Not for a woman. No woman would give a tip like that to another woman – particularly not to a dancing girl.'

Alexine shrugged. 'They were all trying so hard.'

'With sadly little result.'

'Poor dears,' Harriet said.

Alexine, with her usual extravagance, now took some more money out of her bag. She turned to the Governor's nephew. 'This is for the other girls,' she said.

'You're very kind, mademoiselle.' He slipped the money into a pocket of his jacket.

'I hope he passes it on,' Harriet said in Dutch. Reluctantly she admired Alexine's generosity, even though she herself was always prudent in her handling of money.

'I doubt if he will,' Addy responded. Then she once again shifted uneasily. 'Isn't it time to return? I'm sure we've spent long enough here not to offend him by leaving.'

'There are all sorts of things I have to ask him to do for us,' Alexine said.

'Well, couldn't you come back tomorrow with Osman?' Addy suggested.

'Yes, I suppose so.'

The Governor staggered uncertainly as he accompanied them back through the house and out into the bare, dusty oval of ground beyond the front garden. The carriage was nowhere to be seen. Angrily he told his nephew to find it. The nephew passed on the order, no less angrily, to one of the servants.

'I'm sorry to keep you waiting, ladies.'

Addy involuntarily cringed, as a bat swooped above them.

Alexine smiled. 'It doesn't matter. It's so beautiful out here at night.' She looked up at the sky. 'So many stars. At home we never see so many stars so clearly.' She was enchanted.

When the tired horses eventually appeared, drawing the ancient carriage, its hood hanging askew, the Governor suddenly announced, on a whim, that he would accompany them back to the camp.

'Oh, no, that's not necessary, not necessary at all. Many thanks, Your Excellency, but really . . .'

The Governor would have nothing of Harriet's intervention. 'No, no. So late at night. In any case, I'm not in the mood to sleep. I'll enjoy the ride in the company of three such charming – and remarkable – ladies.' He clambered into the carriage, after having assisted them to do so, and sat down heavily next to Alexine. 'This is a unique occasion for me. I've never before entertained three foreign ladies, never in all my years in Barbar. Once I entertained one foreign lady – her name was, yes, yes, Pullar, Madame Pullar – but she was with her husband.' He turned to Alexine: 'Not as young or as beautiful as you, mademoiselle.'

Alexine ignored the compliment. 'Your Excellency, we have to replenish some of our supplies. Water is one of our problems. That well in your garden . . .'

He nodded, not pleased with the practical direction in which she had so abruptly switched the conversation. 'Yes, tomorrow, I suggest that my nephew . . . He can discuss all these matters . . .'

Alexine persisted in mentioning other problems to him, but each time received the same sort of reply.

When they had reached the camp, she handed a tip, lavish as always, to the coachman, and then handed some money to the Governor: 'Your Excellency, please do not be offended. This is a little present for your staff.'

The present was not little; the Governor was far from offended.

'Dear ladies, dear ladies! How kind you all are! Now, please remember, I am here to help you, to do whatever you command me. Tomorrow morning, my nephew will come to see you. Please be sure to tell him of all your needs, all, all! Then he'll report to me and I'll ensure that action is taken. Of course, we'll meet again. I've so much enjoyed our meeting together. I hope that you've also derived some pleasure from it, dear ladies. I sincerely hope so.'

He went on for a considerable time, while the two horses tugged at the scant vegetation around them and the women shifted uneasily, the breeze disordering the hair so patiently coiffured for them by Nanny Rose and two of the Egyptian maids, and fluttering the carefully laundered and ironed flounces of their dresses.

'Oh, what a bore!' Addy exclaimed, as at last the carriage trundled off. 'I must go and see how my Mister is getting on. I've neglected the poor little poppet for most of today.'

'I thought that a wonderful evening,' Alexine said.

Harriet pondered. 'It was *interesting*.' For her that word was never a pejorative. That things should be interesting was always more important to her than that they should be enjoyable.

∽

That was the first and last of such meetings that Addy was ever to attend with them during the journey to Khartoum. She became increasingly reluctant to leave the stifling cabin on the little boat, even to lie out on the camp bed in the comparative coolness of her tent each night. Each time that, at Alexine's and Harriet's insistence, she left the cabin, she felt as though they were prising her from a protective shell, and her spirit felt raw and bruised.

Day after day, oblivious to the shouts between the near-naked, sweating men pulling the craft up the river, to what was happening on either bank and to the constant buzzing of flies around her, she read on and on. For much of the time Mister lay on her lap. If, in search of a cooler place, he attempted to jump off the bunk, she would tell him 'No, no, darling, no! Stay! Stay!' and clutch at his collar. He was ceaselessly scratching and gnawing at himself for fleas, and her own fragile arms and her bony chest were covered in flea bites.

But, curiously, she felt a widening, placid contentment, as hour succeeded hour and nothing happened except what Balzac made happen in a far-off provincial town that she had never visited and was never likely to visit.

7 ALL THROUGH HER TRAVELS, Alexine had constantly taken photographs. Sometimes the whole long, straggling caravan would be halted when something – a formation of rocks, a cluster of trees, a group of nomads – caught her attention. The tent that served as her darkroom would be unloaded, the cumbrous equipment unpacked.

If there were people involved, then they were often frightened of this one-eyed monster glaring at them, and overawed by the imperious white woman in her flowing robes, a silk scarf wrapped round her head, who, when not endlessly fidgeting to get a pose exactly right, would order them in an oddly accented Arabic: 'Don't move! Don't move at all! Still! Absolutely still!' Their reluctance to participate – what was she doing? was this some way of putting a spell on them? might not the monster gobble up their souls? – was only overcome by lavish presents of goods or money. Sometimes even these inducements could not win them over, and the intended victims would then scuttle off on their camels, horses or donkeys, without even a backward glance.

Until Sunny's arrival, Harriet had usually acted as Alexine's assistant. This task, devoid of any opportunity for artistry such as the photographer herself enjoyed, had eventually begun to pall on her. But equally devoted to her duty and her daughter, she continued to carry it out, even in the intense heat of the midday sun, without even a murmur of complaint.

Sunny avidly watched the two women at work, either standing beside one or other or squatting near the landscapes or the peoples being portrayed. When he finally viewed the picture, he would draw in his breath and his eyes would widen with wonder. Magic! From time to time, in an effort himself to work the same sort of magic, he would draw with a finger in the dust beside him, attempting a recreation, however ephemeral, of what he saw before him. But he was never satisfied with the resulting image and would hurriedly erase it with a palm.

Harriet eventually came to depute some of her tasks as assistant to the boy – would he please hold this, carry this, wipe this, wash this for her? He was an amazing learner in this, as in everything else. Eventually, when she was occupied, usually with Osman as interpreter and Daan in attendance, in settling one of the innumerable wrangles that took place between the servants, Sunny took over entirely from her. Self-importantly he rushed hither and thither, whereas she, in similar circumstances, would merely stoically drag herself about, wan and weary from the heat and the endless travelling.

His English was soon good enough for him to indicate, a beseeching expression on his face, that he would like himself to attempt to take a photograph. Alexine smiled and shook her head. 'Not yet. Too difficult.' Then, because he looked so crestfallen, she relented. 'All right. Have a try.'

He pointed at her. 'You.' It was she and not, as she had supposed, two men approaching on donkeys, whom he wanted to photograph.

'Me?'

'You. Wait. Please.'

He went and fetched a folding chair from the half-dozen set out under a gaudy blue-and-red striped awning, where the four women and he would soon be eating their midday meal. Then he pointed to it, to indicate that she should sit on the chair. She had always been the photographer, not the person photographed. She felt uneasy sitting motionless before the camera instead of fidgeting behind it.

In an eerie mimicry of her own procedure, he went forward, knelt and began to twitch first at the folds and then at the lace flounces at the bottom of her dress. The Egyptian maids would scrupulously unstitch and stitch back these flounces, so that, unlike the dress, they could be laundered after only a single day of wear. He gazed at her, head on one side. Tentatively he put out a hand, gathered courage, and held her chin in his fingers. He tilted it slightly. 'Yes. Yes. Good.' He stood back, he gazed at her. 'Yes.'

When that plate had at last been successfully processed and she had handed him the print, he stared down at it for a long time. He touched the image where her right arm was slightly out of focus. He shook his head. She was amazed by this perfectionism. During the long exposure, she had moved slightly, as many of her sitters moved. Unless the result was a whole area out of focus, she never bothered about this blemish. But he clearly did.

Soon, they were alternating as photographer and assistant. Then, with an increasing assumption of authority, it was he who would supervise the setting up of darkroom tent and equipment, while she rested in the shade of the awning until he indicated to her that everything was ready.

Their collaboration gave her a strange, almost sexual thrill, such as she had experienced when, as photographer and sitter, she and Adolph had collaborated in creating image after image. She had brought all those images with her in a lacquer box. Sometimes, alone at night, she would take them out and stare down at them with a mixture of anger and regret.

Inevitably, she began to irritate Harriet and Addy with the increasingly long delays caused by her and Sunny labouring to produce a photograph of something or someone that struck the two older women as totally unremarkable.

'If only that wretched machine had never been invented!' Harriet grumbled as yet again they waited for the order for the caravan to start.

'And if only she had never bought that wretched boy!' Addy said.

8 LUCY WARBURTON SUPERVISED THE TWO MAIDS, one so stunted that she was almost a dwarf and the other so huge that Lucy's husband, Roderick, referred to her as 'the elephant', in their sweeping and scrubbing of room after room. The Khartoum house, which had been abandoned by a previous Governor for one newer and more central, was really a series of houses, linked to each other not merely by roofed-over passages but by the luxuriant creepers, the haunt of birds, small animals and snakes, that, long unpruned, cascaded everywhere. She was not domestic and she hated domesticity. That, as much as love, had been the reason for which, in defiance of his prohibition, she had quit her father's Lincolnshire rectory, had married an ailing man, son of a carpenter, many years older than herself, whom her father described as 'nothing better than an adventurer', and had then set sail with him to East Africa.

'In this corner. Here! Here!'

When she had received from Cairo the request to let out a number of empty rooms to these three eccentric, apparently immensely rich Dutch women, her first impulse had been to refuse. But her husband had returned not merely ill from a year-long journey into the interior but also almost penniless, having been cheated by his Arab partners in a series of deals so complex that, when he had irritably tried to explain them to her, she had been totally unable to understand them. Now he lay upstairs, no longer suffering from the fever with which he had returned but, as she put it, *smashed*. He did nothing, he rarely said anything. He would eat a little of the food that one or other of the maids carried up to him on a tray and then would push it aside. Occasionally, as she stood looking down at him with a mixture of pity and exasperation – she rarely now felt any love – he would turn his head up to her and, to her horror, his eyes would begin to fill with tears. He was, for the moment at least, past earning any money. Letting the rooms now would earn some. The gossip was that the three women splashed money around.

She looked on in indifference as the squat little maid ran after a scorpion, dislodged from a dusty corner by her broom, and then, broom raised high above her head, brought it down with impeccable aim to pound it into pulp. The maid screeched with delight at her success.

Lucy pointed at the windows and told the maids: 'Those must be cleaned.' After years in the country, she spoke the language almost as fluently as English.

'Tomorrow,' the elephant said.

'No, today. They may arrive at any time now. Any time. We don't know. Everything must be ready for them.'

A firm shake of the head. 'Tomorrow.'

'Oh, all right, tomorrow.' Lucy gave in to them, as she always did. Tomorrow, and tomorrow, and tomorrow, she thought. She knew not merely such hackneyed quotations but much else of Shakespeare by heart. Regarded as both plain and a blue-stocking in Lincolnshire, she had been destined by her father for a career as governess to the children of the wealthy patron who had appointed him to his living.

She wandered away, progressing through a honeycomb of empty rooms, almost all empty of furniture. She hoped that the rumour was true that these three women were travelling not merely with a number of cats and dogs and innumerable wardrobe trunks, but also with every sort of furniture, including a piano. There were not enough things here to furnish even one bedroom to their standards. High up in a corner of one room she noticed that, no doubt having entered through a broken window-pane, birds had built themselves a large, dishevelled nest. In another room, spider webs festooned the brass bedstead that was the only piece of furniture in it. In a bathroom, also containing an earth-closet, there was a terrible stench. She lifted the lid of the closet, and saw that it had not been emptied for who could say how long.

Eventually, she gave up on this depressing voyage from one high-ceilinged, empty or half-empty room to another, and returned to the wing, its walls recently painted by the gardener who also doubled as handyman, to which in recent years she and her husband, having at last wearily despaired of having any children, now confined themselves. In this wing, she had what she had come to call 'my den', a small addition to the house, built out into the garden from the main structure, in which, in the days of the Governor's occupation, the guards used to sit during the day and sleep during the night. Every wall was covered with bookcases. There was a desk, piled high with papers and books; a chair and a table made locally of unvarnished wood on which there were a few ivory objects, obtained in barter on those increasingly rare occasions when she had joined her husband on his travels; a pile of letters, most of them unanswered; and an ebony box riddled with worm-holes.

She raised the bunch of keys that dangled from her waist – she had learned that everything had to be kept under lock and key if it were not to be in danger of being filched – and, having inserted it, opened the box. Carefully she took out what looked like a ledger, an ink-well and a pen. She sat down, the ledger before her on the table, and began to riffle through the pages, reading at random here and there. Then, having reached the end, she smoothed the pages before her with a large, bony hand, the wedding-ring perilously loose, and picked up the pen.

At that moment, she heard his voice: 'Lucy! *Lucy!* Where the hell are you?'

She was tempted to ignore it. But with a sigh she put down the pen between the open pages and got to her feet. 'Coming,' she called. 'Coming! What is it?' She always tried to suppress the note of exasperation in her voice but, as now, usually failed to do so.

She went into the room. He looks as if he were on the rack, she thought. He was only forty-three but he might have been mistaken for sixty. His hair and straggly beard were white and the deep criss-cross wrinkles on his yellow, pulpy face looked as if a fine wire mesh were containing a deliquescent cheese. She felt a sudden horror and remorse. What had happened to him? She had once asked him that question, soon after his return, and he had made no answer. Now she put the question only to herself.

'Did you want something, darling?'

'When are those infernal women arriving?'

'According to the last news they've left Barbar. They ought to be here any time now.'

'I don't want them. It's the last thing I want.'

'We have to have them. You know that.' She had learned, of necessity, to be implacable in this quiet, patient manner. 'We're almost down to our last farthing.'

'If those scoundrels –'

'What's the use of talking about it?' She wanted to add: 'You've so often cheated others. Now it's your turn.' But she restrained herself. Instead, forcing herself to be solicitous, she asked 'Some tea? Or some lemonade?'

He shook his head frenetically from side to side. She might have said: 'Some arsenic? Or some cyanide?' Then he got out hoarsely: 'Water. Just some water. But make sure it's boiled.'

'It's always boiled.' She turned away.

Having brought him the water, she returned to her room and again took up the pen. But the words that had flowed like molten lava the previous day now refused to come. She raised her head and once again watched the giant spider that for days had been building its web above an empty cupboard. If the spider was so indefatigable and persistent, why could she not be like it? Again she picked up the pen and plunged it into the ink-well.

But it was no use. The words would not respond to her bidding. She was too full of panicky expectation.

∞

The women's voices, echoing about the high-ceilinged rooms, jangled like bells. Everything about them had amazed Lucy: the elegance of their clothes; the size of their retinue; their perfect English and French; the perky black boy whom they treated not as a servant but as though he were a member of their family. They might have arrived not as tenants in this hell-hole but as guests in the elegant Georgian mansion of her father's patron.

'I think this would be best for Addy. There's a lovely view from this window.'

'How about the piano going here?'

'Oh, no. There's a patch of damp. Look!'

'I wonder where we can find someone to tune it.'

'Sunny'd better have this little room next to mine.'

'This cupboard must be put in store. It takes up too much room.'

'Would you be happy here or would you like that other room up the stairs?'

They were so eager, decisive, cheerful: all the things that Lucy no longer was. In her plain brown dress, her hands clasped before her, she followed behind them, saying nothing unless one of them first addressed her.

'It's a lovely house,' Harriet told her.

Lovely?

'So surprising,' Addy took up. 'Fascinating. A real labyrinth. One never knows where one's going. Or where one's going to end up.'

'It needs so much doing to it. Even if we could find the workmen, we couldn't find the money.'

'Well, if you could find the workmen, then we'd be perfectly prepared to produce the money,' Alexine volunteered. 'Do try. Please.'

'I wonder how we're going to accommodate all our staff?' Harriet pondered. 'There's room here for our old Nanny and our dear, grumpy, faithful old retainer Daan. And Sunny is to be next to Alexine. But the others . . . I suppose there might be room for some of them here but . . .' She mused, plump hand to chin.

'Our two maids sleep upstairs. There are another two little rooms there, next to theirs.'

'Oh, that would be perfect for our two little Egyptian girls – the ones that look after my sister, my daughter and me. After a fashion.' Harriet laughed. 'But what about the rest?'

'There are some outhouses at the back. We could clear them of their junk.'

'Oh, we don't want to put you to too much trouble. But that would be a solution. Our local people are not at all particular – as you'll know, I'm sure, from your own experience. They've been sleeping out in the open for weeks and weeks on end during our journey.'

'We must think about a kitchen,' Alexine said. 'I have a feeling that our best choice might be that large room at the back. You know the one I mean?' She turned to Lucy. 'Could you spare that as well?'

'Of course.'

'We've brought all our own kitchen things with us. Pots and pans. Ice-box. Water filter. Even a range!'

In the next room, which contained no furniture other than the brass bedstead still festooned in spider webs, Alexine rushed over to the bed, threw herself on to it and bounced up and down, laughing like a child. Suddenly Lucy, who had been previously alienated by her imperious manner, was drawn to her. She had so much gaiety, energy and zest. 'Oh, what bliss to be on a bed that actually has springs! That camp bed was torture.'

Lucy marvelled as, sweating and grunting, the servants began to carry in an endless succession of valises, crates, wicker baskets, pieces of furniture, carpets, curtains, and even pictures, while Harriet and Alexine, sometimes prompted by Nanny Rose or Daan, issued their directions, often countermanded not merely once but two or three times. Far away from all this activity, Addy sat in Lucy's den, her feet on a stool, reading a book. Lucy's own maids looked on, goggle-eyed. From time to time, with a lot of giggling, they would make a half-hearted attempt to give clumsy assistance or would appraise, under low-ered lids, the younger and the more handsome of the men, who would surreptitiously return their interest.

'Oh, no, Flopsy, no, no!' The dog had cocked a leg against the brass bedstead and a stream of urine was snaking across the floor.

'Luckily the carpet hasn't been put down,' Harriet said.

In the early afternoon, Lucy, assisted by the three maids, laid out a meal. There was rice, a stew of extremely tough goat with aubergine and tomato, some sour-tasting bread, and oranges, pithy and almost juice-less, that had been roughly peeled and cut into quarters. Sunny gobbled up what was given to him and then eagerly accepted a second helping. Because of the quality and quantity of his diet in recent weeks, he was growing fast. The rest merely picked at their food. Their own cook would certainly have done far better than this.

'I really must apologize for this dreadful meal. But there's a shortage of most things at present. Supplies are so erratic here.'

'We still have masses of provisions with us,' Alexine said. 'Haven't we, mama? We can spare you anything you need. Just tell us. We could feed a whole regiment.'

You almost have a whole regiment with you. Lucy wanted to say it but managed not to do so.

Near the end of the meal, Addy asked the question that all of them had been wanting to ask.

'Is Mr Warburton away?'

'No.' Lucy had dreaded this. 'He's ... he's not well, I'm afraid. He went on one of his trips and returned ... Nothing serious,' she added. But from the way that the trio now looked at her, she knew that they knew that that was not the truth.

'We have a large medicine chest – full of all the latest remedies,' Harriet volunteered. 'My daughter's responsible for it. She's really very knowledgeable about medicine. As about most things.'

Lucy hesitated. 'That's kind of you. Very kind.' She laid down her knife and fork. She had eaten even less than the others. 'There's a doctor here, just one. A Greek. He used to be good but now ... Mr Warburton says that he's gone native. But to hit the bottle in a Moslem country is hardly to go native, is it?' She gave a dry laugh.

∽

Later, Lucy was standing out alone on one of the many verandas, a hand to a trellis from which a rose, long deprived of water, was drooping, its once white blooms rusty at the edges. From behind her she could hear the men still carrying in their burdens. They were shouting to each other, and from time to time loud laughter erupted. Above those deep voices, Alexine's sharp, clear voice, an intermittent descant, issued her orders.

Lucy gazed out, across the film of heat shimmering above the flat, yellow-brown expanse of uncultivated land beyond the overgrown garden, towards the far horizon. She sighed. She wanted to get back to her den and to her writing. But all this din and movement were too distracting. Well, at least the sum offered by the visitors for their quarters for a period of three months was more than ten times what she had expected. She was ashamed now that she had not at once told them that it was far too high. But, if Roderick continued as he was now, they would need all that money and more to see them through the months ahead.

She turned at a rustle behind her. It was Addy, delicately stepping out through the French windows, a forefinger inserted between the pages of the book that she was carrying with her.

'I see you're a reader like myself,' Addy said.

'Yes. There's little else to do here.'

'I've read so much on this journey of ours. It's the only thing that's kept me sane.'

Now, as previously with Alexine, Lucy felt a sudden, unexpected rapport with this emaciated, heavily rouged woman, dressed as though for a stroll in St James's Park. As a result, she felt that she could put the question that she had been wanting to put throughout that shamefully awful meal. 'What made you start on such a journey?'

Addy opened the book and looked down at it, as though the answer were in it. Then she snapped it shut. 'I can't speak for the others. But life there – in the Netherlands – had become so dreary and pointless. The same people, the same parties, the same things . . . An awful monotony. I wanted – wanted – something different.' She gave a brittle laugh. 'Well, I certainly got it.' She moved over to one of two wicker chairs standing in a corner, dusted it off with a hand, and sat down. Lucy hesitated for a moment, then joined her on the other chair.

'And you, my dear? What brought you to Khartoum?'

Lucy gazed once more at the horizon, a wavering line shimmering through the heat-haze. Then she turned her head and smiled at Addy: 'Love. Oh, and one or two other things too.'

Addy again gave her brittle laugh. 'One must be careful of love. It makes one take decisions one later regrets. I know that from my own experience.'

'Yes. That's what happened.' There was despair in Lucy's voice.

'And what brought your husband here?'

'Money. His family was a poor one. He wanted to make money. And at first he did, lots of it. That's how we came to buy this ludicrous house – which, as you can see, is far too big for us. Then . . . things began to go wrong . . . His Arab friends cheated him, his English friends . . .' She paused. 'Rumours. They started rumours.'

'Rumours? What sort of rumours?'

Lucy hesitated, biting on her overfull upper lip. 'That he was not just dealing in ivory and things of that kind. That he was also . . . also . . . dealing in slaves.'

'Oh, my dear!' Lucy had expected Addy to be shocked but instead she merely burst into laughter. 'And was he?'

Lucy was indignant. 'No! Of course not. No. They were jealous. That was all.'

'Why should they be jealous?'

'Because he was making money. And because he was made honorary consul here. As you know.'

Harriet was calling: 'Mrs Warburton! Mrs Warburton! There's a small problem here. I wonder if you could spare a moment?'

Wearily Lucy got to her feet.

'I'm sorry we're being such a nuisance,' Addy said.

'Oh, no, not at all, not at all.'

Once again Addy opened her book. She was more interested in the problems of Balzac's characters than in those of this melancholy, resigned, faded woman.

9 HARRIET HAD STACKS OF LETTERS with which to deal. But before she could attend to them, she must, with her usual thoroughness, ensure that her room was precisely as she wanted it.

'No, Nanny, I don't think it's a good idea to have that chest under that window. I think it would be better over there . . . Oh, this carpet has got terribly dusty in transit. You'd better call two of the men and tell them to beat it . . . Those curtains look dreadful – far too short for such high windows. Perhaps we could swop them for those in Alexine's room. Her windows are far less high . . .'

Nanny Rose listened patiently and then no less patiently carried out these often contradictory instructions and others like them. She no longer wore her hair in a small, hard bun at the nape of the neck but cut short and dressed in stiff ringlets. This, like the change in her usual expression from a suppressed irritation to a smiling benevolence, made her look much younger. She summoned the men back to work again on windows from which, at their first lazy attempt, they had failed to remove all the dead flies and wasps. She stood over the elderly woman and her daughter whom she had ordered once more to scrub the stone floor. She placed the carriage clock precisely where Harriet could see it when she woke, on a console table at the foot of her bed, and oversaw the installation of Harriet's own commode, washstand, wash-basin and ewer, the last of these covered with a crisp, newly laundered towel, in the bathroom adjoining the bedroom.

As a result of all these efforts, Harriet could at long last walk about the room and out on to the veranda in the certainty that nothing dirty, broken or out of place would catch her eye. Now, after so much delay, she decided that she could settle to those letters. She sat down at her desk, took up the silver paper-knife that had once belonged to the Admiral, and slit open the first of them. It came from one of the closest of her women friends, a baroness. How were they getting on? the baroness asked. They were so much missed. Were they getting proper food to eat? Was the heat too terrible? So much had been happening since their departure. But what had been happening seemed more and more distant and trivial to Harriet, as she turned over stiff page after page, a coronet embossed on each, and read yet another paragraph, written in letters the bold swagger of which seemed to be an oblique indication of the importance of the writer.

The next letter was from John. He had concluded all the financial transactions requested by Alexine, but he must confess that he was frankly worried about the recklessness of her expenditure. Certainly she was an extremely rich young woman, but even the extremely rich had to be provident. Only recently one of the richest men in England, similarly heir to a fortune derived from the West Indies, had gone bankrupt and been obliged to escape to Paris with his wife, his wife's jewellery and what scant funds he could manage to lay his hands on.

Harriet put the letter down half-read. She would pass it on to Alexine. Since the money and the extravagance were both hers, why did he not write to her direct? He was a good, decent man but, oh dear, he did so often irritate her.

Having read all the letters, she began the next day conscientiously and carefully to answer them. Since her friends might pass round her letters, she struggled to find different ways of giving the same news. In such circumstances, many people might have been tempted to exaggerate the perils and hardships of the journey, but that was not Harriet's way. She wrote lightly and flippantly, even when describing some close encounter with disaster or even death. Her style, colloquial and relaxed and generously scattered with dashes and exclamation marks, lacked any of the formality of the majority of her correspondents. But she was an observant woman, and she described what she had seen in a manner so vivid that, weeks later, reading what she had dashed off, the recipients would be as much enthralled as by any book or newspaper article.

The letter-writing finally concluded, she began on yet another of her lists. This was a list of all the things that, filched, broken, mislaid, or recklessly consumed, would now have to be replaced, if possible in Khartoum, before the next stage of their journey. But where were they going, and when would that be? She did not know. When she had last asked Alexine, the reply was: 'Oh, don't let's think about it yet, mama. I have all sorts of ideas and it's difficult to choose between them.' Harriet sometimes wondered whether Alexine had any ideas at all.

It was as she was writing down:

> Dried haricot beans
> Dried apricots
> Flour (wheat, maize?)

that Addy appeared, still clad in peignoir and slippers although it was almost noon. Having entered the room, she gazed around it, appraising everything. She approached the desk and examined the two neat piles of letters received and letters to be mailed.

'You've been working hard.'

'Yes, very hard. I've got cramp in these fingers.' Harriet wriggled them. 'I was hoping to practice a little on the piano.'

'I must have received almost as many letters as you. But I'm not going to bother with any of them.'

Harriet was shocked. 'But you must, Addy!'

'Why must I?'

'Well, if people go to all that trouble to write, then the least one can do is –'

'Oh, please! The only advantage of being in this dreadful country is that one is out of their range.'

'They're your friends.'

'Fine friends! Have your forgotten how they gossiped about us?'

'Oh, everyone gossips. That's a fact of life. From what Mrs Warburton tells us, they even gossip here. Soon, we're going to be as much a topic for gossip in Khartoum as in The Hague. You mark my words.'

Once more, like a caged animal, Addy paced the room. She picked up the clock and stared at it, and then, to Harriet's concealed annoyance, failed to put it back exactly where Harriet and Nanny Rose had long ago decided that it should stand. Lowering her head, she gazed at a photograph of her brother-in-law in an elaborate silver frame. It was one of those taken by the Baron.

'Do you miss him?'

'Who?'

'Philip.'

Harriet thought. She was an unusually truthful woman. 'Sometimes. Less and less. You know' – she ran a hand through her hair – 'I've almost forgotten him. Not what he did – or we did together. But what – what he was actually like.'

'Did we ever know that?'

Harriet did not answer.

Addy lowered herself into one of the six Chippendale chairs brought with them, to Lucy's amazement, from The Hague. Termites would destroy the chairs, Lucy had warned. Termites had a burglar's instinct for what was valuable. They had devoured a pretty little mahogany sewing-box, once her mother's, that she herself had brought to Khartoum. Now, she said, she kept everything of value in tin boxes.

'Do you realize that Nanny and Daan are sleeping together?'

'Yes, I *imagine* they must be.' Harriet was offhand. Weeks had passed since a late evening when, emerging from her tent, she had seen the two of them walking arm-in-arm, at a leisurely pace, beside the Nile. Nanny was wearing a black bonnet, a black shawl and high-buttoned black boots. Daan had on his wide-brimmed straw hat and was carrying a cane. They might have been a long-married couple going for an evening stroll along one of the Dutch canals.

'You imagine they must be!'

'Well, why not? What other company is there for them? Each has the other – and no one else.'

'But even so . . .'

Harriet shrugged.

'You wouldn't take such a relaxed attitude back at home. Would you? If you knew that they were sharing a room. As they are. Yes, yes, they are! What do you suppose Mrs Warburton will think if she finds that out? Nanny Rose's room is never slept in. I passed it late last night, the door was ajar, and so I peeped in. No sign of her.'

'Well, I hope they'll be happy.'

'But it's immoral. They're not married, Harriet.'

'You never used to be greatly concerned about morality. I was. Once. But out here . . . That's the wonderful thing. To be free of it. I mean, of that rigid, bourgeois idea of what's moral and what isn't. Wonderful!'

'This trip has changed you!'

'Yes, it has, it has.' Harriet nodded her agreement. 'It's changed us all. For better or for worse. Yes, you too.' She laughed, head on one side. 'If Daan did decide to make an honest woman of her, how would he do it? Who'd marry them? There's a Roman Catholic mission but they're not Roman Catholics. Perhaps there's also a Lutheran one. Or do you think that an honorary consul can conduct a marriage service? But if Mr Warburton is so ill . . .' Again she laughed. 'It looks as if they'll have to go on living in sin until we return to civilization. The only consolation is that Nanny, unlike Philip, is unlikely to produce a bastard.'

'It's no joke!'

∞

Not for the first time, Alexine studied the Colonel's creased and tattered map. During the journey, late at night, when she could not sleep despite her tiredness after a day of almost incessant riding and walking, she would often light a candle, take the map out from her pocket or her bag, where she carried it folded up in a small leather purse and, holding it up to the flickering illumination, would try to discover from it what she should make her next objective once they had reached Khartoum. It was as though she believed that, through the erratic, fine, scarlet lines, branching hither and thither like innumerable blood-vessels, the far-off Colonel could somehow direct her.

This time it was by the light of a colza lamp, not a candle, that she gazed down at the map. There was Cairo and there, far south of it, was Khartoum. In the area around Khartoum the red network was particularly complex and dense. There were so many arrows that to attempt to follow them, even with a magnifying glass, merely confused her. Eventually, frustrated, she once more folded up the map and replaced it in the purse. Then she put the purse under her pillow, as though she expected it to speak to her in her dreams since it so obstinately refused to do so while she was awake.

The next day, after breakfast, when she, Lucy and Sunny were sitting together in the garden, Alexine said: 'You know, Mrs Warburton, I'd so much like to meet Mr Warburton.'

'Lucy. Please call me Lucy. In a place like this, when we're living so close to each other and there are so few other Europeans – it seems somehow ridiculous to be so formal.'

'May I? May I really?' Alexine was delighted. 'Yes, I'd like that. And you must call me Alexine. That'll mean we're really friends.'

'You'd like to meet my husband?'

'Yes. I want his advice.'

'I'm not sure that he's up to giving anyone any advice. He was a great one for giving advice in the past,' she added, surprising Alexine with the bitterness of her tone. 'But now . . .'

'Please ask him. Tell him I need some advice. Badly. He knows this whole area so well. Doesn't he? He's lived here so long. He's known – and helped – all the great explorers.'

'And a lot of gratitude he's got for it!'

'Do please try. I promise not to tire him. Please.'

'I'll see if I can persuade him. I'm never very good at that. But I'll try.'

Sunny, who had been squatting on the floor at Alexine's feet, now tugged at her sleeve. 'You said you'd take me to buy clothes this morning.'

'Yes, yes. In a moment.'

Lucy was amazed. The boy certainly had charm, but it was ludicrous how Alexine spoiled him.

'Where do you think I can get some clothes made for Sunny? Something really smart.' Alexine still did not realize it that, in buying clothes for Sunny, she was repeating what, by taking him to his expensive tailor, her father had done for Sammy.

Lucy made two suggestions: an Egyptian with a shop in the market, and a Greek tailor. The latter could copy well enough. She ran a hand down her plain, ill-fitting brown dress. He had made that for her, she said, copying it from one from England that had worn out.

In no way to Lucy's surprise, Alexine was clearly not impressed.

∽

The Egyptian's shop was little more than a rickety wooden shed with an open drain, choked with refuse, running in front of it. Daan leapt across the drain with remarkable agility for someone of his years, to be followed by Sunny. Then they both held out their hands for Alexine. But ignoring them, one hand raising her skirt while the other held her parasol aloft, she too leapt across.

'This doesn't look much of a place,' Daan said, peering up at it.

'Shall I take a dekko first?' But, as he spoke, Sunny had already entered.

'Oh, let's all go in.'

Having so often been importuned to buy, buy, buy, Alexine was surprised by the indifference of the old man who, gazing vacantly into space, hands clasped in his lap, now rose slowly to his sandalled feet, and merely looked at them with a vague enquiry. One of his eyes was clouded with cataract; the other was red-rimmed and gummy in one corner with a yellow-green pus.

Daan, who had already begun to wander round the premises, said: 'This is just a junk shop.' He picked up a fork, bearing an elaborate monogram, its twin tines bent askew, which rested by itself beside a letter-rack on the top of a rickety table. The shop-keeper at once swivelled round to watch him, until he had replaced the fork.

'He thinks I'm going to pinch it.'

Alexine greeted the man in Arabic and explained: 'I want some clothes for my friend.' Sunny was examining, head tilted up, a row of ancient hats on a shelf above him.

The man, who had not returned her greeting, silently shuffled to the farthest end of the shop, turned and beckoned. Hanging from a long row of pegs, Alexine saw a jumble of western clothing, men's, women's, children's, all dusty, most stained, many so tattered that, in their own countries, the owners would most likely have consigned them to the rubbish dump.

Even her dead father's clothes, so clean and in such perfect condition, had filled her with revulsion when, having gone into his room to ask her mother something, she had found her sorting them out with the aid of Hans and the valet. On that occasion, having received an answer to her question, she had at once retreated. She felt an even more intense revulsion now. Most of the people who had once owned these clothes, brought with them when they had set out, full of hope, from their own temperate countries for what Lucy called this hell-hole, must now be dead. There were many children's garments. Most of those children must also be dead. She put out a hand to an embroidered pinafore, touched it, then at once withdrew the hand. The shop-keeper was watching her suspiciously with that one, pus-tacky, red-rimmed eye.

Then Sunny was beside her. Straining on tiptoe, he reached up to hitch some corduroy breeches off their hook. He held them up against himself, chin tucked in as he looked down. With the amazing serendipity that he so often showed, he had at once alighted on a perfect fit. For the first time, the shop-keeper smiled. He pulled back a curtain over what seemed to be little more than a closet and indicated that Sunny should go behind it to try the breeches on.

In a few moments, Sunny marched out. He stood in front of Alexine, hands raised, in the manner of an acrobat seeking applause after the performance of a particularly difficult trick. Gazing at him, she realized with amazement how much he had grown and filled out in the past few weeks. 'Good? Good?' He whirled round.

'Perfect. A perfect fit for the lad,' Daan said.

Alexine thought of the boy, no doubt dead of some insidious or peremptory tropical disease, who had once worn the breeches. She was filled with horror at the thought of Sunny now wearing them. But they looked almost new; they were, as Daan had said, a perfect fit.

'Please,' Sunny said, misinterpreting her hesitation for an uncharacteristic reluctance to spend money. 'Your present for me. Please!'

'Oh, very well!' She turned to the shopkeeper. 'How much?'

'You must bargain, miss!'

'Oh, I can't be bothered. Why waste the time?'

The man named a sum and she at once accepted it.

Sunny now began to forage for other things, running hands along a shelf or reaching up to jerk some other garment off its hook. As with the breeches, he showed an astonishing flair for finding exactly what was right for him. Daan also began to hunt, pulling out a pair of yellowing combinations, a heavily creased cravat, and a boater hat with a sweat-stained ribbon.

In one corner, boots and slippers were piled high. Sunny knelt down and began to scrabble among them, like one of Alexine's dogs looking for some edible morsel in a garbage-heap. Eventually, he extracted a pair of black patent-leather boots, which he dusted off on the sleeve of his jellaba before extending a bare foot and then pulling one on.

'Wrong boot! Wrong boot!' Daan shouted.

Sunny threw it aside and grabbed its pair.

'Try the other now,' Daan said.

Hands on hips, Sunny strutted up and down the shop in both boots. It was the first time in his life that he had not been barefoot. Yet again, the fit was perfect. Yet again, Alexine thought: 'He's no longer a child!'

He grinned: 'Yes, missie?'

Alexine nodded, his joy all at once communicating itself to her.

'I might buy these,' Daan said. He held up a pair of boots. 'Those boots of mine are on their last legs. What d'you think, miss?' Noticing the look of distaste on her face, he said: 'I've no feelings about wearing dead men's boots. Or anything else.'

'I'll buy them for you. If you really think they fit.'

'Oh, no, miss! I'll settle for them myself.' The protest was a token one.

'I'd like to.'

'You must get him to give you a lower price for everything together. You've bought more than he probably sells in a month of Sundays.'

But again Alexine could not be bothered to bargain.

'How are we going to get all this clobber home? There's too much to carry.'

Although Daan had spoken in Dutch, the shopkeeper somehow guessed what he had said. He went to the doorway of the shop and shouted something in a hoarse voice. Then he coughed and spat out a green glob of phlegm, which landed on the bedraggled corpse of a bird upturned, feet in air, in the gutter. 'Wait, madame. Wait, please.'

Eventually a lanky boy arrived pushing a cart.

Pointing at him, the shopkeeper said in Arabic: 'Tip for boy, madame. Yes?' Then he repeated the word in English: 'Tip, tip, tip!' Probably it was one of the very few English words that he knew, perhaps even the only one.

'Later,' Daan told him loudly and clearly in Dutch. 'When we've got back home.' He always imagined that if he said something with sufficient volume, then somehow his Dutch would be understood.

The shopkeeper nodded, having again somehow guessed what Daan had said. He laughed and, once more extending his head out of the door, coughed and spat another huge glob of phlegm into the open drain. Then: 'Tip, tip, tip!' he sang out happily in English.

'What about the tailor?' Daan asked.

'Oh, another time. Let's get all this stuff home. Mrs Warburton gave me directions but I never wrote them down. I'm not at all sure where he is.'

'You could ask.'

Alexine shook her head. She felt oddly disorientated so that, looking around her, she was not even sure of the way back home. This disorientation, creating a feeling of vague panic, seemed to her to be merely an extension of the general disorientation that had afflicted her since her arrival in Khartoum. As in the city itself, so in her life there was a labyrinth of routes and she was dizzied by the struggle to decide down which to plunge.

'It's so hot.' She put a hand to her forehead.

'Oh, I thought it was rather cooler, miss. There's this nice breeze now.'

Nice! As they stood beside the open drain, the breeze, fluctuating capriciously, struck Alexine as being like a series of breaths from a giant mouth full of rotting teeth.

Fortunately, Sunny knew the way. He strode out ahead both of them and of the youth with the hand-cart, from time to time looking round to see if they were following but chiefly gazing down at his newly acquired boots. He was also wearing the breeches and one of the two jackets that Alexine had also bought for him. She had told him that he would be far too hot in these clothes but he had insisted that no, no, he would be fine.

'Well, you look like a real macaroni,' Nanny Rose told him, when they entered the house. 'I hardly recognized you.'

'What do you think of these?' Daan held up his boots.

Nanny Rose inspected them, screwing up her eyes. 'Not bad. They must have cost you a pretty penny.'

'They cost Miss Alexine a pretty penny.'

'You're too generous! I keep telling you.' Nanny Rose shook her head in disapproval.

'Oh, what's money for? One might as well spend it while one has it.'

Nanny Rose, who had repeatedly heard Alexine express this sentiment, again shook her head, her mouth pursed.

Sunny, having seated himself on a stool, began to tug off his boots. In the heat of the walk home, his feet had swollen and his tugging was unsuccessful. Seeing his predicament, Alexine knelt down on the floor – really it was too absurd, the way she pandered to him, Nanny Rose thought – and began to tug at one of the boots herself. Eventually, she all but fell over backwards as it came away.

'Oh, you've got a blister! Look where it's been rubbing!' She looked round at Nanny Rose: 'Do bring me some of that Salve Benoît, Nanny.'

'We're running low. Miss Addy used a lot of it for her sunburn.'

'Oh, never mind that! Bring it.'

Muttering under her breath, Nanny Rose moved off.

Alexine touched the blister gently with a forefinger. It was over the toe that overlapped the one next to it. Sunny smiled up at her, showing the gap where one of his front teeth had been knocked out.

When she went out later that evening, Sunny, as so often on such occasions, attached himself to her without asking for her leave. He was once again wearing the boots, but now, where the leather had rubbed against the toe, he had neatly cut out a diamond-shaped hole.

∽

'Do you really want to meet my husband?'

'Of course. If he's willing to meet me.'

'He's curious about you. About all of you, but about you particularly. He's not been curious about anything for weeks.'

'Well, that's a good sign.'

'I hope so.'

Alexine, whose moods of depression or doubt were always so transient, could not understand how a woman relatively young and in apparent good health could so constantly suffer from both. Like Harriet, she felt sorry for Lucy; unlike Harriet, she was also irritated by her. It was often with difficulty that she restrained herself from scolding her: 'Come on! You can't spend your whole life brooding and moaning!'

With his sheet thrown back and his nightgown rucked up so that it revealed his white, oddly hairless legs, one crossed over the other at the ankles, and even a thigh, Alexine thought of the greyish grubs that the porters had avidly seized when they had seen an army of them on a clump of low trees, their branches already half-ravished of their leaves. The porters had at once begun to thrust these grubs, often two or three at a time, into their mouths, before swallowing them, whole as it seemed, with greedy relish. Roderick looked like a magnified version of one of these.

Lucy fetched a chair from where it stood against a wall. 'Sit,' she said.

'What about you?'

'Oh, I've so many things to do. I'll leave you both alone together.'

Alexine felt a swelling panic. How was she to initiate a conversation with this man who had not returned her greeting with more than a grunt, and who now stared up at her with dazed, puzzled eyes? For several seconds after Lucy's departure, they were silent. Alexine looked out of the curtainless window at a tree from which a number of fruit bats were dangling; Warburton continued to stare at her.

Suddenly he spoke: 'You're very elegant.'

'Thank you.'

'You're all very elegant. I was watching you from over there' – he raised a flaccid arm and pointed – 'one afternoon when you were in the garden, and I thought how elegant all of you were. But you were the most elegant of all.'

'People usually say that my aunt is the most elegant.'

'Do they? Do they? Then they're wrong. Anyway ... anyway ...' He seemed to have lost the thread of what he had been planning to say. One hand, the yellow-tinged nails for so long uncut that they looked like the talons of some bird of prey, moved restlessly over his thigh as though in search of that lost thread. Then he said: 'You must be an extraordinary woman. A prodigy.'

Alexine laughed and shook her head. 'There's nothing extraordinary about me – about any of us.'

'You have courage – travelling in this godawful country, by yourselves, three women.'

'Four women,' Alexine corrected. She now thought of Nanny Rose, as she had never done in The Hague, as one of themselves.

'Yes, that needs courage.'

'Not really. We can always give up and escape. Tomorrow or the next day we can decide that we'd rather be in The Hague – or London, or Paris, or Vienna – and, pfft, the magic wand can carry us there.'

'Magic wand?'

'Money. My money. I know it's bad manners to talk of money, but I find that, travelling like this, I talk about it and think about it constantly.'

He gave a small, twitchy smile. 'How lucky!'

'Yes. Lucky. Our luck is that, because of money, we're free. It doesn't require courage to come to a place like this if one is free to leave it whenever one wants. The real courage is to come to a place like this knowing that one can never leave it.'

'You're thinking of my wife.'

'And of many other people.'

Again there was a silence, with Alexine once again staring at the fruit bats dangling like black handkerchiefs from the tree outside the window and him once again searching her half-averted face.

'You wanted to ask me something?'

'I wanted to ask you two things. The first question is about you. The second is about myself. I don't know if you're able – or prepared – to answer either.'

'Try.'

'What's the matter with you? Your wife doesn't seem to know.' He winced visibly at the brutality of the question. Then he was grateful to her for it. It was as though a surgeon had lanced a boil: a moment of excruciating agony, then relief.

'I wish I knew.' For a time he pondered, head turned sideways, away from her, and hand to cheek. She waited with growing impatience. At last, in a dreamy, puzzled voice, he said: 'Everything has lost its taste for me. Everything – sickens me. I don't want to do anything – eat, get out of this bed, read a book, talk to anyone, even perform my natural functions. Imagine a clock which has all its other components in perfect order but mysteriously has lost its mainspring.'

'Money,' she said. 'People say that money is the root of all evil but it can also cure evils. Your wife tells me that you have financial problems.'

Once again her directness first pierced him agonizingly and then brought a gush of relief. 'She shouldn't have told you that.'

'Well, she has. And I don't blame her. We were here. Whom else could she tell?'

'Yes.' He sighed. 'Yes. I've made a mess of things. No doubt of that. I was overconfident. It's when you think that you can cheat someone else that you're most likely to be cheated.'

'I want to help you.'

'Help me? Why?'

'Because I've become fond of Lucy. I feel sorry for her in a way that I can't feel sorry for you. I feel sorry for you, yes, of course I do, but I hardly know you and so . . . But because of Lucy I want to help you.'

'And how do you propose to do that?'

'I told you. Money. Tell me what you need to get on your feet again.'

'On my feet again? Do you mean that literally or figuratively?'

'Both. I want you out of that bed. But I also want you back in business – whatever that business is.'

He stared at her. Then he burst into laughter. The laughter prolonged itself. He put a hand over his mouth, like a child trying to suppress its giggles under the eyes of a disapproving adult. 'Are you proposing to be my fairy godmother?'

'Yes. Why not? I can afford it.'

Suddenly, as though leaping up and away to avoid some imminent danger, he swung his legs aloft and then down from the bed. As the legs described an arc in the air before her, she saw for a second the plump white cock, another enlarged grub, the loose, wrinkled scrotum and the luxuriant, sweat-moist bush above them. There was something both ludicrous and pitiable about the sight.

He perched on the edge of the bed, knees together, one inturned foot over the other, leaning forward towards her. She could smell his breath. It reminded her of the breeze that, putrid gust on gust, had fanned over the open drain in the market. 'Are you serious?'

'Perfectly.'

Suddenly he raised one arm above his head and then the other, and exhaled a tremendous yawn, almost a groan, his whole body shuddering as he did so. 'Let's think about it. Both of us.'

'I don't have to think about it. I decide what I'm going to do. I do it. Does that sound terribly arrogant to you?'

He nodded, smiled. 'Yes.'

'But in one matter I can't decide what to do. So that's my second question to you. Where do I go from here?'

Either he genuinely misunderstood her or he pretended to do so. 'From here? Aren't you happy in our house? Hasn't Lucy . . . ?'

'We love it here. And Lucy has been immensely kind to us. But I have to push on. That's why I came here – not to stay here but to push on. We've been here long enough already but . . .' Again she looked out of the window at the motionless fruit bats. 'I can't be like one of those bats – just hanging on. Tell me. Where do you think I should go?' When he did not answer, merely staring at her, his eyes narrowed, she went on: 'I want to find something that no one else has found. To go somewhere where no one has gone before me.'

'There's nowhere where no one has gone before you. This whole continent is teeming with people.'

'I mean – no one white.'

'Ah! I see.' He spoke ironically.

'So what do you suggest? You know this whole area so well. You've travelled all over it. You've seen more of it than anyone else. That's what they told me in Cairo, and what they now tell me here.'

'The Grail,' he said. 'The Holy Grail. Did any women go out in search of the Holy Grail? I don't think so. I don't remember.'

She was mystified. 'The Holy Grail?'

He nodded. 'There always has to be something in Africa that people are obsessed with finding. The finding of it doesn't mean that the people of this wretched continent – or anywhere else for that matter – become richer or happier or even better. It's just the singularity of the find that makes it – for some idiots – worth suffering for and even dying for. But the nature of the Holy Grail constantly keeps changing. Until recently it was the source of the Nile. But that search is virtually over.'

'So what are the idiots searching for now?' Alexine spoke drily. If all the men who had ventured out, palpitating with excitement, ambition and dread, into the vast darkness of this continent were idiots, then surely she herself, a mere woman, was also one?

'The source of the Congo.'

'The Congo?'

'Yes, the source of the Congo. You might say – or, better, I might say – who cares about its source? The river is there and all the riches – minerals, ivory, slaves – around it are there. What does it matter where the river originates? Human beings want to know where they originate – from the dust or from monkeys or from the hand of God. That's natural enough. But a river, for heaven's sake, a river! None the less ... People are prepared to die to find it.'

Alexine was hardly listening to him. The one word 'Congo' had been like the report of a rifle fired just over her head, deafening her to anything else. The Congo!

She was eager to question him but, knowing how jealously explorers guarded their knowledge for fear that someone might steal a march on them (her father, she remembered, guarded his insider knowledge of the markets with equal jealousy), she hesitated. Might not he too be in secret search for this Holy Grail despite his contemptuous remarks about the 'idiots' who were obsessed with finding it?

'Yes?' As though guessing the reason for her hesitation, he abruptly prompted her.

'That's an idea,' she said. 'The source of the Congo. Why did I never think of it? Colonel Scott once spoke about it to me. But for some reason I hardly took it in.'

'Well, if I've been of some help . . .' His tone was sardonic.

'Oh, you have, you have!' Then an idea suddenly flashed at her. 'Why don't you join us?'

'Me?' He pointed to his narrow, emaciated chest, the long, yellowing, talon-like nails resting on a rib-cage of which every bone was distinct.

'Why not? You know the country. Lucy told me that you spoke some of the languages. Arabic will be of little use, I imagine. You could be such a help to us. Yes, it's a tremendous idea!'

He was looking across at her, his hand still on his chest, his head tilted to one side and a mocking but not malign smile on his lips.

'I'd pay you. Of course I'd pay you. Generously, I have the reputation for being generous. So that would be a solution to your financial problems. Of a kind. Oh, do say yes!'

'If you wanted me to go on an expedition to find copper or gold or ivory, of course I'd say yes. But the sort of expedition that you have in mind – for me it's pointless, absolutely pointless. Why risk our healths and even our lives for something so pointless? No, no.' He shook his head. 'Count me out.'

'But think about it!'

'I've often thought about it. Yours isn't the first invitation of that kind. Far from it. Not long ago Pullar asked me to accompany him and his wife. I said no then. I must say no now.'

Alexine was not used to being refused. 'Think about it,' she repeated. 'Please. I promise I'd go along with anything you suggested. I know that people say that I'm far too obstinate and bossy but I promise . . . Please!'

Again he shook his head.

Alexine abandoned any further attempt to make him change his mind. Instead she began to press him for advice. Where did he himself believe that the source of the Congo was located? What route should they take?

'A lot of what I say is only supposition. I may be wholly wrong. But my advice is to begin by sailing for Bahr-al-Ghazal. I've been there myself – trading. Not easy. From there I estimate a march of at least five hundred miles south by west. With luck you'll then come on the watershed between the White Nile and the Congo. With luck! Well, unlike me, you're clearly a lucky person. Anyone who inherits so much money can only be lucky.'

She continued to question him. But he soon lay back on the bed, drawing the sheet up over his emaciated body, his eyelids fluttering as though in an effort to ward off sleep. His voice became almost inaudible, falling away at the end of every sentence and sometimes of every phrase.

At last, taking pity on him, she got up from the chair. 'I've exhausted you. I'm sorry. When I get excited about something, I can think of nothing else. I must let you rest.'

Again the eyelids fluttered. 'Never mind. My wife told me that your aunt calls you the girl who always gets what she wants. Perhaps – who knows – you'll get the Holy Grail. That would be something – a woman who found the Holy Grail!'

'May we talk again? Soon?'

'Why not?'

'And meantime – tell me how much you need. Yes?'

'How much I need? Oh – oh, you mean money.' His mouth opened as though he were again going to emit another of his prodigious yawns, and the dry, rattling sound of laughter emerged from the back of his throat. 'The root of all evil. Well, if you insist.'

'I do insist.' In gratitude for that one word 'Congo', she impulsively put out a hand and laid it over the one still resting on his rib-cage. 'Get well soon. Please. Make an effort.'

'Patient, heal thyself.'

'Oh, yes, there was one other thing I wanted to ask you. Do you know what happened to Colonel Scott?'

'Scott? That old mountebank! The last I heard he was somewhere in America. Married a rich widow. In Chicago, was it? Yes, that was it. She was the widow of some railway or meat baron. A wise move on Scott's part. Every move in his life has been a wise one. He was finished, health ruined, no money, when he met her. No more Africa for him!'

Lucy was behind her. 'I think he's getting tired.' Passing the door, she had halted and, with a feeling of shame, had begun to listen. She was sure that there had been an intimacy between her husband and Pullar's wife. Perhaps a similar intimacy was now about to take place between him and this bossy, opinionated, intrepid girl – or had already done so. Although no longer in love with him, she could, much to her surprise and chagrin, still feel jealousy. 'He tires so easily.'

'Yes, I was just going to go.'

'She's going to bail us out,' Warburton said. 'Think of that! She's going to bail us out.'

Lucy turned in surprised questioning to Alexine.

Alexine nodded. 'Yes. I want to do what I can to get you both out of your troubles.'

Lucy's pale face suddenly flushed. For a moment she looked angry. Then, tugging straight the sheet under her husband's body, she said:

'Well, that's very generous of you. I don't know what we've done to deserve such generosity.' Irony gave her tone a dangerous edge.

'You've been so kind and hospitable to us. And your husband has given me a wonderful idea.'

'My husband's wonderful ideas all too often end in disaster.' Warburton might not have been present, his eyes moving back and forth between one of these commanding women and the other. 'I hope that won't happen in your case.'

10 SUNNY AND ALEXINE RODE OUT SIDE BY SIDE, as she and Sammy had so often done in a past that now often seemed to her to be no more than a smoke-like puff of dream, suddenly drifting across her mind and then, strand by strand, disintegrating.

Like Sammy, Sunny had from the start been fearless on the pony bought for him by Alexine, with Osman as intermediary; but, unlike Sammy, he had no natural aptitude, so that it was fortunate that his shaggy, skinny mount, still to show the benefits of its change of owner-ship, was rarely to be coaxed into a trot, let alone a canter. When he did trot, Sunny gripped the pommel of the saddle and, legs dangling bare-foot alongside the stirrups, bounced up and down, often giving a hic-coughing laugh as he did so. Alexine told him to put his feet in the stirrups and to raise himself as the pony rose. But he could not grasp something to her so simple, and in consequence, since he clearly felt no hardship, she soon gave up.

'Look, missie, look!'

They were riding through a grove of Palmyra palms when, letting go of the reins, Sunny pointed upwards. In the branches above him, bul-bous fruit dangled like orange globes of light. He jumped off his pony and, without bothering to tether it, miraculously, prehensile toes to trunk and hands around it, shinned up the tree. 'Take care! Take care!' Alexine shouted. He answered with a laugh. Had she not, when first set-ting eyes of him, been reprimanded by Harriet for calling him 'Monkey'? He was now showing a monkey's insouciant agility.

When he descended, he had one of the fruit precariously clutched under an arm. He had flung another down, only for it to smash, spilling its pulp.

'Smell.' He held the undamaged fruit up to her.

She lowered her head to smell. She breathed in deeply.

'Wonderful! Like a melon!' The smell, sharp and cool, even seemed to assuage her growing thirst.

Now he rode lopsided, bare feet still dangling and one arm cradling the fruit. Once back in the house, he would scamper off to the kitchen and, to the displeasure of the Egyptian cook, who was busy preparing dinner, take down a large, curved knife from a rack, and hack the fruit into pieces. Alexine, to whom he would offer a slice, would meditatively munch the orange flesh – 'Not bad, not bad' – but the others would refuse and Lucy would then jump up, take the plate from him and say that the servants could use it to make some flour for their bread.

As they returned by way of a street flanked with white houses that made Alexine screw up her eyes at the glare reflected off them, a group of five mounted men, all in Arab costume, emerged from around a corner. They were talking in loud, vibrant voices, seemingly all at one and the same time, so that Alexine had difficulty in grasping what they were saying. At the sight of the tall, pale woman, her hair bleached almost white by the sun, and the small black boy, they reined in and turned their heads to stare. Sunny kicked at the sides of his pony. Alexine averted her eyes.

Then, on an impulse, she looked at them. All the faces were almost wholly covered; but, with a shock, she was sure that she recognized one. Wasn't it Fielding? When she had last spoken to him in Cairo he had said nothing of being in Khartoum when she was there. But that meeting had been a long time ago and perhaps it had only been after it that he had decided on the journey. Should she say something? But the eyes above the white cloth showed no recognition. She must have been mistaken! During the trek, she had often found that the heat and tiredness had tricked her mind into mistaking something for something else – so that, briefly, a distant tree had been transformed into a motionless figure, a drooping liana into a sleeping snake, a long shadow cast by one of the tents in the dusk into Osman's waiting presence.

Over long glasses of lemonade, she asked Lucy: 'Do you know – is someone called Fielding – Tim Fielding – in Khartoum again?'

'I hope not. I haven't heard that he is.'

'Why do you hope not? I met him in Cairo. I rather took to him.'

'Most people do take to him. At first. But there's always trouble where he goes. He's partly – perhaps largely – responsible for what happened to my husband.'

'How?'

'Oh, it's too complicated to go into it all. But they were once friends, partners. Then Fielding betrayed my husband.'

Alexine persisted in trying to extract more details, but Lucy merely shook her head: 'No, no. Let's not talk about it. It's too boring, it's too painful. I don't want to see him again, I don't want to talk about him. I want to forget him.'

∽

For the first time since their arrival, Warburton came down to dinner that evening. They were all seated round the dining-room table, half-way through their meal, when suddenly there he was, in his night-shirt, feet bare.

'I thought I'd join you.'

Harriet jumped up, took his arm, and guided him over to her chair. She then signalled to one of the two servants, now dressed in white, starched uniforms that she had had the Greek tailor make for them, to bring her another chair. The day before she had at last been admitted into Warburton's bedroom. Addy and Nanny Rose were now meeting him for the first time.

'But this is your chair,' he protested.

'It doesn't matter. They'll fetch me another. Please. Sit.'

He staggered to the chair and sat down.

Lucy's eyes were fixed on him. 'Dear heart, I hardly think that you're properly dressed for dinner with these ladies.'

'Oh, it doesn't matter!' Harriet cried out, as she lowered herself into the chair brought by the servant. 'I must introduce you to my sister.' Addy gave an abrupt nod of the head. Unlike Harriet, she was affronted by the sight of this unshaven, cadaverous, rheumy-eyed man in nothing but his nightshirt.

'And this is our dear companion, Nanny Rose.'

He made no response.

Lucy leaned across the table. 'Darling – please ... Do go upstairs and put on –'

'Oh, shut up, damn you!'

Sunny put a hand up over his mouth and laughed behind it. He himself was wearing his newly purchased breeches and a white linen shirt and cravat.

∽

Lucy emerged, eyes stinging and arm aching from working at her book, to find Addy outstretched on a *chaise-longue* brought from The Hague and placed in the cavernous ante-room because Harriet had been unable to think of anywhere else for it. Addy looked up from her book.

Lucy paused at the foot of the stairs, deliberated for a moment, then turned.

'I'm sorry about that unedifying scene over dinner. But, as you know, my husband has been ill. And I suppose that for the ill – for people who are ill in their minds – one has to make allowances.'

'Of course one must. I was once ill like that myself. Fortunately I found this wonderful man in Slovenia, by a lake called Bled. People said terrible things about him – that he was a quack and a crook and a pervert and so on – but he cured me. I wish your husband could go to him. But he's getting better anyway, isn't he?'

Lucy nodded. 'Yes, I think that your niece has begun to bring about a cure.'

'Alexine?'

Lucy nodded. 'She seems to have the key to the door of his cell.'

What key was she talking about? Addy wanted to ask but was embarrassed to do so. Had he fallen in love with the girl? Might they even be having an affair? Lucy's tone was so bitter. She decided to change the subject.

'Forgive my asking, but what exactly is it that you do when you go into your – your den?' By now she had got used to Lucy using that word ('Well, I'm going to disappear into my den for a little', 'My den summons me', 'I must put in an hour or two in my den').

'I write.'

'Write? You mean, letters?'

'No. Not letters. I have none of your sister's enthusiasm for receiving and sending letters. Which is just as well, since I so rarely have occasion to do either.'

'In that case – ?'

'I'm attempting to write a book.'

'A book? How interesting!'

'I doubt if it is.'

'Perhaps one day I'll be able to read it. As you must have realized by now, I'm a tremendous reader.'

'Even a tremendous reader might not be attracted by my book.'

'What – what sort of book is it?'

Lucy had been looking out of the window at the dangling fruit bats at which Alexine had stared the day before. Now she turned. 'A novel.'

'A novel! But that's my favourite kind of reading. I've read everything written by Dickens and Thackeray, and I'm now on my second journey through *La Comédie Humaine*. How exciting!'

'I'm afraid there's little excitement in my novel.'

'What's it about?'

Lucy considered, as though she were trying to sum up the contents of a novel by someone else, read years before. 'Well, let me see. What's it about? It's about a girl whose father is an impoverished rector in Norfolk. He keeps losing what little money he has – and what little faith he has. She goes as governess to the family of her father's widowed patron. He lives in a grand house on a hill, in a park of several acres. Designed by Repton. Well, she suffers all sorts of humiliations but then, in the end, he notices her and falls in love with her. His domineering mother and his sister are against any marriage, since they don't think her worthy of him – socially, I mean. But in the end – as always in the end in novels – true love conquers and the little governess becomes mistress of the grand house and all those acres.' She looked sardonically over at Addy. 'How's that for a story?'

'It sounds fascinating.'

'Yes, it's a kind of cross between *Pride and Prejudice* and *Jane Eyre*.'

'Yes, yes, it sounds fascinating.'

Lucy leapt up from her seat. 'No, I'm only joking with you. That's not it, not it at all.' Again she went to the French windows and peered out. Damp strands of hair were sticking to her wide, low forehead.

'When you mentioned *Jane Eyre*, I was thinking that you looked rather like Charlotte Brontë.'

'Is that a compliment?' Then Lucy took pity on Addy, so eager to be friendly and sympathetic and so much puzzled by all that she had heard. 'I suppose that mine is really a Gothic novel.'

'Oh!' Addy's disappointment was plain. 'I don't know why, I don't really take to –'

'It's a Gothic novel of an unusual kind. It's not set in some castle in the Alps or the Highlands of Scotland, but here, here in Africa, here in Khartoum.'

'Well . . .' Addy was bewildered and flustered. 'Well, that seems a very – very original idea.'

'Yes, I suppose that the idea *is* original. The only question is – is the execution any good?'

'Oh, I'm sure it is.'

'You're so encouraging. Thank you.'

Lucy began to mount the stairs. With a pang, she realized that Alexine was once again in her husband's room. She could hear them talking to each other and then, as she put her hand on the handle of the door, he gave a clear, joyous laugh, such as she had not heard from him for many months.

She pushed the door open.

'Oh!' She stared coldly at Alexine. 'What a surprise!'

∽

Harriet tore open the envelope that a servant had just delivered on foot, and stared down at the invitation inscribed in French with a number of extravagant curlicues. The servant, squatting out in front of the stable block that now housed most of the domestic staff, had said that he would wait for an answer.

'It's extraordinary how many invitations are coming in. These people' – she held out the card – 'have never met us and I've no idea who they are.'

Lucy lowered her head to squint down at the invitation. Before the arrival of the Dutch party she had broken her glasses, dropping them on the stone floor of the kitchen, and their replacement had still not arrived from Cairo.

'Oh, it's from Monsieur Thibault. The French consul. His wife's name never appears on an invitation. She was a Sudanese slave.'

'I don't think we can be bothered to go,' Alexine said. 'Not because his wife was a Sudanese slave,' she added hastily. 'That doesn't trouble me at all. But because I find all these parties so dull.'

'You won't find Mr Thibault dull, I think. You might even find him interesting. He's been here for years and years. He first came here, as Roderick did, merely as a trader. He's the man who sent the first giraffe to the London Zoo.'

'Oh, we saw it!'

'Well, that's something you can talk to him about.'

'Since they've never met us – and, in most cases, we haven't even got introductions to them – I don't know why all these people keep asking us to their houses,' Addy said.

'Well, you can imagine how things are here,' Lucy responded. 'Nothing ever happens – except that each year a number of bores die and a number of bores replace them. You're a novelty. You're not interested in gold or copper or ivory or slaves – or even in exporting animals to some zoo or other. You're aristocratic and rich and you have a vast retinue. To them, it's like a visit from royalty.'

'Shall we go?' Harriet pondered, tapping the invitation against her mouth.

'No!' Alexine said.

'Yes!' Addy said.

They spoke simultaneously.

Harriet turned to Lucy. 'I suppose you'll be going?'

'Then I'm afraid you've supposed wrong. No, we are no longer *personae gratae* in that little circle.'

'Oh! How's that?'

Lucy shrugged. 'You must ask my husband that question.'

∽

As they were frantically preparing for the party – Addy had mislaid a cameo brooch and had convinced herself that it had been stolen, Harriet was dissatisfied with the ironing of her dress by one of the Egyptian maids so that Nanny Rose was now hurriedly re-ironing it for her, Alexine had returned late from a ride with Sunny and had then insisted on water being heated up for a bath – the ponderously dignified, grey-haired servant whom they now regarded as their butler announced the arrival of the Mudir's barge.

'The Mudir? The Mudir? Who on earth is he?' Harriet asked Lucy, who happened to be sitting with her while she was awaiting her dress.

'The Governor,' Lucy said. 'A Turk.'

'But why should he send a barge for us? I thought we were dining with Monsieur Thibault.'

'Yes, you are. But those two are thick as thieves. Which is, in fact, what both of them are. Each helps the other. Old Thibault pushes a bribe in the direction of the Governor, and in return the Governor does him a favour. The most usual favour is to make his barge available to him. Three years ago that favour turned into a disaster. The barge was hit by the Governor-General's steamer, the crew all panicked, and some of Thibault's guests, who had never learned to swim, were drowned.'

'Well, I hope that we're not going to drown. Alexine can swim but Addy and I never learned. Our father thought that swimming was a lower-class pastime.'

'You'll travel in the new barge, which was brought all the way from Cairo.'

'In The Hague, we had a magnificent black and yellow brougham – made in England. Just as the Governor's barge seems to be used chiefly for transporting Mr Thibault's guests, so our brougham came to be used chiefly for transporting the guests of our friends and relations. It was borrowed so frequently that I often had to travel in more humble fashion myself, in one of our smaller and older coaches.'

The barge was magnificent – the only really elegant thing that they had seen since their departure from Cairo, Addy declared. Painted red and green, with armchairs upholstered in red and green damask and with a crew attired in uniforms of the same two colours, it was propelled majestically down the river by six oarsmen clearly in no hurry, so lethargic was their rowing.

Addy, fearful that the breeze would disorder the elaborate coiffure created for her by the two maids whom she shared with Alexine and Harriet, fingered now it and now the cameo brooch that she had imagined to have been stolen until Nanny Rose had come on it in a drawer. 'Wouldn't it be wonderful to have a barge like this to get us about the city?'

'Oh, don't say that!' Harriet cried. 'The next thing will be that Alexine will order one from Cairo. Or offer to buy this one for a sum so huge that the Governor will be unable to refuse.'

Alexine, who had been watching the crew as they went about their tasks, suddenly said: 'Isn't that man beautiful?' With her ostrich-feather fan she pointed at one of the sailors.

'Oh, please!' Addy protested.

Harriet raised the jewelled lorgnette which she wore only on important occasions. She peered through it with her small, alert eyes. 'Yes,' she said. 'Yes. They *are* a beautiful race, no doubt about it. When one sees someone like that, it's like finding a diamond lying in the dust.'

Addy again put a hand up to her coiffure. 'What nonsense!'

The Thibault house was set back from a surprisingly green lawn that sloped down to the river. 'It looks like an even more *petit* Petit Trianon,' Addy commented as, guided by a sprucely uniformed major domo who, standing motionless with arms folded across his swelling chest, had been waiting for them, they made their way up from the landing-stage. Lucy had told them that Thibault was the richest foreigner in the city. It was obvious that she was right.

To their amazement Thibault was attired not, like his guests, in European formal dress but in what appeared to be the uniform of a high-ranking Turkish officer. He was even carrying a curved dagger in the red silk cummerbund encircling his vast girth. 'Delighted, delighted,' he murmured, as he lent over their hands to brush them with his full, moist lips.

There was no sign of the Sudanese wife who had once been a slave. Later Addy was to say to him, 'We're so disappointed not to meet Madame Thibault', to be told: 'Yes, she is most disappointed not to meet three such distinguished guests. But the sad truth is – she is a martyr to migraine. And when the wind is in this direction – the Sudanese equivalent of the mistral – she is particularly vulnerable.' Later still, as they waited endlessly for the arrival of the entrée at dinner, they heard a female voice, from behind the baize-covered door leading from dining-room to domestic quarters, raised in angry hectoring of the dilatory staff. Clearly her migraine had not prevented Madame Thibault from acting as behind-the-scenes stage-manager of the lavish occasion. No doubt Monsieur Thibault preferred it that way.

The other guests gawped openly at the three Dutch women as they made their entrance into a long, low-ceilinged drawing-room, lit by elaborate, multicoloured chandeliers – 'brought from Murano', Monsieur Thibault said when Addy, who in fact thought them extremely vulgar, remarked on how 'striking' they were. Every object in the room – chairs, picture-frames, mirrors, even false Ionic columns – appeared to have been gilded. Monsieur Thibault triumphantly moved the women from group to group, making his introductions. This invariably began: 'I am sure that you have heard of these three remarkable ladies,' and then continued with references to their connections with the House of Orange and the extravagance of their progress, accompanied by a vast, polyglot retinue, from Cairo to Khartoum.

It was clear that Monsieur Thibault had gathered all Khartoum 'society' – of which the Warburtons were no longer a part – with the purpose of impressing on everyone the importance and wealth of his three Dutch guests who, dressed in the height of fashion, at once became a focus for everyone's eyes. 'Look at that necklace. Diamonds and rubies. Have you ever seen anything like it?' 'Even those shoe-buckles must have cost a fortune.' 'I love those ear-rings. They must be French, don't you think? That bow shape could only be French.' 'Have you seen the diadem the girl is wearing? It reminds me of that one worn by the Empress Josephine in that portrait of her.' Their clothes elicited even more excited comments. Most of the other women were dressed with an ostentatious lack of taste, to be ridiculed later by Addy during the journey home – if one must wear such an elaborate white collar and cuffs, then at least they ought to be spotless, maroon was such an unflattering shade for a woman with that sort of muddy complexion, had they noticed how one of the pleated panels of that dress garishly embroidered with humming-birds worn by that elderly Greek woman was not merely coming away but was actually hanging loose?

Before the summons to dinner Monsieur Thibault's three daughters, beautiful girls with glowing brown skins, vivacious eyes and ample haunches and breasts, self-consciously arranged themselves on the floor around Alexine, as though they were about to pose for one of her photographs. One admiringly fingered the torchon lace trimming of her white muslin dress. 'This must be from Paris.' Alexine nodded, not wishing to say that no, it had been made for her by Madame Molnar in The Hague, since the Hungarian dressmaker was someone of whom she still did not like to think, much less speak. Another put out a brown hand and stroked the black patent leather toecap of one of her otherwise white slippers. The third raised Alexine's wrist to examine the bracelet on it.

Excitedly they began to question her. Had she been to Paris? And to London? The eldest had travelled as far as Venice with her father – it was on that occasion that the chandeliers had been purchased – but the other two had never travelled farther than Cairo. The French magazines arrived so late in Khartoum, and some that were sent never arrived at all. Oh, they so much envied her her voyage! From time to time, their mother had travelled, chiefly as interpreter, with their father on his journeys into the interior, but he would never allow any of them to go too. He was terribly strict in that way, old-fashioned, unaware that times were changing.

'When will you start on your travels again?' the eldest asked.

'As soon as possible. But there are so many preparations to be got through first.'

'Oh, couldn't I come with you?' another of the girls asked.

'Couldn't we all come with you?'

Alexine shook her head. 'I don't think your father would allow it.'

The girls groaned and sighed.

At dinner, Harriet was seated on Monsieur Thibault's right. As dish after dish appeared, he kept telling her of the difficulty with which this or that ingredient had been procured. Good milk, he explained, was hard enough to come by, but cream of this quality was virtually impossible. This was lamb, not goat, from some sheep brought from Greece. The *petits fours* were not local but imported from France. His florid face was sweating and from time to time he raised his heavily starched linen napkin to mop at it.

'Your father was an Admiral, wasn't he? Yes, Admiral Van Capellen. Very distinguished. And didn't his brother marry – was it a cousin of your King?'

Harriet was soon bored and longing for the evening to end. But her natural good manners prevented her from in any way betraying this. Addy was less self-controlled. When Harriet's eyes met hers, she raised a hand and went through an elaborate charade of yawning behind it. She was seated between a middle-aged Italian engineer, sent by his company to explore the possibility of laying a railway track from Cairo to Khartoum, and an elderly English businessman who had recently arrived to shoot big game.

After dinner, Monsieur Thibault asked Harriet if she would play for them. 'Your fame as a pianist has preceded you even to this cultural desert,' he proclaimed, not realizing that this was hardly flattering to his other guests. Harriet was at first reluctant, but eventually acceded. She wished that she had not done so: having wiped her palms on a lace-bordered handkerchief, she practised a few arpeggios. Clearly, no piano-tuner had visited the house for months, perhaps even years.

What would be suitable for a company like this? She decided on some of the Mendelssohn *Songs Without Words*. Everyone listened with attention but with little evidence of pleasure. When she had played five of the pieces, she thought that that was enough, and the company seemed to agree with her. But Monsieur Thibault jumped up, applauding more vigorously than anyone else, and asked her if she would accompany 'one of my little girls'. The little girl was the oldest and largest of the trio, who came forward with an album of Tosti songs. Did she know them? she asked Harriet. Yes, Harriet did. She had frequently played the accompaniments in drawing-rooms in the Netherlands and England. She sighed as she squinted short-sightedly down at the score spread out before her by the girl.

The voice, a powerful contralto hoot – Addy later said that the girl had sounded like a cow in labour – was excruciating. Monsieur Thibault beamed, as she went through 'A Last Dance', and his other two daughters beamed with him. The rest of the audience were no doubt wishing that the last dance was also the last song. But her father clapped even more vigorously than he had clapped Harriet and cried out: 'Encore! Encore.' The girl was only too happy to oblige.

Suddenly Alexine was thinking of Sophie's clear, sweet, artless but unfailingly tuneful soprano. She seemed to hear it, a silvery descant, above the chesty bawling resounding round the room. She closed her eyes. She had so seldom thought of Sophie since her arrival in Africa. From Shepheard's Hotel she had despatched a brief reply to the three long letters that she had found awaiting her there. Here in Khartoum four more letters had been awaiting her, their girlishly enthusiastic chatter so much grating on her that she had postponed writing an answer, despite Harriet's urgings – 'Oh, you must write to the poor little thing. She'll be so disappointed not to hear from you. It's so cruel of you.' Now Alexine was consumed with guilt, as she closed her eyes and visualized Sophie standing by the piano, her small, plump hands clasped before her and her throat quivering as she released a particularly high note.

Alexine opened her eyes. There, not sitting in a chair but leaning against the wall opposite her, was Fielding. She stared intently at him, willing him to look in her direction, but his face remained averted. Unlike all the other men, he was clad not in formal evening dress but in the sort of loose tweeds that he might have worn when walking around his father's now cruelly diminished ancestral estates near Ennis. His trousers, patterned with large squares of black and brown, were of peg-top design, the upper part cut very loose. His waistcoat was yellow checked with black, with heavy brass buttons. He was shod in Hessian boots. Was he not embarrassed at appearing in such clothes for such an occasion? From his negligent stance and slightly contemptuous expression, his eyes half-closed, it was clear that he was not.

At last the performance was over. Having gone on clapping long after everyone else had stopped, Monsieur Thibault first told his daughter, 'Thank you, my dear, that was a beautiful experience,' and then took Harriet's hand – she was still seated at the piano – and bowed over it and kissed it. 'Madame – all that we have heard about your musicianship has proved to be no exaggeration. You were truly inspired.'

Harriet shook her head. 'I badly need practice.' She restrained herself from adding: 'And the piano badly needs tuning.'

It was then that Monsieur Thibault noticed Fielding. 'My dear friend!' As the Frenchman rushed over, Fielding straightened himself and took a step back. Monsieur Thibault threw his arms around him and kissed him on either cheek. Then, gripping both his forearms, he looked him over, beaming idiotically. 'What happened to you? A place was laid for you at dinner. We waited.'

'I had a meeting. Something I could not avoid. My apologies.' Fielding was coolly offhand. 'I didn't even have time to change, as you can see.'

'Oh, that doesn't matter. You look far more elegant in your casual clothes from Savile Row than we do in our formal ones from our Greek friend.' Monsieur Thibault guffawed, throwing back his head, hand to the dagger at his waist. 'Have you met our guests of honour?'

'The three intrepid Dutch ladies? Yes, I have. In Cairo.'

'Well, come and meet them again. Didn't you enjoy Madame

Thinne's playing? Exquisite. And she accompanied my little girl with so much tact. The voice is beautiful but it still needs a lot a training – which could, alas, also be said about the character of the singer.'

'Oh, you're doing her an injustice. In my experience, Lola always behaves impeccably.'

Thibault took Fielding's arm and began to push him ahead of him to where Harriet was seated on a sofa, with a citron-faced middle-aged woman perched eagerly on its edge beside her. But Fielding had other ideas.

'Oh, Miss Thinne!' he called out. 'We meet again.' He jerked free of Thibault's restraint, and hurried over to Alexine. 'Monsieur Thibault told me that the three of you were to be here. That was what decided me to come to one of these singularly tedious gatherings. Was the food as indigestible as the caterwauling? It usually is.' Monsieur Thibault was still hovering in their vicinity. Alexine feared that he might have over-heard these far from flattering remarks.

She shook her head. 'No. We had an excellent dinner. The teal was particularly good. I tried to shoot some on the journey here, but had little luck.'

'*Shoot* some! So you shoot! You're an even more remarkable woman than I thought. The amazon not of the Amazon but of the Nile. May I sit down here beside you?' He pointed to one of the fragile gilt chairs.

'Please.'

He moved the chair round, in such a way that the burly American trader to whom Alexine had been talking was totally excluded.

The chair creaked perilously as he lowered his powerful body into it.

'So you arrived here safe and sound!'

'Yes. We arrived here.'

'I knew that you would. You had that sort of determination. And when are you going back?'

'Oh, we're not going back. We're going forward.' The moment that she had said it, she wished that she had not done so.

'Forward! Where to?' He was astonished.

'We haven't decided. We don't yet know.'

Like every other explorer, wary of any rival, she was deliberately vague. It was she, not he or anyone else, who would find the Holy Grail. That determination was now the central pillar of her life.

'Well, you'd better hurry up. Once the rainy season arrives, progress will be difficult.'

He began to question her about both the voyage on the steamer and about the overland trek that had followed it. When she spoke about her photographs, he at once said, 'Oh, I'd like to see those!' Then he added: 'But that'll have to wait until I get back from my journey.'

'Your journey? Where are you going?' Could he be preceding her on the route that she herself was planning to take?

'Oh, into the interior,' he said vaguely. 'I've heard of a cache of ivory. The price keeps soaring in Europe and America, thank God. It makes it worth all the discomfort – and danger.' He leaned forward. 'I do hope that you're going to be careful – very careful. It's one thing to make the journey as tourists from Cairo to here. It's another to push on – yes, often literally to push on, through mangrove swamps and lianas and thorn bushes and God knows what else.'

'I don't think of ourselves as tourists,' Alexine said, nettled.

'Well, not quite. But according to all accounts, you had a cook from the French legation preparing food that wouldn't have disgraced Shepheard's – not to mention ice-boxes, carpets and commodes, and maids washing and ironing your frocks.'

'I rarely wore a frock. Unless you call a jellaba a frock.'

He laughed, enjoying her combativeness. 'What is all this I heard about your buying a slave?'

'I didn't buy a slave.'

'Then who was the black boy I saw riding with you two or three days ago?'

So she had been right: it had been he whom she had seen mounted and in Arab costume with that party of Arabs.

'I bought him, yes, but not to be my slave. I bought him to free him. He's free now. I treat him as – as if he were my nephew. Or son. He has to do what I tell him, of course he does, because he can't be more than twelve or thirteen. But he has his pocket money, just as my nephew or son would have it, and I treat him no differently than I'd treat them.'

'All that may not be so easy when you return home.'

'*If* I return home.' At once she wondered: Why had she said that? Until that moment, she had never consciously thought that she might not return home and might instead opt to settle here in Africa.

'Forgive me for offering some advice.'

'Yes?' The upward inflection was sharp.

'I think you must be careful. The rumour has been – it's even reached Cairo – that you bought yourself a slave. It's all nonsense in my view but, as I'm sure you know, there's this obsession with putting an end to slavery in Africa. When people are slaves to hunger, disease and the murderous caprices of their neighbours, slavery to foreigners is usually no worse and often an improvement. But that's not how most civilized people' – he put the last two words into ironic inverted commas – 'see it, I'm afraid. So – my advice is, be careful – be very careful. People talk, people exaggerate. Look what has happened to your host.'

'Our host?'

'Well, your landlord. That poor, pathetic ass Warburton.'

'What has happened to him?'

'He's ruined himself, that's what's happened. You must know that. First he got in with some Arab rogues, who managed to fleece him. Then, to recoup, he started dealing in slaves. Transporting them through this area to the Gulf. Soon everyone knew what he was up to – it's not easy to keep secrets in that business these days – and that finished him completely. A year ago he would have been at a party like this. Now no one wants him around – not, of course, for moral reasons, but for fear of guilt by association. So there you have it. You three must have been a godsend to that couple. Otherwise they'd have been on the next ship back to England – with no return ticket.'

She was shocked by the contempt with which he spoke.

'We've become fond of them. I admire her.'

'Admire her? With all those intellectual airs she gives herself? And that razor tongue of hers?'

'She's gallant. I admire gallantry.'

At that, Alexine decided to move off. But, before she could do so, she heard her mother's voice behind her.

'Alexine! I suppose that I'm regarded as the senior lady here, and so perhaps we ought to make a move.'

'Yes, let's do that.'

'Good evening, Mr Fielding. I hadn't noticed you before.'

'Good evening, Madame Thinne. I've been hearing all about your adventures. And I gather that there are more to come.'

'Yes. My daughter is greedy for more. I sometimes feel that I've had enough. And so does my sister.' She turned: 'Come, Alexine. Let's get Addy.'

'Then I'll say goodbye to you two ladies. I hope we'll meet again. As I said to you before, Miss Thinne, this is such a vast continent and yet people keep running into each other, as though it were a village.'

He bowed to them each in turn.

∽

Monsieur Thibault accompanied them across the lawn and down some uneven steps to the barge. 'Take care, dear ladies! Don't slip! Don't fall!' He put out a supporting hand but none of them took it. 'My dear wife fell here only two or three weeks ago. We feared that she had broken a wrist but it proved to be only a sprain.'

'I wish that we could have met her,' Harriet said.

'Yes, indeed, indeed. She was most disappointed. Apart from everything else she would have loved to inspect your magnificent dresses and jewellery. It's so unfortunate that she's so often prone to migraine.'

'It was so kind of you to have us to such a delightful party,' Addy said, as the barge edged alongside the jetty.

'It was so kind of you to come. If there is anything that I can do for you, please do not hesitate to ask. I flatter myself that, after some thirty years, I now know everyone in this city – or, at least, everyone who is anyone.'

Impulsively Alexine stepped forward. 'There is one thing, Monsieur Thibault.'

'Anything, anything, dear lady! Big or small!'

'Well, this is rather big.'

'No matter. Tell me what it is.'

'Soon we'll be setting forth on the next stage of our journey. As you may have heard. And for that we need – we need a steamer.'

'A steamer! But such a thing doesn't exist in the Sudan. Surely you know that?'

'We heard that the Governor-General has one.'

Monsieur Thibault was astonished. 'Well, yes. But that's the only one here. It was transported here in sections. Some people – including a Scottish engineer – died in the process.'

'Well, couldn't we hire it?'

'Hire it! But the Governor-General might need it.'

'We could ask him.'

Monsieur Thibault shook his head and smiled indulgently. 'My dear lady, the Governor-General is rarely here. At present he's in Egypt. That's where he spends most of his time.'

'Then he's much less likely to need his steamer. Who is deputizing for him?'

'The Mudir. The Governor of Khartoum.'

'Well, as we're about to travel again in his barge, perhaps he'll also allow us to travel in the Governor-General's steamer.'

Harriet was shocked by all this importunity: 'Alexine, I really don't think . . .'

'I could arrange for you to meet the Mudir,' Monsieur Thibault unexpectedly volunteered. 'After that – it's up to you. He may ask a large, a very large, price. If he's prepared to agree, that is. To hire the only steamer in the country . . .'

'Oh, we don't care about the cost. But we do care about travelling in that steamer.'

'Well, in that case . . .' He gave an indulgent smile. 'What a forceful character you are, mademoiselle.' He laughed. 'Almost as forceful as my wife.'

'You promise me that you'll try to arrange a meeting?'

'My word is my bond.'

'If there is anything we can do in return . . .' Harriet said.

'Well, yes, madame, since you mention it, there is. You accompanied my daughter, you heard her voice. It's a beautiful instrument, as I'm sure you agree, but she has yet to learn to play on it properly. If you would be willing for her to visit you from time to time – to practise with you . . . Your remarkable musicality can only lead to an improvement.' He cocked his head on one side. 'What do you say, Madame? Yes? Yes?'

'Yes, of course.'

'Then I'll speak to the Governor tomorrow. Once I have his reply, I'll send Lola round to you with his answer.'

∽

As the barge glided through the night, the six rowers grunting with each tug at their oars, Harriet and Addy laughed and chattered away together. What an extraordinary occasion! That house – it was a masterpiece of ostentatious vulgarity! Fancy allowing those three young girls to rouge their cheeks so obviously and to wear all that native jewellery! And that singing!

Alexine sat apart from them, gazing out to the glimmering bank opposite. She was still smarting from the mocking way in which Fielding had spoken to her. All too clearly he thought little of her as an explorer. To him she was merely yet another of the tourists who made their way from Cairo to Khartoum. The only things that differentiated her from them was that she was a woman and travelled so much more lavishly.

Odious man!

But, even while she had become increasingly angry with him during their conversation, she had, against her will, felt a more and more insistent tug of sexual attraction. She thought now of his strong hands, with the black hair on their backs, and their far from clean nails; of his luxuriant side-whiskers; of his hooked, powerful nose.

She told herself that she never wanted to see him again, but at the same time she could not bear the thought that she might never do so.

11 ALEXINE WAS WAITING ON THE JETTY for the red and green barge once more to pick her up. She had told Osman that she wished him to accompany her on her visit to the Mudir, since Harriet, who was suffering from dysentery and so could not come herself, had insisted that she must have someone with her. But he had mysteriously disappeared, as he so often did, never asking for leave of absence and never explaining or apologizing when Harriet later took him to task. In consequence, it was Daan, dressed in a frock coat and top hat bought from the shop in the bazaar and his new pair of boots, who now stood beside her. He had, in the course of their travels, acquired a commanding dignity, so that anyone seeing him would assume that he was some newly-arrived member of the business community of Khartoum. To confirm this impression, he was, like Nanny Rose, becoming less and less subservient to his employers, often arguing with them, offering them his advice, unasked, or disregarding their instructions.

'They have no sense of time, miss. Why don't we go back to wait in the cool of the house?'

'Oh, no, it's lovely here. I wish I could take Flopsy with me. He loves the water. But my mother said that a Muslim wouldn't like a dog brought into his house.'

'There are lots of Christians who don't like dogs in their houses.' Daan did not like them there himself.

Before the arrival of the barge, Lucy joined them. 'Roderick would have been only too happy to accompany you, but he didn't think his presence would have helped things. Quite the reverse.'

'It was wonderful to see him eat so much breakfast. And later I heard him whistling in the garden.'

'You're the one who cured him.'

An elderly, uniformed man with a bristling moustache and a large wart on a cheek, ushered Alexine and Daan into the Mudir's house, followed by a straggling platoon of soldiers. He indicated a divan to them, but, whereas Alexine at once went over to it, Daan shook his head and walked across to a chair. The usher frowned. Time passed. Outside a window too high for Alexine to see anything beyond it, some men were talking in loud, vehement voices. A slave came in carrying a dented tin tray, on which two glasses, full of a pinkish juice, were set out. Alexine sipped, smiled, sipped again. 'Pomegranate,' she told Daan, who was staring down into his glass, wary of trying what was in it.

'Oh, I can't do with pomegranate. Now if it was a glass of really cold beer...'

Eventually, they were summoned into the Mudir's presence. Once again, Alexine placed herself on the divan indicated, opposite the one on which the Mudir himself was lounging, and once again Daan opted for a chair.

The Mudir was a small, grey-haired man, with feverishly bright eyes and a sudden, high-pitched cackle. He spoke stilted French with an odd sibilance, spit showering from his mouth as he did so.

'I am afraid that you must find this heat very tiring, mademoiselle.'

'On the contrary, monsieur. Heat invigorates me. But my poor mother and aunt – they suffer, I'm afraid.'

He continued to talk of the weather in the Sudan. From the topic of conversation, one might imagine that one was in England, Alexine thought.

He broke off and pointed at Daan: 'Your friend speaks French?'

Alexine did not reveal that Daan was not a friend but a servant. She shook her head. 'Only Dutch.'

'I thought that all people in your country speak French.'

She laughed. 'No, no, by no means!' Would they never get to the subject about which she had come?

'Do you like this house?'

'Yes. It's even bigger than Monsieur Thibault's. And this room is even larger than his drawing-room.'

'It was built by an Italian bricklayer about fifteen years ago. Pietro Agati, that was his name. He was the first man to build a house of brick in Khartoum since the time of the Pharaohs. Yes, this was the first house of brick in the whole of Khartoum. Can you believe it? Now there are brick houses everywhere. Anyone who has any money has a brick house. But when I was a child every house was made of straw and mud.'

'Is he still alive?'

'Oh, yes, indeed. Very much so. Recently he built a new house for my harem.' He crossed over to a window and then turned. 'Come, please!'

Alexine got up from the divan and joined him.

He pointed. 'There it is.'

The long building, its regularly spaced windows fixed with iron bars, might have been the barracks of the slovenly soldiers who had lounged about, chattering to each other, picking their noses or teeth, or wandering restlessly hither and thither, in the anteroom in which she had waited.

He turned. 'I have eleven wives.' He smiled. 'Muslim men are luckier than Christian ones.'

'And Muslim women are unluckier.'

'It is better to have a share in a good husband than a bad husband to oneself. That is one of our sayings. You have a husband?'

'No. I'm single.'

'Excuse the question, mademoiselle, but how is it that no man has married you?'

'I'm only twenty-two. There's plenty of time. There's so much I want to do before I marry.'

'Everyone here thinks that you are very beautiful.'

'Not many do in my own country.'

'Do you know what they call you here?'

Alexine shook her head.

'They call you "The Daughter of the Queen".'

'How flattering! But which queen is that?'

'Queen Victoria, of course, the Queen of England. Everyone here who sees you in the street thinks that you are English. Few foreign women come here. Some French, some Italian, some English, some Greek, some German. No Dutch. Never.'

'My father's first wife was English.'

'Ah! So he had two wives.'

'Only one after the other. The first died.'

'Do you wish to see my harem?'

She really wished to get to discussion of the hire of the boat, but she nodded. 'Thank you. Yes. That would be interesting.'

'But – I am sorry – your friend' – he indicated Daan – 'must wait here. He is old, but even so . . .'

Alexine gave Daan a few words of explanation, and then followed the Mudir to the door opposite the one by which they had entered, at the far end of the room.

A pebbled pathway led to the harem. Half-way along it, the Mudir paused and turned. 'My wives are not beautiful like you. Dark, dark skins. In my country we think fair skins more beautiful. Only one has fair skin and she is now old, too old. But . . .' He shrugged. A moment later, he once more halted and turned. 'Do you know Mrs Pullar?'

'Mrs Pullar? You mean the explorer's wife?' Ever since their arrival in Khartoum people had been asking if they knew this woman, never if they knew her husband. Clearly, wherever she had gone, Mrs Pullar had made an impression. 'I'm afraid not. I wish I did.'

'She is not as beautiful as you. Much older. But she has a white skin and golden hair, hair like yours but longer. She wears her hair loose, down to her waist. Very unusual. Like a young girl.' He laughed. 'Charming! She and I became good friends. I lent her my barge many times.'

'You were so kind to send your barge for me.'

'I am always pleased to help a beautiful young lady.'

They had walked only a few more paces when he turned yet again. 'She was a slave. Did you know that?'

'Who?'

'Mrs Pullar. That is what they say. She is his second wife. A Circassian. He saw her in a slave-market and he bought her. Like you buying your black boy.'

Alexine frowned. The story of her purchase of Sunny had clearly spread.

Two guards were seated on the ground on either side of the iron-studded door to the harem. One got lethargically to his feet and pushed the door open for them to enter. Since there were bars on the windows, Alexine was surprised that the door was not locked.

As she entered the room, excited squeals erupted from the women. All of them jumped up from the divans on which they had been sprawling, and rushed forward in a powerful cloud of scent. The tips of their finger-nails were orange with henna, and many of their palms, outstretched to her in greeting, bore geometric patterns in black. One of them, the youngest present, little more than a girl, was nibbling at a sweetmeat. She now pushed all of it into her mouth and, having swallowed it, began daintily to lick at one finger after another. Another, gaunt and hollow-eyed, stooped and, without a word, examined the lace fringe of Alexine's dress, lifting it in a hand. Looking down at this one's bowed head, Alexine saw that the roots of her dyed black hair were grey.

'Come! Come over here!' The Mudir collapsed on to one of the divans and beckoned Alexine over. She went across and perched uncomfortably on its edge. The women now lined up raggedly, facing them. All of them stared fixedly at Alexine.

'You like them?'

'Yes, they're charming. And all so different.'

He laughed. 'I like change. Every man likes change. Now.' He pulled in his chin and adopted a serious expression. 'They wished to greet you with a song, but they know no Dutch song. So they will sing you a song taught them by a Scottish missionary lady. Sadly, now dead. She was bitten by a snake when looking for wildflowers. But she taught them this song.' He said something to the women and then raised a forefinger. 'Listen.'

Hesitantly and raggedly at first but then in confident unison the women began to sing. What was the song? At first, Alexine was puzzled, rarely able to distinguish one word from another. But then she heard it – 'Bring back, bring back' – and she realized that, yes, it was 'My bonnie lies over the ocean'. The women's heads swayed from side to side in time to the beat – they might have been the well-drilled chorus of an operetta – and their bodies, some dumpy, some tall, some emaciated, some vast, some beautiful, also swayed. When they had finished, they all covered their faces with their hands and burst into laughter.

'Now I wish you to hear an African song. This wife comes from the far south. She was a slave. I bought her two, three years ago.' He leaned forward and called out something.

In response, a tall, extremely thin woman, her hair elaborately plaited close to her head so that it looked as if her pink scalp was enclosed in a net, picked up a stringed instrument propped against a wall and seated herself on a stool fetched for her by the girl-wife. She placed the instrument on her lap, her legs wide open, so that it looked like the upsided half of a water-melon, with a long, stringed neck sticking out of it.

She plucked a few notes meditatively, and then a few more. She paused. She looked up at Alexine and gave a small, slow smile. There was another plucking of notes, seemingly at random, one after another, with long pauses between. Then, suddenly, she gripped the instrument even more tightly between her knees, and began to produce a jangled frenzy of sound. She shut her eyes, she began to sing. Alexine stared at her, mesmerized. She wished that Harriet were present. The voice had a plaintive, husky quality, now gleaming as it soared and now darkening as it sank to what was little more than a gruff whisper.

At the conclusion, Alexine clapped. She was the only person present to do so. Without any acknowledgement, the woman got up off the stool, handed the instrument to the young girl, and then wandered off. She seemed to be deliberately making a point: she had sung for herself, not for this stranger, not for her husband, and not for the other wives.

'Did you like that?'

'Very much.'

'Better than the English song?'

'Not English, Scottish. Yes, I liked it better.'

'The two songs are similar. A woman longs for the return of a man. Two places are so far apart but the feelings are the same.' He said the last sentence as though he were making some profound observation. 'Shall we leave now? We have our business to discuss.'

Back in his room, she was surprised to see that Daan had vanished.

'Where is my friend? He hasn't gone has he?'

Without answering, the Mudir took her arm and, holding it, guided her over to the divan on which she had been previously sitting. When, to her surprise, he lowered himself on to it beside her, he was so close that she at once shifted away from the inevitable contact. He looked sideways at her, smiling. 'Monsieur Thibault has told me of your wish. I think there is little hope.' He edged towards her. 'I will see what I can do, of course. For a woman as beautiful as you, I am willing to do any- thing. If the steamer were mine ... But I merely look after it for the Governor-General in his absence. I do not know if he would wish ... He might return at any time and demand to have the use of it. However...' He sighed. 'For you...' He again shifted abruptly, so that his body was once more pressing close against hers. She could retreat no further from him, since she was already pressed against the wall. His hand descended on her knee. 'Dear mademoiselle – we must try to reach some sort of agreement. However difficult that is.'

Alexine jumped to her feet. She would have done so sooner, had she not been so curious to see what would follow next. She walked over to the window and once more gazed out at the prison-like building oppo- site. There were louvred shutters behind the bars. There was no way of looking in or of knowing whether anyone was looking out. The two squatting guards were both now asleep, their half-recumbent bodies resting against the iron-studded door. One of them had his mouth wide open.

'Why have you gone off there?' His voice was querulous.

Alexine turned. She laughed. 'Please, Your Excellency. Please. I beg you. Let's understand each other.' She felt no anger and no fear. She knew herself to be totally in control of the ludicrous situation. 'I am not looking for a husband, I am looking for a steamer. I'm prepared to pay for a steamer. But the only thing with which I'm prepared to pay for it is money.'

Now he too laughed. 'Yes, you could be the daughter of the Queen – of Queen Victoria.' He jumped up from the divan and went behind his desk. 'Well, let us talk frankly. It is always best to talk frankly when doing business. May I put a frank question to you? How much money are you prepared to pay?'

'How much do you want me to pay?'

It was one of the rare occasions on which Alexine was willing to bar- gain, taking the same pleasure in the contest as she took in playing piquet with Addy or chess with Daan. As usual, she paid far more than the other party had dared to hope for, but far less than she had feared.

∽

When she eventually left the Mudir, she found Daan seated on a chair under a tree, puffing at his pipe.

'What happened to you?'

'They said I couldn't smoke in that room of his. I thought you'd be much longer in the harem. Sorry, miss. Did you need me?'

'No, thank you. I managed perfectly well on my own.'

12 HARRIET WAS COMPILING ANOTHER OF HER LISTS. She had not fully recovered from her sudden bout of dysentery, even though Lucy had been dosing her with a morphine mixture brought with her from England, and an injudicious walk by the river that morning had given her a headache.

First she listed the boats at their disposal:

> Steamer
> Dahabiah (first-class accommodation)
> 2 other dahabiahs
> 3 nuggars

Then she listed the animals, which were to be carried in the two inferior dahabiahs:

> A.'s horse
> S.'s pony
> 4 camels
> 2 mules
> 40 donkeys
> 50 sheep
> 70 (?) hens

That completed, she began to add up, hand to brow, the number of people taking part in the expedition. In addition to themselves, the six local servants and Sunny, there were sixty-five soldiers, who on the advice of Monsieur Thibault were all to be armed with muskets, and six more soldiers allocated to them by the Mudir as an additional protection. There were even more porters than on the journey from Cairo. Alexine had also announced, after consulting with innumerable people, a few expert but most merely ignorant busybodies, that further recruitment of porters would have to be made as soon as they had left the river to penetrate inland.

Lucy came into the room. 'Sorry to disturb you. I wondered whether you wanted our cook to prepare the dinner or whether you'd like yours to do it.'

'Oh, let ours do it. We pay him enough. And he's demanding even more to accompany us on the expedition.'

'You look done in.'

'I am done in. These preparations are endless.' Harriet threw down her pen. 'The problem is that we don't know how long we'll be away.

Three months, six months, nine months, a year? No one can tell us because no one can predict what will happen. So we have to assume that it'll be a year and take enormous quantities of supplies to last us for that period.'

'I hate to say this, but your whole party is far too big. The more people you are, the more food you need. The more food you need, the more boats, porters, donkeys and camels you need to transport them. And the more mouths you have to feed ... Well, you can see. It's a vicious circle. On his journeys, Roderick never takes more than a dozen or so people with him.'

'Yes, I know, I know! But I've no idea how to break the vicious circle. Everyone says that we must have a large number of soldiers to protect us.'

'I don't envy you.'

'I wish we weren't going.'

'Well, don't go.'

'If I don't go, then Alexine will go on her own. Addy certainly won't accompany her without me. I couldn't let Alexine set off by herself.'

'Why not?'

Staring into space, Harriet did not answer the question.

'You're very close to each other.'

'She's all I've got.'

A terrible weariness suddenly overwhelmed her. She crossed her arms on the desk and then rested her left cheek on them.

She felt Lucy's hand on her shoulder.

'It's hard for you.'

Harriet suddenly brightened. She raised her head. 'But fun.'

'That girl's here.' Nanny Rose was at the door.

Harriet looked down at the diamond-encircled watch pinned to her bodice. 'Isn't she early?'

'She's always either early or late,' Nanny Rose said. 'No sense of time.'

'How can you bear to listen to that hooting and squalling?' Lucy asked.

Harriet laughed. 'She's improving.'

Three times a week Lola came over for a singing lesson. Sometimes she arrived by carriage, but often she walked over alone, striding out vigorously under a parasol one shaft of which was broken. She would often examine the shaft as she was closing or opening the parasol and say that she wished that she could find someone to mend it. On their departure, Harriet was planning to give her one of the three parasols that she had brought with her from Europe.

250

By now Harriet's piano had been tuned, by the nineteen-year-old son of the Greek tailor. He had served only a brief apprenticeship to an elderly piano-tuner uncle in his native Smyrna, but was fortunate in possessing perfect pitch. After tuning the piano, he would beg Harriet to play on it for him and then, leaning forward, one knee crossed over the other and eyes closed, would listen enraptured. Harriet said that at last to be playing on a piano totally in tune was like waking up one morning and finding that all one's rheumaticky aches had disappeared.

'Lola!' Harriet had already grown fond of the girl, so eager, so enthusiastic, and so full of ambitions for a singing career that would never be realized for lack both of opportunities and of talent.

'Madame Thinne!' The girl swooped across the room, threw her arms around Harriet and kissed her on both cheeks. She smelled of healthy sweat from her walk as well as of the lavender water that Harriet had given her on their last encounter. 'Are you better?'

'Oh, it was nothing.' Harriet hated to discuss her health.

The lesson over, Harriet and Lola set off for the market in the carriage that Alexine had rented for the period of their stay. The girl, overhearing Harriet complaining of the difficulty of communicating with those traders, the majority of whom did not speak any language but their own, had offered to accompany her. This had now become a routine at the close of every lesson.

As they set off, Harriet cried out: 'Oh, I've forgotten my list!'

Lola laughed. 'Oh, Madame Thinne! You and your lists! I've never kept a list in my whole life and I'm sure mama never has.'

'Oh, no, here it is! I wonder why I put it in that pocket.'

Harriet had ticked off some items on previous expeditions to the market. But as she now glanced down, she saw how many things still remained to be bought: wine, pale ale, tea, tins of soup, pearl barley, soap, biscuits, packets of seeds, pins, needles, cotton, pens . . .

Suddenly she remembered something not listed. Monsieur Thibault had advised her to acquire a gutta-percha inflatable boat. It would be useful if they wished to explore some channel too narrow for their other craft. She searched her reticule for a pencil to add that item.

∽

When Harriet returned, she was exhausted, and at once went up to her bedroom, drew the curtains, and, without removing even her dusty boots, lay down on her bed. But almost at once she was aroused by Addy's voice outside the door: 'Harriet dear! May I have a word with you?'

Harriet wanted to ask whether the word could not wait, but she knew how her sister was constantly fretted by impatience – often repeating the Dutch proverb 'Do it and it's done', when it was suggested that something trivial but regarded by her as urgent might be deferred.

'Yes. Come in, come in! What is it?'

'I've been thinking about something. For days.' Addy crossed over to the bed and sat down on it. She bounced. 'You need a new mattress.'

'Oh, I can't be bothered to look for one on top of everything else ... What have you been thinking about?'

'Our trip. I know how upset you're going to be – and how upset Alexine is going to be – but I'm afraid' – she played with a tassel of the bedspread – 'I just don't think I'm up to it.'

'Why? You've been perfectly well for weeks. Of course you're up to it!'

Addy shook her head. 'I've – I've lost my nerve. I can't face it. As you know, I almost died on the journey here. I really thought that I was dying. I can't go through all that again. If I go with you, I know that this time I'll die. Yes, I know it, I know it!'

'Oh, you mustn't have these morbid ideas. Anyway, at our ages, it won't be all that long before both of us are dead. But we're just as likely to die in our beds back at home as out here in the jungle.'

Again Addy shook her head. The two women gazed at each other. Harriet's first feelings of shock and dismay had been transitory. Relief was now sweeping away all her previous feelings of weariness and discouragement. Why this relief? she was later to question herself with guilt and shame. Her love for her sister was second only to her love for Alexine; they had spent most of their lives together. But not to have Addy, constantly ailing and constantly complaining, with them was to be free of a responsibility as heavy as that of caring for that multitude of often stubborn, lazy, inefficient, demanding and quarrelsome employees.

'But what you are going to do while we're away? It may be months and months before our return. You're not thinking of travelling back home by yourself?'

'No. I don't mind waiting for you. Here. I'm sure Lucy and Roderick won't mind my staying on. Lucy and I get on well together. We've become good friends. Really, we're so unlike each other, but we have one thing in common. We're both great readers. That's a strong bond.' She got up off the bed. 'Oh, Harriet, don't be cross with me! And I hope Alexine won't be cross. I hate to let you both down. But I haven't got your spirit. Not now. I did once, I think. But not now, not now.'

Harriet swung her legs down from the bed. 'Well, it's sad, very sad. But I understand, of course I understand. Do you want me to break it to Alexine?'

'Oh, would you, would you? Please! You know – I've never confessed this to you before – I've always been rather frightened of her. Even as a little girl.'

Harriet smiled. 'Sometimes I'm also frightened of her. Napoleon's marshals must have been frightened in the same way of him.' She hobbled towards the door. Her legs felt leaden and her feet were aching. 'I must do something about finding that gutta-percha boat. I had no luck in the market. I wonder if Roderick has any ideas.'

13 ALEXINE WAS INFURIATED by the slowness of their progress.

'Why can't be get a move on?' was her constant, increasingly angry question, as she marched about the steamer or, when they were merely adrift as the captain debated with members of the crews and even one of the porters or a servant which of two entirely similar channels they should take, listened in mounting impatience to a conversation that she was unable to follow. 'French, French!' she would often order, ignoring the fact that, though the pilot could speak rudimentary French, as could the cook and the two personal maids, scarcely anyone else could do so.

The captain tried to explain: the problem was the constantly changing appearance of the sudd.

'Sudd? What is this sudd?' She had never heard the word in Dutch, English or French.

Again the captain tried to explain: it was a barrier, perpetually shifting hither and thither – he made a sinuous gesture with a hand – of floating vegetation, trees, roots and impenetrable mud.

'Well, can't we hack through it?'

He laughed, infuriating her even more.

'Do be reasonable, dear,' Harriet implored.

But to be reasonable was something of which Alexine was now incapable.

There was the further problem of the paddles of the steamer, which was making its maiden voyage up the river. Repeatedly they became choked with floating plants. The crew then had to descend into the viscous water and, naked but for their exiguous loincloths, perilously balance themselves on the paddlewheels and hack and pull until at last they were freed. At one moment, such was her impatience, Alexine herself was about to join them in this task.

'No, no!' Harriet cried. 'No!'

'But they're such idiots!'

'No!'

Eventually, the flotilla reached Mashra Ar Riqq, a trading-station, and anchored in a curve of the river, where alligators were said to make any entry into the water extremely dangerous. Huddled on the bank, chained to each other by neck-collars, were groups of slaves, impassive under a heavy, coppery sky that presaged a storm. Harriet preferred not to look at them, playing patience by herself under an awning on the main deck. But Alexine, accompanied by Sunny, ventured out.

Sunny clutched her hand and remained close to her, as though terrified that one of the Arab dealers might suddenly snatch him up and away. He stared intently into the faces of the slaves, as though looking for someone he knew. Eventually, on an impulse, Alexine swung round and began to march back to the steamer, dragging him with her. She returned with a tin of biscuits, which she began to apportion first to one group and then to another, until they were all exhausted. The recipients stared at what they had been given, turning them over and over in their hands. Then one of them, an elderly woman, raised a biscuit to her mouth, nibbled at it, and at once began to gobble. The others followed her example. The lucky ones began to laugh and chatter among themselves. The rest held out their hands and set up a weird keening.

'I can't stand this,' Alexine said. 'What can one do?'

Sunny gazed up at her, without an answer.

Two nearby Arabs began to laugh.

'What are you laughing at?' Alexine demanded in Arabic.

The men laughed again.

∽

The storm broke that night. Alexine looked out of her cabin window and saw the humped shapes of the slaves lying out in the pelting rain. They looked little different from the provisions, covered in tarpaulins, two shrouded soldiers armed with muskets seated beside them on guard, that next day would be carried aboard. Sunny was asleep on a pallet on the floor of the cabin, beside her bunk. He preferred that to climbing up into the upper bunk or even, as she had offered, taking the lower bunk while she went above.

Eventually, she got off the bunk, pulled a mackintosh cloak over her shoulders and went out onto the deck.

Nanny Rose and Daan were already there. They were standing close to each other but at once moved apart as they heard her approach.

'What a downpour!' Nanny Rose exclaimed. 'I've never seen anything like it.'

'I hope this doesn't mean that the rainy season has started,' Daan said. 'I was woken by all that thunder and so was Nanny.' It was as 'Nanny' that he now always referred to her, as though that, and not Mabel, were her Christian name.

'I feel sorry for those poor devils out there. It's so cruel to leave them there, tethered like animals, with no shelter.' As soon as she had spoken, Nanny Rose hurriedly raised her hands to her ears as the sky swung open like an iron shutter, letting in a glaring flash of lightning, and then slammed shut again. A tremendous thunder-clap followed, echoing back and forth and ringing in Alexine's ears.

'What can one do?' Alexine asked, as she had asked before.

She drifted away from them and re-entered the cabin. Sunny stirred, whimpered, then went back to sleep.

She sat on the edge of the bunk, her feet almost touching him.

What can one do?

She was filled with despair. She could hand out biscuits or, as she had repeatedly done with the porters, medicines and bandages. But even if she were to hand out her entire vast fortune, it would make virtually no more difference than the scattering of a handful of sawdust in a vast abattoir.

∽

Harriet was playing patience, Alexine was staring down at the Colonel's map. Once again the whole flotilla was doing a U-turn and retracing its passage. The network of scarlet lines on the creased, soiled parchment might have been a tracing of their own journey, back and forth, east and west, north and south.

'Don't you know where we're going?' Alexine demanded more than once of the captain.

Each time he merely shrugged and muttered: 'The sudd, mademoiselle. The sudd.'

The sky was now always still and leaden except when sudden spectacular thunderstorms erupted, followed by rain that fell down in what seemed to be a solid sheet, obscuring the mangroves and water-hyacinth that continued repeatedly to choke the paddles.

Eventually, at an even more remote trading station, the captain announced that he could proceed no farther.

'What do you mean? Of course you can!'

He shook his head.

Alexine raged at him. It was ridiculous. Many people in Khartoum had told her that they could go much farther.

'Few, if any, of those people have travelled this far.'

Like a fencer who suddenly realizes that his sword has buckled, Alexine realized, with mingled rage and panic, that even her all-conquering will could not move the steamer on.

She did not sleep that night, but brooded on what to do next. It was clear that the rainy season had started and that the expedition could not proceed by land until it was over. Over breakfast, she announced to Harriet, Nanny Rose and Daan – all of the Europeans, along with Sunny, now fed together – that she would be setting off the next day with Osman, a dozen of the most trustworthy of the soldiers, two porters and a local guide, to the Gossinga mountains – some sixty miles ahead, so she had been told by the guide – where she would prospect the possibility of their camping there on high ground until the rains were over.

The others all protested that she could not possibly make the journey. She must send Osman with the others and stay behind herself. But she was adamant.

'If I don't go with them, the others may never come back. You know what they're like.'

'They'll come back, dear, never worry,' Nanny Rose said. 'They'll come back to get their money.'

'I must go.'

'I will go with you,' Sunny, who had been silent all through the conversation, suddenly announced.

Alexine laughed and shook her head. 'No, no. You're far too young.'

'I will go too! I will go!' Suddenly he was shouting in fury.

'No. You must stay here to help Daan look after Mama and Nanny Rose. Will you do that for me? Yes?'

He pondered. Then reluctantly he nodded.

'Good. Then that's settled then.'

On the first day the rain fell remorselessly, so that, despite her mackintosh cloak and hat, Alexine was eventually soaked to the skin. Then, suddenly, early the next morning, the sky lightened and, after little more than an hour, the sun was beating down. Soon, the thick bush gave way to wooded country. There were flowering shrubs and fruit trees all around them, and a constant screech and twitter of birds. Even the guide, an elderly man who had been morosely taciturn throughout the previous day despite Alexine's attempts to draw him out in French and in Arabic, now brightened up. He called for a rifle, and after two or three failures, brought down a guinea-fowl. Alexine took the rifle from him and almost at once, with mingled triumph and dismay, brought down a gazelle.

Soon she was dismounting to jot down notes on the flora and even to draw rough sketches of it. When they passed through a wood of gardenias in full flower after the recent downpours, the grass beneath them an astonishingly luminous green, Alexine was enchanted.

'Do you think that the rainy season is over?'

Osman shrugged. 'Who can say? Nothing is regular here.'

Alexine's enchantment intensified when they passed through a gallery forest, a precipitous ravine full of huge trees entangled with creepers. She remarked on the beauty of it to the others, but they merely looked at her in bewilderment.

Eventually, in the foothills of the mountains, they arrived at about four o'clock at a small village of neat *tukuls*, with a stagnant pond as its centre. Soon, summoned by some of the inhabitants, the local Sheik arrived on a mule, kicking at its lean sides with his bare heels. A tall, handsome man, he seemed not in the least surprised by Alexine's presence and at once offered to clear a family out of the largest of the tukuls in order to accommodate her. She protested that they were travelling with tents, but he would have none of it. All that night, she was devoured by fleas.

The next morning, she said to Osman: 'We could make our camp here. What do you think?'

He was dubious. 'Yes. Possibly. But if the rainy season is really over, then there is no reason to loiter here. We can push on.'

Push on. Alexine liked the idea of that. She derived intense pleasure from pushing her huge cavalcade on and on merely by an exertion of her formidable will.

'Then that's settled. We'd better return.'

But she returned with regret, making a succession of detours and lingering whenever a place took her fancy. Warburton had been right. It was so much easier and better to travel with just these few, chosen companions, sleeping rough and living off what one could either shoot or acquire locally in return for some of the china beads, mirrors and knives that they were carrying with them, rather than with a vast retinue of animals and men.

∽

Without Alexine's enthusiasm, determination and energy to hold it together, the expedition began to unravel. Sitting around chatting, the servants were either dilatory about doing things or failed to do them at all. The steamer had by now set off on its journey back to Khartoum, with a promise from the captain that it would return to fetch them when he received a message by runner telling him that they were ready. It affronted Harriet that many of the goods unloaded still lay in a jumble instead of being tidily stacked and covered. It affronted her even more that, without asking permission, some of the porters, natives of the area, took themselves off to their villages, with only the vaguest assurances that they would ever return. At first she bustled about issuing commands through the cook or anyone else who could speak any French or English. But the commands were all too often ignored. Discouraged, she increasingly came to let things slide, and instead spent more and more of her time in her tent writing letters. She despatched one batch of these letters with the steamer, and a few days later another batch with a runner.

Such were her innate optimism and her ability to relegate to an attic of her memory whatever was unwelcome, these letters gave little indication of the difficulties, discomforts and unpleasantnesses of the journey. She constantly wrote of the beauty of the countryside and the people, and when she described something untoward, it was always with dismissive humour. To her step-son John, she wrote of a time before Alexine's departure:

Alexine and I felt restless. So, by a fine moon, we wandered through a wood near our camp. We laughed at the idea of being in the heart of Africa, *nous deux*, she on foot and I on a donkey, only attended by an old man with a lantern and our negro foster-child! We were no more afraid of lions and tigers or of the local inhabitants than on the downs *chez nous*. Oh, it's a beautiful country and richly repays all our trouble, fatigue and expense!

To Lucy:

In comparison with ourselves, the others seem to eat so simply and scantily. But they have magnificent physiques, as you will know. Among the porters I have my special favourites, as Alexine has hers. These are the men who are particularly kind, thoughtful, cheerful. Of course we cannot communicate with words but they have an almost supernatural ability to guess what one is feeling or wanting.

∽

When not overseeing the two personal maids in their tasks, Nanny Rose now spent most of her time knitting under an awning projecting from the tent that she and Daan openly shared. What she was knitting was a woollen sweater for Daan, who certainly would not need it until their return to Europe. Beside her, sometimes cross-legged on the ground and sometimes on a stool, he would patiently whittle away with a penknife at one amateurish wood carving after another. He was attempting to create carvings similar to those that he had seen on their journeys. When they returned, he planned to sell them, as genuine native artefacts, in Cairo and The Hague.

One day, the cook announced that the whole of a recently slaughtered sheep had been stolen. 'Well, there's nothing I can do about it,' Harriet told him. 'Report it to the *vakeel*.' The next day Nanny Rose announced that an amber comb had disappeared from her tent. 'Oh, I'm sure you must have put it down somewhere and forgotten where.' Harriet now shrank from being involved in these recurrent dramas. She could barely conceal her exasperation when yet again someone bothered her with a complaint, query or request. Oh, if only Alexine would return!

The Egyptians and Sudanese were constantly quarrelling among themselves. Late in the night, the Europeans would hear their voices raised in anger. One day a token scuffle broke out, with two groups of men measuring up to one another, shouting insults, their teeth bared, and eventually pushing, elbowing and kicking. On that occasion Harriet got up from her chair and marched towards the trouble: 'Now stop that! Stop that at once!'

She was amazed that her intervention was immediately successful: the men slunk away.

The Europeans were all asleep when they were aroused by a clamour far louder than on that previous occasion. Through the darkness they could see figures racing hither and thither. A lone man hurled a cauldron at a group advancing on him and then raced off, shouting as he did so. The tent used by the Europeans as their dining-room and drawing-room suddenly tipped sideways, as three or four men tumbled over its guy-ropes, wrestling with each other.

'You'd better read them the riot act,' Nanny Rose, in her flannel nightdress, her grey, unbraided hair falling down her back, told Daan. 'Go on! What's the matter with you?'

Sunny emerged from the tent that he usually shared with Alexine, rubbing his eyes.

'Go on!'

Still Daan hesitated. Then, repeatedly halting as he cocked his head on one side to listen to the uproar or peered into the half-light, he ventured slowly forward. All at once, he halted, turned abruptly and ran back to them.

'They've got knives, some of them. I saw. I'm not going to risk my life for them. Let them fight it out.'

Nanny Rose looked at him with contempt. 'I just hope they don't decide to do us all in.'

'It's a quarrel among themselves. We've got nothing to do with it. Let them fight it out,' he repeated.

Eventually, the rumpus was over as quickly as it had started. As soon as the dawn had broken, Harriet and Nanny Rose busied themselves with treating the wounds. 'What a way to carry on!' Nanny Rose kept muttering, as she now dabbed with iodine, taking pleasure in seeing the men wince as the soaked cotton-wool made contact with their raw flesh, and now unrolled some more lint or a bandage. For the most part, the wounded were amazingly cheerful when submitting to her and Harriet's ministrations, laughing and shouting amiably to each other, however deep their gashes.

Harriet's favourite porter, beautiful, young, constantly smiling and constantly eager to do something for her, suddenly became silent and still. He no longer smiled, he no longer volunteered for any duty. When asked to do something, he would go about the task as though he were sleep-walking, trudging along jerkily on his heels, his hands behind his back and his once lively eyes dull and glazed. Was he ill? He merely shook his head when, through the *vakeel*, Harriet put this question to him.

After four or five days of this, he lay motionless under a tree, knees drawn up to chin and eyes shut. He ate nothing, he appeared to perform no natural functions. When people, Harriet among them, tried to rouse him, he did not answer or even move out of his catatonic trance. Sunny knelt beside him and took his hand in his. The man made no response; the hand was preternaturally cold in that heat.

The *vakeel* said that someone had put a hex on him. Sunny said the same thing – 'Someone has made magic, bad, bad.' Sunny no longer went near the man. Everyone seemed to avoid him, as though some contagion were emanating from him. Nanny Rose took him sweetened tea but he did not stir when she approached him with it and spoke to him. Harriet wiped his forehead, face and bare, muscular chest with a sponge soaked in water. Again there was no response.

One midday, when the sun was at its zenith and the four of them had retreated to the communal tent, they heard a shouting. Sunny jumped up and looked out of the tent and then called, at the same time beckoning frantically, to the others to join him. The man had leapt up from his motionless position on the ground and was now blundering hither and thither, back and forth, as though blind, between the tents, the trees and the high-piled stacks of goods. Everyone was watching him, rapt. No one was doing anything. The man began shouting one word, over and over again. Sunny later told them that it was 'home'. It transpired that the man had originated from the same area as he had.

Suddenly the man stopped his racing in erratic circles and headed for the river. He ran out onto the jetty and, with a cry of triumph, threw himself down into the murky water.

'Oh, the crocs, the crocs!' Nanny Rose cried out. 'They'll get him.' Again she turned on Daan: 'Do something!'

'I'm not going to do anything. I can't swim. And I'm certainly not prepared to be eaten by a crocodile.'

Harriet, followed by the others, hurried down to the jetty. A number of people had collected there but no one was making any attempt to rescue the man, who was now floundering around in the water, clearly unable to swim. His face, mouth stretched wide open, appeared and disappeared repeatedly.

Then a man appeared with one of the poles that supported the chair in which Nanny Rose or Harriet often took it in turns to travel. He pushed between the gaping onlookers and held the pole out into the water. The man snatched at it, went under, re-emerged, and snatched at it again. He clung to it, gasping for breath, as the other man pulled him in.

On the jetty the man shook himself like a dog, scattering water over Harriet and the others. 'To think that I washed and ironed that dress for you only yesterday,' Nanny Rose protested. 'Now it's got all that filthy river water over it.'

The man threw back his head and laughed. When he did so, all the others began to join in. The man said something, they answered. In a group, all of them trudged back to the camp. Someone produced a flat loaf of bread and the man began to tear at it with his white, even teeth. Someone else produced some water. He gulped at it.

The hex – if it had been a hex – had clearly been lifted.

∽

'How can she be taking so long?'

'Oh, don't worry, dear. Nothing can have happened to her.'

'But it's only sixty miles or so. And she's been gone for eleven days.'

'You know what the countryside is like. Remember how long it took us when we made that trek on the journey from Cairo. It'd have been quicker to stay on the boat until the water rose again.'

That night, Harriet could not sleep. She rarely worried about anything, but now her worry was intense. Perhaps the little party had lost its way; perhaps it had run out of food; perhaps it had been attacked by wild animals or hostile natives; perhaps Alexine, always so tough, had now fallen ill?

Two days later a delegation of porters came to see her. The long, enforced idleness away from their womenfolk had made them mutinous. The ringleaders crowded into her tent; the rest waited, silent and tense, outside it. The *vakeel* was with them and it was he who now spoke for them. He explained to her in his barely adequate French that he did not support the men's demands; but he thought it only proper to bring them to her attention, since otherwise they might desert *en masse*. What was the problem? Harriet asked. Laying down the pen with which she had been writing yet more letters full of the delights of the journey, she got to her feet, since she felt that by doing so she would gain more authority.

The *vakeel*, a native of Alexandria, explained: the men had no corn to eat, and the ration of meat was small. They had never been told the destination for which they were making or for how long they would be absent from their homes. Why were there no maps? He went on to list a number of other minor grievances – some had had to carry heavier loads than others, the Muslims among them resented having to look after the dogs, the mosquitoes from the river tormented them and prevented them from sleeping.

For the first time since they had started out from Cairo, Harriet felt afraid, as she looked round the sullen, threatening faces. Once again she thought: If only Alexine were here.

What did the *vakeel* propose?

He shrugged. What he proposed would cost money.

Oh, never mind that! She had always in the past urged Alexine not to be extravagant, but now fear put her in a mood to be extravagant herself.

The *vakeel* explained that there was a nearby *zariba*, some ten miles or so away, from which a small expedition could bring back corn. But at this time of year it would be dear. It might also be possible to buy sheep or goats there, which they could slaughter and distribute.

How much would all this cost?

He could not be certain. He named an approximate figure.

Nanny Rose, who was present, exclaimed: 'It's ridiculous, absolutely ridiculous!'

But Harriet nodded. 'Very well. Come back in an hour. I'll have the money ready for you.'

Gradually, singly or in groups, the men dispersed, with one exception. This was the man whom the others thought to have been under a spell. He was now his usual smiling, always helpful self.

Slowly he approached Harriet, knelt down before and reached up and took her hand. He placed her hand on his bare chest, on the right side. The skin was smooth. She thought that she could feel, through her palm, the steady beat of his heart.

He looked up at her and stared.

Then he released her hand and got to his feet. He walked backwards out of the tent, a hand now raised to his forehead as though in salute or valediction.

She did not know what it all meant. She felt alternately elated and troubled by the incident.

'What do you think it means?'

Nanny Rose shrugged. 'One never knows what they're up to, does one?'

∽

It was not until another eleven days had passed that Alexine returned.

'What happened to you, what happened to you?' The long period of anxiety made Harriet ask the question in a tone of anger. 'I was so worried.'

'Well, we found a perfect place for our next stop. But it looks as if all that rain was only a false alarm. If the rainy season hasn't, in fact, started yet, then we could push on, without a halt there.'

'But why did it all take you so long?' Harriet persisted.

'Oh, I wanted to collect some botanical specimens. And there was another slave market that I wanted to see for myself. And . . . well, there was so much else that was interesting. We've brought back vegetables and fruit – and pigeons, partridges, guinea-fowl and even an antelope. Some of them shot by me but most by Osman. So we're going to have a number of feasts.'

'I expect you want a bath,' Nanny Rose said.

'Yes, I've been longing and longing for one. There was a pond, but the water was filthy. And there was a stream on the journey back.'

'I'll tell the girls to get everything ready.'

'And how have things been here?'

'All right. Some complaints, some rows. The problem has been that the men have had nothing to do. They can't spend their time writing letters like me, or knitting like Nanny Rose. And if any of them have been carving wood like Daan, I haven't seen them at it.'

∽

That night Alexine slept deeply and contentedly. It was wonderful to be in the privacy of her own tent, on her own folding bed, with her own mattress beneath her. It was no less wonderful to hear Sunny's regular breathing from his pallet on the floor and to know that, within call, her mother, Nanny Rose and Daan were at hand.

One night, maddened by flea bites in that *tukul* that the Sheik had had peremptorily emptied of its inhabitants so that she could inhabit it by herself, she had had a terrible dream about Harriet. It had been so vivid that she had feared that it might be prophetic. Harriet was standing on the rickety jetty, looking out over the river, as though waiting for a ship. Alexine and Sunny were at the summit of the little hill below which they were all encamped. All at once, the jetty moved away from the land and began to float down the river. Harriet still stood motionless on it, with no sign that she realized what was happening. A huge wave appeared, a moving wall of yellow-green water, so smooth and shiny that the mangroves were reflected in it. It approached the gently gliding jetty and thrust it ahead of it. In a moment, wave, jetty and Harriet had all vanished round a bend.

On the last leg of the journey, Alexine had been so superstitiously worried by this dream – what did it mean, what did it mean? – that she had half expected to hear Nanny Rose or Daan tell her that her mother had mysteriously disappeared. But there Harriet had been, looking well, as she always looked, her pen still in her hand, since, at the moment when Sunny had excitedly called to her to tell her that he had sighted the party appearing over the hill, she had been making a list of all the animals recently bought for eventual slaughter at the nearby *zariba*.

Alexine was awoken out of her deep, contented sleep by the sound of voices outside the tent. Sunny had already jumped to his feet. The voices sounded angry. Sunny behind her, she went out to see what was happening.

To her amazement she was confronted by some dozen of the soldiers. All of them were carrying their muskets. In nothing but her nightdress, her feet bare and her hair hanging loose, she felt extraordinarily vulnerable. But in a loud, clear voice, she demanded in Arabic: 'What is all this? What do you want?'

At first no one seemed disposed to answer the question. There was a lot of muttering, but she could make nothing of it.

'Well? Who's prepared to speak? Come on. Either tell me what you want or let me go back to sleep.'

Sunny had moved in front of her, as though to protect her. She put a hand on his shoulder.

'Well?'

One of them, a man with black hair but a grey beard, stepped forward. He was an Egyptian and spoke Arabic. In a nasal, sing-song voice, he began to complain of the scarcity and sameness of the food. Alexine listened attentively. Then he spoke of their pay. It was not enough, he said. When they had agreed to the sum offered by the *vakeel* on her behalf, they had had no idea that they were to come to a place as distant as this, for such a long period. As with the porters and Harriet, there were other trivial complaints.

Osman now appeared. He was standing to one side of the men. She hoped that he would intervene, but he did not do so. His arms were crossed and he looked in turn at Alexine and the men, a vaguely contemptuous smile on his lips.

'Is that all?' The man had at last fallen silent.

There was no reply. One man shouted out something, but it was not in Arabic, and so she did not know what it was. It sounded like a threat.

'Is that all?'

Again there was silence.

'Now listen to me. But before I speak, you must put down those guns.' She pointed at the musket in the hands of the man closest to her. She glared at him. 'Put it down! Down!'

The musket fell from his hand. She waited. Another man rested his musket against a pile of crates beside the tent. She went on waiting. Gradually, reluctantly, in twos and threes, the soldiers laid down their arms. She had never doubted that they would do so. After she had given that decisive command, she had, miraculously, experienced not a moment of fear.

'Good. Now listen to me! The first thing that I want to say to you – I say it first because it is the most important thing – is that you were given those guns not to threaten me but to protect me. Do I make myself clear?' They shifted uneasily. 'If you do not protect me – if you harm me or even threaten me – how do you think that the Mudir will treat you when you return to Khartoum? You want to return to Khartoum, don't you? Or do you want to stay on here – in this place that you tell me that you so much dislike? You talk of the money that I agreed to pay you. You know that it is a far larger sum than anyone has ever paid you in the past. We agreed that I should give you some of the money when we set out, some every week that we were away, and the rest on our return. If you harm me, you will not get that money, and you may even be too frightened ever to return. Think about that.'

The men had begun once more to mutter among themselves. Some had turned away from her, as though frightened of her defiant, compelling gaze.

'Think about it.'

She waited.

With a change of tone from anger to emollience, she said: 'I know that this long wait has been hard for you. I will therefore give the *vakeel* enough money to prepare a feast. And I will give orders for an increase in your rations. All right?'

Some of them nodded. Once more they turned to each other. First one sullen face and then another broke into a grin. Then she could hear their voices raised in noisy jubilation. They thought that they had won a victory.

Harriet had been watching Alexine aghast, from the opening of her own tent. Now she rushed forward.

'Darling! You were magnificent. You might have been your father. That's how he would have dealt with them.'

Alexine gave a small smile. 'I must have some more sleep after that long journey yesterday. Why couldn't they have waited until I'd had my breakfast?'

14 ADDY SAT IN A SHADY CORNER OF THE GARDEN, reading the three letters from Harriet that the runner had brought that morning. She was not surprised that there was no letter from Alexine. She was rarely pleased to receive a letter and was reluctant to write any. Out of sight, she could hear the gardener watering the plants that Lucy so much cherished. The water was raised from a well by a constantly circling, blinkered, mangy donkey, and the gardener then carried it in two pails, supported on a yoke over his muscular shoulders. Today, she had noticed, with surprise, that there were no bats in the trees above her, but she had seen an emerald tree-frog, squatting motionless where the lowest branch of the nearest tree joined its trunk. She and the frog had stared at each other for several seconds before, with a flip, it had vanished into the undergrowth. At its disappearance, Addy had laughed in delight. She was laughing far more now, usually at the absurdities or surprises of her daily life, than for many years.

Eventually Lucy joined her. 'It's too hot to write.' She sank into a cane arm-chair. 'Sweat kept dripping off me on to the paper.' She noticed the letter held in Addy's hand. 'So what's the news?'

'Oh, they seem to be having all sorts of adventures. Nothing is going according to plan but that doesn't seem to cause them any worry. My sister's quite extraordinary. She's clearly enjoying every minute of it. She says the countryside and the people are both ravishing.'

'That's not Roderick's view. But then Harriet always strikes me as someone who makes the best of things. Whereas Roderick is always determined to make the worst of them. Are you now regretting not having gone with them?'

'Oh, good heavens no! I'm far happier here with you. Do you know, next Monday they'll have been gone for five months.'

For more than three weeks now the women had been alone in the house. Warburton, again solvent thanks to Alexine, was away on one of his mysterious expeditions. If there was any consular business, which was rare, Lucy handled it in his absence, far more efficiently than he would have done. From time to time, lying in bed or working alone in the garden, she would have the exhilarating, guilty thought that life might be not merely preferable but even possible without him. She would travel with Harriet, Alexine and Addy to The Hague, when they had decided, as she had herself decided long ago, that they had finished with this continent. Perhaps, now that the two of them were so close, Addy would employ her, as she was in effect already doing, albeit without any spoken agreement and without any pay, as her companion. If not, then no doubt Addy would be able to find her work as a governess with one of the many rich families related or known to her.

Addy was now showing Lucy the sort of generosity that Alexine showed to everyone. They often strolled out together, arm in arm, a single parasol raised above them and Mister at their heels; if Lucy saw something that she needed or wanted, she had only to indicate that she did so, in however indirect a manner, for Addy to insist at once on buying it. Even in so short a space of time, they had ceased to have any secrets. Addy had talked at length, to Lucy's amazement, about her affair with the Tsar and its terrible aftermath; Lucy about the runaway marriage which had seemed a glorious liberation and had ended in her being the prisoner of a man whom she no longer loved, in a country which had come to fill her with alternating boredom and horror.

When Lucy was not at her work on her book – that was the one subject about which she was evasive with Addy, since she nursed a superstitious dread that, if she revealed too much about it, it would die on her – the two women would spend much of their time either reading in silence together or else eagerly discussing what they had read. Lucy had never read Balzac and she had always previously doubted if her French were good enough for her to do so with any ease or pleasure; but now, encouraged by Addy, who would provide her with translations of any difficult words and so save her having to consult a dictionary, she was almost half-way through *La Cousine Bette*.

Mister suddenly began to yap. Lola, holding aloft the parasol that Harriet had given her after their last lesson together, now appeared at the far end the garden. She would often pay such unannounced visits, using the pretext of wanting to practise on the piano since, she said, the one in the drawing-room at home was so dreadfully out of tune. Why didn't she suggest to her father that he should employ the Greek youth to tune it? Addy had asked. 'Oh, what a good idea! Yes, I never thought of that. I'll speak about it today.' But she continued to come over, each time asking, as though for the first time, if she might use the piano for a while, and then, when that all-too-brief while was over, would join them, often literally sitting at their feet.

Addy, who had previously commented on the vulgarity with which Lola and her sisters dressed and who had found the girl's exuberant behaviour 'gauche' or 'common', had now taken to her. She and Lucy agreed that she was generous-hearted, intelligent and kind. Both sighed that it was a pity that, like her sisters, she had failed to receive a proper education.

On this occasion Lola had brought with her, as she often did, two bunches of huge, garish flowers with an overpowering scent from her father's garden. Addy used to say that she could not bear to have such flowers in her room, and so her gift was usually placed, in a vase, on a chest in the hall. Lola now stooped and rested one bunch in Addy's lap and another in Lucy's.

'How kind of you, my dear! I have a little present for you. Something I rarely wear, which will look far better on you than it has ever done on me.' Addy got up from the wicker *chaise-longue* on which she had been reclining. 'I'll fetch it for you.'

'A present! Oh, how lovely! I love getting presents!' Lola was always demonstrative, in a way that Addy never was. That had at first irritated Addy but now it touched and pleased her. 'What is it?'

'Wait and see.'

Addy walked back to the house, from time to time pausing to sniff at a flower or to brush it with her fingertips.

Lucy was far more perceptive than Addy. When Addy was out of ear-shot, she said: 'Something's on your mind. Isn't it?'

'On my mind? Oh, no! Nothing.'

But Lucy persisted: 'I just had this feeling the moment that I saw you . . .'

'No, truly, there's nothing.'

Addy returned with a velvet-covered box, which she carefully opened and then held out.

Lola let out a scream of pleasure. 'Is that really for me?'

A brooch nestled on cotton wool inside the box, its one flaring diamond surrounded by modest rubies. Lola had noticed it on Addy on two or three formal occasions. On the last of those occasions she had even commented admiringly on it, adding 'It must be worth an awful lot of money' – a remark that Addy had later condemned as 'crude'.

'It belonged to my mother,' Addy said with assumed indifference. 'I never greatly liked it. It's yours.'

'But why? Why?'

'Why?' Addy was vaguely offended as she began the gather up Harriet's letters. 'Why? Because we're friends. Aren't we?'

'Oh, yes, yes! Of course.'

∾

Two days later it was not to Lucy but to Addy that Lola confided the reason for her worry. The two of them had taken the carriage down to the market while, fretful at the interruption to her work on her novel, Lucy was dealing with some consular business.

The two women were jogging along in silence, an unusually cool breeze on their faces; Lola turned and, in a voice totally unlike her usually loud, confident one, said: 'Mademoiselle Van Capellen – I wonder if I might consult you about something?'

'Yes, of course. What is it?'

'I'm rather worried.'

'Worried? What are you worried about? You're far too young to have any worries.'

'Well, the thing is...' Her voice trailed away. She turned her head aside and gazed out of the window.

At that moment, the elderly Englishman who had come to the Sudan to hunt big game passed them on a horse. He raised his hat. 'Good morning, ladies!' he boomed out. 'Good morning to you!'

Addy graciously acknowledged the greeting; Lola did not.

When he had gone, Addy prompted: 'So?'

Lola's face looked yellow and pinched and Addy now noticed the acne breaking out on the line of her right jaw.

'I'm – I'm late,' she muttered.

'Late?' Back at the house, Addy was to curse herself for her obtuseness. '*Late?* What do you mean?'

'Well, I haven't – haven't – bled for more than seven weeks. And I'm – I'm frightened.'

Addy stared at her. All at once she was reliving her own joy and then terror when, all those years ago, she had slowly begun to realize that she was pregnant.

'Oh, but that sort of delay's not at all uncommon. With Mrs Van Capellen and my niece it's always been like clockwork, but I used to have endless problems. Sometimes I bled so much that I had to take to my bed.'

'I've never been late before. Never, in my whole life.'

'You're probably just run-down. Or it may be because of this unseasonable heat.'

Lola shook her head. 'No, I feel it. I just know.'

'When did you last' – Addy sought for a conventional phrase since convention, despite the scandal of her youth, had always been important to her – 'have intercourse.'

Lola thought, eyes screwed up and the fingers of one hand pressed to her full lips. 'Almost two months ago.'

'And you'd had it a number of times before?'

Lola hesitated to answer, fingertips still to lips.

'I'm sorry to ask you these questions, but if I'm to be of any help to you...'

Lola shook her head. 'Not a number of times. Three.' Her voice was attenuated to a wispy thread so that Addy, who was beginning to go deaf, could hardly hear her.

'And are you still ... still seeing him?'

Again Lola shook her head. 'He's gone away. I think ... feel...'

'Yes?'

'I don't think he'll want to see me again.'

'Why? Did you quarrel?'

'No. Not quarrel. But that's – that's his way.'

'How do you know?'

'People say. Another girl – a friend of mine – they – they *did* things – two, three times. Then . . .' She raised her hands and dropped them.

'He sounds a thoroughly bad sort.'

'He is, he is! But . . . I love him. Loved him.'

Addy put a hand over the girl's. 'Poor dear.' Then, after a few seconds' silence, she asked: 'Have I met him?'

Lola did not answer, biting her lower lip.

'Have I? Yes?'

Lola nodded.

'Where?'

'At that party, the first party.'

With a triumphant leap of intuition, Addy at once knew who it must be. 'Was it that Mr Fielding?'

Silence.

'It was, wasn't it?'

Lola nodded.

'The brute! I never took to him, even on our first meeting in Cairo.'

'What am I to do?'

'You haven't said anything to your parents?'

'Oh, I couldn't! I couldn't! They'd turn me out of the house.'

'I'd better speak to Mrs Warburton. She knows this place. She may have some idea. Let me do that. May I?'

'But I don't want anyone else to know.'

'I'm sure she'll be discreet.'

∽

'Well, there are these old women – and some young ones. They prepare potions that are said to be effective. But they could be dangerous.'

'What's the alternative for the poor girl? She says her father will turn her out of the house.'

Lucy thought. She said, 'Well, if that were to happen, I suppose she could come to live here. Perhaps once the baby was born – and had been adopted – her father might then relent. Yes, she could do that.'

'But would you want her here all the time?'

'No, not really,' Lucy retorted drily. 'But what's the alternative – if we can't get her an abortion?'

'And you think Mr Warburton . . . ?'

'I'm sure he wouldn't in the least welcome the idea. But – I really don't care a jot about that.'

Both women laughed. They were now accustomed to speaking with contempt about Warburton.

∽

Lucy enquired among the two women servants employed by her and the three employed by Addy. Eventually one of Addy's servants, a Sudanese, reluctantly came up with the name of an old woman living in a village seven miles from the town. She was famous, the servant said, as an expert in such matters. Deciding not to take Lola with them, Addy and Lucy set off in the dusty, dilapidated carriage. The road was little more than a stony track, and they were constantly thrown against each other. In the best of humours in spite of the nature of their errand, they merely laughed each time their bodies collided.

The old woman lived in a thatched hovel, where the small, crowded village petered out in a few shacks, some pens for sheep, and a patchwork of cultivated and uncultivated smallholdings. She was seated on a stool, a naked child of two or three in her lap. Shortsightedly she was peering down at the child's head through half-closed, hooded eyes, as she diligently picked out nits and then crushed them between her long fingernails. Lucy spoke to her in Arabic, but she shook her head, not understanding, and then resumed her task.

'I ought to have realized we'd have this difficulty.'

'What about the coachman?'

'We don't want the whole world and his wife to know our business. And in any case his Arabic is so poor . . .'

At that moment a young man in shabby Western dress and dusty boots sauntered past. He smiled at the two women and, when Lucy smiled back, raised his hat, bowed and said in French: 'Good morning, ladies.' He was later to tell them that he was a tax official.

'Good morning.' It was Lucy who answered. Addy would never have done so.

He walked on, hesitated, halted, and then returned.

'May I help you?'

'Well, yes,' Lucy said. 'Thank you. But we don't want to take up too much of your time.'

'My time is all yours, madame.'

A three-sided conversation ensued between the stranger, the old woman and Lucy. Addy, taking no part, opened the fan that she was carrying with her, and began vigorously to wave it before her face. Beads of sweat were pushing through the powder on her cheeks and neck, and the curls artfully created for her that morning by her maid with a pair of tongs were limply sticking to her forehead.

Alexine had once said that all conversations between Europeans and Africans ended in discussion of money, and this was no exception.

'But that's absurd! That's far too much!'

'She says this medicine is special to her. No one else has such medicine.'

'But one could buy a mule for less than that!'

'If you want the medicine, and not a mule, then she says that that is her price.'

Lucy argued so vigorously that, pushing the child off her knees to the ground, the woman eventually got up off the stool in order, arms akimbo, to confront her on the same level.

At long last, the contestants agreed a sum, and Addy, insisting that Lucy must pay no part of it, produced the money from her bag.

'I congratulate you, ladies,' the man said.

The old woman disappeared into the recesses of the hovel, followed by the child, who crawled after her, wailing as he did so. When she reappeared she was carrying a bottle that proclaimed in French on its grubby, scuffed label: *Vinaigre*.

'Well, I hope you've paid out all that money for something more efficient than vinegar,' Lucy said, pointing to the label.

As they walked over to the carriage, the old woman, bent almost double, shuffled after them. Lucy and Addy quickened their pace, convinced that she was going to ask for more money. When she put a hand on Addy's arm, Addy at once jerked it away. But the woman's intentions were, it emerged, entirely benevolent. She smiled, said something, smiled again, said something more.

'She is wishing you good luck. You and the woman who will take the medicine. She is asking the gods to bless you.'

'Well, that's very kind of her.' Addy now felt guilty for her former suspicions. She inserted a hand into her bag, drew out a coin and, smiling, stooped to give it the child in the dust at her feet. He grabbed the coin and was about to shove it into his mouth when the old woman snatched it away from him.

The young man asked if he could have a lift with them back to the city. They were far from eager to agree to this request, but felt that, after he had given them so much help, they could hardly refuse. He sat opposite to them, one leg crossed high over the other. His boots, though dusty, looked expensive, but he was wearing no socks. His legs were thin and extremely hairy. He pulled some amber beads out of his pocket and began to click them between his fingers, smiling now at one and now at the other.

Addy fanned herself more and more vigorously. Then she coughed and coughed again. In recent days she had become breathless after any effort, and there was an intermittent feeling of constriction in her chest. The man put down the beads on the seat beside him, and again foraged in his pocket. This time he produced a box of pastilles. He held it out.

She shook her head, forced a smile. 'Thank you. I'm all right. Thank you.'

He put away the box, and a long silence followed.

Then he said: 'Is the medicine for one of your servants?'

Each woman waited for the other to tell the inevitable lie. Then Lucy said: 'Yes. Yes, that's right.'

'These country girls . . . Is she a country girl?'

'Er – yes.'

'It's always the same sad story.'

To change the subject, Addy asked him whether he was from Khartoum or elsewhere?

He was from Aswan, he said. Did they know Aswan?

Of course, Addy answered. Then she said: 'We passed through it on our horrendous journey from Cairo.'

'Horrendous?' He was surprised.

Addy laughed. 'Well, far from comfortable. I'm a creature of comfort,' she added.

⌒

The next day Lola arrived at the house, as arranged, and Lucy and Addy watched her as she drank the first of three doses from the bottle. The liquid was sticky, a dark-brown with strange, grease-like orange globules in it. However much first Addy and then Lucy shook the bottle, these globules refused to disperse. Lola pulled a face as she swallowed the draught from the glass, and then lurched forward, retching. Tears appeared in her eyes.

'It's horrible!'

'Well, anyway you got it down. And kept it down,' Lucy said.

When Lola arrived on the following day, she looked even yellower than ever and the acne was now a bright red along her jaw.

'Any luck?'

She shook her head miserably. 'I was sick,' she said. 'Twice. During the night. I woke my mother. I told her I must have eaten something bad.'

'Well, you'd better take the second dose,' Addy said.

'Oh, no! No!'

'Yes!'

Again Lola bent over, retching; again her eyes filled with tears. Her lips were drawn back, and her teeth were stained a murky brown. She walked out with them on a shopping errand but soon said that she felt exhausted and, having kissed each of them perfunctorily, turned for home.

On the day after that, still nothing had happened. 'I don't believe

274

that medicine's any good. She cheated us. Who knows what it really is?'

'You must take the third dose.'

Again Lola protested, and again, bullied by them, she eventually swallowed the draught.

The next day Lola dolefully told them that there had still been no result.

'Well, that's it. Perhaps you're right. Perhaps she did cheat us.' In sudden rage, amazing the other two women, Lucy flung the empty bottle against the kitchen wall, where it shattered. Lola stooped to pick up the fragments but Lucy ordered her: 'Leave it, leave it! The maids can see to it.'

Out in the garden, the three drank lemonade. The birds were even more noisy than usual, and the fruit bats, hanging motionless upside down from the trees, had returned. The bats always made Addy feel uneasy. Suppose one were to detach itself and drop on her head?

'Well, what are we going to do now?' Lucy voiced the question in all of their minds.

'I'll have to have it,' Lola said, in a despairing voice.

'Yes, perhaps that would be best,' Lucy said. 'If you can't have it at home, you can have it here. Why not?' That previous night she had toyed with the idea of adopting the baby. Before, she had been thankful for her childless state, but now, suddenly, she had begun to regret it and to long for it to end.

'You are very kind.' Lola eyes filled with tears. 'My best friends.'

～

Four days later the three of them were playing cards. Lola, though the game was new to her, was constantly winning. Piled up before her were the sweets which, at Addy's suggestion, they had been using as counters. She was staring down at her cards when, suddenly, she put a hand to her stomach and let out a scream. She let out another scream and jumped up from her chair. On the pale yellow damask seat there was now a scarlet patch. As she raced into the house, Addy and Lucy both saw that the back of her dress was also drenched in blood.

Lucy flew after her, followed by Addy, at a slower pace.

'Are you all right?'

Lola had locked herself in Addy's bathroom. She made no answer.

Lucy rattled the door handle. 'Lola! Let me in! Let me in!'

Addy sat down on the upright chair beside the bathroom door and crossed her hands in her lap. Acutely now she felt that constriction in her chest.

For a long time Lola would not open the door, even though Lucy continued to rattle at the handle and call to her. When at last she emerged, her face was yellow-grey and streaked with sweat. She had got out of the dress and stuffed it into the commode, before putting on a peignoir belonging to Addy that she had seen hanging behind the door. One hand was raised to hold the folds of the peignoir together, the other was in her damp hair. Later, Lucy, pulling a face, would rescue the dress and one of the maids would wash it and iron it.

'It's gone. Over.'

She said it not merely with utter exhaustion but also, to the amazement of the other two women, with a furious anguish.

15 THEY HAD NEVER BEEN HAPPIER. 'Oh, it's so beautiful, so beautiful,' Harriet kept exclaiming as they passed through the gallery forest, previously visited by Alexine, camped on a vast plain with herds of buffalo in the distance, or watched some dozen elephants processing majestically down to a pond surrounded by gum trees to drink.

On one occasion, as a stretch of downland gently rose, a luminescent green before them, Harriet even remarked: 'It's as good as Scotland.'

'As good as Scotland!' Alexine exclaimed. 'It's a hundred times better. From then on, she would constantly mock her mother by asking 'As good as Scotland?' when she remarked on the beauty of some view.

Eventually they arrived at a river, little more than swollen stream, that the two guides, who would constantly argue with each other, on this occasion both agreed they would have to cross.

'At last we can use that gutta-percha boat,' Nanny Rose said. 'I thought we were never going to.'

Although they cried out in dismay when the boat appeared to be about to capsize as the two of them climbed in, Nanny Rose and Harriet were eventually ensconced in its bows.

'Come on, Daan! Come on!' Nanny Rose gestured vigorously.

'No, I'm all right. I'm all right. I can wade. The water's not deep.'

'Well, you come, Alexine!' Harriet cried out.

'No, no. I'm going to wade.'

'You can't! No, no!'

But, as always, Alexine got her own way.

When the boat, hauled by a number of men stripped of every piece of clothing except their loincloths, had deposited its first cargo of the two European women and their terrified maids, and then returned, it was found to be too small for many of the animals.

'What we need is an ark,' Daan said, in so serious a tone that Alexine wondered whether he might not really mean it.

'They'll just have to wade or swim.' Alexine pulled up her jellaba and knotted it round her thighs. 'And I'll have to wade or swim with them.'

There were shouts, screams of laughter and apprehension, and the constant sound of splashing water, as the animals, some acquiescent and some rebellious, were either coaxed or bullied across. One sheep swam over at once, but the others, to everyone's surprise, refused to follow, and had to be half lifted and half dragged. The cats in their panniers on the boat set up a tremendous caterwauling. Two dogs suddenly began to fight each other in the water, but Flopsy, head raised, paddled effortlessly across, as Alexine preceded him dragging her horse behind her. Some of the soldiers insisted that they must cross by boat. Others, lifting their muskets high above their heads, waded over. Osman cut an imperious figure, as the waves parted before him astride his whinnying horse. Sunny, who had by now learned to swim, struck out boldly.

'What an adventure!' Nanny Rose remarked as the porters began to put up the tents, everyone having at last safely crossed the stream. She then turned on Daan: 'But you were a fool to wade! You could pick up anything in that water. There's that worm we were hearing about from Lucy.'

'Bilharzia,' Harriet put in.

'Well, whatever it is. It's the last thing anyone wants.'

'I laughed and laughed,' Harriet said. 'Particularly when the *vakeel* slipped and went under the water.' She had never cared for him, suspecting that he often fomented the little mutinies in which he then offered to act as mediator.

Two nights later, after a day of downpour, the vast, clear sky was blazing with stars. They all craned up at them.

Sunny pointed at the brightest. 'Look, look!'

'Oh, if only we could travel there!' Alexine exclaimed, putting her arms around his shoulders.

'Aren't you satisfied with travelling as far as we've got?' Nanny Rose asked.

'Nothing satisfies her, Nanny. You know that by now. She must always have more, go farther.' Harriet grabbed Alexine's hand. 'But I'm so glad that you insisted on our leaving dreary old Khartoum. This is a hundred times better.'

'I wonder how Addy is getting on.' Alexine suddenly realized that she had not given a thought to her aunt for days.

'It's so sad she's not with us.'

'Just as well,' Nanny Rose said. 'This isn't the sort of life for her. Did you know that we're soon going to run out of soap? Imagine Miss Addy without any soap!'

'Yes, I know, I know about the soap!' Harriet wailed. 'I totally miscalculated.'

'If you ask me, there've been thieves around.'

∽

Eleven days later, they arrived in the late afternoon at a mission station, set in what appeared, from far away, to be the idyllic surroundings of a lake ringed with low, wooded hills. A church bell was ringing, the single, tiny note echoing back and forth. They could make out the steeple of the chapel, and around it thirteen straw huts. Beyond it blue smoke drifted up into the air from what must be a native village.

'Oh, it all looks so peaceful,' Harriet cried out.

'Heaven on earth,' Nanny Rose concurred.

But the nearer they approached, the more apprehensive they became. Fields that had once been cultivated were now overgrown. The thatch of the huts looked dishevelled and patchy. A gate to an enclosure hung askew and there were no signs of the animals that once must have been penned there.

The young man who emerged from one of the *tukuls* to greet them was painfully emaciated, with a straggly beard, reaching almost to his waist, made up of black and white strands, matted together. At first, they thought that the brilliance of his eyes was due to his delight in seeing them in this place of extreme isolation. Then, as he began to cough, endlessly, on and on, bowing over as he did so, they realized that he was ill.

He was, they were later to learn, one of the only two French priests left of the eleven who had come out some dozen years ago. There were also five black laymen. He introduced himself, in a soft, hoarse voice, in English, as Père François. His superior, Père Thomas, was taking a service in the chapel. It was for the service that he himself had been ringing the bell.

'Do you have a big congregation?' Harriet asked.

He gave a small, sad smile. 'People come. A few people. Why do they come? For God? For food?' He shrugged. 'But people who first come for food sometimes later come for God. We hope.'

'Are the local people ever hostile?' Alexine asked.

'Oh, no! They are kind, good, helpful.'

By now they had moved from the overgrown garden, with its pungent odour of mint crushed under their feet, into the *tukul* that served as a dining-room and living-room. There were only five chairs, which the priest indicated that the three women, Daan and Sunny should take.

'No, no,' Alexine protested. 'Sunny can sit on that step over there. Or I can. You must have a chair.' It was essential, she thought, that sick as he was, the priest should be comfortable.

'We heard you were coming.'

'Heard? How is that possible?'

'Some Arab traders passed through. And an Englishman. They told us. They brought us some supplies. And letters.' He jumped up. 'Tea. They brought us some tea. We have had no tea for five, six months. Now you can have some tea.'

He moved stiffly, like an old man, into an inner room, from where they heard him giving orders. After what seemed an extraordinarily long time, a barefoot male servant pattered in, carrying a tray with the tea on it.

'If you're still short of any supplies, do tell us,' Alexine said. 'We can probably help you.'

As they were sipping their tea, Père Thomas entered the room. 'You've arrived.' He was a tall, elderly man, as emaciated as Père François, with a totally hairless skull. His collar was loose on him, and his habit was tattered. He gave each of them a formal greeting.

'You will have some tea, Father?' Père François asked.

Père Thomas shook his head.

The laymen now entered. Having been introduced, they squatted on the floor, leaning their backs against the wall. For the most part they were silent, staring at the visitors with a dazed, bewildered curiosity. All of them were little more than gawky boys.

Unlike his colleague, Père Thomas spoke with a sardonic edge to his slow, quiet voice. They were travelling like royalty, he told them. Even the Governor-General on his rare visits did not travel with such a vast retinue. So many people had never before been congregated in their little mission station. 'We are honoured, truly honoured.' His eyes glittered in his yellow, drawn face. Accommodation was, as they could see, limited to a few *tukuls*. But they would be happy to put one at the disposal of the ladies.

'That's very kind of you.' It was Harriet, not Alexine, who answered. 'But we have our tents and our beds – and everything else that we need. We don't wish to put you to any trouble. We'd – we'd like to invite you to join us for dinner. All of you.'

'But we have a duty of hospitality to you.'

'Oh, don't let's talk of duty. We have plenty of provisions and an excellent cook. Shall we meet in, say, three hours?'

They ate out in the overgrown garden. The laymen dragged out some trestle tables and benches, and then added some chairs. Some of the expedition servants set out the cutlery and crockery. When the visitors returned, they had all bathed and were wearing formal clothes. Priests and laymen gawped at them in amazement.

'We try to make our own wine,' Père Thomas said. He raised his glass: 'But this of yours is much better.'

'I'm afraid so much travel hasn't improved it.' Harriet sipped from her glass. Then she raised it: 'A toast to the mission.'

They all raised their glasses.

Père Thomas was draining glass after glass in rapid succession. Red spots appeared on the high cheekbones above his sunk-in cheeks, and his speech was getting slurred. Harriet, who was seated on his right, began to ask him about the mission.

He mumbled his answers, his head now sagging on his neck, as his hand circled the stem of the glass. It had been there for nine years now, and he himself for seven. Père François had arrived two years ago. At first things had gone well: they had built the *tukuls*, they had created the gardens, the animals brought by them had multiplied. But now ... 'It's as though God decided that he'd had enough of us. And why not? The animals fell mysteriously ill and most of them died. And then we fell mysteriously ill and most of us died. My younger brother was with us. He died – for me most terribly of all.' Again he gulped wine. 'We expect that, any day now, we will be recalled and this little station will vanish, as though it had never been. But by then will there be any of us left here to recall?' He raised a bony hand and hiccoughed behind it.

Alexine leaned across the table. 'Is there nothing that we can do to help?'

'Help?'

'Is it a question of money?'

He shook his head. 'No. Of God's will.' He got the words out with difficulty. Again his gaunt, totally bald head swayed on his long, thin neck.

At the far end of the table the laymen were more cheerful. Daan, who had brought a pack of cards with him in the back pocket of his tail-coat, was performing some tricks for them. 'How did you do that? How? How? Tell us.' But he shook his head triumphantly, smiling to reveal his crooked, yellow teeth. Sunny, in the same group, grabbed the cards and performed a trick of his own, learned from Daan. 'This is your card! Yes? Yes?' he shouted in triumph.

Nanny Rose raised a hand to her mouth, yawned behind it and said to Harriet, who was looking over to her, to see if she was all right: 'I'm ready for Bedfordshire. That was a long journey today. We started so early.'

Alexine had had her bed placed not in her tent but out under the stars. She gazed up at them, amazed, as she constantly was, by their multitude and brilliance. A lamp gleamed from the half-open doorway of the *tukul* inhabited by Père François. She had sat next to him at the dinner, and in the course of their conversation they had begun to speak of French literature. 'Oh, I wish my aunt were here,' she told him. 'She reads so much and she would have been able to pass on so many books to you.' She added that she herself had some books with her, now read, which she would be happy to give him. There was a resigned desperation about him, as there was a savage one about Père Thomas, and it had filled her with sadness. Everything in the mission seemed to be dying – the animals, the men, the men's faith in God and in themselves and in the world around them. She suddenly thought that she would like to hold Père Thomas's body in her arms, like a child's, her lips to his fevered forehead or cheek, to comfort and console him. He would be as light as one of her cats, she thought, and far more fragile.

Again she stared up at the sky, until she began to feel dizzy and confused by all that illimitable recession of stars beyond stars. She shut her eyes. She fell asleep.

∽

Père François walked with Alexine down through the garden. His soutane and her full skirt constantly brushed against long, reed-like grass and overgrown bushes. The morning was clear and cool. From time to time he stopped and, bowed over, hands on knees, gave his dry, interminable cough. On more than one occasion, having straightened after coughing, he banged on his breastbone with a fist, as though furious with his own body for letting him down.

At the bottom of the garden, some vegetable beds still survived. 'We still work these. Tomatoes. Aubergine. Maize. A few other things. You can see. Père Thomas was interested in such work – his father was a farmer – but now ... We are all weak.' He sighed. 'There has been so much sickness among us – as though we were cursed.'

'Are you taking quinine? I have a lot with me. We find it wonderful.'

'Quinine? Yes, yes!' He nodded wearily. 'Of course. Quinine all the time.'

They now came to a wall built of irregular blocks of stone, with creepers cascading down it. Père François told Alexine that, when the mission had first arrived, full of hope and ardour, Père Thomas had decided that they would build a chapel not of wood, like the present one, but of stone. With the aid of some men recruited from the village, they had all set to work. The chapel had begun to grow out of the ground, like a sapling, constantly spreading itself. Its fame even reached Khartoum. Then a rainy season of unusual ferocity had swept in over the distant mountains. The torrents, often accompanied by lightning and thunder, had fallen remorselessly for days on end, terminating all work on building the chapel and cultivating the fields and the vegetable garden. Suddenly, one night, everyone had been woken by a strange, subterranean rumble, like a train travelling at speed through a tunnel, followed by what sounded like a huge explosion. The missionaries had all run out to investigate, and had found that the chapel was now no more than a heap of rubble.

The village workers refused to take part in any rebuilding. They said that the gods were angry, and that it was they who had brought about the destruction. For many months there was no chapel at all, and the missionaries used one of the *tukuls* for their services. Then they had built the wooden chapel, with its metal steeple like a bent needle, tilted to one side.

All that now remained of the stone chapel was this wall – he pointed – with its arches. He lifted some of the fleshy, dark-green creepers with a hand. 'Look!' In the arch, there was a headstone, also covered with creepers, leaning so far forward that it looked as if it were in imminent danger of falling. Now it was Alexine who lifted up the glossy leaves, starting back as a vast, hairy spider emerged from the centre of them and then retreated again.

'Père Thomas's brother.'

The clumsy carving of an inscription was now, even after so short a space of time, almost indecipherable.

In the other arches, there were other headstones, all carved from the same friable sandstone and all similarly difficult to decipher. Sometimes a headstone stood alone, but more often two or three leaned towards each other. Alexine was appalled.

'How did they all die?'

'How do people die in this country? Suddenly. With fevers and chills. With pain. With delirium. With terror.' He was briefly lost for words, swallowing twice with apparent difficulty and raising his emaciated arm in a wide sweep. 'This continent doesn't want us. Why do we force ourselves on it?'

'Because it has what we want.'

'They were all young. Except for one father – an old man. He had lived in South Africa, he had travelled with Livingstone. He died of old age. This continent had accepted him. The only one. He was never ill.'

Flopsy, who was with them, began to root around in the undergrowth by one of the graves. Alexine stooped and tugged at his collar. 'Stop that!'

They walked on, down a narrow path to the lake. Like the mission station, it had looked so beautiful from afar; but now Alexine saw that the water was murky and that this end was choked with mangroves.

The priest pointed. 'That tree has berries that one can eat. Look! Up there!'

The berries looked like huge mulberries, a purple colour shading to black.

'What is it?'

'I don't know the name in French. The natives have a name for it.' He said a word.

'You speak their language?'

He nodded. 'I'm trying to translate the Bible for them. That was my task when I came here. Another father helped me but ... Gone. Père Thomas isn't a scholar. He's something more important here. He can do practical things and show others how to do them.'

Alexine was on tiptoe, trying to pick one of the fruit. The sun was in her eyes, piercing through the branches. She reached and reached again. Each time she had the illusion that, just as her fingers were about the close on the fruit, the branch sprang away from them.

'Let me pick.'

He reached up, also on tiptoe. Then he was again convulsed with coughing. He put a hand first to his chest and then to his mouth. He swayed, extended the hand seemingly towards her, and toppled forward.

She knelt beside him, not caring that she was soiling her dress with the faeces-like mud. She put fingers to the side of his neck and felt the trembling pulse. So he hadn't died, as, in terror, she had at first assumed. She waited beside him for him to recover consciousness but he did not do so. 'Father! Father!' She took his hand in his and squeezed it. There was no response.

She looked around her. There was no one in sight. The dog sniffed at the priest's extended hand and then put out his tongue to lick at one of his hollow temples.

'Stop that! No!'

Alexine scrambled to her feet and, on an impulse, bent over and scooped the body up in her arms. She had expected that his weight would prove too much for her; but, as in her reverie of the previous night, she might have been holding one of her cats. Lurching from side to side, sweat streaming down her face, she mounted the narrow, slippery path with the body in her arms.

Eventually she came on a wooden bench, presumably once placed there so that the priests could sit and enjoy the view of mountains and lake. By now she was exhausted. She set him down on the bench, his body occupying most of it, his legs dangling, and gasped for breath. Then she saw the blood that was trickling out of one of his nostrils. She stared down at it, a scarlet thread that became two threads and then three. Suddenly she thought of the Colonel's map, with those erratic scarlet threads constantly dividing, subdividing and joining up again. She was both fascinated and terrified.

Slowly she put out her hand and extended a forefinger. Even more slowly she placed the forefinger against the nostril from which the blood was trickling. She put the forefinger in her mouth and sucked on it.

She thought: I am tasting his life.

She thought: I am tasting his death.

Alexine and Nanny Rose emerged from the *tukul* in which Père François was lying. It was the heat, he had kept insisting, nothing more. He had fainted from the heat. He seemed even more eager to persuade himself of that than to persuade his visitors.

Nanny Rose had brought a number of medicines. He had been reluctant to swallow any of them, but she had stubbornly insisted, as she used once stubbornly to insist when Alexine declined a childhood dose of rhubarb or worming powder. 'Now I want you to be sure to take this powder. This is the important one. Don't forget! I'll be very angry if you forget. You must take it if you want to get well.'

He closed his eyes, his face expressionless.

'Don't forget!' she repeated.

Outside the *tukul*, she said: 'Poor fellow! I don't give him long. It's a strange thing. I always seem to know.'

'Seem to know?'

'When someone's about to make the journey.' Nanny Rose was full of these euphemisms. They always exasperated Alexine.

'Oh, I'm sure he'll recover. At his age, why not?' But at heart Alexine shared Nanny Rose's pessimism.

'It's odd. There's that poor fellow – not much more than thirty – and it's all but over for him. And here am I – nearing my sixties – and I feel as though I were reborn.'

'Reborn?'

'Yes, as soon as I arrived in Africa, I felt that. All that went before now seems to like a dream. And Daan says it's the same for him. He says that before he was always living other people's lives and now he's at last living his own. I suppose that's one way of putting it. You know, I don't think I ever want to return to England or the Netherlands. Isn't that strange?'

'I sometimes feel the same. I just want to go on and on, farther and farther, deeper and deeper.'

Alexine and Harriet had been playing piquet, a lantern beside them.

Harriet put down her cards. 'My eyes are tired. Let's stop.'

'You say that because you're losing.'

'I always lose with you. But this is the first time I've said my eyes are too tired for me to go on.' She picked up the cards and began to shuffle them.

Alexine jumped up. 'Let me show you something.'

'What? In the dark?'

'It's not dark.' Alexine tilted her head and gazed up into the sky. 'There's that huge full moon. And all those stars – so many stars. It's

lighter than on a foggy day in London – or The Hague for that matter.'
She beckoned. 'Come!'

Harriet got up from her chair, hitching at her shawl. After the intense
heat of the day, the nights were often cold. 'What is it you want me to
see?'

'The graves. The graves of all the priests who have died here.'

'Oh, I don't want to see anything so morbid!'

'Please! It's very moving. Beautiful too. You can't really make out
the inscriptions – just part of a name here, part of a date there – but you
imagine all those men leaving France to come all this distance out here.
And for what?'

'For God, I suppose.'

'Do you – do you really believe in God? Tell me truthfully, mama.'

Harriet thought for a while. 'I used to think that God had created
the world. But, having come here, I now think that, on the contrary, the
world created God.'

'What does that mean?'

Harriet did not answer.

Alexine slipped an arm through her mother's as they took the downward path to the overgrown garden and the little cemetery beyond it.

'You know, I can never think of you as my mother.'

'Thank you!'

'I mean, for me you're really like a sister – or like a closest friend.'

'Yes, we *are* close, aren't we?'

'And all these adventures have made us so much closer. We were
never as close as this before.'

Harriet halted and Alexine halted with her. In the undergrowth near
them there was a rustle.

'What's that?' Harriet asked.

'I hope it's not a snake.'

A cat, not one of theirs, whisked out. It was carrying something
small and wriggling in its mouth. It was too dark to see the precise
nature of its prey.

'Horrible!' Harriet said.

'It's only being a cat. Just as when humans do horrible things, they're
only being humans.'

They walked on for a while in silence. Then Alexine jerked her mother's arm, bringing her to a halt.

'What's the matter?'

Alexine put a finger to her lips. She pointed.

Below them they could see the arches with the creepers cascading
from them. In front of the arches the headstones stood out a bleached
white. A man and a woman were there. She was on her knees before

286

him, and he, hands on hips, was looking not down at her but straight out ahead. Harriet and Alexine had never seen the woman before, but they could see that she was not white. The man was Père Thomas. He was in front of his brother's headstone.

By mutual consent, saying nothing, they turned and retreated.

It was only as they neared Harriet's tent that she said: 'Poor devil! What terrible lives they lead here!'

∽

The next day, Alexine told Harriet that she wanted to photograph her down by the headstones. As she had lain awake the previous night, she had, as so often, clearly visualized the image. She had known precisely where and how she would position her mother. There would be the dark foliage behind her and a headstone beside her. The sun, filtering down through the cascading foliage, would chequer her dress, but it would also strike full on her face and hands, so they stood out starkly white.

'Oh, no, dear, no. The last thing I want is to be photographed in that dreary place.'

'Oh, please, please!'

They argued and eventually Harriet gave in.

'I'll just call Sunny to give us a hand.'

'Oh, do we really need him? I can help you.' The resentment that Harriet had felt when Sunny had begun to supplant her as Alexine's assistant, had intensified as he had become more and more her partner, often himself posing sitters or choosing a scene.

'We can't carry all that equipment all that way – and then back again – by ourselves.'

'Oh, very well. But I'd much rather be photographed out here, by the chapel. It's so picturesque.'

'I want a picture, not something picturesque.'

As Sunny tightened the head clamp, Harriet cried out: 'Oh, do be careful! You're hurting me! And you're ruining all Nanny's work with the tongs.'

'It's essential that you don't move,' Alexine said. 'Pretend you're a corpse.'

Harriet's body stiffened. She stared unblinking ahead of her. Oh, if only that wretched boy would stop gawping at her! She felt an involuntary tremor of an eyelid. That mustn't happen again or the likeness would be ruined.

'Lovely! Perfect. Don't move yet. Don't move!'

A fly buzzed round Harriet but she did not move.

'You're my best model.' Alexine removed the plate from the bulky camera and handed it to Sunny. The she stooped for another and inserted it. 'Just one more.'

'Oh, please!'

For the rest of the day, Alexine and Sunny continued to take photographs. Alexine even tried to photograph the dogs. But though she posed them on the laps of either Sunny or Nanny Rose, whom she instructed to clasp them firmly, they always somehow managed to move, so that, when the plates were at last developed and printed, there was Nanny Rose or Sunny perfectly solid, but the dogs were merely ghostly, evanescent blurs or scratches of whiteness or blackness.

'It's as though they didn't exist,' Nanny Rose commented to Alexine. 'And yet they have far more life in them than anyone but you.'

16 WHEN THEY LEFT, they presented the mission with bags of dried beans and apricots, coffee, sugar and some bottles of brandy. Nanny Rose added some medicines – 'though we can't really spare them, our stocks are running low,' she told Harriet and Alexine.

The two priests and the five laymen all came out to see them off. Père François staggered, as though drunk, towards each of them in turn, shaking their hands. He was deathly pale and his adam's apple was even more prominent than ever. Père Thomas avoided their gaze as he too shook their hands, almost as though he knew that Harriet and Alexine had been witnesses of that scene in the cemetery. He had a morose, almost angry expression, and he did not smile even when, in front of them, Sunny performed a whole series of exuberant cartwheels. The laymen stood motionless, their black faces devoid of any expression that might give a clue to their feelings. Alexine wanted that clue. What would become of them when the last of the priests had either died or been recalled and the mission was closed? Were they truly believers or did it suit them to appear to be believers? What did they feel about the two white men, both so frail, one physically and one morally?

Alexine and Sunny rode not ahead of Nanny Rose and Harriet in their makeshift palanquins of chairs supported on poles, as they usually did, but beside them. All of them, even Sunny, were in a sombre mood. The two fathers had said that they were looking forward to seeing them if they were to return the same way, but the visitors all knew that, even if that return were to happen, their hosts would probably have vanished.

When they could no longer glance back to see the lake, the hills round it, the steeple of the chapel and the blue smoke drifting up from the nearby village, their spirits at once lifted. Daan, jolting along on his donkey, began to sing an old ballad in his nasal tenor. Alexine pointed out trees and bushes with particularly spectacular flowers on them. Harriet leaned back, eyes closed, a smile on her face, as she felt a cool breeze wafting over with an illusory smell of the far-distant sea.

'I'll race you,' Sunny said. 'Yes?'

'Yes.'

'But I must have a start.'

'All right. I'll wait here and you can begin running when you reach that rock over there.'

Nanny Rose muttered: 'I could do with a bite.'

17 THERE HAD BEEN A NUMBER OF DAYS when she had been so happy, riding on and on, over hills, beside streams, across woods or through villages, that she had not wanted or, on many occasions, even been able to sleep. She would hum tunelessly to herself as she jogged along on her horse and then she would break off and look over to Sunny beside her and for no reason at all she would smile at him. At night, long after the others had gone to bed, she would lie out on the bamboo-and-wicker *chaise-longue* that Harriet had bought in Khartoum and stare up at the sky. At such moments, she had a strange sense that she had become both omnipotent and immortal.

Then, one afternoon, everything changed. They had halted for some food, but she had no appetite and she felt her body twitching with restlessness. There was a curious sensation at the back of her neck, as though the muscles were constantly contracting, and her fingertips were tingling. 'Oh, come on! Let's get moving again. We want to arrive at that town they spoke about before nightfall.'

Soon after they had moved on again, she was aware, with a sense of bewilderment and dread, of a change in the sky. It was no longer limitless and translucent. Now it was as though a huge glass bowl had been inverted over their straggling party, imprisoning them within it. The rim of the bowl, where the horizon extended, had been smoked to a blue-grey. She peered into the distance, twisting from side to side in her saddle. Was it some optical illusion of light and dust? The blue-grey began to darken, even though it was long before nightfall. Sunny said something to her but she hardly heard him and did not reply. There was a sensation of grit under her eyelids and a metallic taste in her mouth.

The town sprawled far farther than they had expected, and its muddy streets were thronged with people. Normally she would have delighted in all the movement and noise, but now when the good-natured crowds stared, shouted and gesticulated as the interminable cavalcade, repeatedly held up, wound its way between them, she cringed, as though fearful of some sudden attack.

Mechanically performing a task long since grown familiar to her, she asked a dignified-looking shopkeeper for the head man and followed him when, striding out beside her horse, he took her to him. She presented a letter from the Mudir, she handed over the usual gift of money. Her throat felt dry, she still had that metallic taste in her mouth and, once so fluent in Arabic, she now stumbled over the simplest of words.

As she, Osman and the *vakeel* were returning to join the others, it was with amazement that she heard her name being called in English. It was Fielding, strolling on the other side of the street in the company of two Arabs.

'I was expecting you!' Having hurried over to her horse, he placed a hand on a stirrup. She stared down at him. His face was blurred, its edges dissolving.

'You!'

'Why so surprised? I've been hearing about all your adventures.'

'How?' She felt the monosyllable fall from her mouth like a stone.

'Oh, one hears, one hears. Eventually one hears everything.'

She tried to smile down. 'You got here before us.'

He laughed. 'Of course. I haven't got all your baggage to hinder me. Are you coming to the festivities this evening?'

'The festivities?'

'Don't ask me what they are. But they're celebrating something – the birth of a God, some victory over their enemies, something of that kind. There'll be dancing and singing. It might even end in an orgy – who knows? It'll be interesting for you. Just what an explorer ought to explore. I'm sure you've never been at an orgy before.'

She thought, once again experiencing that strange sensation of the muscles contracting at the back of her neck, while her fingertips tingled.

'All right. Yes.' She licked her lips. 'Yes.'

'Shall I call for you at, say, eight or so? I'll be able to find you, no difficulty about that, since there are so many people accompanying you on your royal progress.'

'Yes. Thank you. Good.'

She was aware of him frowning up at her, half puzzled and half anxious. Clearly he realized that something was amiss. Then she kicked at the flanks of the horse, without saying anything further, and moved off, followed by Osman and the *vakeel*. She had often thought and even dreamed of Fielding during the journey, longing for him and yet disgusted with herself for doing so. Now she had met him again and she felt neither pleasure nor disgust but merely an inexplicable weariness.

∽

'You don't look well. You look exhausted. Why do you have to go?' Nanny Rose was helping Alexine into her frock. Harriet, seated, was watching them.

'Because it's something I want to see. He said – he said it's the kind of thing every explorer ought to explore.'

'I shouldn't be surprised if you had a touch of the sun. You're not yourself.'

'What is myself?'

Harriet and Nanny Rose exchanged worried glances.

'Nanny is right,' Harriet said. 'You should get to bed and have a good rest.'

Alexine shook her head. She longed for the oblivion of sleep but she must not give in. It was, after all, she who constantly looked after the others, not they her. A tremor ran through her body, making her put out a hand to the frame of the pier-glass.

'Are you sure you're all right?'

'Sure.'

∽

Earlier, in the street, Fielding had looked dirty, bedraggled and unshaven. But he had now bathed, shaved and changed into formal clothes. Briefly, Alexine once more felt as she had felt throughout her travels: vigorous, eager, euphoric, in control both of herself and of everything around her. The old dizzying pull of his attraction had become even stronger than ever. She wanted him, she was going to have him. Was she not the girl who always got what she wanted?

'Who are those men?' Six barefoot men slouched behind him, muskets over their shoulders. All had identical red cloths wrapped round their heads. A seventh man, also with a red cloth round his head but without a musket, was carrying a lantern.

'Oh, the head man sent them. They're here to protect us. Or, rather, you. I said that you didn't need any protection, you were perfectly capable of looking after yourself and that I was perfectly capable of looking after you if you weren't. But he insisted. He said that there's lot of lawlessness during these festivities. People drink – or take things even more intoxicating.' He looked around. 'Aren't you going to travel in a chair?'

'Oh, no! I want to go on foot.'

'Then I'll leave my horse here.'

As they set off down the first of a labyrinth of narrow streets, he took her arm in his. She moved not away but even closer to him.

'Now tell me all the things that have *not* been reported to me!'

'What things?'

'About your adventures.'

'Oh, we've had some wonderful days! Unforgettable!' Like a once dry cistern suddenly and miraculously filling with water, she was continuing to feel energy and joy pulsing up and up within her. It was no longer an effort to respond to his questions; she laughed with total naturalness whenever he made one of his sardonic remarks or teased her.

Crowds were surging along in the same direction as themselves, with a lot of pushing, shouting and laughter. To protect her, Fielding removed his arm from hers and instead placed it round her shoulder, drawing her against him. 'Don't be afraid. They're in a happy mood.'

'I'm not afraid. Not in the least.'

She felt his jacket rough against her cheek.

'We have a place beside the head man. He's a friend of mine. And in any case you gave him such a handsome present, you earned it with that.'

They turned a corner and there, in front of them, was a vast, bare, uptilted stretch of ground crammed with people and blazing with bonfires. Each time they passed one of these bonfires, the leaping flames seared her face and bare arms.

There was a beating in her head, louder and louder, more and more insistent. She put a hand to her forehead, pressing her temples with her fingers, as though in an effort to squeeze out the sound. Then she realized that the beating was not in her head but came from a row of drums beyond the leaping, stamping, swaying masked dancers in the circular space kept clear for them by men with the same red cloths around their heads as those worn by their own guards.

As the dancers rotated, so the whole scene began to rotate around her. She clutched Fielding's arm, swaying against him. The drum beats coalesced into each other, until there was just an arhythmic rat-tat-tat-tat, more and more deafening. Everything seemed to be darkening at its edges, as the horizon had darkened during the long ride of that day. A darkness was invading her, flooding in through her straining eyes, her gaping mouth, her flaring nostrils.

A vast woman capered zig-zag towards them, shaking her naked breasts and buttocks, her eyes half-closed in a near-trance. Close to Alexine, she opened her eyes wide in a round face streaming with sweat. Her tongue, large and purple, popped out of her mouth. Then her eyes focused on the long pearl necklace around Alexine's throat. A hand shot out, like the paw of a lioness, and grabbed at the necklace, with such force that the string cut into Alexine's flesh. The woman tugged and tugged again. The string broke, and two or three pearls scattered to the ground. Because of its careful knotting, pearl separated from pearl, the rest of the necklace remained intact. With her booty, the woman dashed away with an amazing agility and speed for someone of her size.

Alexine was aware that Fielding had let go of her and had started off in pursuit. Then, like a slap to the back of her head, a rifle shot rang out and she smelled the powder acrid in her nostrils. Alexine had seen gazelles and antelopes leap and plunge when she had shot them, precisely as the woman now did. She lay on the ground, her mouth distorted in agony, a hand to her thigh. Then she screamed.

Suddenly, as though she were being carried up some uneven mountain path in the chair by the porters, Alexine felt everything around her tipping sideways. The fires roared up, circling her, the white-painted faces and bodies of the dancers merged into a chalk wall, moving towards her.

Although she felt no pain, she thought: I must have been shot.

Tasting the priest's blood, she had thought: I am tasting death.

Now she thought, as the smell of the gun-powder filled her whole body and everything became totally black: I am swallowing death.

∽

Later, when she gabbled to them of what had happened or what she thought had happened – she would never be wholly able to differentiate between the two – Harriet, Nanny, Daan and Sammy would all tell her that it was all only the effect of her illness, she had imagined it, it was only part of the delirium that accompanied such a dangerously high fever.

... The woman leaps up skyward and crashes down to the ground. She screams on and on, endlessly, on a single high, yelping note. She is pressing her hand to the wound, where the bullet has left a deep furrow in the blubbery thigh. Alexine feels no horror, much less any impulse to go to her rescue. Well, you've got what you deserved. Frantically, the woman looks about her for help, but the crowds are advancing from all around with a totally different purpose in view. As the woman, the string of pearls still clutched in a fist, struggles to raise her huge bulk, yellow fat begins to coil out of the gaping wound. Fascinated, Alexine watches its extrusion. Then the man leading the crowd pounces. In snatching the necklace, the woman was like a lioness. Lithe and swift, the man is like a panther. He tears at the fat, dragging it out, with both his hands and then he stuffs into his mouth. The woman goes on yelping on that single high note. Others, more and more, now join the man. They jostle and push at each other as they too now pull out the yellow fat from the wound. There is a limitless supply of it. Voraciously they devour it.

Then a woman, immensely tall and thin, appears with a hatchet. She pushes through the crowd, raises the hatchet and hacks off the wounded woman's arm. She and two other women fight over it, until, as she snarls and threatens them with the hatchet, they back off. She lifts up the severed arm, and sinks her teeth into the elbow. A man comes up behind her, puts one arm around her neck and all but strangles her before the arm drops from her grasp. He now seizes it.

Alexine watches. She is filled with the longing to join them. But as she steps forward, she feels the strength draining out of her body and crashes to the ground ...

∽

... She is hungry. She must eat. She is tired of lying out in this *chaise-*

longue, hour after hour, looking at the stars. What has happened to the servants? Why have they brought her no food? She calls but no one answers, even though the tents occupied by Harriet and by Nanny Rose and Daan must be in earshot. Perhaps they have gone off to eat somewhere else, leaving her here alone?

She gets up off the *chaise-longue* and, staggering, makes her way down the baked track to where the others are encamped. But of them too there is no sign. Where is everyone? She has rarely been into the tents housing the kitchens, since that has always been Harriet's province. But she now raises the flap of one and, her eyes slowly accustoming themselves to the murk after the afternoon glare outside it, makes out the man, the head cook from Cairo, who is squatting on the floor, chopping onions. There is a large pan beside him, and he keeps dropping the chopped onions into it. He looks up at her and smiles, with those narrow, light-brown eyes of his. The colour of them has always fascinated her. She smiles back and edges farther in. Then she sees that there is a basket beside him and in the basket there is lying a naked baby. The baby is white, a boy, with a protuberant belly and a tassel-like penis. The baby smiles when it sees her.

'What are you doing with that baby? That baby is mine.' She has never had a baby but she knows that the baby is hers.

He shakes his head, then reaches out for a knife.

She knows what is going to happen. She screams.

He transfixes the baby with the knife. Then, with a swift gesture, he sweeps the remains of the onions off the chopping-board and lifts the baby's body on to it . . .

∽

. . . She is feeling better. She has drunk a gruel, with Nanny Rose holding the invalid cup to her mouth with one hand, while the other hand raises her head from the pillow and then supports it. The gruel has no taste. Is it meant to be like that? She tries to say something but somehow the words will not come. Or is it that the words are willing to come but her mouth is unwilling to release them? Nanny Rose's lips are on her forehead. As the old woman bends over her, her loose dress falls away and Alexine can see her large, sagging breasts. She has nursed children at those breasts. Alexine knows that she will never herself nurse children, because the cook has killed that baby of hers. 'There, there!' Did she say that or did Nanny Rose?

Suddenly Nanny Rose has, as though by magic, been transformed into Harriet. 'He was here to ask after you. He's leaving this afternoon. I told him you were in no state to see him.' Alexine feels a terrible sense of loss. She makes a low, keening sound from the back of her throat. Harriet says, 'That place was cursed. I felt it all the time that we were there.' What place? Then Alexine remembers the mission. She remembers the priest standing in front of his brother's headstone and the black woman kneeling before him. What was the priest saying to the woman? Was he giving her absolution? Was he saying: Go in peace, sin no more?

∽

... Sunny is seated on the chair opposite to her bed. He sits in one corner of the chair, his knees drawn up, and his eyes, large and sorrowful, are fixed on her. She knows that he has been there for a long time. She would like him to jump up and execute some of his cartwheels for her, to speak to her, to laugh. But he merely stares. She closes her eyes, she is drifting off, the bed moving outward and outward and then up and up, soaring away.

She opens her eyes. He is still there. But now both of his feet are on the floor, spaced widely apart, and his knees are also widely spaced. There is no longer that sorrowful, brooding expression on his face, but one full of mischief, roguish, coquettish. He is still gazing at her as he fumbles with the buttons of the trousers bought – so long ago, it now seems – from the second-hand shop in Khartoum. He looks down at the buttons and then up at her. He is inviting her to look. She is fascinated. Excitement pulses through her. He draws out his penis. She is astonished by its size. She had never imagined that a boy of only twelve or thirteen – no one, not even he, knows his exact age – could have one so large. It reminds her of the snake that, when she was once out riding with Osman, they had seen gliding zig-zag along a sand dune. Osman had jumped down from his horse, drawn his sword, raised it above his head and then severed the snake neatly in two. Later he had skinned the snake and offered her the beautiful green skin, chequered with black. But merely to touch it, as she had done briefly, had filled her with revulsion. It was Addy who had eventually accepted it – 'I'll have it made into a belt.'

Searching her face for a response, whether of horror or delight, Sunny begins to massage his penis. It grows and grows. It reaches monstrous proportions, reminding her of the donkey on which Daan rides. She puts out a hand. But the hand is leaden. It falls back on the sheet. She stares down at the hand. What is the matter with it? Why won't it move for her? When she looks up again, Sunny has vanished. What has happened to him? How could he have gone so quickly? ...

∽

... Where is the revolver? Captain Scott showed her his Robert Adams revolver. It was cold, heavy and hard in her palm. She decided there and then that she would herself have such a revolver, unique in its design. John reluctantly bought it for her and sent it out to Cairo. Every night, before going to bed, she has placed it under her pillow. Waking up during the night, she has comforted herself by putting her hand under the pillow and holding it. As though by magic, it has unfailingly helped her to fall asleep again. But now, when she puts her hand under the pillow, it is no longer there. One of them must have taken it from her. But she needs it, she needs it! Anyone could come into the tent and kill her and she would have no protection. 'Where is it?' she repeatedly asks them, always to receive the same answer: 'What are you talking about?' from Nanny Rose or Harriet. Once Harriet adds: 'Who is this Robert Adams?' Without the revolver, she is often too fearful to sleep. Once she even staggers off the bed to look for it and collapses, knocking over a folding table and smashing it beneath her. Sunny finds her and somehow gets her back on to the bed again . . .

∽

'Your delirium lasted for four days.'

Alexine was lying out on the *chaise-longue* and Harriet and Nanny Rose were seated beside her. The air was cool. Alexine ran a hand up her arm and felt her cool flesh. For so long it had been burning, as though the flames from those bonfires had been constantly playing on it.

'We thought we were going to lose you. I think it was the quinine that saved you. Or the Good Lord,' Nanny Rose added, not believing that.

'You said such extraordinary things. And you seemed to be seeing such extraordinary things.'

'Such as?'

'Oh, I don't remember.' But Harriet remembered perfectly well. 'Rubbish. All jumbled together. Nothing of any importance.'

'Mr Fielding wanted to bring you an Arab doctor, but we said no thank you to that. He'd have probably finished you off. No, I said to him, the best hope for her is quinine and good nursing. But, as I said, there were times when I really thought . . .'

'Oh, don't let's talk any more about it,' Harriet interrupted. 'Let's talk about something more cheerful. The good news is that Trudy has had four puppies.'

'Oh, how wonderful!'

'Sunny was present with Daan at the birth. He wants to bring the puppies to show you but I told him it was early days for that.'

'He was so sweet when you were barely conscious. So attentive. He would sit for hour after hour by your bedside, never stirring. We had difficulty in getting him to come and eat his meals.'

'He's become absolutely devoted to you,' Harriet said. 'He adores you.'

∽

During those days of convalescence, Alexine would struggle to differentiate between the things that had really happened and the things that had happened in her delirium. Those things in her delirium were so much more vivid than the things before it and now after it. Her walk through the village with Fielding, the leaping flames, the jostling crowds, the music and the dancing: all were hazy, as though now seen through a window streaming with rain. Hazy too were the appearances of people who bent over to ask her how she was, told her what preparations were being made for the next stage of their journey, or attempted to cheer her up or at least elicit a smile with some gossip of the camp or the town. But those scenes of the crowd tearing the woman apart and devouring her, of the matter-of-fact killing of the baby, of Sunny masturbating before her: all those scenes and others hardly less terrible, still had a devastating vividness.

As she made the comparison between the one set of happenings and the other, she was overwhelmed by horror and disgust. How could she have brought out of some deep, dark recess of her being prodigies far more terrible than even this huge, frightening, fascinating continent was capable of spawning out of its pitch-black womb? That question haunted her, perpetually coming between her and the world in which she had once taken so much pleasure.

18 HARRIET, ALONE IN HER TENT, was writing to Addy. Before her, on the desk that had come all the way from the house in The Hague, three other letters were piled, awaiting the runner who never came and was less and less likely to come. In those earlier letters she had written of Alexine's long and bewildering illness ('We think that she must have picked up something at that terrible mission station, where everyone was dying')', of her eventual recovery ('When the crisis came, her sheets got sopping wet, so that we were constantly changing them'), and of their thankfulness that they still had her with them ('We really thought that we had lost her forever').

Now she wrote:

Alexine stands the journey surprisingly well. Well, you know how courageous she is, allowing nothing to daunt her. She is still terribly pale and thin, and Ahmed has to tempt her with all sorts of delicacies if we are to get her to eat. Sunny has been wonderful. He is no longer the child whom you will remember, but a little man, fully aware of his responsibilities to this woman whom (I am sure) he has come to look on as his mother.

To travel she has a stretcher with a canopy above it to keep off the sun – you know how trying it can be. There's a mattress on it, so that she rests very agreeably and often takes a refreshing nap. I have a chair, as we both had when you were with us. Nanny Rose now has your chair. She, too, has been a boon and blessing. I don't know how I'd have managed through those terrible days without her support. She was a rock.

We are each carried by four negroes, with eight in reserve, so that they can take turns and so get some rest. The twelve men are always the same, with the result that we have become very fond of them, always so cheerful and kind, and they – I sincerely hope and think! – have become fond of us. We now have fewer negroes for our immediate baggage than when you were with us – some 120 in all. Over the months a number have deserted.

All today was lovely – the ground a vivid green full of flowers, and everywhere groups of tall, elegant trees. I defy any part of Europe to show anything better.

∽

'More letters!'

Harriet laid down her pen. 'How are you feeling, darling?'

'Perfect.'

'You mustn't overdo things. You must remember that you were very ill indeed.'

'This is my idea for where we go next. I wanted to show you.' Alexine began to unfold the Colonel's tattered map.

'Oh, no. I can't read maps, you know I can't! I leave all that to you. What's worrying me is the maize.'

'The maize?'

'We ought to have bought more in that town where you fell so ill. We could have done. That was my fault. I miscalculated, I'm afraid. Osman says that we'll soon reach another town, quite prosperous, where we can buy some. But you know how unreliable he is, much of the time one can't believe a word he tells one.'

Alexine raised a hand and yawned behind it.

'You're tired! See! I knew you were overdoing things.'

'I'm not tired. It's just that all this talk of provisions bores me. I leave all that to you and Ahmed.'

'Oh, he's a rogue!'

'Well, then to you alone.'

'Now go and lie down for a little. Before we eat. Our supply of oil for the lamps is also running out.'

∽

The last of all Harriet's letters to Addy began:

> This will only be a brief note, since I have a terrible headache and feel generally rather under par. Nanny has doubled my daily dose of quinine. The old dear, in her usually pessimistic way, has decided that I must be coming down with African fever. But if I were going to get it, surely I'd have got it long ago? If it's anything, I think that it may be a recurrence of that dysentery I had a few weeks back. It was very inconvenient but the Dr James Mixture soon put a stop to it . . .

She gave up there, deciding that she would complete the letter on the following evening. Ahmed had reported that there had been more thefts from the kitchen stores – this time of sugar and jam. She must see to that. She must also have a word with the two personal maids, who had been quarrelling again, each accusing the other of not doing her fair share of the work. Oh, why were so many of them so often at loggerheads? She put a hand to her forehead. Yes, she must have a fever. Her forehead was hot but a chill was beginning to rattle her bones. Oh, well, she'd better get over to the kitchens . . .

∽

Next evening, she sat making one of her lists.

Provisions urgent – to be purchased as soon as possible:
    Flour
    Sheep (for mutton)
    Hens? (Poor layers to be slaughtered?)

Then she got up stiffly, her teeth chattering, and, without even removing her shoes or her shawl, lay out on her narrow bed. She closed her eyes but, so violent were the rigours that now shook her, she could not sleep.

Alexine entered. 'We've been wondering what's happened to you. Don't you want any dinner?'

'No. Thank you, dear. I think I'll give it a miss. Somehow – I feel too tired to eat.'

'Let me get one of the servants to bring you something here on a tray.'

'No. No, please. The thought of food ... I'm all right. Don't worry. Just tired.'

Alexine approached the bed and looked down at her mother's face and dull, dazed eyes. Despite her hatred and fear of illness, whether her own or others', she now sat down on the edge of the bed and took her mother's hand in hers.

'You have a fever.'

'Oh, nonsense!'

'Of course you have!' Now Alexine raised her hand to her mother's forehead. 'If only there were a doctor in this godforsaken place.'

'Thank goodness there isn't. Most doctors only make one worse.'

'We can't move on tomorrow. It's out of the question.'

'Oh, do stop fussing! Oh, leave me alone! I want to rest, rest, rest!'

'Oh, very well!' Affronted, Alexine got to her feet and made to leave the tent.

'I'm sorry, darling. Forgive me! You know what I'm like when I'm tired.'

But even when she was tired, Harriet was rarely ill-tempered.

Alexine hesitated, then returned to the bedside. Her lower lip caught between her teeth, she squinted down at her mother. Then she said: 'It's strange. Long, long ago, there was a time – a short time – when I really hated you. Yes, hated you.' She nodded as Harriet gazed up at her with bewildered, frightened eyes. 'You sent Sammy away. I told myself I'd never forgive you for that. And now – now I love you more than anyone else in the world.' Harriet turned her head aside, with a little gasp. 'I mean that. Truly I mean that.'

There was a silence. Then, her head still turned away, Harriet said: 'It was for the best – for you, for him, for everyone. Or, at least, I thought it was for the best.' She drew a deep sigh. 'One does what one thinks was for the best and one never knows whether it may not have been for the worst after all. I'm sorry.'

'Oh, I don't know why I said that! It's all so long ago. Who knows? Anyway – anyway, Mama, get well soon. You're – you're so precious to me. I don't think I could go on without you.'

Harriet now looked up at Alexine. 'Of course I'm going to get well soon. There's nothing really wrong with me. Nothing.'

She put out a hand and Alexine bent forward and grasped it in both her own. The hand was burning. It also felt inert, but for a strange throbbing that, at erratic intervals, pulsed through it.

∽

Harriet had got out of bed and was playing the piano. But by now, with all the travelling, it was horribly out of tune, and after a while she could not bear to continue. In any case, her mind had become as blurred as her sight, and she kept forgetting the notes of the Chopin Nocturne, once so familiar to her that she used to say that she could have played it in her sleep.

Nanny Rose had heard the jangling from the next-door tent.

'What are you doing? Get back into bed! At once!'

She spoke to Harriet as to a refractory child. In the past she would never have been so peremptory. 'Come along! Let me help you.' She softened. 'You poor dear. You *are* having a tough time of it. But these fevers burn themselves out. You'll see. You know how it was with Alexine.'

Harriet banged down the lid of the piano. Then, supported by Nanny Rose, she staggered across the tent to her bed. 'That piano badly needs tuning.' Her voice was now no more than an unravelling thread.

'Yes, I know, dear. But we're not going to find anyone to tune it out here, that's for sure. Once we're back in Khartoum that nice Vassili can see to it.'

'Vassili?' Harriet subsided on to the bed.

'That Greek. You must remember him.'

'Oh, yes, yes,' Harriet said vaguely. She closed her eyes. Then she muttered: 'I feel terribly thirsty. I drank all that lemon-essence and water' – she indicated the empty glass on the table beside with a trembling hand – 'and now I already I have this terrible thirst.'

The thirst intensified. She had always been so moderate in her appetites but now she drank endlessly – more lemon-essence and water, wine mixed with water, arrowroot with wine, chicken-broth, the making of which Nanny Rose supervised. But, as though her body rejected all this liquid, it streamed endlessly from her, soaking the sheets and the mattress beneath them.

When she had become so weak that she had difficulty in swallowing,

Nanny Rose soaked some lint in water and then repeatedly placed the lint between Harriet's lips. The first time that she did so, Harriet stirred and gave a small chuckle. 'Is that extreme unction?'

Alexine entered the tent and for a while watched what Nanny was doing. The lips moved feebly on the lint. Drops ran down on either side of the dying woman's fallen-in mouth. Then she made a desperate sucking noise.

'Let me do it! No, let me do it!' Alexine's voice was sharp with the anguish that she was determined to suppress.

'All right, dear. You have a try. She seems to be taking something in. I'll go and get some more sheets.'

Alexine sat down by the bed and leaned forward. Then she soaked another piece of lint in the water and placed it between her mother's lips. But this time it merely rested there. The lips did not move.

Her mother opened her eyes and stared up at her:

'I must.'

'Must what?'

'Up. Get up.'

'Don't be silly, darling.' Like Nanny Rose, Alexine now spoke to Harriet as though she were a child. 'You can't get up until you're really better.'

Soon Harriet again opened her eyes. She twisted her head from side and side and then put out a hand to thrust the damp, grey hair up from her forehead. She repeated:

'I must.'

'No, no! You can't get up.'

'Must – list – letters . . .' She raised an emaciated arm, the almost black veins standing out on it, in the direction of her desk. Then the arm fell back.

'Oh, forget all those!'

Harriet closed her eyes. Her mouth opened and she gulped in air. Then she expelled it in a long, shuddering breath. She lay quiet.

Alexine stared down at her mother, exerting all her formidable will: *Get well, get well, get well.*

After a long time, Nanny Rose returned, some sheets over her arm. 'Would you believe it? There were only these two clean sheets. I don't know what those wretched girls have been doing. One of them is too taken up with that Mohammed to have any notion what she's at, and the other can no longer be bothered.' She went across to the bed. 'I'll move her over and then, if you'd . . .'

She stared down. In a puzzled, aggrieved voice she said: 'I do believe she's gone. Yes, I do believe it.'

Alexine jumped up from her chair. She opened her mouth wide, as though she were about to scream, and then snapped it shut. She leaned over her mother and stared down at her, her face immobile, without any sign of emotion. She drew back. She walked over to the chair, sank into it and covered her eyes with her hands.

'There, there, dear!' From behind, Nanny Rose put her hands to Alexine's bowed shoulders and rested her cheek against hers.

'Oh, please!' Alexine jerked away.

'I'd better tell Daan. You'll be all right? Only a moment.'

Nanny hurried out of the tent to the one that she and Daan occupied. With mounting agitation she cried 'Daan! Daan! Daan!' as she jerked back the tent-flap.

Then to her amazement, she saw him on his knees by his bed.

'What are you doing?'

He looked up guiltily, tongue caught between his yellow, irregular teeth.

'Praying!' Nanny Rose exclaimed angrily. 'It's no use praying now! She's gone!'

∽

Osman supervised the digging of the grave. The twelve porters, each team of which had so often complained that its stint of carrying Harriet's chair had gone on for too long, now argued about who was to have the honour of doing the digging.

That evening Harriet's body was placed in the makeshift coffin, lined with the tasselled, heavy cloak that she had worn to parties, and was carried out on the shoulders of Osman, Daan, Ahmed and Sunny. Because Sunny was so much shorter than the others, it listed perilously to one side. Nanny Rose had thought it foolish to give him a task for which the *vakeel* would have been so much better suited. But Alexine had insisted that, no, he must be one of the bearers. Her mother had been so fond of him, Alexine said, and he of her. But Nanny Rose thought that nonsense; the mistress had never really accepted him.

Alexine stood waiting by the grave, her white face as immobile as ever and her hands clasped before her. Nanny Rose had at first stood close to her, but Alexine had at once moved a step away.

The size of the grave had been miscalculated, so that the porters had to hurry off to retrieve their spades in order to widen it. While this went on, everyone waited in silence, except for Nanny Rose who demanded of Daan, 'Do they never get anything right?'

Nanny Rose had told Daan that he must conduct the service.

'Me! But I'm not a priest. How can I do it?'

'Well, who else is there?'

'But I –'

'You must. *Must.* You owe it to her.'

Alexine's head was bowed. Then, suddenly, while Daan was still mumbling from the Prayer Book held in his trembling hands, she turned to Nanny Rose.

'How can I forgive myself?'

Nanny Rose spoke out of the side of her mouth, her eyes squinting angrily: 'What are you talking about? No one could have asked for a better daughter.' She drew in a sharp breath.

'No, no!'

Then Alexine was once more motionless.

Sunny, who was beside her, looked up at her and, when she made no response, nudged her and pointed. As though with difficulty, she focused her gaze.

A small, bald hill swelled up beyond the encampment; marshalled on it, totally still and silent, were all the African members of the expedition. Their white robes fluttered in the wind, so that they looked like some giant wave arched on the crest, its spume reflecting the dying light of the sun.

As the little party of Europeans, Sunny, Osman, Ahmed and the grave diggers moved off, there all at once burst from these onlookers strange wails of lamentation. Later Nanny Rose was to tell Daan that it had sounded like the howling of a pack of wolves – not that she had ever heard one. Then, as suddenly as it had started, it had stopped.

Alexine hurried off ahead of the others. Sunny ran to catch up with her and then placed a hand on her arm. But she ignored him. She lifted the flap of her tent, turned and once more looked up to the bald crest of the hill.

Everyone had gone.

∽

Nanny Rose now, in effect, took over the leadership of the expedition during the long retreat back to Khartoum. Having for all her life been obedient to the orders of anyone not a child or a servant, she was now the one who issued orders. At first, there were mutterings of rebellion – who did this woman think that she was? But then everyone reluctantly came to respect her. She had, by some miracle, acquired the decisiveness and force of will that they themselves had never possessed and that Alexine had lost.

At first Nanny Rose went through the formality of consulting Alexine at the beginning or end of each day's trek. Usually she would find her either lying out on the *chaise-longue* in the shade of a tree, dozing or staring up at the sky, or else at the desk of what had once been Harriet's tent, assembling and annotating, with painstaking slowness and thoroughness, the floral specimens collected over almost a year.

'Do you think that we should send another runner about the steamer?

Something might have happened to that man. I have a feeling we were wrong to trust him.'

As she raised her head, Alexine's neck now seemed extraordinarily frail and vulnerable. Nanny Rose was stabbed with pity. Poor darling! She had first seemed to take her mother's death so well, and now she was taking it so badly. 'Do what you think best. I leave it to you.'

I leave it to you. That was what she constantly said. Or: *I trust you.* Or: *You know best.* In the past, Alexine had never left anything to anyone, had never trusted anyone to carry out her wishes precisely as she wanted, and had never thought that anyone knew best.

When they travelled, Alexine did not ride, but was carried in the palanquin-like chair which Harriet used to occupy. She had told Sunny that he could ride the horse and this he now did, maintaining an ambling pace beside her. The *vakeel* complained to Nanny Rose that, if anyone rode the horse, he should be the one to do so and not that boy. She replied that it was nothing to do with her, he must speak to Mademoiselle Thinne about it. Restrained by a grudging reverence for her grief, he never did.

If Nanny Rose was now the commander, then Daan and Sunny were her two trusted lieutenants. At last, so late in life, Daan had also learned how to issue orders – barking out unintelligibly in a Dutch peppered here and there with some mispronounced Arab words and phrases learned on the trek: 'No, here, *here!* ... Not that one, you idiot, the other one! ... Bring it, bring it! Quick, quick!' The imperious tone was the same that Philip had so often used to him and his fellow servants. It also carried echoes, albeit fainter, of Alexine.

Under the stress of Harriet's death and Alexine's near-death, Sunny had all at once ceased to be a frisky, erratic, laughing, demonstrative child and had become an adult. He had grown rapidly, his shoulders had broadened, wisps of hair were visible on the firm line of his jaw and on his chest. His expression was melancholy, grave, ruminative. He spoke in a low, gravelly voice, totally unlike his previous excitedly high-pitched one. Alexine, watching from her *chaise-longue* or her chair but saying nothing, realized that there was some sort of flirtation going on between him and one of the two personal maids. The maid was at least five years older than he was, and she had a hard, determined look to her. But she was certainly beautiful, and moved with a swift, pantherine grace. Once Alexine might have felt jealous and possessive. Now she did not care.

As they retraced their steps, she was constantly reminded of her mother. It was in this valley that they had seen what her mother claimed was an eagle, huge wings outspread, and she herself was sure was a vulture. There, far away in the distance, she could make out the mission chapel and the eleven *tukuls*, but she had no desire to approach them and, for once decisive during this interminable retreat, told Nanny Rose that they must push on, not stop. She, too, now believed that the place was cursed. Perhaps the curse had had something to do with her illness and those terrible dreams. Perhaps it had also had something to do with the death of her mother. It was under that rock that three ancient shrouded women had been squatting. Seeing the vast caravan they had at first jumped up in terror, preparatory to fleeing. Then they had shyly approached, hands holding their veils high up over their faces, with only the eyes visible, and Harriet, without their asking, had given them some money. There, shimmering through a gauze of heat ahead of them, was the village in which they had sat by a well, while Sunny, with indefatigable persistence, practised the cartwheels that he was later to master.

All these places now seemed to bear the same relationship to the places of the past as sepia photographs to the colourful realities from which they had derived. The sky had been clearer then, the grass more vivid, the sounds of the birds circling about them far louder. Life had now bled away, and what remained lacked all tone and edge.

Alexine had ceased to worry about changing her clothes, about washing her body, about having her hair combed and curled by Nanny Rose or one of the two maids. Nanny Rose would tell her, 'You know, dear, I really think it's time to change that dress of yours,' or 'I'll tell the girls to bring the water for a bath as soon as the tents are up', or 'Let me do something about that hair'. Alexine would protest for a while and then, when Nanny Rose persisted, would at last acquiesce with a sigh.

Everywhere, she kept the revolver close beside her. She would touch it or hold it obsessively. It gave her the same consolation as a baby derives from a comforter.

∽

After many weeks of travel, they once again reached the shallow stream and Nanny Rose ordered the gutta-percha boat to be readied for the crossing.

'You'd better come with me and the cats,' she told Alexine.

But Alexine was hesitant. 'You go ahead. I'll wait here a little.'

Sunny was talking, as he so often now did, with the little maid. She was giggling behind the hand raised to her face. He was shaking a finger at her in mock reproof.

As on the previous occasion, there was a chaos of struggling humans and animals, shrieks, panicky shouts, splashing, laughter. But to Alexine it was all at first forlornly attenuated and pale. Then, on an impulse, seeing that Sunny was leading some of the dogs down the water's edge, she once again tucked up her voluminous jellaba and knotted it round her thighs, kicked off her shoes, and strode down to join him. He looked up at her in amazement, then smiled and handed her two of the leashes.

She strode on into the water. Flopsy and a mongrel acquired during their travels paddled, heads raised above the muddy stream, beside her.

'Good dogs! Good! Good!'

The returning boat neared her. One of the two oarsmen leaned out of it, extending a hand. Did she want to come aboard?

She threw back her head to get her hair out of her eyes. She laughed, with a sudden access of joy. 'No. No, thank you.'

The opposite bank seemed to have acquired a new effulgence. She could see Nanny Rose gesticulating at the porters, instructing them where to stack their burdens. Daan was tethering the donkey. But, good heavens, what was that lazy head porter doing, sitting under a tree and devouring a slice of melon, instead of lending a hand?

'Hey! Hey!' The water streamed off her as she emerged, followed by the dogs, which at once began to shake themselves. 'Get up, do something! You're not paid to sit there eating.' She swung round. 'Oh, Nanny, I honestly don't think that's the best place to stack those boxes. It's directly in the midday sun.'

Alexine was once more in command.

19 'MADAME WARBURTON! Mademoiselle Van Capellen! Mademoiselle Van Capellen!'

It was Lola, who had entered the house unannounced, as she always did now, and who was calling their names. At the sound of her voice, Mister began to yap.

In her den Lucy pulled an exasperated face, put down her pen and, having hastily blotted what she had been writing, pushed the sheet of paper into a drawer of her desk. She turned the key in the drawer and then put the key into a pocket. Roderick used to tell her that if she took as much care about locking up the stores as she did about locking up her precious manuscript, they would lose much less to thieving.

'Oh, hello, Lola. Mademoiselle Van Capellen has had some bad news.'

'Bad news?'

'Yes, I'm afraid so. Two runners arrived almost simultaneously. They brought letters from the expedition.'

As soon as Addy had seen that the first of the letters had been written by Nanny Rose and not by Alexine or Harriet, she had known at once that something terrible was wrong. Nanny Rose had difficulty in writing and her letters were full of grammatical and spelling errors. She rarely put pen to paper.

'What's happened?'

'Let's go into the drawing-room. I don't want to disturb Mademoiselle Van Capellen.'

They both sat down. Then Lucy jumped up and closed the door.

'Yes?' Lola prompted.

'I'm afraid that Madame Thinne has died.'

Lola put a hand up to her cheek and let out a little squeak. Her eyes widened, the colour drained from her face. '*Died?*' Suddenly her mouth twisted to one side and she began to sob uncontrollably.

Lucy had not expected such extreme distress. She nodded. 'Yes. I'm afraid so. Of course, she *was* sixty-six. You may not have known that. It's amazing that a woman of that age was able to go through all that she went through. I couldn't have done so even at my age.'

Leaning forward in the chair, her hands gripping its arms, Lola was still sobbing. Then, after a number of attempts to stem the sobs, she got out: 'She was my teacher. Without her – what will I do? Where will I find another teacher in this place?'

'She wouldn't have been here for very long anyway.'

'I know, I know. But maybe she could have persuaded my father. I think he would have listened to her – someone so important. My dream was to go to Italy – to Napoli or Roma. Or perhaps I could have gone to the Netherlands with her, and she could have continued to teach me.' Speaking of all these opportunities now lost forever renewed her anguish. Again she leaned forward in the chair and again the sobs jerked out of her.

'Yes, it's sad. Very sad. I'm sorry. And it's even sadder for Mademoiselle Van Capellen. They were so close, the two sisters. In recent years they had rarely been separated.'

The door had opened.

'Oh, it's you, Lola.'

Lucy and the girl looked across at Addy, who remained standing in the doorway. One hand rested on the jamb for support, the other was clutching a sodden handkerchief up against her chest. Her hair was hanging loose round her shoulders, her cheeks were unrouged, and she was wearing only a peignoir with a nightdress beneath it. Her eyes were red from weeping, the wrinkles round them looking like small scars.

'Oh, Mademoiselle Van Capellen, I'm so sorry, so sorry!' Lola ran towards her.

Addy did not yet realize, as Lucy did, that the girl's sorrow was largely for herself. Moved by the apparent sympathy, she all but gave way to tears once again, her lips quivering. 'I ought to have been with her. I feel so guilty.' Trembling hand to wall, she staggered across the room, towards the sofa.

'Nonsense,' Lucy said. 'If you'd gone with her, you might also be dead.'

Addy sank on to the sofa with a small moan. 'I keep getting this terrible pain.'

'There's a French doctor here at the moment. He was brought from Cairo to see one of the Mudir's wives. I'm going to ask Roderick to get him to come and see you.'

'Oh, no, no! I'm all right. All I need is to get back home again. That's all.' Then, realizing how wounding this might be to this woman with whom she had struck up, against all expectation, such a close friendship, she rushed on: 'Except that I shall miss you, oh, I shall miss you so much, Lucy.' An idea flashed to her: 'Why don't you come back with me? For a visit – or even forever! Why not? I'm going to be lonely, oh, so lonely without my sister.'

'You'll have Alexine.'

'Oh, Alexine! I don't think she cares a hoot about me. Not really.'

'How can you say that?'

'Not a line from her, not a single line, during all these ten, eleven months . . . Not even when her mother dies. She leaves it to Nanny Rose to tell me. Can you imagine?'

'She was very ill herself. And no doubt Harriet's death . . .'

Lola had been following the conversation avidly, turning her head back and forth from one of the speakers to the other. Now she asked:

'You'll go back to your country – you and Mademoiselle Thinne?'

'Of course. As soon as possible. Before anything else can happen. You know, in one of her last letters, my sister wrote of visiting a mission, where all but two of the eleven – or was it twelve? – priests had died. She wrote that she thought that there must have been a curse on it. Perhaps that curse followed her.'

'Nonsense!' Lucy exclaimed.

'It's possible. Perfectly possible. Anything is possible in this country.'

∽

'Dearest!'

Addy held out her arms, expecting Alexine to run into them. But instead Alexine moved deliberately, almost hesitantly towards her, with a puzzled, dazed expression on her face, and then halted too far away for them to touch each other. Mister sniffed at the hem of her jellaba. She gazed into Addy's eyes, her head tilted to one side. Her sunburn had faded, so that her face and arms shocked Addy with their whiteness. Her eyes were huge above her gaunt cheeks, and her nose seemed much larger and more aquiline.

'What you've been through!' Again Addy held out her arms.

At last Alexine allowed her aunt to embrace her. As Addy put her lips to her niece's cheek, she was amazed that, on a day so hot, the flesh should be so cold. She sensed a corresponding coldness in Alexine's whole demeanour.

Sunny, Nanny Rose and Daan were standing some distance away.

'Nanny! Thank you for your letters. You must also have gone through a terrible time.'

'I did all I could for her. We all did.'

'Oh, I'm sure, I'm sure!'

'I'm not really one for writing letters. I hope you could understand what I wrote.'

'Oh, yes! Of course! Both letters were so beautiful.'

Soon, after that vacillating beginning, Alexine was once more in command. 'We'd better decide what we want the porters to bring up and what to store. We must also set about making the final payment to them. You know, we had to pay about twice as much for the steamer on the return journey than we paid going.'

'I wish you could have brought back the body,' Addy said.

'Well, you can understand the problems. In any case, I think that that's where she would have been most happy. It was a beautiful place. She loved places like that far more than Khartoum – or probably The Hague.'

'If anything were to happen to me, I'd want to be with my own people.'

'That was the difference between you and mother. All people were her own people.'

∽

'Your aunt is far from well. I got a French doctor to see her – he was here to attend to one of the Mudir's wives, but the poor woman died the day after he got here. After a lengthy examination of your aunt, he diagnosed a serious heart condition.'

Warburton and Alexine were walking alone together in the garden. The dogs, which he secretly detested, were either frisking around them or dashing off into the undergrowth.

'What did he prescribe for her?'

'Digitalis. The usual thing. She's not young. She undertook a journey that would have taxed a woman half her age. She's now had the shock of your mother's death.'

Alexine sensed an undercurrent of accusation in his words, and it sharpened her ever-present guilt. For a while she was silent, her head lowered. Then she asked: 'Are you warning me of something?'

'No. I'm merely giving you the facts. Lucy and I – particularly Lucy – have become very fond of her during all these months. What we like most about her is her . . .' – he paused, seeking for the right word – 'her gallantry. And her gaiety, of course, that too. Your mother had that gallantry. Perhaps it's a family quality? Perhaps an aristocratic one? I don't know anything about your family other than that it *is* aristocratic. And I'm far too lowly to know anything about the aristocracy.'

'I want Lola to have the piano. I mean the one here, the large one, not that dreadful little one we took with us. That other one we can give to some mission or other. No doubt someone will enjoy thumping out hymns on it.'

The irrelevance of this to what they had been previously saying took him aback. 'That's kind of you. Typically generous.' He was thinking: *Typically extravagant.* He mused for a while, as Alexine stooped, picked up a stick off the baked earth, and hurled into the bushes for the dogs. 'It's sad we'll never hear your mother play again. She played so beautifully.'

Alexine stooped for another stick. She was thinking of that terrible jangling from the hideously out-of-tune piano when her mother had played on it for the last time. She should have gone into her then, to sit with her and give her what comfort she could, instead of thinking, as she had done at the time, 'God, what a din!', before resuming her sorting of some photographs.

'Yes, she played beautifully. But I know so little about music.'

∽

Addy's lips were blue and her nostril flared as the struggled to breathe. She had come down to dinner and now wished that she hadn't. It was disturbing that not merely Nanny Rose and Sunny but also now Daan should be sitting with them at each meal. Alexine had insisted on that.

'But, Alexine, you can't be serious,' she had protested, after she had overheard her telling Lucy that in future Daan would also eat with them.

'I'm being perfectly serious. We all ate together throughout the journey. Mama never minded. She was happy to have him with us along with Nanny and Sunny.'

'Yes, but that was something different –'

'If people are prepared to share your dangers, then it's only fair that you should be prepared to share your meals with them.'

'What an odd girl you've become!' Constant pain had given an edge to Addy's voice.

'Become? Wasn't I always odd?'

Warburton was staring quizzically at Alexine as, head lowered, she raised a full spoon from her soup. In the five days since her return, she had already begun to look far better. But, perversely, she had attracted him far more when she had been so haggard and pale that anyone might have thought that she was suffering from some mortal illness. Next to her, Daan was wiping his soup-plate with a hunk of bread. Addy, appalled, was frowning down at the hand holding the bread.

'So what are your plans?'

'My plans? Well, eventually, I suppose I'll have to start all over again.'

Alexine was wholly unaware that, at the words, Addy had jerked up her head to stare across at her in horror.

'Well, that shows courage after all you've gone through.'

'Or obstinacy.' Alexine laughed. 'I never like to give up on things.'

'So – so when is the next royal progress planned to take place?'

Alexine ignored the sarcasm. 'It's not going to be anything like a royal progress. You were right. To have a hundred people accompanying one is far less effective than having twenty. Yesterday someone told me that Mr Pullar and his wife were expected back soon. If they plan another journey, then perhaps they'd agree to our joining forces.'

'That sounds to me like a recipe for total disaster. He wouldn't take kindly to your giving him orders, and she wouldn't take kindly to the company of a woman younger and more attractive than herself.'

'And what's to happen to me?' Addy demanded.

Alexine, who had given the matter hardly any thought, hesitated. 'Well, of course, I'd be happy for you to come along too. But I know you wouldn't want that. You could stay here. I'm sure that Lucy and Mr Warburton would be happy to have you.' She looked first at Warburton and then at Lucy.

After having waited in vain for her husband to answer, Lucy said: 'Of course!' She turned to Addy. 'We'd love that. Your company has been the best thing that has ever happened to me here.'

'Or I could take you back to Cairo and from there we could find a ship for you,' Alexine put in.

'Oh, thank you, thank you! How kind! How thoughtful!' This was not Warburton's playful, glancing sarcasm but one full of previously suppressed bitterness. 'But please, *please*, don't worry about me. I may be old and ill but I'm perfectly capable of looking after myself. Do by all means set off on your next hare-brained expedition. But all I ask of you is not to force other people to go along with you.'

'What do you mean – force, *force?*'

The witnesses to this sudden confrontation were aghast. Lucy extended a hand and put it over one of Addy's, as though, without any words being spoken, her touch alone would calm her and restrain her. But Addy ignored this.

She sucked in her breath, with a high-pitched, wheezing sound. 'Oh, you know what I mean!'

'No, I don't, I don't.'

'If it hadn't been for your nagging and bullying, your mother would never have dreamed of coming out to her death in this dreadful, dreadful place.'

Hating any scenes, Sunny jumped up from the table and, head lowered, hurried out of the room, as Alexine shouted across the table: 'What are you talking about? She wanted to come. She didn't *have* to come. It was what she wanted. And she was happy here. You may not believe it, but she was happy. She often told me that. She said that her time in Africa was the best time of her life.'

Addy once more sucked in her breath, then gave a laugh of derision. 'She only put up with it all because of you. She pretended, for your sake, that she was enjoying herself, but she hated it all, hated it! And why do you think that I came?'

'You asked to come. I didn't ask you.'

'I asked to come because I felt that I had to be on hand to protect your mother.'

'To protect her? To protect her from what? You'd have hardly been of much use if we'd been attacked by natives or wild animals.'

'To protect her from you.'

Lucy picked up the handbell before her and tinkled it. 'If no one wants any more of the mutton, shall we go on to some fruit? I found some wonderful peaches in the market.'

But neither Addy nor Alexine paid any attention.

'The trouble is that you've always been spoiled. You've always had your own way. If it hadn't been for you and your ridiculous ideas of being a great explorer, your mother would still be with us and I wouldn't be the wreck that I am.'

'I'm not responsible for the state of your health.'

'It was that illness of mine that ruined it. I've never been the same since. That French doctor agreed with me. He said that that sort of strain on the system can weaken the heart. You're to blame for that. You'd better face it.'

Alexine's chair grated back. 'Excuse me, Lucy. I can't listen to any more of this.' She stalked out of the room, slamming the door behind her.

Addy gave a scoffing laugh and put out a hand for one of the peaches on the dish just placed before her by the maid. 'She doesn't like to hear a few home truths. But I felt I had to have it out with her.'

'Oh, Addy, I wish that you hadn't. What's the point? She's suffered so much.'

'Well, I've suffered too. And I'm still suffering. No one was closer to me than my sister, no one, no one. And now I'm in this constant pain.'

With trembling fingers she began to peel the peach.

'We're all tired,' Nanny Rose said, as though to a group of quarrelling children. 'It will seem quite different tomorrow. When we're tired we say things we don't really mean.'

'Oh, Nanny Rose, one can always rely on you to come out with the right thing,' Warburton said, tipping his chair so far back that he was in danger of falling over. 'I do like that about you.'

Not sure whether he was making fun of her or not, Nanny Rose nodded. 'Thank you.' Once she would have said, 'Thank you, sir,' but since Harriet's death she had dispensed with that sort of subservience. Even Addy was no longer 'madam' to her but merely Miss Van Capellen.

'And what are your plans?' Warburton asked.

'Well, you might as well know them sooner than later. Mightn't they, Daan?' She smiled fondly across at the old man, as she wiped the corners of her mouth with her heavily starched linen napkin. 'First, Daan and I are going to get married.' Again she smiled. 'Well, it's never too late. We made enquiries yesterday at the Lutheran mission.'

Addy put down the slice of peach from which she had just taken a bite. She stared at it with an expression of melancholy disgust. She was in no mood to offer her congratulations.

'That's wonderful, Nanny,' Lucy said. 'I'm sure that you're both going to be extremely happy.'

'Do you plan to make your home in The Hague or in England?' Warburton asked.

'Oh, neither. We want to live in Cairo.'

'Cairo!'

'Yes, that's our plan. We like that city. And Daan' – she looked over to him – 'has become interested in the antique things they dig up here. Also in those objects made by the natives. They're not really to my taste, but foreigner visitors pay a lot for them. As I'm sure you know. Daan's quite an expert now. An American in Cairo told him he had a real flair. Didn't he, Daan?'

'That seems a wonderful plan,' Warburton said. 'And you think you'll like life in Cairo?'

'Oh, yes! We'll like life there because it'll be a new life – another life – for us.'

Lucy put her napkin down on the table, to indicate that the meal had ended. 'I wish I could find a new life, another life.'

'It's never too late to do that,' Nanny Rose said. 'Look at us.'

20 ALEXINE HAD FALLEN INTO A DEEP SLEEP as soon as she had gone to bed that evening. But then, less than two hours later, she had woken, imagining that it must be morning until, having pulled back the curtains, she gazed out into the dark. Once more she stretched out on the bed, so much more comfortable than the one which she had used for so many months, but she could not sleep again.

She had been furious with Addy, and for the rest of the previous day, after their confrontation, they had barely spoken to each other and then only as though they were strangers. But now she was consumed with guilt both for what she had said and for what, before that, she had done. It was cruelly untrue to say that she had forced her mother to accompany her; but perhaps from the first she should have told a woman of that age that the journey was unsuitable for her. Yes, yes, but for months on end, Harriet had never once been ill. Her constitution, even in her sixties, was phenomenally strong. She had merely died, as the priests at the mission and so many other Europeans far younger than herself had died, from one of the sudden fevers as common in Africa as a cold anywhere else.

Having fumbled for a box of vestas and lit the candle on the table beside her, she got out of bed, pulled a crocodile-skin valise out from a cupboard and, having placed it on the bed, rummaged in its contents. Eventually she found the large, battered cardboard box that she wanted. It contained the photographs taken of Harriet during the journey.

Seated at the desk beneath the window, the flickering candle beside her, Alexine began to go through them slowly, one by one. Yes, Mama had been happy, happy! She was smiling into the camera, always smiling. Happiness vividly emanated from each of the sepia images, however badly posed or blurred, so that that happiness even briefly communicated itself, a flash of light in the enshrouding darkness, to the sad, guilty young woman now staring down at them. Yes, here Mama was actually laughing, as she lay back in the chair with the porters on either side of her and a parasol held above her.

Then Alexine came on the last photograph of all. It was odd that her mother, who had dispensed with mourning as soon as they had set off from The Hague, should on that day have opted to dress wholly in black, so that she stood out starkly against the white of the ruined wall behind her and of the titled headstone beside her. She was not smiling on this occasion. The eyes were screwed up and there was an odd look of apprehension in both them and the tenseness of the mouth. Oh, no, she was imagining these things! Surely she was! Again Alexine rummaged in the valise and took out the magnifying glass that had once been Harriet's. She held it over the picture and peered down. Was that really apprehension or just the result of having to hold a pose, the clamp gripping her neck, for so long a time? Alexine could not be sure, and the uncertainty tormented her.

She left the photographs scattered about the desk, got up, went to the window again and pulled back the curtain. The dark was thick, velvety, suffocating. It reminded her of the fleshy leaves of the mangroves, crowding against the steamer, as she and Harriet sat out late on the deck, swatting at the gnats and mosquitoes settling on their bare arms or necks. They had been careless about those mosquitoes. Warburton had warned them about them. Perhaps one of those mosquitoes had been the bearer of her mother's death and her own near-death? Hastily, Alexine dragged the curtains closed again.

Yet again she stretched out on the bed. She began to think of all those occasions when she had been impatient with Harriet – 'Oh, you and your lists, lists, lists – I'm so bored with them!'; of Harriet's chagrin when increasingly it was Sunny whom Alexine employed as her assistant when taking her photographs; of her disappointment when Alexine refused to play yet another game of piquet with her, to ride beside her chair, or even (a dismissive wave of the hand as Harriet ventured into her daughter's tent) to chat to her.

Then she began to think of Addy. All the difficulties, dangers and deprivations that had sweetened Harriet's nature and strengthened Nanny Rose's had soured, weakened and finally broken hers. She had started out with so much enthusiasm, such a readiness to adapt herself to changing situations, so lovable an ability to find every setback a joke. She had been a woman of a totally different world, that of the Court, to which she had been attached for most of her adult life. But she had stepped out eagerly to embrace this new world of clamorous challenges and people wholly different from those that she had had to deal with back at The Hague. Then, sadly, she had drooped, lost heart, finally failed altogether.

Alexine raised her fist to her mouth and bit hard on the knuckle of her forefinger with such force that she all but broke through the skin. That afternoon a darkening bruise would begin to appear. She had so often made cruel fun of her aunt's inability to do the sort of things that she, with her natural athleticism and her mother with her natural endurance and strength, were able to do. 'Oh, I can never get the hang of using these steps!' she would exclaim as she clumsily struggled up and down the companionway of the steamer. When she rode on a camel, there was endless fussing – 'I'm falling, I'm falling! Oh, do keep the brute still!' Even to get her into or out of the chair she so often used for travelling could be a protracted business. But until her near-fatal illness she had been determined never to abandon her sister or her niece – 'You two are all I've got,' she would repeatedly say.

Why, oh why, had she never written to her aunt after Mama's death? True, she had descended into that black pit in which every action had been an effort and every thought had been tinged with despair. But that was no excuse. She ought to have made the effort, however demanding. She had watched as Nanny Rose, tongue between teeth and pudgy fingers stained with ink, had laboriously inscribed not one letter but a series of them – 'She's going to be in a terrible state, she was so used to hearing regularly from your mother.' Only two of those letters ever arrived but that was not important– Warburton had said that the others might yet turn up, since one could not rely on the punctuality of runners in Africa as one could on that of postmen back in England; what was important was Nanny Rose's determination in writing them. ('How does one spell village, dear? Does it have one *l* or two? I can never remember'). She herself had lacked that determination.

Once Addy, in the course of her interminable reading, had said to Alexine: 'Isn't this a wonderful phrase? It's Anglo-Saxon or something like that. The *agenbite of inwit*.' She repeated the words, savouring them. 'Thackeray quotes it in this preface. Apparently it means the remorse of conscience.' Now Alexine repeated the phrase to herself. *The agenbite of inwit*. That was what she was suffering from now. It was like one of those rodent ulcers that she had seen on the legs of the porters – not disgustingly visible like theirs, however, but gnawing away insidiously within her.

As she was dressing, Alexine heard her aunt going down the corridor past her own room to the bathroom they shared. She almost went out to speak to her and than shrank from doing so. She did not like the idea of humiliating herself with an apology. If she owed Addy one, then equally Addy owed her one. But to think that was ungenerous, she hurriedly told herself. Addy was old, in constant pain, no doubt anxious about a future without her inseparable companion, Harriet. Here, in Khartoum, she and Lucy were close. But if she were to take Lucy back to The Hague with her, as she was talking of doing, could that closeness survive differences in their respective social status, their interests and their characters, when suddenly brought into cruel relief in a different environment?

Yes, she must go and apologize, or at least heal the rift. She pulled a comb through her hair and then marched decisively out of her room and down the corridor. There was no reply to her rap on the door. She rapped again. Addy must be in there, she had heard her returning from the bathroom, her slippered feet shuffling past the door.

'Aunt Addy!'

She tried the handle and, finding the door unlocked, pushed it open.

The first thing that she saw was Mister, looking up at her from the bed. Then she saw Addy sprawled on the floor beside her dressing-table chair. On the table, among the hair tongs, the bottles of perfume, the jars of pomade and the half-open copy of *Quentin Durward*, there was an open pot of rouge. The brush had fallen from her hand and lay on the floor beside her. Scatterings of rouge covered one side of the white peignoir wrapped around her.

∽

Later, Alexine and Lucy sat talking in the garden.

'We so often sat here,' Lucy said. 'She was fascinated by the bats.' She pointed. 'She was afraid that one of them would suddenly fall out of the tree and land on her head.' She laughed. 'I kept telling her that it couldn't possibly happen but she never believed me. The funny thing is that, though she was frightened of them, she always wanted to sit here, under the tree, nowhere else. Oh, we had such fun together. And she was so intelligent about everything she read. She would draw my attention to things – in *Tom Jones* or *Les Liaisons Dangeureuses*, for instance – that had somehow totally escaped me.'

'Yes, she was fun,' Alexine agreed, restraining herself from adding 'once'. 'People always said that about her back at home.'

'Where will I find someone else to talk to as I used to talk to her? I mean, in a place like this.' She sighed and put a hand over her eyes. 'She made all the difference to my life during her months here.'

Now Alexine gazed upwards at the bats. 'I behaved badly to her. I'll never be able to forgive myself for that.'

'Oh, people so often say that, when someone has died. But in the end they forgive themselves. They do!' Lucy did not want to console Alexine, she wanted to make her suffer even more. That scene with the mortally ill woman in the dining-room had been, in her opinion, a disgrace.

Alexine shook her head. 'Was I responsible for my mother's death? And hers? I just don't know. I wish I did.'

Suddenly Lucy felt sorry for this girl in the loneliness of her anguish. She would never like her – so tough, so ruthless, so determined to achieve her own aims, regardless of others – but, now that she had been brought so low, yes, she could feel sorry for her. 'None of us has ever done all that we could have done. So it's pointless – and unfair – to reproach yourself.'

Again Alexine shook her head.

'You and I are so unlike each other,' Lucy said, after musing for a while. 'I'm a coward, you're so valiant. You want action, and I want only to be still. But we have one thing in common. I was thinking about it in bed this morning.'

What could she mean? Alexine gazed at her, frowning in puzzlement.

'We are both after something that's probably unattainable. And we're prepared to go to endless sacrifice – of ourselves, of course, but also, sometimes at least, of others – to attain it. I have that wretched novel upstairs, on which I've been slaving for, oh, three years and really getting nowhere. And you have your dream of discovering something that no one else has discovered, which so far has brought you only frustration and grief. But, obstinately, we'll both go on with our quests.' She looked over at Alexine. 'Won't we?'

At first Alexine seemed not to have heard her. Once again she stared up at the motionless bats. Then she shook her head. 'No. I don't think so. I feel – I feel that my quest is over. Enough.'

Book 4

1

IN NAPLES ALEXINE WAS AN OBJECT OF ENVY, amazement, curiosity and derision.

The white 200-ton yacht, which John had had built in the Isle of Man to her constantly changed specifications, lay anchored out in the bay when not carrying her around the Mediterranean. Its original name was *Seagull*, but Alexine had translated that into Dutch and it had become *Meeuw*. Sometimes she slept aboard it even though, ever since its arrival, she had complained to John in innumerable letters that its main cabin was too cramped. Sometimes she would occupy the suite that, with its five rooms and balcony overlooking the sea, she kept rented at the Hotel Splendido. Seated out on the balcony, she could watch through binoculars everything that was happening on the yacht. Other guests in the hotel complained of the noise and smell of the dogs; but she was too valuable a client for anything to be said to her by the management. She was paying a vast sum weekly for the suite and, as always, she tipped constantly and lavishly.

In the narrow streets, people would stop to stare at her and her retinue with impudent frankness. Urchins would even shout and point. She had eventually come to dress the members of this retinue in European clothes, since that way they were less likely to be mobbed; but she herself, once so fashionable in her attire, now wore shapeless, billowy gowns, more oriental than western, with a wide-brimmed straw hat, a turban or merely a scarf or shawl wrapped around her head. Sunny would often be beside her, carrying her portmanteau-like bag and leashes for the dogs. Following her there would often be a rabble of servants originally recruited for the African expedition. When she had been about to pay them off, they had begged her to retain them. Otherwise, they told her, they would be at once taken back into slavery. The dogs would scavenge in the gutters or bark at anyone who dared to approach too near.

∽

Having been in Rome on business, John travelled on to Naples to see his half-sister. They had last met, in the immediate aftermath of the two deaths, when he and his wife had arrived in Cairo, determined to take her back with them either to the Netherlands or to England. But she had been adamant in her refusal to accompany them.

'No, no! I can't possibly return! No, no!'

John had been taken aback by the note of panic in her voice. Later, he and his wife had wondered if Alexine's hideous experiences might not have unhinged her.

'Why not?'

'Because they all blame me.'

'Who blames you?'

'Everyone. Everyone who knew us.'

'But why? Why?'

'You know why. They think I killed them. They think I'm a murderess.'

It had been impossible to argue with her then; it was still impossible to argue with her now, almost two years later. Once again he tried to persuade her to return home and once again he failed.

'What's the point of this vagrant life? Don't you get bored?'

'Of course I get bored. I'm bored with Naples and every other place I visit. I'm even more bored with myself. But what's the alternative? I'm not going home to be a pariah.'

'A pariah?' He repeated the word in amazement.

'Like one of my dogs before I've rescued it. Kicked, beaten, stones thrown at it. No, I don't want that. I can't face it.'

He shook his head and pursed his lips. It was useless to argue further, he could see.

'So yours is to be a future of collecting more and more animals and servants and sailing about the Mediterranean?' His exemplary patience, which had enabled him to put up with her peremptory instructions and nagging complaints over so many years, was beginning to fray. His wife had so often told him: Stand up to her. At last he was on the verge of doing so.

Alexine raised the binoculars and stared through them at the yacht. The two Egyptian maids, one of whom had now married the under-cook, were lining the rail. She could see them smiling, almost as though they knew that she was watching them and were smiling back. Lowering the binoculars, she said in a voice of melancholy resignation: 'I don't know. I just don't know. It's as though something had broken inside me. When one breaks a leg or an arm, one's told to rest it until it has mended. So that's what I'm doing – resting whatever it is until it's mended.' She brightened. 'I've been thinking of starting an animal hospital. You can't imagine how horribly they treat their animals here.'

'But that will mean more money – a lot more money! That's something else I wanted to talk to you about. I like to think that I've managed your affairs pretty well. But you must know that you're no longer living on your income. You're eating into your capital at an alarming rate.'

'Oh, please. Don't let's talk about money. It bores me. I leave that to you.'

'But what I'm trying to warn you about is –'

'If the money runs out, it runs out. In the mean time...'

Later, in his bedroom, John was to write to his wife that Alexine had become even more difficult than ever, and that he wished that he could lay down the burden of looking after her affairs. But his sense of family loyalty was too strong. He could never do that.

৩

As Alexine was striding out in the Park with Flopsy, a small, dapper young man, with a pale, translucent skin, a number of rings on his fingers and ash-blond hair reaching almost to his shoulders, passed her, cane in hand, followed by a huge, shaggy, grey dog which, he was later to tell her, was called Tito and came from the Maremma.

Flopsy, always bellicose despite his size, raced after the strange dog, barking wildly. Tito turned. Keeping his distance, Flopsy barked even more furiously until, without a bark or even a growl, Tito suddenly hurled himself on him. Alexine and the young man ran forward simultaneously. He reached the dogs first and at once, with uncharacteristic courage, grabbed both of their collars and somehow managed to hold them apart until Alexine was able to fasten a lead on to Flopsy and drag him away.

The two dogs now safely on their leashes but still snarling at each other, the man examined his fragile wrist. A bead of blood appeared and then another.

'Did one of them bite you? Is it bad?'

'*Niente*. Nothing.'

'I'm so sorry.'

'The dogs should apologize, not you.' He drew a silk handkerchief out of the sleeve of his jacket and delicately dabbed at the wound.

'Oughtn't you to see a doctor?'

He laughed. 'No, no!'

'You speak English. But you must be Italian.'

'I had an English nanny.'

'I also had an English nanny. I sometimes wish I still had her.'

'I don't wish I still had mine. She was horribly strict with me.'

'But taught you excellent English.'

He looked at her and smiled. His teeth were small and white, like his hands. 'I know who you are.'

'Do you?'

'You're the one they call *La Principessa*.' He also knew that they called her *La Pazza*. 'You're famous. With your yacht out there' – he pointed with his cane – 'and all those African servants.'

'And who are you?'

'Well, if you're a *Principessa*, then I'm a *Principe*.' He swept off his hat and gave her an elaborate mock bow. '*Il Principe Massimo di Montebianco.*'

'I've also heard of you.'

On her rare forays into Neapolitan society, she had heard people speak of this young prince, the last of a once famous house, with either mockery or disapproval. For most of the time, she had gathered, he lived with his hypochondriac and rarely seen mother on the diminishing ancestral estates between Naples and Salerno; but he also had an apartment on the *piano nobile* of the family *palazzo* in the city. The rest of the *palazzo* was let to some rich Americans in search of an aristocratic husband for their only child. Later Alexine was to recollect a snatch of conversation, overheard over a dinner table, about this girl and the Prince. A heavily bejewelled and jowly dowager was talking: 'Well, if those poor, ignorant creatures think that Massimo is going to take the girl off their hands, they have a surprise coming to them.' The red-faced old man next to her – a retired diplomat, Alexine was later to learn – laughed: 'If they're really prepared to part with a fortune to buy her an aristocratic stallion, then they should make sure that the man is not merely the first of those things but also the second.'

'What have you heard of me?' Massimo now asked. 'Nothing good, I'm sure.'

'Interesting things. I'm glad I've met you at last.'

Together, they began to walk through the park. The dogs, once so ferociously determined to do battle, now each behaved as though the other did not exist.

'What brought you to Naples?'

'Chance, nothing more than chance. We were making for Patras, when a storm was imminent. I wanted to press on, but the captain insisted that we must put in here until it had blown over. I decided to stay for a few days, and the few days became a few weeks. As things are going, the few weeks might well become a few months.'

Their conversation became increasingly animated, until he asked whether she would take a coffee with him in a nearby café. The place – though he did not tell her this – was much frequented by younger members of the aristocracy, who regarded it almost as their club.

'But what about the dogs?'

'Oh, they don't usually admit them. But they'll admit them if they're with me,' he told her grandly.

Everyone at *La Girasole* seemed to know him. '*Ciao*, Massimo,' people looked up to greet him as he and Alexine made their way through the crowded salon to a small room, containing only three tables, at the back. But the waiters were much less enthusiastic about his presence. Although he repeatedly clicked his fingers and shouted to summon them, they continued either to feign a total unawareness or to respond '*Momento, principe*' or '*Vengo, vengo subito*' and then vanish never to return.

Eventually, he jumped in fury to his feet. 'This is impossible!' He strode out towards the door leading from the little room to the salon and shouted down it: 'Signor Bartelli! *Vieni qua, per piacere! Vieni!*'

The porcine manager arose from behind his cash-desk with a look of annoyance and strutted over in highly polished boots the exaggerated heels of which gave his dumpy body an illusion of height. He bowed ironically and asked if something were the matter. Massimo, his voice edging upwards in pitch and intensifying in volume, replied that, yes, something was the matter, a lot was the matter. The manager expressed his ironic regrets. In a scathing voice he added: 'But you must know, *Principe*, that if customers are prompt in settling their debts, then waiters are more likely to be prompt.' Peering into the little room, the manager suddenly glimpsed Alexine. She had never been a customer of the café, but a friend of his, the head waiter at the Hotel Splendido, had pointed her out to him in the street as the eccentric millionairess who not merely owned the yacht out in the bay but also rented the most expensive suite at the hotel. At once his whole attitude changed. 'Let's not quarrel, *Principe*. I'm truly sorry if my staff have been remiss. As you can see, the café is full and they're exceptionally busy. You are – need I say? – a highly valued customer, as your father was before you. Please!' He indicated the table, with a smile. 'I will myself come to take your orders.'

On leaving the café, Massimo said, 'I hope that we may meet again?'

'Why not? Do you always exercise your dog at the same time?'

'Yes.' In fact, he usually left it to his one elderly servant to exercise the dog.

'Then we could exercise our dogs together tomorrow.'

He was both startled and delighted by her bold seizing of the initiative.

On the second of their subsequent walks in the park, a group of grubby, barefoot boys first scurried along beside them and then, surrounding them, pointed and began to shout derisive abuse. Massimo shouted back, but so ineffectually, in his high-pitched voice, that that merely intensified the mockery. Then he lunged out with his cane. The boys scampered off only to return. When this had happened twice, Alexine put a restraining hand on his arm: 'Don't worry. Ignore them. This is what these wretched people do all the time to me. In the Arab world no one behaves like that. Forget it.' Dismally conscious that he lacked the authority to get the better of the urchins, he felt both ashamed and relieved.

When they next met in the park, he dreaded another such incident. But fortunately it did not occur.

∞

Massimo was sitting with his closest friend, Paolo, an impoverished aris-
tocrat like himself, with a long, narrow face and sloping shoulders, in
the *Girasole*. Paolo lowered a spoon into the *bombe surprise* before him
and sucked on it. 'You know that she's extremely rich?'

Massimo nodded, embarrassed, as he fiddled with the gold fob of
his watch. 'So they say.' He had, from time to time, guiltily thrilled to
the evidence of Alexine's huge wealth – the suite and the yacht, both of
which he had by now visited, the retinue of fourteen people whose chief
task seemed to be no more than to trail around in her wake, the constant
throwing of money, as though to do so were no more than a nervous tic,
not merely at waiters and coachmen but at any beggar, however implau-
sible, who approached her in the street. But at the same time he kept
insisting to himself that, even if she were as impoverished as he was, he
would still value her friendship.

'Aunt Rosa told me that she was the richest woman in the Netherlands. Perhaps the richest woman in the world.'

'Oh, you know how people exaggerate!'

'I wish you could teach her how to dress better.'

'She doesn't care about clothes. At that dance at the Austrian legation
she looked wonderful. She only has to make the effort.'

Again Paolo sucked on the spoon. He was envious of his friend's
good fortune.

'Why don't you marry her?'

'Oh, don't be silly.'

'That would solve all your problems.'

'And it would create a lot more.'

Massimo had already had this discussion with himself. A vestige of
family pride, and a dread of gossip even more unfavourable than was
already going round about him, made him shrink from becoming too
blatant a fortune-hunter. At least the American heiress was both beautiful and younger than he was.

'She has a certain *je ne sais quoi*. A modern Amazon. It's pity she's
so tall and you're so short.'

When walking in the streets with Alexine, Massimo was embarrass-
ingly conscious of that disparity between their heights. Even Sunny was
now taller.

Massimo sighed. 'I don't know what went wrong. When I was eleven,
twelve – do you remember? – I was much taller than you. And then –
then I just stopped growing.'

That evening, Massimo accompanied Alexine to *The Barber of
Seville*. It had been her idea, and it was she who, by dint of some bribery
conducted by the Neapolitan who now served as her general factotum,
had procured the box next to the royal one. 'Would you like to bring

someone?' she had asked Massimo. He had thought for a second or two, wondering whether to invite Paolo. But then, possessive of this woman with whom he had struck up this totally unexpected and thrilling friendship, he had shaken his head. 'I prefer to be with you alone. Unless, of course', he added playfully, 'you're planning to bring a duenna.'

'Oh, no, I've grown out of that. Long ago.'

When he arrived to collect her from the hotel in a carriage borrowed from a cousin, who had been grudging in his agreement to lend it, he was delighted by the elegance of her dress and stunned by the magnificence of her jewellery. In the carriage he put a hesitant hand to the bracelet on her wrist. 'Is that a family heirloom?' His mother had long since sold all but two or three of the family pieces. 'Yes. Yes, I think so.' She was vague. 'It belonged to an aunt of mine.' To her guilty consternation, she had been the sole beneficiary, apart from a few small legacies to servants and a generous one to Lucy, of the will that Addy had secretly made, writing it out herself and then getting Monsieur Thibault and Lola to witness it, only a few days before the return of the expedition to Khartoum.

'Magnificent!'

She turned her wrist from side to side, examining the bracelet: 'I had to have it altered here in Naples. My wrists are so much thicker than my aunt's. Hers were so slender.'

During the opera, each time that the Rosina sang, Alexine found herself thinking about Sophie. It was so long since she had done so. It was even longer since she had written to her. Three letters from The Hague lay in the folding desk, now rarely opened, in the cabin. In them Sophie had written of her two small children, a boy and a girl, of her 'darling' husband and of papa and mama, now once again resident in France after papa's retirement. She had also written – suddenly abandoning all her previous stiltedness of expression – of her longing to see the dearest of all her friends once again after so long a separation. Were it not for the children, still far too young to leave, she would travel to Naples – or to anywhere in the whole wide world – to be with her. Poor little Sophie! Guilt now once again gnawed at Alexine: like Harriet with Lola, she had unintentionally filled the girl with so many aspirations and hopes, all unrealizable.

After the opera, Massimo announced that there was a cold supper awaiting them at the *palazzo*. He linked his arm in hers as he conducted her to the carriage, at the same time pulling out his watch to consult it. *Accidente!* The carriage was supposed to fetch his cousin and his wife back from a dinner-party by eleven at the latest and now it was five past that hour. Should he send the carriage on its way and hire one to replace it? Recklessly, he dismissed the idea, even though the cousin was one of the few of his relatives still prepared to lend him money. He supported Alexine into the carriage and then clambered in beside her.

'That's a wonderful scent.'

'You like it? From Paris. My half-brother brought it as a present for me on his last visit.'

He inhaled. 'Intoxicating.'

'And you're wearing an interesting scent.' During the opera, as he had repeatedly leaned towards her to hand her the opera-glasses, she had thought that his scent was totally different from the kind used by her father or Adolphe or indeed any other man she had ever encountered.

'Do you like it? From Parma. Violets.' He omitted to add that he had asked Paulo, returning from a business visit, to bring it back for him. He had not been able to settle the debt immediately and, though the sum was small, Paolo kept nagging him about it.

Over the supper, which was served to them by the only servant at the *palazzo* apartment – an elderly man with a long, lugubrious face, wearing a pair of gloves so old that his thumb, the nail seamed with dirt, poked through a hole – they talked animatedly of the opera. Massimo knew far more about opera than Alexine did. Eagerly he spoke about Rossini, Donizetti and Verdi, about his favourite singers, and about an extraordinary performance – 'all through I was in heaven, heaven!' – of *Tristan und Isolde* that he had attended in Bayreuth, when taken there by an elderly friend of his long dead father.

Breaking off from talking derisively about the stout, visibly sweating mezzo-soprano who had been the Rosina that evening, he put down his knife and fork and rushed over to the piano standing in the far corner of the high-ceilinged, beautifully proportioned but bare *salone*. He plonked himself down on the piano stool, adjusted the tails of his jacket, and then began to accompany himself as he sang *Una voce poco fa* in a mockery of the woman's frayed, effortful voice. The words were not those of the opera but ingeniously improvised as he went along. There were hen-like cluckings and owl-like hootings, so ludicrous that for the first time for months Alexine found herself laughing uncontrollably. The cruel accuracy of the parody was matched by the outrageous *doubles entendres* of the words – delivered in Italian, so that some of the more scabrous lines were lost on Alexine, despite her growing mastery of the language.

When he returned to the table, she grabbed his hand. 'Oh, that was fun! Such fun!' What appealed to her more than anything else in him was this sense of fun. It was a quality she knew she lacked. 'Oh, I do so enjoy being with you. I'm beginning to feel happy again.'

He raised his glass in a hand on which the rings glittered in the can-dle-light. 'To happiness.'

'To happiness.'

The glasses clinked together and clinked again.

∽

The next day, without the dogs, Alexine and Massimo were wandering through the Galleria. She was now dressed not in one of her loose, billo-wy robes, but in a frock which, like that of the previous evening, one of the two Egyptian maids had meticulously ironed. People now stared at her not, as in the past, because she looked so wild and odd, but because she looked so elegant.

She put out a hand to the frayed cuff that emerged below the sleeve of his tight-waisted jacket. 'That's getting old.'

From the expression on his face she realized at once the tactlessness of the comment.

'All my clothes are getting old. That causes Luigi some dissatisfac-tion.' Luigi was the old manservant. 'Firstly, he doesn't like to see his master go around looking so shabby. But secondly – and more impor-tantly – I can no longer pass on clothes to him, because I have to go on wearing them until they're in rags.'

She felt a pang of pity, not merely for his impoverishment but for the humiliation that he must inevitably have suffered in speaking about it.

When, a short time later, they passed a well-known shirtmaker, she decisively took his arm and propelled him into the shop.

'What are you doing?'

'You're going to choose some shirts.'

'No, no! I can't afford them.'

'*I* can afford them.'

'But I couldn't possibly –'

'Nonsense. Do what I tell you! Choose the cloth, have yourself meas-ured. That's all you have to do.'

'I think they already have my measurements.' They also, though he did not reveal this, had his promissory notes for shirts for which he had never paid.

Alexine found an extraordinary pleasure in poring over the patterns with him. In the past, her father had derived the same pleasure from buying clothes for Sammy, and she from buying clothes for Sunny. 'This would be perfect.' She held the strip of cloth up to his shoulder.

He pulled a face. 'The stripes are too wide.'

'Then what about this plain grey?'

'Better.' He felt it between his fingers.

'Egyptian cotton,' the shirtmaker said.

'Egyptian! I think I'll have a blouse made of that.' Suddenly she was filled with a longing for Egypt.

Massimo felt the cloth again. 'Yes, I think that's my choice.'

'But that's only the beginning.' Alexine pointed imperiously at a bale of cloth high above their heads. 'Please get that down for us. Yes, the second one!'

'You're too generous,' he said as they left the shop. He felt both excited and demeaned by that generosity.

After that, she repeatedly bought him clothes. At first his protests were genuine – it was humiliating to have her pull out a wad of money, with the implication to everyone present that she was keeping him – but then, such was his love of finery, the protests became merely token ones.

On one occasion he even said to her: 'I wonder if I might ask a great favour of you?'

'What is it?'

'I've run out of cash. And I badly need a new pair of boots. I wonder if you could possibly lend –'

'*Lend!* Certainly not. Let me buy them for you.'

As a child, she had shown little interest in dolls. But now he was like that *poupée modèle* that her father had once brought back to her from his travels. She had rejected that doll. But her pleasure in dressing this one was inexhaustible.

∽

Two days later, he took her out to the *palazzo* in the country. 'Unfortunately the carriage is being repaired,' he told her, never having admitted that the carriage that had taken them to and from the opera had been not his but his cousin's. 'We'll have to hire one.'

'I will hire one. I'll tell them at the hotel.'

'Oh, but they're sure to overcharge you.' After the extravagances of his youth, poverty had taught him thrift.

'They always do that! That goes without saying.'

'Wouldn't you like me to see if I can find something cheaper?'

'Oh, why go to all that bother?'

Together they wandered through empty room after room of the *palazzo*. Many were empty, their furniture long since sold. One, a ballroom, open at its far end to the sky, was spattered with bird droppings. Another contained a high-piled heap of rubbish – broken chairs, a rusty enamel basin, a dog basket, clothes, yellowed newspapers, broken-backed books. Yet another, otherwise wholly empty, had at its far end an organ, many of its pipes scattered below it. Massimo became increasingly depressed. Since he and his mother now confined themselves to a wing, he had not visited these rooms for a long, long time. Alexine, on the other hand, was enthralled. She gazed up, mouth open, at a cracked *trompe l'œil* fresco; ran a hand along the back of a dusty sofa, its damask hanging in shreds from the honey-coloured walnut like skin from a burn; stared in wonder out of a long window at a vast parterre sprouting a rash of weeds.

In the garden, he kept pointing. The land over there – and there – was still theirs. But that vineyard was sold, and those barns had also been sold, as had the stables in which his father had kept bloodstock famous all over Italy. He opened the door into a coach-house, revealing an ancient carriage, its hood hanging loose and its leather seats sprouting horsehair. 'We no longer use that one. The other – the one being repaired – is so much more modern and comfortable.' She knew that he was lying; there was no other coach.

After a meal served to them on a terrace overlooking the distant sea by an elderly manservant so like the one in the apartment that Alexine wondered if they were brothers, she asked: 'When am I going to meet your mother?'

'Oh, you don't want to meet her. Why?'

'Why? Why? Because she's your mother. And anything to do with you interests me.'

'But she's so old. Ill.'

'She can't be that old if you're only twenty-three.'

'She's aged since she tried to kill herself.'

Alexine was taken aback. 'How did that happen?'

'My father died. My sister died. No money. She was unhappy. Perhaps it would have been better if she had succeeded, instead of being found by Maria,' he added morosely.

Alexine asked what form his mother's suicide attempt had taken.

'Oh, I don't want to talk about it. I don't like to talk about death – or near-death. Can't we talk of something else?'

When she continued to press him, he said: 'Well, if you must know – she cut her wrists. She bled a lot before Maria went into her room. The loss of blood affected . . .' He pointed a forefinger to his head.

His mother lay propped up on a number of pillows in a four-poster bed. The curtains of the bed were tattered and dusty, and Alexine, who had been so fastidious about cleanliness even on her African travels, was horrified to see how dirty the sheets were. Immediately she decided that she would offer to pay the wages of a servant who could devote herself exclusively to looking after the invalid.

'Who is this?' The Principessa looked so fragile, like some starved, wounded bird up-ended on the sagging mattress, but her voice was strong, even sharp.

Massimo explained. As he rattled on about Alexine, greatly to her embarrassment, he made much of the yacht in the harbour and the suite at the hotel, as though this evidence of wealth would ingratiate his new friend with the old woman.

The Principessa seemed hardly to listen to, much less take in, what was said. Instead, without any further acknowledgement of Alexine, she suddenly announced, apropos of nothing: 'Those two are at it again.'

Exasperated, Massimo protested: 'Mother, they're absolutely honest. I've told you that over and over again. If you go on like this, you'll find yourself with no one to look after you.'

'My ear-rings, the emerald and diamond earrings. They've totally disappeared.'

'You sold them, mother, you sold them. Have you forgotten? Levi came here and made you an offer for them and you sold them.'

'Levi? Who is Levi?'

'Who is Levi? You know who Levi is!' But it was obvious that she had no idea at all. 'He's been buying your jewellery for the last ten years at least.'

Alexine had only now noticed the purple, ridged scars on the old woman's wrists. She stared down at them, horrified but fascinated.

'Is this the one who's buying you all those clothes?'

Massimo visibly cringed. 'Mademoiselle Thinne has been very kind to me.'

The Princess gave a scoffing laugh through her curved, high-bridged nose. 'Poor fool!'

'Let's go.' Massimo turned to Alexine. His face was flushed. He inserted a hand in his collar and twisted it from side to side, as though he had difficulty in breathing.

Alexine nodded.

'Perhaps she'd like to settle some of those gambling debts!' the Principessa shouted out, as he hurried to the door to open it.

He turned: 'Please, mother!'

'Please, mother,' she lisped back in a parody of his voice quite as cruel as his of the opera-singer three nights before.

Outside he turned to Alexine: 'I'm sorry. I told you it was no good. She...' Once again he made that gesture of pointing at his head. *'Pazza,'* he said in Italian, forgetting that the people of Naples so often called Alexine *'La Pazza'*.

'I was glad to meet her.'

'You don't mean that. Why pretend?'

'Yes, I do mean it. She's part of you. I wanted to meet her because of that. And because of that I'm now glad that I've done so.'

Downstairs, in the hall, the two elderly servants were waiting. They looked shifty and morose, as the old man coughed, cleared his throat and then asked, in a hoarse voice, if they might have a brief word with the master.

Massimo pointed to a small room, once his father's study, leading off the hall. 'I'll see what they want in there. Would you mind waiting a moment? I'm sorry.'

'I think I know what they want.'

Humiliated and angry, he stared at her, his usually pale, translucent face suddenly transfused with colour.

'What do you mean?'

'Don't worry. I'll let you have the money for them. Tell them that.' When he lingered, she repeated: 'Tell them that!' She experienced a triumphant sense of possession and then at once felt ashamed of it. Addy had more than once told her: 'You like to buy people.' To buy people was potentially corrupting not merely of them but of oneself. She had at last come to realize that, but could not stop herself.

Alone, she returned to the old woman's room. She wanted somehow to win her over, to make a friend of her. She knocked and there was no answer. She knocked again. Then she entered and approached the high, untidy, four-poster bed. Her mouth wide open to reveal toothless gums, the old woman was snoring loudly as she slept.

With a sudden uprush of pity, Alexine stared down at her.

Then she heard Massimo calling: 'Alexine! Where are you? What are you doing?'

'I'm here. I'm coming.'

But she continued to stare down at the woman for several seconds longer.

∽

In the middle of the night, Massimo started up from one of the wet-dreams that he so often experienced because of the rarity in his life of the sort of sexual contact natural to him. Mopping with a handkerchief at his thigh and the rumpled, sodden sheet beneath it, he was filled with astonishment. He had dreamed of Alexine. They were on a high, four-poster bed, the dusty hangings of which fluttered around them in gust after gust of wind. Moonlight poured in through a diagonal rent in the ceiling at the other end of the otherwise totally empty room. She was astride him, gripping his wrists, so that he was unable to move. In mounting excitement as she rode him, he twisted his head from side to side, pleading 'Let me go, let me go!' But she was remorseless, smiling down with half-closed eyes and shaking her head. It was only as he felt the convulsion of the semen shooting out of him, that she relaxed the punishing grip of her hands and her thighs.

Why should he have had such a dream? Only once in real life had he ever had an ejaculation with a woman, and this was the first time that he ever had one with a woman in a dream. As a boy of fifteen, his father already dead, an uncle had taken him to a brothel. 'It's time you learned about this sort of thing,' the uncle had told him before they had entered the establishment. 'The one I have in mind should be ideal. Mind you, she's a bit long in the tooth, but she's a delightful creature, very kind and patient. She's learned a lot over the years and so she can teach you a lot.' In the event, the woman, a Sicilian, had needed all her kindness and patience with her virgin client. As he became more and more embarrassed and ashamed, so she, her exasperation almost slipping out of control, became more and more like the English nanny who, along with his mother, had dominated his childhood. Finally, by dint of some laborious fellatio, she at last brought him to a climax. When that occurred, he burst into tears, partly of disgust and partly of relief. Scrambling off the bed, the naked flesh of her thighs quivering, she spat into a basin and then reached for a towel. 'Well, that's it.'

He had never been conscious of any sexual desire for Alexine. Sitting up in his bed and pondering, he even felt repelled by what had just happened. Disgusting! He jumped out of the bed, hurried to the bathroom, and having filled the bidet, splashed cold water, each time gasping at the impact, over his crotch and thighs. He felt as if he were washing away the bloodstains that were the evidence of a crime.

∽

'Tell me about your travels.'

They were once more seated in the small room of the *Girasole*. Alexine would have preferred to be in the *salone*, with all its bustle, colour and noise, but when she had indicated this he had replied crossly, 'No, no, let's be private.' The truth was that he did not like to sit with her under the eyes of all those people who greeted him with so much outward friendliness but who, he was certain, mocked at him as soon as he had moved out of earshot. Besides, if they sat in the *salone*, he would be under an obligation to introduce her to these so-called friends, and he was far too possessive of her to wish to do that.

'My travels? Oh, they eventually ended in disaster. I had dreams of making some new discovery and of becoming famous because of it. But' – she pulled a face – 'it all came to nothing. Or, rather, it all came to disappointment and death.'

He attempted to draw her out further, but had little success. She answered his questions perfunctorily and volunteered nothing. More than once she said, 'Oh, I just want to forget all about it!'

'You know, I once dreamed of becoming an explorer.'

'*You* did!'

'Well, it was only a dream. I wanted to escape from here and that was the way in which I dreamed of doing it. I met this man,' he added.

338

'What man?'

'I was only sixteen. An Englishman. He was called Colonel Scott, Colonel Mark Scott.'

'But I knew him! I knew him!' Alexine cried out in excitement, leaning across the table. 'Perhaps if I'd never met him, I'd now be leading a boring life in The Hague, married to someone boring and with a number of boring children. What a coincidence! How did you meet him?'

'He was here, on his way to Cairo. Just for a few days. A ship had brought him from England and another ship was going to take him on. He was waiting here for the ship. Staying not in the Splendido or anything like that, but in a cheap hotel down in the harbour. My mother still went about then, and she and I were at a party at the British Legation, and he was one of the guests. For some reason, he came over and talked to me, just like that, without any introduction. I think he – he took to me. Yes, he must have done, because he wanted to see me again, invited me to dinner not in his hotel but at *Le Tre Fontane*, asked me to go with him to Pompeii. When he left, he told me he'd write to me. But he never did.'

Massimo said nothing of the thrilling, mysterious sense that he still had of an unfulfilled and even unspoken sexual attraction between himself and the far older Englishman. But the excitement with which he spoke of the encounter transmitted itself to Alexine, suddenly revivifying her memories of those far-off days with Scott in Bled.

'He never wrote to me either. I wrote to him, but he never wrote back. Strange man.' She pondered, gently stirring her coffee. 'In a way, he was my destiny.'

'And he could have been mine – if I'd been older and if I'd had more courage. Sometimes I still think I want to set off for Africa. If he were to come back here again, on his way to another journey of exploration, I'd beg him to take me with me.' He nodded, lost in this dream. 'Yes, I think so. I'd be prepared to follow him to the ends of the earth.'

'And I'd probably feel the same.'

'I remember that he once spoke of what he called "the greatest journey of all", and at once I thought, "That's the one I want to make!" From Tripoli, across the Sahara, to Lake Chad, and on to Khartoum.'

Alexine again leaned eagerly forward and put a hand over his. 'But that was my dream too! Only – it seemed too difficult, the distances too great.'

'Isn't it your dream any longer?'

'Oh, no! I've finished with that life.'

Suddenly, like a child, coming up with some scheme at which all the grown-ups laugh indulgently, he exclaimed: 'We could go together!

Why not? It would be such fun!'

'Exploration isn't *fun*.'

'We could make it fun. Why not?'

'Oh, I haven't the heart for it. Or the strength.'

'Of course you have! Oh, do let's go.'

'And what about your mother?'

'She hardly knows who I am. And she's never in the least pleased, when she does. You saw that for yourself. If you were being serious when you offered to pay for someone to be there to look after her all the time, then there's no reason why I ... Oh, come on! Let's do it! Let's make the journey of a lifetime! Let's become famous and show everyone who laughs at us and criticizes us!'

'You're crazy. They call me *La Pazza* but you're *Il Pazzo*.'

'Please, Alexine, please!'

Inexorably, sadly, she shook her head.

But that night, in her narrow bunk on the yacht, she found herself thinking about the preposterous idea with a growing excitement. Warburton had spoken to her admiringly about the Frenchman Duveyrier and his intrepid travels deep into the Sahara. She could start by following the same route as his. She jumped off the bunk and searched for an atlas among the books piled in one corner of the cabin. Tassili d'Ajjers – yes, those were the mountains of which she now remembered that Warburton had spoken. Having passed through them, the route would go on to Lake Chad. Then there was the territory of the Sultan of Bornu ... Darfur ...

She lay sleepless all that night.

∽

'You will come, won't you?'

Sunny shook his head.

'Please! I can't travel without you.'

'I can't travel with that man. I'm sorry.'

'Oh, he's all right. What's wrong with him?

Alexine suddenly felt a revival of tenderness for this tall, muscular African, in his formal western clothes, standing before her. She also felt remorse. In the past two weeks, since she and Massimo had met each other, she had seen so little of him; and, until then, he had been her inseparable companion. When she had taken photographs of Massimo and the two family palaces, it had been not, as always in the past, with Sunny as her aid, but instead struggling alone with the heavy equipment, except on those rare occasions when Massimo had made a half-hearted, maladroit attempt to help her. Offended, Sunny had eventually gone off unaccompanied to the slums with one of the other cameras, to take photographs by himself. Later she had inspected these images of elderly women in black seated out on their doorsteps, of washing dangling on lines between narrow streets, or of urchins leaning against a wall, squinting into the lens while attempting not to move even a fraction of an inch, and had thought wonderingly: 'He's become a far better photographer than I am.'

'What's wrong with him?' she repeated when Sunny merely gave a brief shrug and pulled down the corners of his mouth.

'Oh, I just feel . . . He's not *right.*'

'Oh, Sunny, he's kind and amusing. On any journey he'll be fun. And we need fun. That's what was so often wrong the last time. There wasn't enough fun.'

Obstinately Sunny shook his head.

'He'll do what I tell him. And what you tell him. We're going to be the leaders – you and I. He'll just be coming along.'

When she had said that, she sensed that Sunny was relenting.

'He'll have to obey our orders – to the letter!' She laughed. 'Or else!' She gazed fondly over at him. 'Oh, Sunny, do say yes!'

'I'll think about it.'

'Please!'

2 'YOU SAID THAT, if you ever organized another expedition, it would be a small one,' Sunny reminded Alexine, when they had returned to their Tripoli hotel, after having recruited yet more porters. He spoke to her in the now near-perfect English that, the difference of pitch apart, sounded uncannily like her own.

'I know, I know! But everyone says that we have to be safe. So we need the guards. And, if we take the guards, then we have to take the food for them. And if we take the food, then we have to take more porters . . . It's the old vicious circle. Just as it was before.'

For a while they continued with their plans, seated on either side of a rickety table in the dusty drawing-room of Alexine's suite. Then she exclaimed: 'Oh, I've had enough of this for a day. Let's go for a ride.'

Having read in a French newspaper of women bicycling in the Bois de Bologne, she had, with her usual impetuosity, at once written off to John to order her not one bicycle but two. She had at first envisaged not Sunny but Massimo as her cycling companion. But at first with a lot of hilarity and then with exasperation, the Italian had been totally unable to master the art. Eventually he had fallen off when travelling at speed, so that he had torn his trousers and lightly grazed his knee. 'Oh, I've had enough of this thing! I can't be bothered.' He had made no attempt to remount the machine, stalking off and leaving it lying where it had fallen in the road. A passer-by picked it up and, foreseeing a tip, had then wheeled it back for them to the hotel. Sunny had had no such difficulty, showing a natural aptitude that he had totally lacked when learning to ride the pony.

As they bowled along the seafront Alexine was filled with exhilaration. There was only one other bicycle in Tripoli, the property of the youthful French consul, and so, inevitably, everyone whom they passed halted to stop, stare and point. But, for once, this blatant attention in no way annoyed her. Perilously taking a hand off the handlebars and her eye off the road, she would wave and nod in greeting. Before the arrival of the bicycles she had imagined that she would use them to ride out over the sands of the desert. But a brief attempt on the outskirts of Tripoli had at once made her realize the futility of this idea.

'Have you seen the Prince?' she asked the desk-clerk when she and Sunny returned to the hotel. Massimo had not been at breakfast and she had had no glimpse of him since.

'I'm sorry, mademoiselle. His key is here but he isn't in his room.'

Alexine sighed and the line of her mouth tautened. Increasingly,

Massimo would disappear, sometimes for two or three days. When he returned, his clothes would be crumpled and grubby, his shoulder-length hair dishevelled, his eyes bleary, and his chin covered in a golden stubble. Where had he been, what on earth had he been doing? Alexine would demand, with a mixture of anxiety and anger. He would either then make no answer at all or else petulantly tell her, as he had so often in the past petulantly told his mother, that he had to lead his own life, that he was under no obligation to explain his movements to anyone, that he hated prying and spying, that he refused to be cross-examined. At that, he would stagger upstairs, fall on his bed, and sleep for several hours.

'What on earth does he *do?*'

Sunny shrugged. He had heard something of Massimo's escapades and had made his guesses, but he shrank from revealing to Alexine what he had heard or guessed.

'I must go and write some letters.' Curiously, once so reluctant to write letters, Alexine now wrote them almost daily. It was as if Harriet's final legacy had been to bequeath to her daughter an occupation that had soon become not merely a duty but also a pleasure.

As so often, it was to John that she wrote, her hand moving over the paper with the same rapidity that Harriet's had done. Even the way in which she expressed herself was Harriet's: informal, unliterary, often even ungrammatical, vivid and full of eagerness and optimism.

I have ordered seventy camels which should come in about twenty days, and I am busy whilst waiting with preparations that are as odd as they are complicated and tiresome. It seems that to travel into the interior here one must turn oneself into a sort of grocer – but one that does not get paid for his goods! On the last expedition the food that we carried was almost wholly for ourselves. Now we must carry large quantities for others. In addition, Sunny and I spent most of yesterday buying an extraordinary variety of other things, destined to be presents for the grand folk met on our way – cotton stuffs, knives, needles, beads, red mantles, Turkish caps, no end of things.

Because of all this expenditure, funds are once again beginning to run low. I must therefore ask you, I'm afraid, to instruct Glyn's Bank...

She broke off at the sound of an uneven tread down the stone flags of the corridor outside her room. She jumped up and pulled open her door.

'Massimo!'

He swung round. There was a dark-brown, diamond-shaped stain down one side of the elegant white cotton jacket that she had bought him only a few days before, and a bruise on his cheek. One of his boots trailed its laces. His face was, as on similar occasions in the past, unshaven, and the left eye was bloodshot.

'Where have you been? You've been gone so long! I was thinking of sending out a search party.'

'Please!' His voice was hoarse. 'I've told you and told you! I can't share my whole life with you – or with anyone else. I must be free.'

She felt no annoyance, only a baffled pity. Where did he go? What did he get up to? Had he found friends whom he was determined she should never meet or even see? Was there some woman? The always unanswered questions now nagged at her with even sharper importunity.

'You worry me,' she said. 'I can't help it. I care too much for you not to be upset when you disappear for a day, two days, and then return in that state and refuse to –'

'Oh, shut up! Shut up!'

Once so elaborately courteous, he increasingly spoke to her with such rudeness.

He hurried into his room, slamming the door behind him. She heard the key turning in the lock.

∽

That evening followed the pattern of other evenings after one of his fugues: it was as though nothing untoward had ever taken place. There was still the bruise on his cheekbone and the one eye was still bloodshot. But he was immaculately dressed, he had washed and shaved, and he was, as he could so often be, the most entertaining of companions. Looking at him across the dining-room table, she forgot her hurt and anger at the way in which he had spoken to her and was overwhelmed, as so often, by a dissolving, relaxing tenderness. He was so beautiful, she thought, as she so often did when looking at him. Constantly she was amazed by the regularity of his features, the transparency of his skin, the sheen of his hair, and the extraordinary violet of his eyes under arched brows. But what she felt on each of these occasions was not so much a sexual as an aesthetic excitement.

She could not resist giving words to the thought that had suddenly come into her mind, though she knew that he would find them ridiculously gushing, as she did herself. 'You look exactly like Antinous.'

'*Antinous?*'

'In Rome we saw that statue of him. I thought him the most beautiful man I had ever seen.'

'Well, thank you for the comparison.' He spoke drily; but she knew that secretly he was delighted by the compliment.

When, the meal over, they settled down to a game of chess, she noticed that his fingernails, dirt-seamed when she had confronted him outside his room, had once more been scrupulously manicured. It was her own Egyptian maid who each day performed this task for him. Even the nails, with their pinkish glow and generous moons, struck her as beautiful.

3 ALEXINE WAS WRITING A LETTER TO SOPHIE in her tent:

We have now reached the fine remains of a Roman town called Bondjem. It is extraordinary to find such a remote and lonely place full of archways and buildings – now of course all in ruins – of immense stones. I haven't seen any architecture so massive and grand since I was in Malta last year. Sunny has collected some bits of Roman pottery – a peculiar red colour. I myself prefer to collect flowers. But they quickly wither in the icy cold of the nights . . .

She broke off there, as Sunny stormed into her tent.

'I'm going to kill that man!'

'Oh, Sunny, what's happened? What's the matter?'

'He's disgusting! Why doesn't he leave me alone? That's all I want. I want him to leave me alone. Not to talk to me, not to come near me.'

'But you were getting on so well.' At the outset of the expedition she had feared trouble between the two; but she had been amazed to see how, from the outset, Massimo had been at pains to ingratiate himself with Sunny – choosing a place beside him at meals, often riding beside him, constantly attempting to draw him, taciturn as he was, into any discussion. Now, within the past week or so, all that had changed. What had Massimo done?

'He's loathsome!'

Bewildered, she persisted: 'But I don't understand. What is it? You seemed to be such good friends.'

'Thank you! I don't want to be his friend.'

After that, Sunny slept not in the tent that he and Massimo had so far been sharing but, wrapped in blankets against the cold, out under the stars.

Clearly, there was now some irreconcilable difference between the two; but what it was continued to baffle her. Perhaps Sunny disapproved of Massimo's bout of drinking at the end of a long day's journey or even sometimes during it? The Arabs, strict in their avoidance of alcohol, might certainly do so. He would carry a bottle of wine with him in his saddle-bag and drank from it openly, even ostentatiously, with his head tilted up and a hand tipping the bottle up against his lips. Or perhaps Sunny disapproved of Massimo's way of quitting the dinner-table as soon as the meal was over, in order to squat with the porters or the guards, as they passed a hookah around in a circle from one to another?

The sweet, acrid smell would waft over to the tent in which Alexine and Sunny would still be seated at the dining-table, often discussing their plans for the forthcoming day. About these plans Massimo now showed a total indifference – 'Oh, I leave it to you both', he would tell them, or, sarcastically, 'You both must plan all these things in your infinite wisdom. Leave me out of it. I really have nothing to contribute.'

∾

One night, while completing yet another letter to John, Alexine laid down her pen and hurried out of her tent, having suddenly decided that she would wander for a little among the ruins before she retired. Sunny had often told her that it was dangerous for her to go out like that unaccompanied, but she had always laughed at him. The desert, she told him, was not like the African jungle. She looked up at the sky, once again marvelling at the multitude and the brilliance of the stars, with a sense of dizzying breathlessness.

Beyond some of the stunted trees that surrounded the miniature oasis, she came on a row of ruined arches, which at once reminded her, even though they were totally devoid of foliage, of the ruined arches of the tumble-down mission church. But there were no gravestones in front of these, to gleam eerily in the moonlight. What there was, though – only now did she notice it – was a cave receding back and back from one of the arches. Without a lantern, it was impossible to estimate the depth of the cave or to discover what, if anything, was in it. For a while she peered into its darkness, as though expecting some flash of lightning to reveal everything to her. She felt a sudden, inexplicable urge to venture in, to lie down, to be sealed in a cocoon of its stillness and darkness, to fall asleep there, far from the problems of coping with the enmity between Sunny and Massimo and the inefficiencies and demands of so many servants, porters and guards. Then she braced herself and turned away from it, to retrace her steps.

From the encampment of the porters she heard the sound of singing and hands clapping. A voice shouted out something she could not catch, and then another voice: 'Yes, yes, yes!' This was followed by laughter. A moment later, someone began to beat monotonously on a drum, the same note repeated over and over with no variation of rhythm.

As she edged towards the encampment, the previously unvarying rhythm began to quicken. From a slight eminence, separating the rest of the encampment from the area occupied by Sunny, Massimo and herself, she saw someone was dancing before the fire blazing up into the icy desert air. It must be one of the Egyptian maids – though they usually kept themselves separate from the porters, regarding them as their inferiors. The body swayed, jerked, circled the fire, casting huge shadows

347

on the sand dunes. There was now a tinkle of thumb-bells, in time to the accelerating beat of the drum. Somewhere one of the dogs was barking, on a single desperate note. Once more the onlookers raised their voices in encouragement and delight. 'Yes, yes, yes! That's it! That's it!'

It was then that Alexine realized with a shock that the figure dancing round the fire under the huge, almost full moon, was not a girl but Massimo.

What an idiot! Her first feelings were of annoyance and contempt, followed by a chill. She drew her cloak closer about her and hurried on.

Later that night, she was woken by the sound of Massimo cursing, as he tripped on a guy-rope of her tent, so close to his own, and all but fell over. Then she heard him singing, as he had once sang for her in Naples, that aria of Rosina's, *Una voce poco fa,* in a parody of a coloratura diva.

4 IT WAS SO BEAUTIFUL AMONG THE ROMAN RUINS that, although it conflicted with her previous plans and Sunny's impatience to get moving, she decided to stay on for another two days.

'What's the hurry?' she asked when Sunny complained.

'It's you who always want to hurry. What's changed you?'

'I love this place. I feel totally at peace here. And I want to take some photographs.'

Helping Alexine to carry the cumbersome equipment and himself from time to time halting to take a photograph, Sunny was soon reconciled to the delay. Set in a niche, he spotted half a marble head of a woman. He made Alexine stand beside it and took three photographs, frowning in concentration as he did so.

'If only we could take it back with us!'

'Far too heavy,' he said.

'It's probably some Roman goddess. I wonder which.'

'She looks rather like you.'

'Do I really look so stern?'

When they returned from this expedition, they found Massimo lolling against a tree, a bottle beside him. Raising a hand to his forehead to shield his narrowed eyes from the sun, he squinted up at them. His cheeks were flushed and, when he at last spoke, his voice was slurred: 'Ah, here are our two photographers! Always busy! Always up to something!'

'You should have come with us.'

'Not with the sort of hangover I have!'

'That bottle won't improve things,' Alexine said.

'The hair of the dog.'

Later, when Alexine left her tent, Massimo was asleep, his chin on his chest and his mouth half open with a thread of saliva trailing from it.

At the midday meal, however, he seemed once more to be himself. Once or twice he asked Sunny a question. Sunny's answers were offhand and barely audible.

'What's the matter?' Massimo eventually challenged him.

'The matter?'

'What have I done to you?'

'Nothing.'

'Then why the hell can't you give me a friendly answer?'

'Children! Children!' Alexine intervened, in an echo of Nanny Rose's interventions when she and Sammy used to squabble. At that moment she did, indeed, see them as her two children, in constant rivalry with each other for their mother's love and respect.

'Let's go over to those ruins that the guide was speaking about,' Massimo suddenly suggested when the meal was over.

'How? Riding?' Alexine asked.

'Why don't we walk?'

'In this heat?'

'It's not all that bad.'

'All right.' It was unusual for him to show so much initiative and energy.

The three of them trudged off across the burning sand in the direction pointed out to them by the Arab guide. The guide asked, reluctantly, if they wished him to accompany them, and Alexine said no, no, it wasn't necessary. The guide was clearly relieved. From time to time Massimo picked up one of the reddish brown stones and handed it to Alexine, who placed it in the bag slung over her shoulder. Sunny walked a short distance behind them. He was carrying Alexine's parasol for her and two bottles of water. At one point he asked why she did not put the parasol up. She replied that her wide-brimmed straw hat was sufficient protection against the sun.

The temple consisted of little more than a dozen or so stones, an arch and the shattered remains of a mosaic floor. But some distance from it Sunny came on a lion's head, its nose chipped away, half buried in the sand. He had always shown that sort of serendipity. Eagerly he began to extricate it.

'In perfect condition,' Alexine said.

'We could take it with us. It's not too large.'

'And this.' Massimo held up what looked a shard of emerald-green pottery. It was as though he were trying to vie with Sunny in making a discovery.

Surprisingly, Alexine was more excited by the shard, turning it over and over in her palm, than by the lion's head. Eventually she slipped it into her bag.

'Shall we take the lion?' Sunny asked.

'Yes. Why not?'

At some distance from the temple, some scrub bristled up from the side of a sand dune. They went over to it and crouched in its shade. Sunny produced one of the bottles of water and then a beaker. He filled the beaker and handed it to Alexine.

'Wonderful!' She drank greedily.

Sunny filled another beaker and himself drank from it.

'What about me?'

Sunny refilled the beaker from which he had drunk and then, without a word, handed it to Massimo. Massimo frowned at him, then began to drink, not as they had done with one greedy gulp after another, but with delicate sips.

The sun was beginning to sink as they started the walk back to the camp. Sunny was carrying the lion's head, now in both hands in front of him, and now, supported by one hand, on his shoulder. 'God, this is a weight!'

'Why not let Massimo help you with it?'

But Massimo, walking at some distance from them, whistling softly to himself, made no move to do so.

It was only when they had arrived at her tent that Alexine suddenly realized that she had left her bag at the temple. 'I put it down when we having that rest. Oh, how idiotic of me! Didn't either of you notice?'

Neither of the two men answered.

Then, with weary irritation, Sunny said: 'I'll have to go back for it.'

'Oh, I'm sorry! I'm so sorry. Ride. You must ride.'

She stood in the entrance of her tent watching the silhouette of horse and man moving slowly away against the setting sun. Then they passed over the brow of the sand dune and were lost. She was overcome with an inexplicable feeling of valedictory sadness. Glancing over to the encampment, she saw that Massimo was now squatting, as so often, with the Tuareg guards, the hookah yet again circling among them. Going into her tent, she began to continue her letter to Sophie. But soon, with a gasp of impatience, she gave up and, having removed her boots, lay out on her bed.

She was awoken by a loud altercation. People were shouting. Then a shrill scream rang out. Giddy with sleep, she stumbled off the bed and went to the opening of the tent and raised the flap. The sun had almost sunk, the air was already chill. A fight was taking place, with some four or five men milling around together, while the others surrounded them. In Cairo she had once seen a crowd ringing some fighting pariah dogs in the same way. Then she realized that one of the men was Massimo and that two of the other men were holding him while the others viciously kicked and punched him. He saw her, she was sure of that, as he began to scream: 'Help me! Help me!'

She ran in her bare feet towards the fracas. 'Stop that! Stop it!'

But they paid no attention to her, did not even look at her.

'Stop it! Stop it at once!'

'Help me! Help me!'

She ran back to the tent and, with trembling hands, pulled her revolver out from under the pillow of her bed. She cocked it.

'Leave him alone! Leave him! Or I'll shoot you.' She raised the revolver and fired up into the sky.

The men were briefly frozen by the sound. Then she heard their baying, like a pack of frenzied dogs.

Again she cocked the revolver and again she raised it. She must not kill Massimo. She trained the sights on the man who was tugging at one of his arms, a few inches distant from him.

As the shot rang out, she felt as though the kick of the revolver had been hugely, agonizingly magnified. She recoiled, she collapsed on to the ground. She heard a confused hubbub all around her. She saw a man with a sword rush at Massimo. She screamed, 'No, no!'

Then, as the blood gushed out, she knew that the same sword had all but severed her arm.

On top of the far-off dune, horse and rider were motionless.

Epilogue

IT IS ALL NONSENSE. Why do people, twenty-six years later, still go on writing such nonsense? He told everyone what happened, and others, straggling back to Tripoli either with him or in small groups, confirmed his story. But the nonsense continues.

It was an Englishwoman, one of his most frequent clients, who this morning brought in the copy of the *Morning Post*, when she arrived with two of her six children to have them photographed. 'This may be of interest to you,' she said. Fearful that he might start reading the article there and then and so delay her, she added: 'I'll leave it with you. No hurry to return it.'

The article is by a well-known Algerian journalist, who claims that, during a journey that he made among the Tuareg, he learned from an old man, once one of the guards on the expedition, that Alexine did not die but, after the murder of Massimo, recovered from the wound, was captured and then sold to a wealthy chieftain by whom she had three children, all still alive. She herself, the journalist says, is dead.

Sunny puts his head in his hands. It is once more bursting with all the old exasperation, anguish and despair. Nonsense, nonsense! Similar nonsense has repeatedly been written in the past. What is the matter with these people? He was with her when she died, too late to do anything about the nearly severed arm from which the blood was gushing out over the sand. He was with her, he held her in his arms, he tried to staunch the bleeding. When he realized that she was dead, he howled like a dog, endlessly, on and on and on. Later, much later, he and three other men dragged her body to that cave and, having wrapped it in her mackintosh cloak, buried it there, under a cairn of stones. It was he who, as an afterthought, placed the lion head on top of the cairn, as a memorial to her. He remembers exactly the tone of voice, reverential and sorrowful, with which one of the others, a porter from Luxor, said 'Yes, that's right, that's right. She had the heart of a lion.'

On his return, he recounted this over and over again to all the people, some hostile and some sympathetic, who questioned him. John, of course, believed him at once, because, having known him before, he was certain of his total loyalty to his half-sister. It was John who bought for him the studio and the house that stood beside it, and who told him that he could keep all Alexine's photographic equipment – which the guards had not looted, since they had no idea of its value or even of what it was. But, none the less, dark, dangerous rumours persisted. People who had never met any of the three of them and knew nothing of them would wonder to each other if his story was really the true one. Might it not be that he and Massimo had both been her lovers and that, in the course of a violent quarrel between the two of them, he had killed Massimo, and she, attempting to intervene, had somehow also got killed? She was, after all, a woman who always defied convention. So why be surprised that she should have had an Italian Prince and an African savage as her lovers at one and the same time?

In the immediate aftermath of the tragedy there was talk of sending an expedition to recover the body. But John at once rejected the idea: she was resting where she would be happiest to rest, not in some cemetery in England or the Netherlands but in Africa, which had always obsessed her and which she had so much loved. In any case, a French military mission, despatched to explore the possibility of laying a trans-Saharan railway, had recently ended in disaster, with its eighty members all either killed by Tuareg or dying of starvation and thirst. Why risk more lives?

Although constantly busy with the work of his studio – he is the only photographer in the city and he is now far more expert than Alexine ever was – Sunny finds that, after all these years, he thinks far more often and far more intensely about Alexine than in the immediate aftermath of her death. Before locking up the shop and going next door to join his Italian wife and their daughter for dinner, he often takes out the photographs of the expedition and pores short-sightedly over them through the glasses that have a way of slipping down low on the bridge of his nose. He wants answers to his questions: Why did she ever come to Africa? Why, in that stinking market, crowded with slaves, did she decide to buy him and not one of a host of other people? And did she realize that he was there, up on that sand dune, looking down at the carnage and looting below him, cravenly not riding down at once to her aid because he knew that, if he did so, he too would be murdered?

Having dropped the Englishwoman's newspaper to the floor, he stares yet again at the many ghostly, tantalizing images of her. Sometimes the mouth and the widely spaced eyes smile up at him. But far more often the whole face is tense with an implacable resolve. He cannot find his answers.

Giving up, as in the end he always gives up, he reaches for the bag, soiled and battered from the long, desolate trek back to Tripoli. He was bringing it back to her from the patch of scrub on that last, terrible day. Later, he handed over to John everything of value that he found in it – a bracelet, once Addy's, that she must have removed and slipped into it during their walk; a small jewelled box containing some pills; another box, made of tortoiseshell, containing visiting cards (as though, in the desert, she would hand out to the inhabitants of some oasis these proofs of her identity!). But two things he kept.

One is a map of Africa covered in a fine network of lines in red ink, criss-crossing each other, doubling back, appearing never to arrive at any destination or perhaps even to have one. The other is a bright emerald shard from some pot made by unknown hands hundreds and hundreds of years ago.

He stares down at the map. He balances the shard in his hand.

He is aroused from his meditation by the entrance of his plump, grey-haired but still beautiful wife. 'What are you doing? What's happened to you? We're waiting to eat!' She leans over him and looks down at the evanescent, enigmatic images spread out before him on the desk. Once again she asks that question that she has so often asked.

'What was that woman to you?'

But instead of giving his usual reply, 'Nothing', this time he says: 'She was my mother.'

At that his wife bursts into laughter. 'She was white. You're black. How can she have been your mother?'

This is a work of imagination, not of record. But I owe a profound debt to Pauline Gladstone's biography of Alexine Tinne, *Travels of Alexine*. My other outstanding debts are to Samuel Baker's *Albert Nyanza*, Frank McLynn's *Hearts of Darkness*, and Timothy Severin's *The African Adventure*.